Lindsay
Stanberry-Flynn

The
Broken
Road

About the Author

The Broken Road is Lindsay Stanberry-Flynn's third novel. Her first two novels have received several awards. She has an MA in creative writing from Bath Spa University, and combines writing with her work as a creative writing tutor.

www.lindsaystanberryflynn.co.uk

Also by Lindsay Stanberry-Flynn

Unravelling

The Piano Player's Son

Non-fiction A Writer's Alphabet

Lindsay
Stanberry-Flynn

The
Broken
Road

Poetry
Sarah James

RAVELLING BOOKS

A CIP record for this book can be obtained from the British Library.

ISBN: (ebook) 978-0-9934182-1-1
(paperback) 978-0-9934182-0-4

Published by Ravelling Books

Formatting and cover design by
JD Smith Design www.jdsmith-design.co.uk

Printed and bound in Great Britain by Clays Ltd, St Ives plc

For Debbie and Daisy

... I have spread my dreams under your feet;
Tread softly because you tread on my dreams.

He Wishes for the Cloths of Heaven
WB Yeats

One

If Ollie had been a lark, things would have been different. He envied larks: the glow of sainthood flooded their lives. They caught the worm; they got things done. If Ollie had been a lark, he'd have been up hours before his mobile buzzed at nine o'clock. He'd already have been for a run, dashed off half a dozen paintings, and made breakfast for Jess and Flo. But Ollie was an owl, not a lark, so he reached a hand from under the duvet, slammed the phone into silence and went back to sleep.

He was sorting through the paintings stacked in the hallway when it rang again. He let himself dream of good news. That new gallery in Highgate might be offering him an exhibition. Or there was a chance the American customer had come good and wanted to commission more of his Hampstead Heath scenes. He studied the painting in his hands: an avenue of lime trees in Alexandra Park. Sunshine pierced the canopy of leaves, spreading a lacework of light on the path below. He'd painted it during a period of inspiration last summer. Jess had loved it: 'Hey, that's good!' she said. 'You've got your magic back.' She'd kissed him, the sort of kiss she used to give him when they first met.

A dog barked in the street below. A hacking, insistent noise, like a consumptive's cough. It dragged him away from that summer day made forever idyllic by his painting. Traffic noise from the Holloway Road rumbled through the open window in the kitchen; a magpie screeched in the gardens behind the flats. The mobile had stopped, but rang again almost straight away. He propped the picture in front of the others and ran into the bedroom, snatching the phone from the chest of drawers.

The screen lit up: two texts and a voicemail. He listened to the message, his father's West Country burr reverberating in his ear: *I'm in London for two days, son, staying at The Queen's in Highbury. Are you free for lunch or dinner today? And why the hell don't you answer your phone?*

The voice brought back all their disastrous meetings. What was the old man doing in London? He hardly ever left Plymouth. Mum was always asking if they could go on holiday, but, no – his precious hotel came first.

Ollie checked the time: eleven forty-five. He could make lunch. There were several pubs with lively bars near The Queen's. Noise. A buzz. That's what they needed. No chance for conversations of any significance.

He clicked on his father's name in his contact list and waited. It rang several times, and he was poised to leave a message when his father answered: 'Oliver, at last! I've been trying to get you all morning.'

Ollie gritted his teeth. 'Hi, Dad. What brings you to London?'

'Meetings, money, the usual stuff. I needed specialist advice.'

Mm. What was that about?

'So, are you going to squeeze me into your busy day or not?' his father said.

Ollie shifted the phone to the other ear. 'I can meet you in an hour for a sandwich.'

'Oh, I was hoping ...' Disappointment puffed out of his father's voice. 'Maybe dinner tonight. Bring Jess and Flo along. Your mum told me to make sure I saw them.'

A memory snaked its way to the surface:

I'm in the cricket team this Saturday, Dad. Will you come and watch?

Sorry, son, I've got to work on these accounts.

'It will have to be lunch, I'm afraid,' Ollie said. 'There's a pub round the corner from your hotel, the Orion. How about I meet you there?'

The pub was all wooden floors, high ceilings, sofas, lots of glass. Two huge abstracts, streaks of red and mauve, dominated the walls. Ollie's watercolours wouldn't stand a chance here. He scanned the room and found his father standing at the bar. It was lined with people ordering drinks and lunch, but an oasis of calm surrounded his father. He'd always had this sort of power: people didn't jostle him, push in front, overstep the mark. There was some sort of inbuilt authority, probably a genetic bonus from his long line of hotelier ancestors. Whatever it was, Ollie hadn't inherited it.

He stared at his father's back, at the blue shirt, the immaculate grey trousers. He hadn't expected seeing him again after so long to generate such a jolt. The iron-grey hair, the square shoulders, the upright stance were unchanged. He squeezed between the knots of people.

'Hello, Dad.'

'Oliver! Good to see you. What are you drinking?' A whisky already stood on the bar.

'A lager. Thanks.' Ollie waited until the barman placed the bottle in front of him. 'Do you want to order lunch?'

His father looked up, and Ollie noticed the deep grooves running from his nose to the corners of his mouth. He didn't remember them being there before.

'No, son. Let's get out of this crush. I can't hear myself think. And as for the price of the drinks – it's daylight robbery!'

They found a table on the pavement outside the pub. It was one of those days in April when summer infiltrates spring. The sun was hot on Ollie's back. He fished in his pocket and pulled out one of Flo's scrunchies. He felt his father's eyes on him as he dragged his hair into a pony tail and fixed the band round it: he wouldn't approve. Nor would he think much of Ollie's paint-streaked T-shirt, the torn jeans, but for once he didn't say anything.

Ollie lifted the neck of the bottle to his lips, savouring the cold liquid slipping down his throat. 'Cheers, Dad. Good health.'

His father raised his glass. 'And to you, and those lovely girls of yours.' He took a sip and returned the glass to the table. 'So, how's life treating you?'

Ollie thought of the unsold paintings in the hallway of the flat. 'Yeah, it's good. Everything's good.'

'What about Jess? Sill slaving away in that school of hers?'

Ollie tapped the bottle against his teeth. 'She's still teaching if that's what you mean.'

'And little Flo? Not so little now, I suppose.'

'Flo's great. Doing well at school. She never seems to be at home what with drama club, choir –'

'And you? Still daubing with the old paints?'

'That might be how you describe it, Dad.' If his father was trying to needle him, he'd succeeded even sooner than usual. They'd been circling this argument since Ollie's sixteenth birthday, when his father had spread his arms wide in the hotel reception: *One day this will all be yours, son*!

'How much money have you made this year?' he asked now.

Ollie gulped back some lager. 'Life's not all about money, you know.'

His father laughed. 'Can't get far without it though, can we?'

Ollie rubbed his forehead and his palm felt sticky with perspiration. The money his father put into his bank account every month seemed to materialise on the table between them. What had been acceptable when he was at college didn't sit comfortably these days.

'How's Mum?' he asked.

'Come and see for yourself.'

'What about Louise? How's she doing?'

'She's fine. Seems to have put all that trouble behind her at long last.' His father gripped the edge of the table, spreading his fingers wide. 'But let's cut to the chase, eh?' A line of dark hairs sprouted above the knuckles, and the familiar gold signet ring decorated the little finger of his left hand. Physically, Ollie took after his mother's side of the family, tall, skinny, dark-haired, but his hands with their wide palms and square-tipped fingers were identical to his father's.

'You haven't been down to Plymouth for over a year.'

'Our last meeting wasn't exactly positive, was it?' He fixed his eyes on his father's face. 'I seem to remember you said, "Don't come back until you're ready to discuss the next steps".'

'It's breaking your mother's heart, you know.'

'Don't do the emotional blackmail, Dad. I phoned Mum last week, and she's fine.' Ollie indicated the empty glass. 'Another one?'

His father shook his head. 'We need to talk business. I'm sixty-four this year. I'm getting tired, and I want to secure the future of the hotel.'

'We've been through this before. You know how I feel.'

His father's fingers drummed on the table. 'I need you

down in Plymouth, Oliver. One day the hotel will be yours –'

'No, Dad!' Ollie had been determined to keep his cool, but the words exploded from his mouth. The couple at the next table stopped talking and stared at him. 'I've told you. I'm not interested in running the hotel.'

'The South-West is renowned for its light. You could do a bit of painting on the side.'

'I don't want to do *a bit of painting*. I'm an artist; it's all I've ever wanted to be.'

'It's your inheritance, Oliver. The hotel has been in the Anderson family for generations, father to son, father to son. You're my first born –'

'You've only got one child, Dad.'

'What are you talking about? There's you and Louise.'

'The hotel has always been the only child you care about.'

'Just because I took my responsibilities seriously. I regarded running the hotel as an honour and a privilege.'

'Even at the expense of your family?'

'You're thirty-nine –'

'Thanks, Dad. I'm well aware of my age.'

'Come and join me in the hotel.' Beads of sweat on his top lip were the only sign his father was agitated. 'I can pay you a proper salary, show you the ropes, and when the time comes, you'll be ready to take over.'

Ollie thumped his balled fists against his knees. 'You haven't listened to anything I've said. You can't ride rough-shod over other people's feelings.'

'I could have been all sorts of things. I was good at science. I'd like to have been an engineer.'

'Then you should understand what it means to feel passionate about something.'

'What I understand is duty. I promised your grandfather on his deathbed that I'd pass the hotel to you, his namesake. And it's your duty –'

'You can't promise on someone else's behalf, Dad.'

'A deathbed promise is sacred. I can still hear your grandfather's voice now: *Another Oliver Anderson to take over the hotel. I can die in peace.* You're asking me to break that.'

'And you're trying to make me to feel guilty about something that was nothing to do with me.' Ollie jumped up, his hand knocking against the bottle. It crashed on the ground, and the glass splintered. 'I'm not taking on the hotel, Dad. Sell it. Do whatever.'

His father looked up at him, grey eyes glinting in the sunlight. 'I can't believe it's come to this. I always told your mother you'd see sense one day.'

'Leave Mum out of it. Just because she's had to do as she's told, doesn't mean I have to.'

His father stood up and faced him across the table. 'You'll regret that.'

Ollie dragged the band from his pony tail and shook his hair free. 'I doubt I will, Dad. And you needn't bother with the allowance any more. I don't want your money.'

The silence grew around them and he sensed other people's eyes on them. His father's fists were clenching and unclenching. Their stares locked for several seconds. Then Ollie pushed back his chair and walked away.

Two

Matt turned out his bedside light. 'Goodnight, beautiful.'

Louise reached over and kissed his shoulder. 'I won't be long.' She tucked the duvet round her and balanced her notepad on her knees. An orange glow from her reading lamp pinpointed her list for the next day, her second wedding anniversary: (1) early morning run (2) coffee with Emily (3) buy Matt's present (4) new dress.

Every moment had to be planned in meticulous detail. When things got out of control, the mess could suffocate you. In the drawer of her desk, she kept hard-backed A5 jotters, one for each of the last four years. What had started as a safety rope to clutch through the turmoil had become a necessity. The notebook she'd begun, at the counsellor's suggestion, soon after her return to Plymouth, was dark blue. The early lists were painful to read: (1) wake up (2) make a cup of tea (3) have a shower. Every tick in those days marked a triumph. The subsequent jotters were brighter, one red, another apple green, and her current one was purple with white circles. She added two more items to her list: (5) see Mum & Dad (6) dinner, pushed the notebook under her pillow, and switched off the light.

She opened her eyes, and felt the wet on her lids. She hadn't cried in the night for ages, but knew instantly what the time would be. Still, she moved her head on the pillow to see the clock. The red digits glared back at her: 03.50. Ten to four.

Matt was snoring lightly by her side. Her foot met the warmth given off by his sleeping body. Why now? When she thought she'd conquered it all. She turned on her side, and rolled into a ball, clutching her knees. The window was ajar and an occasional ripple of the curtains made her imagine a breeze on her cheeks, and the scent of the sea in her nose. She'd read a magazine article about reasons for a run of nights broken at a specific time. A portent of things to come, she recalled it saying. A whisper of the future like a sigh along a telephone wire. But the article had got it wrong. In her case, the awakening wasn't a link to the future, but a dreadful reminder.

'Louise?' Matt's voice was muffled in the duvet. 'What's up?'

She rolled onto her back. 'I thought you were asleep.'

'You've been tossing and turning for ages. What's the matter?'

She threaded her fingers between his. She loved the feel of his hands, powerful and capable, roughened by his passion for woodwork. They made her feel safe, like her father's did. Eugene's hands were slim, his fingers long and tapering: she should have taken more notice.

'I don't know.' She did know; of course she knew. And Matt did too, but somehow across the space between them, they'd created a shadow-world of half-truths.

He stroked her palm, moving his fingers higher and massaging her wrist.

'I'll call in for holiday brochures on the way home from work.' He moved his hand further up, and his fingers danced in her armpit. 'Sun, sea, and ...'

She pushed him off. 'That tickles!'

Matt had his heart set on a holiday on a Greek island. 'It will be romantic,' he'd said last time they discussed it. 'And we can

9

start practising for ... you know.' She'd pulled away, wondering how the agreement to try for a baby first came about.

When she woke next, sunlight streaked across the duvet. She reached out to Matt's side of the bed – cold. A greasy film smeared the surface of a mug of tea on the bedside table. She sat up and leant against the pillows. The dreams crashed back into her brain. Glueing. Clogging. Scarring. The clock showed ten-thirty: she'd missed her run. Early morning was best: her legs powering along Hoe Road, Grand Parade, the Mayflower Steps. Back again. Today her limbs felt leaden.

She stared at the painting on the wall opposite, a view of The Hoe and Plymouth Sound her brother had painted and sent to her and Matt as a wedding present. He knew it was her favourite spot, and at the time, she'd thought it was a peace-offering. Despite everything, she missed him.

It was cool in the bedroom, and goose bumps prickled her arms. She pulled the duvet up to her chin and heard a thunk as something slid to the floor. Glancing over the edge of the bed, she saw the rectangle of white on the pale grey carpet, and next to it, a small package with rose-decorated wrapping paper. She reached down and clutched at the envelope.

Pulling the card free, she ran her fingers over the raised velvet heart, adorned with silver glitter and minute red jewels. She opened the card:

> *Every day in every way*
> *I love you more and more.*
> *Your beauty makes my heart race*
> *Without you I'd be sore.*
> *I can't believe that you are mine*
> *But I am yours for sure.*

Underneath the rhyme in Matt's untidy scrawl, it said: *With all my love, my darling wife on our special day. Your loving husband.*

Matt's cards were always effusive: lots of hearts and flowers, rhymes expressing his love. He was a 'doing' man as he liked to say, happiest sanding a plank of pine for their new living room floor, sailing his dinghy, going to the gym. She'd rarely seen him read a book. So, his attempts at poetry touched her immeasurably, but sometimes she would have welcomed an elegant, restrained card, with the simple message *I love you, Matt.*

Emily was in the coffee shop when Louise arrived. She beckoned and pointed to the coffee and croissants on the table. Louise hung her jacket on the back of the chair and leaned forward to kiss Emily's cheek. 'What happened to the diet?'

Emily took a large bite from her croissant, a smudge of chocolate lingering on her top lip. 'We're celebrating! I've got news.'

Louise sat down. Emily was always celebrating something and it usually involved cake. Theirs was an unlikely friendship, but they'd known each other since primary school, and when Louise first returned from London, Emily's undemanding chatter had been like a warm blanket round her chilled frame.

Louise sipped her coffee. 'What are we celebrating?'

'I'm twelve weeks!' Emily's hands curved round her stomach. 'I've been dying to tell you, but David said I had to wait.'

Louise felt a hole open up inside her, a cavity where maggots crawled. 'Congratulations! That's wonderful news.' She stretched her face into what she hoped resembled a smile.

'Oh, God, I'm so sorry.' Emily reached for her hand. 'I can't believe I sprang it on you like that.'

'Don't be silly.' Louise managed another smile, a better one this time. 'You don't have to wrap me in cotton wool. Tell me all about it.'

By the time she escaped from Emily, her head was thudding. She walked to the shopping arcade and bought painkillers from the chemist. She sank onto a chair and downed three tablets. These last few months, she'd felt so much better, Matt's love a cocoon of security. She wouldn't let Emily's news push her off course.

She pulled her notebook from her bag. Only one item on the list achieved so far. She glanced at her watch: already gone midday. She had to pass the outdoor pursuits shop on the way home, so she could get the new anorak Matt wanted then. It wasn't a very romantic present, especially when she compared it to the jade earrings he'd bought for her, so perhaps she'd buy him a new shirt as well. And she'd seen a green dress that she knew would look good against her dark hair and olive skin.

She was in the middle of paying for the dress when her phone rang.

The assistant hesitated. 'Do you need to get that?'

Louise pushed her credit card into the slot. 'I'll ring back in a minute.'

The assistant layered white tissue paper over the dress and folded it carefully. 'It's a wonderful outfit,' she said as Louise tapped in her pin number. 'The silk material hangs beautifully, and of course you've got the figure for it.' She slipped it into a carrier bag, which she sealed with white ribbon. 'Your husband is going to love it.'

Louise smiled. While she'd been trying on outfits, she'd

confided in the assistant that it was her anniversary. As she replaced the credit card in her wallet, her phone started up again.

'Someone's keen to get hold of you.' The assistant's mouth curled in a smirk. 'Hubby, I expect.'

Louise snatched up the carrier bag from the counter. 'Thanks for your help.' She'd reached the door when the phone stopped and then rang again immediately. Stepping onto the pavement, she clicked accept. 'Mum, what's the panic? I was going to phone –'

'It's your dad!'

'What? What's happened?'

'He's collapsed.'

It seemed to Louise that she'd stepped into the road, heard car horns blaring, dodged the motorbike bearing down on her. But when her brain cleared, she was still standing outside the dress shop, gripping the carrier bag.

'Where is he? Can he talk?'

'He's on the sofa.' Her mother began to cry. 'I think he's unconscious.'

'Phone the ambulance!' Louise heard herself shrieking. 'An ambulance now!'

The assistant in the shop must have been watching. She appeared on the pavement next to Louise. 'Here, come back inside. You're as white as a sheet.'

'I need a taxi!'

The woman's eyes widened.

'Please, ring for a taxi for me.'

Three

Seven rejections in two hours. Ollie stomped along the pavement, his portfolio banging against his knee. The Aztec gallery was his last hope. Charlie, the owner, liked his work and had sold several watercolours for him. He hesitated at the door and breathed in: *I'm depending on you, Charlie, boy. Don't let me down.*

Inside, he propped the portfolio against a chair and removed what he thought was his best painting. He looked round, identifying the spot with the most beneficial light. The gallery was different. Instead of white, the walls were dark grey. A metal sculpture, constructed from spanners, nails, screws, washers, stood in the centre of the space.

He heard a cough behind him and swung round. 'Charlie, I was hoping ...' The words died when he saw a tall, skeletal man standing there, glasses perched on the end of his beaky nose.

'Can I help?' The man's voice was surprisingly deep.

'I was hoping to see Charlie.'

'He's not here. Are you looking for anything in particular?'

Ollie gestured towards his painting. 'Some gallery space. Charlie usually takes my work.'

'I'm afraid you're out of luck.'

'Will he be here tomorrow? I can come back.'

'Charlie's gone.'

'What do you mean?'

'Decamped. Vamoosed. Scarpered.' The man shrugged. 'Take your pick.'

'Who are you?'

'The new owner, Guy Norton.' He slapped his hand against the sculpture. 'What do you make of this piece? I love the way it challenges the eye. Forces the viewer to interrogate their aesthetic limitations.'

Ollie hated that sort of pretentious talk about art, but it wouldn't do to let the man know. He held out his hand. 'Ollie Anderson. I work mainly in watercolours.' When Guy Norton made no attempt to shake hands, Ollie gestured to the picture he'd laid out on the low table. 'I was hoping you'd take a look.'

He watched as Guy Norton's finely-manicured fingers flicked at the painting. 'It's not without merit. You've clearly got an eye for perspective, and I like the interplay of light and shade.' He stroked his goatee beard. 'But I'm afraid realism went out with photography.'

'It's not realism. If anything, it's a development of –'

'I'm sorry, but the punters want new ways of looking at the world.'

'But you're not giving *the punters,* as you call them, the chance if you won't even hang my painting!'

'No need to shout. It's not my fault pieces like this are passé. What about Gallery Eight on North Street? I understand they take these little scenes.'

Ollie had already visited Gallery Eight that morning, and he wasn't about to give Mr High and Mighty the satisfaction of knowing they'd turned down the work as well. He snatched his painting away from the fingers that were picking idly at the top left-hand corner. 'I painted this scene on a day when I was sad. I was cold; I'd had an argument with my partner; my daughter didn't want to go to school. It's all there: look at the way the trees are bent. The bleached sky ... A photo can't create atmosphere like that.'

Guy Norton's hand moved from his goatee to his red bow tie. 'That's as maybe. But gallery space is expensive. I can't afford to hang a painting I know no one will buy.'

'You can't *know*!'

The plucked eyebrows lifted in the direction of Guy Norton's hair line. He tapped the side of his nose. 'Trends, old boy. Though I say it myself I can spot a trend at fifty metres, and I'm afraid this depiction of trees on – Hampstead Heath, did you say? – belongs to a trend last seen disappearing over a distant horizon.' He straightened his waistcoat, so that the points lined up exactly with his red braces. 'Now what about a glass of something to show there are no hard feelings?'

'How come Charlie liked my work if it's so unfashionable?'

Guy Norton turned his head to the right, and then to the left, his gaze prowling the room. 'And where is Charlie? Do you see him anywhere?'

'Of course I don't!' Spears of pain radiated down Ollie's neck and across his shoulders. 'I presume he sold the gallery to you.'

'And why was that exactly?'

'Don't ask me. Charlie was a nice guy. No idea why he'd sell to an arsehole like you!' As he saw the expression on Guy Norton's face, Ollie knew he'd gone too far. Chances were he'd be badmouthed in all the galleries in North London.

'This conversation is at an end.' Guy picked up his mobile from the table. He prodded Ollie in the chest with it. 'Out now!'

Ollie shoved his painting back into the portfolio. He tied the ribbons across the top, conscious his hands were shaking.

'On the count of three.'

How could such a roar emerge from such a puny man? 'One ... two ...'

Ollie let the door bang shut. He glanced over his shoulder, glaring at Guy Norton's face looming behind the glass.

He caught the Tube from Highgate. The train was packed, and he had to strap-hang, the upended portfolio balanced on his feet and jammed against the knees of the woman in the seat in front of him. Ripples of irritation emanated from her. He tried to shift away, but was trapped by a suitcase behind him.

At last they reached Kings Cross. He arrived at the escalator and stepped on, his portfolio cradled in his arms. Kings Cross to Piccadilly: five stops of humiliation, ten minutes of misery. Fuck Guy Norton. Fuck his goatee beard, his poncy red braces, his arched eyebrows.

At Piccadilly Circus, he longed to call in at the Royal Academy to spend a moment with the Joseph Abbotson snow scene he loved. He was due at the gallery at one, but it was only twelve thirty.

He headed down Piccadilly and threaded through the crowds to stand in front of the painting. A couple of sheep in the foreground, branches, dark and desolate, silhouetted behind them, the mountain looming in the background. The misty sky, its greyness lightening to sulphur, and thin sunlight casting long shadows across the snowy fields: the scene was rich with brooding winter.

Outside again, he hurried past the craft market in the churchyard of St James's, and then stopped. Stalls were wedged together under an immense magnolia tree, thick with pink and white blossoms. He might find a present for Jess. Help make amends for the row this morning. Show her he still loved her even though times were tough.

He studied a tray of bangles, circles of reds, purples, gold, three or four inches wide.

'Pretty, aren't they?' The stall holder said. 'They're hand-made in India.'

'The colours are vibrant.'

'Are you looking for anything special?'

'My wife deserves a present.'

'What a sweet thing to say.' The woman moved to the other end of the stall. 'I've got some exquisite rings as well.' She placed one in the palm of her hand and offered it to Ollie. 'This is one of my favourites.'

'I like the design,' he said.

'Gorgeous, isn't it? It's called a heart-knot ring. This one's an unusual rose gold, but there's also the more traditional gold, or silver.'

He took it from her palm: it wouldn't even go as far as the knuckle on his little finger. 'It's very delicate.'

'You can have one, or some people buy all three. The different materials look wonderful when they're interlocked.'

'Damn it! I'll take the three.' He was already overdrawn, so what difference was fifty quid going to make?

'Good choice,' the stall holder said. 'What's your wife's name?'

'Jess.'

The woman wrapped the rings in pink tissue paper and placed them on a velvet pad in a black box. 'I'm sure Jess will love them.'

As he left the church forecourt, he checked his watch again. Hell! Ten past one. He ducked through a gap in the traffic and turned down a narrow side street. He stopped outside The Serendip, its name picked out in gold lettering on a green background.

He pushed open the door. Light, reflecting off the

polished wooden floor, flooded the airy, high-ceilinged space.

'Hi Angel,' he called. 'Sorry I'm late. Any coffee on the go?' He dropped his portfolio behind the desk and flopped down on the brown leather sofa. Angel, the full-time assistant, was probably out the back sorting through a load of catalogues. 'Have you been busy?'

'Glad you were able to make it, Ollie.'

His eyes shot open. Simone. He jumped to his feet, running his hands over his hair, trying to smooth it down. 'Hi, Simone. How are you? We weren't expecting you today.'

'Clearly not.'

'I had a bad night.' Ollie tried to laugh it off. 'Where's Angel?'

'She had a family emergency. She sent you a text, but you didn't reply, so I had to step in.' Simone pursed her lips. 'Luckily, I was in town, but I did have other plans.'

He pulled his mobile from his coat pocket: it was turned off. He'd done it before he went into the Aztec Gallery and forgotten about it. He turned it on and shoved it back in his pocket. It pinged with texts coming in. Then it started to ring. After seconds that plucked at his nerves, it stopped.

'Sorry about that,' he said. 'It won't happen again.'

'Good, because I was going to offer you some extra shifts, and I need one hundred per cent commitment.'

'Extra shifts? What did you have in mind?' Ollie asked. His time for painting was squeezed as it was.

'I've been checking sales, and you've been doing remarkably well the last couple of months.'

He was taken aback. He'd always suspected Simone didn't rate him highly.

'You'll get your commission at the end of the month, but in the meantime, what about an extra day a week?' Simone scribbled something in her folder. 'Angel's got a good eye, and I want to free up some time for her to buy.'

Ollie's mind whirled as he calculated how much that would mean a month. The job might be crap, but he could take on the electricity bill, and Flo wanted those new shoes.

'Sounds good, Simone.'

'But if Angel's out of the gallery more, you'll have to pull your weight. No more slumping on the sofa expecting her to bring you coffee.'

'No, no, of course not.' Christ, it was like being back at school. 'While we're talking, Simone ...'

'Yes?'

'We've got some space in the main part of the gallery, and I wondered ... well ... I was hoping you might consider hanging another one of mine.'

She frowned. 'Ask me again when the paintings of yours we've already got have sold.'

The door opened and a middle-aged couple came in. Ollie smiled at them. 'Do take a look around' ... 'Lots of different periods and styles' ... 'And just ask if you want to know more about any of the artists.' He pointed through the curved archways on the left and right to the smaller galleries beyond. 'More to see through there. We've recently acquired a rather nice Jacob Hargreaves' portrait.'

As the man and woman moved through to the gallery on the left, Simone gathered up her bag and folder. 'I'll leave you to it, Ollie. And you'd better not let me down.'

He pulled the door open. 'You can rely on me.'

Ollie spent the next hour with the couple, answering questions on almost every work in The Serendip. They left without buying anything, but promised they'd be back when they'd measured their wall. 'We don't want the painting to overpower the room, you see.' The woman gave Ollie a broad smile. 'And thank you for your patience – you've been wonderful.'

He bowed. 'My pleasure. And look forward to seeing you again.'

The man thrust his hand into Ollie's. 'I didn't expect to have to pay so much, but she's got her heart set on that one with all the swirls.'

'It is beautiful,' Ollie murmured.

He closed the door on them and pulled out his phone. Two texts from Angel, and a missed call from Louise. Why was his sister ringing? They rarely spoke since all that crap with Eugene. If she'd been able to keep him interested, none of it would have happened.

He retreated to one of the inner galleries, where Simone had agreed he could hang four of his own paintings. They were watercolours of the same stretch of woodland, a path disappearing into the trees. He'd painted one in winter, a bleak scene with branches stripped of their leaves, a fox slinking across the foreground. Another was done in early May, trees blossoming, a drift of bluebells mirroring the sky. Two further paintings showed the same scene in summer and again in autumn.

They were good; he knew they were. Why wouldn't anybody see it?

Four

As he came out of the tube station, Ollie thrust his hand into his pocket, curling his fingers round the box with the rings. He could turn to his right – to the flat, Jess, tight-lipped at the cooker, Flo, working on her science project, one eye on the television. He could wrap his arms round Jess's waist. 'I'm sorry, my darling. I'm sorry,' he'd murmur.

But why should he be the one to apologise? The memory of the row she'd forced on him this morning as soon as he opened his eyes, polluted his senses like stale cigarette smoke. A motorbike flashed past, its horn blaring. He stared after it – Dan. He'd know that pink helmet anywhere. Decision made.

He propped his portfolio against the bar and ordered a pint of bitter. One quick one and he'd be ready to face what home might throw at him.

The cold beer tasted good. He hoisted himself on to a stool and stuck his elbows on the bar. The pub was quiet, apart from a gang of young men over at the pool table. Ollie liked the background noise, cheers and jeering when one of them hit a shot or failed miserably.

Tomorrow he'd make another trawl of the galleries: Kentish Town – contemporary painting and sculpture; Finchley – abstract and expressionism; Hampstead – ceramics, jewellery, eclectic collection of prints and paintings. Eclectic enough to include Ollie Anderson's work? *Watercolours – not at the moment … Naturalism is so old hat.* Of course, they'd suggest, if he'd like to hire some gallery space, they should be able to sort something out. But where was he supposed to get the money for that?

He raised the glass and knocked back the remains of his beer. 'What the –?' The thump on his back forced beer from his mouth into his windpipe. A spasm of coughing made his eyes water and liquid trickle down his nose. He turned to find Dan next to him, grinning.

'Careful where you're spraying that beer, mate!'

'I wondered if you'd come in, but no need to attack me.'

'So long since I've seen you.' Dan tapped a coin on the bar. 'Thought you must have buggered off to Venice like you always said you would – before you met the lovely Jess, of course.'

Ollie swallowed hard. 'I've been keeping my head down.'

Dan turned to the barmaid. 'Two more of whatever he's drinking, please.'

Ollie shook his head. 'Count me out. I only dropped by for a quick one.'

'One more won't hurt.' Dan caught Ollie's arm. 'My shout.'

'Okay, half an hour max. I'm in Jess's bad books as it is.'

'No worries. I've got a jamming session with the guys at eight.'

Ollie had met Dan twenty years ago at art college, but the two of them couldn't have been more different. Dan was noisy and confident: Ollie, quiet and insecure. Dan was always out there doing stuff, promoting his band: Ollie liked days spent alone with his paints. Dan had girlfriends all over London: Ollie had only ever loved Jess.

Dan took a long swig of beer. 'Nectar. Nothing like the first taste of the day.' He drummed his fingers against the bar. 'So, what's with the hangdog expression, man?'

Ollie shrugged. 'Just hit a rough patch.' He didn't want to make a big deal of it, but Dan knew a lot of people, maybe even someone with gallery space going begging. 'Money's tight at the moment.'

'Responsibilities, mate. Responsibilities. If I get stuck for cash, I can kip on someone's floor.'

'I need one decent sale and I'll be okay.'

'I thought buyers were swarming all over you.'

'I had a good run last year, but the pond's dry at the moment.'

Dan downed the last of his beer. 'Hey ho. Win some, lose some.' He picked up his helmet from the barstool. 'Have to go. Catch you soon.'

Ollie was staring into his empty beer glass when his mobile vibrated in his pocket. He looked at the screen: Louise. Again.

'What's up?' he asked.

'It's Dad.' Louise's voice clacked out of the phone.

'Don't tell me – he's been having another go. I should be down there taking over the hotel –'

'He's had a heart attack.'

It was suddenly unbearably hot in the bar. Ollie snatched up his portfolio and stumbled to the door.

'Did you hear me?' Louise's question reached into his brain.

'Course I heard you!' He staggered, thrown off balance. Two young boys on skateboards had hurtled towards him, one of them careering into him, sending a flame of pain through his shin. 'You stupid wanker!' he yelled.

'Oliver, what's going on?'

The boys disappeared round the next corner, their laughter thrown back at him. 'Sorry,' he muttered. 'I wasn't shouting at you, Loulou.' Without realising, he'd used his sister's pet name, something that hadn't come to his lips for years. 'Tell me about Dad. Is it serious?'

'We don't know yet. He started having chest pains this afternoon. Mum tried to get him to lie down, but they were still serving lunch in the dining room, and he wouldn't leave.'

'Stubborn old bugger.'

'Don't talk about him like that!' Louise's voice grew shriller. 'It was horrible.'

'You were there?'

'Mum phoned and I rushed over. Dad looked terrible ... trembling and sweating ... he was sort of collapsed on a sofa in the guests' lounge ...'

'Why didn't someone phone for an ambulance?'

'Chef already had by the time I got there. And the paramedics were brilliant. He went off in the ambulance, and they were preparing him for theatre to have a stent fitted by the time Mum and I got to the hospital.'

'Where is he? The Derriford?' Ollie visualised the ward where his grandfather had died, remembered the smell.

'They're keeping him in to run more tests. Oliver...'

He heard the wobble in his sister's voice.

'Oliver ... can you come?'

Images competed in Ollie's mind: his father, hooked up to wires and tubes; Jess, mouth taut as she marked endless exercise books; Flo, curled up on the sofa, waiting to tell him about her day. 'I'll ring you in the morning. You'll know more then ... and give Mum and Dad my love.'

Ollie clicked off his phone. He ran his hand over his face. Jess – he needed Jess.

Five

Ollie hesitated at the front door, searching for his keys. Louise's call had knocked him for six. The old man was as strong as an ox. He'd worked sixteen-hour days for as long as Ollie could remember.

He found the keys and climbed the stairs to the flat. He hung his jacket from a peg, tapping his pocket to check for the box with the rings. The murmur of the television came from the living room. He looked in.

Flo was sitting on the sofa on her own. She was still dressed in her school uniform. She glanced round. 'Hi, Daddy.' She sounded subdued and turned back to the television immediately.

'Where's Mummy?' Ollie was surprised not to see Jess at the table, a pile of books beside her.

'She's in the bedroom getting ready.'

'For what?'

'She's going out.'

'Oh, I didn't know.' Ollie sat down next to Flo. 'Sorry I'm late, sweetheart.'

She shrugged. 'It's okay. Where have you been?'

'I called in for a pint.'

'Are you drunk?'

'I said a pint, Flo. Of course I'm not drunk!' He took her hand. 'Have you been biting your nails again?'

'Mummy shouted at me.'

Some singer was screeching on the television. 'Shall we turn this off?'

'No, it's my favourite song. I told you yesterday.'

'Why did Mummy shout at you?' Jess had been edgy with him for weeks – stress at work, she claimed – but it wasn't like her to take things out on Flo.

'I couldn't find my cardigan after PE.' Flo sucked a strand of hair, something she'd started doing when she was tired or upset. 'One of the boys must have nicked it.'

Nicked? What was happening to his baby? 'Did you try lost property?'

She rolled her eyes. 'Course I did. Mummy said the other one's in the wash, so I'll have to be cold tomorrow.'

'Flo!' Jess's voice called from the bedroom. 'Can you have your shower and get your pyjamas on.'

Flo didn't move. Ollie nudged her. 'You'd better go.'

She gave a huge sigh and stomped out of the room. The bathroom door banged. Ollie clicked the off button on the television. What the hell was wrong with Flo tonight? She was usually such a sunny child.

He forced himself upright and went along the hallway to the bedroom. Jess was putting on make-up. Her eyes, circled with black liner, met his in the mirror. 'You're late.'

He watched her stroking mascara through her lashes. 'I met Dan and we had a beer together.'

'You could have texted.'

'I know, sorry. Any food left? I'm starving.' He hadn't eaten since a quick sandwich at lunchtime.

'Lasagne's in the oven. Expect it's dried up by now.'

Christ, this was hard going. It wasn't as if he was that late. 'Flo doesn't seem very happy,' he ventured.

'Well, I'm not happy with her. That's the third cardigan she's lost. We can't afford to keep replacing them.'

Money. That must be what this was all about. 'I'll talk

to her. She'll have to contribute some of her pocket money.'

'You'll talk to her?' She laughed. 'That's rich – Mr Responsibility himself.'

Ollie bit back his reply. He wanted to crawl into bed and sleep. Wipe out all the horribleness of today. 'Jess.'

'Mm?'

'My dad –'

'Don't start all that again, Ollie.' She snatched up her hairbrush. 'You and he don't get on. We've discussed it endlessly. What else is there to say?'

Tears prickled at the back of his nose. He had to change the subject quickly. 'I didn't realise you were going out.'

'It's just a drink with some of the other teachers.' She ran the brush through her hair. It was one of the first things he'd noticed about her, blonde and falling around her shoulders. He loved to bury his face in it and breathe in its apricot scent.

'I had a call from Louise today.' He waited for her to turn round. There was no love lost between her and Louise. But she was slipping a top over her head, something in black and white. She smoothed it down over her hips; it was low cut and skimmed her breasts.

'Don't stare at me like that, Ollie.' She swung round from the mirror. 'It's unnerving.'

'I was only thinking how nice you looked. Is that a new top?'

'No, you've seen it before.'

He lay back on the bed and clasped his hands behind his head, staring up at the ceiling. 'Where are you going?' She never went out during the week.

'We're meeting in that new bar at Archway. After that, I don't know.'

'Who's we?'

'For heaven's sake, Ollie, what's with the interrogation?'

He risked a glance through half-closed eyes. She'd piled

her hair in a knot on top of her head. Her neck looked pale and vulnerable. He wanted to kiss it. 'What's up, Jess?'

'You.' She threw the brush into her handbag.

He heard Flo come out of the bathroom and the click of her bedroom door. 'Don't be like this. I've had one hell of a day.'

'*You've* had one hell of a day?'

He sat up. *My dad's had a heart attack.* If he could say the words out loud, maybe they'd lose some of their power. But something in her face stopped him. Instead he whinged on about trawling round the galleries, being stuck in The Serendip –

'The Serendip? Would that be the gallery with the polished floors, the chandelier, the subdued murmurs of potential buyers?'

'Don't be sarky. Just because it's a nicer environment than your school, doesn't mean I like being there.' He needed to pee, and he got off the bed. 'Hang on. I'll be back in one sec.'

In the bathroom, his mind cleared as the pressure on his bladder eased. Okay, he was late, and she'd obviously had a bad day. An evening out would do her good. He'd tell her about his dad in the morning. He flushed the loo and rinsed his hands and face. Making sure he squeezed the toothpaste from the bottom, he ran the brush over his teeth and tongue. He felt almost human again.

He opened the bedroom door, his arms poised for the big hug he was going to give Jess, but she wasn't there. He went to the living room: she was over by the window. She stood with her back to it, arms folded, flattening her breasts. The blind was up and the street lamp lit up the flats opposite but cast her face in shadow, so he couldn't make out her expression. He moved towards her.

'Don't come over.'

'But Jess –'

'No more excuses, Ollie. I have to deal with adolescents all day – I don't want to live with one.'

'Hang on: I only went for a pint. I haven't seen Dan for months.' He realised he was holding out his hands like some hammy actor pleading for forgiveness. He shoved them in his pockets. 'I thought a beer might take the edge off the day. I didn't want to inflict my mood on you and Flo.'

'Oh, nice one, Ol.' Jess laughed. 'Somehow you've managed to make it our fault.'

'For Christ's sake! You know I didn't mean that.' He was fed up trying to placate her, and when it came to blame, she wasn't exactly lily white. 'It's not much fun trying to flog other artists' work, when I'm told my own stuff doesn't have commercial validity.'

'Would it be too much to expect you might use your talent to paint something galleries would consider hanging?'

The question knocked Ollie sideways. Jess had always been his biggest supporter, thrilled for him when his work was selling, a buffer when the knock-backs came.

'I thought you rated my work,' he said.

'It doesn't pay the bills.'

'What do you want me to do? Create pyramids of dog turds and say it's a comment on modern society? Cover my prick with twenty-pound notes and take a photo?'

'Shocking people hasn't done Tracy Emin any harm.'

'There's no point pursuing this.' Ollie turned away. 'I'm going to check that lasagne.'

He'd got to the door when Jess said, 'You could always get some teaching.'

He stopped. 'I've tried – you know I've emailed my CV round to all the schools and colleges. But I have got some good news.' He swung round and his knuckles slammed against the back of the chair. He clenched his teeth at the pain. 'Simone's offered me extra work. It will mean less time for painting –'

'And we wouldn't want anything that interfered with genius, would we?'

What was going on? He'd never known her so spiteful, so poisonous. He crossed the room and wrapped his arms round her. Hers were still folded across her chest, and the barrier forced him to hold back, to resist kissing her.

'Let's not argue,' he murmured. 'I love you, Jess.' He rested his head against hers, imagined he could hear her brain ticking. He could fall asleep here, feeling the rise and fall of her breathing, drawing in the sweet smell of her –

The shove caught him unawares, and he struggled to regain his balance. 'What did you do that for?'

Jess's hands were still raised where she'd pushed him in the chest.

'You nearly knocked me over.'

'You stink of beer.'

'But I've cleaned my teeth.'

She pushed past him. 'Grow up, Ollie.'

He heard her heels on the stairs, and then the front door banged. A sudden and complete silence settled round him. He went out into the hallway and hesitated outside Flo's room. A sliver of light shone under the door. He pushed it open. The bedside lamp was on, but Flo's eyes were closed. Panda was clasped against her chest, and a book lay face down on the bed. He crept over and put the book on her bedside cupboard. He studied her for a moment, the long eyelashes shadowing her cheeks. Poor little thing – no one had said goodnight to her. Bending down, he touched his lips to her forehead and turned out the light.

He tiptoed along the hall and into the kitchen. He spooned lasagne onto a plate, and checked in the fridge. There was a can of lager. Settling on the sofa in the living room, he rested his feet on the coffee table. He took a couple

31

of mouthfuls of lasagne, but it was dried up and crusty round the edges. An image of his father slid into his mind. He took a gulp of lager and clicked on his mother's number in his mobile.

She answered in her usual, breathy way as if she'd had to run. 'Hello.'

'Mum, it's me.'

'Oliver, what a relief! Your dad keeps asking if you've phoned.'

'How is he?'

'He seems okay. He was asleep when we left the hospital.'

'He'll be back behind that reception desk before you know it.'

'Not if I have my way, he won't.'

He recognised that stern note in his mother's voice.

'Will you be able to come?' she asked. 'Would do him the world of good to see you.'

'I'll try, Mum, but ... keep me posted, will you? And tell him I called.'

Sleep must have overtaken him because all at once, he was aware of a noise over near the door. It sounded like crying. He forced his eyes open.

'Flo! What are you doing up?' He tried to stand, but his head felt groggy.

'Daddy ...'

Ollie grabbed the coffee table and pushed himself to his feet. 'Did you have a bad dream?'

She rushed towards him and flung herself against his chest. He wrapped his arms round her. She felt thin in her pyjamas, her shoulder blades pushing against the poppy-patterned cotton. He settled her beside him on the sofa and took her hand. 'What's up, beautiful girl? Why are you crying?'

She stared at him – those wonderful green eyes she'd

inherited from Jess. Physically, she was entirely her mother's, but Ollie always thought the real bond, the emotional, the psychological bond was between him and Flo. She had a gift for drawing; they laughed at the same things; they liked to walk in the woods. And she was sensitive – Jess said hyper-sensitive – but Ollie understood. It was what people often accused him of.

'You and Mum were arguing again.'

'What do you mean *again*?' His tone was sharper than he'd intended. 'We hardly ever argue.'

'You had a row last night, and this morning. Mum cried after you went out.'

Ollie recalled snatching up his portfolio and banging out of the flat. He'd regretted it straight away, lugging his paintings around, no breakfast.

'I'm sorry.' From the corner of his eye he could see the can of lager on the coffee table. 'It's what parents do sometimes.'

'Do you and Mummy still love each other?'

Ollie's throat tightened. 'Of course we do, sweetheart. You must never think that we don't.'

'Then why do you keep arguing?' Flo's tears had gone, and her voice was hard.

'You know, grown-up stuff – sharing the chores, being late home, money …'

'Mum said she can't afford for me to go on the school trip.'

It was the first Ollie remembered hearing about a trip. 'Where to? When?'

'To Bath, at the beginning of June.'

'What's it for?'

'Our history projects. We've been doing the Romans, and they've got these amazing baths there.'

'I'm sure we'll be able to find the money.'

Flo threw her arms round his neck. 'You're a star, Daddy!' She planted kisses on his cheek.

He tapped her arm. 'But listen, missy. No more losing cardigans. Mummy was right to be cross.'

'I won't, I promise.' She snuggled closer. 'And you and Mum will make up, won't you?'

'Course we will. In fact, I'll let you into a secret.' He cupped his hands round his mouth and leaned towards her ear. 'I'm going to ask her to marry me.'

Flo pulled away. 'Don't be silly. You're already married.'

'I mean marry me again. Renew our vows. We didn't invite anybody first time round, but this time we'll have a big party.'

'Can I be bridesmaid?'

'You'll have to ask Mummy, but I'm sure she'll want you to be.'

'That's so cool!' She was grinning and her eyes sparkled like frost in moonlight. 'Just the best ever.'

Ollie put his finger to his mouth. 'Don't let on,' he whispered. 'I want it to be a surprise.'

'I promise.' Flo slapped Ollie's palm in a high-five. 'When are you going to ask her?'

'Tomorrow night. Do you think you could stay over with one of your mates?'

'You bet. I'll ask Lauren first thing tomorrow.'

'Right, young lady, back to bed.' Ollie stood up and gave Flo a little push towards the door. 'If she says *yes*, the three of us will go to Pizza Express at the weekend to celebrate.'

'*If*!' Flo shouted. 'She's got to say *yes*.'

Six

Louise slipped from bed and crossed to the window. She pulled the cord on the heavy curtains, frowning as they stalled and she had to tug again. She peered out. Sky and sea met in early-morning greyness. The Breakwater rose like some sea monster at the entrance to the bay. Crested peaks pocked the surface of the waves. A solitary walker, head bent against the wind, strode along The Hoe, his anorak ballooning behind him.

She shivered as she turned away from the window. She pulled her dressing gown over her thin nightdress and put her hand to the radiator: cold. It was late April, but still chilly. She sat at the desk and added *check central heating* to her list of jobs for today.

She'd take over reception at seven, relieving the night porter. Her father was usually there to greet guests on their way to breakfast, and she wanted to be able to report all had gone smoothly while he was in hospital. She'd followed him round the hotel since she was a child and knew his routine without having to be told.

She'd almost backed out of the wedding when Matt insisted they bought their own place. She'd expected he'd live at the hotel with her after they were married. Where else could provide them with a panoramic view of Plymouth

Sound and the buzz generated by the constant coming and going of guests? She'd worked as events manager at the hotel for several years after university, and only constant bitchiness from a certain member of staff had made her leave and move to London.

'I'll die if I have to live in that poky place.' She remembered the conversation with her mother after Matt had first taken her to see the terraced house he'd found near Cremyll Ferry.

'At least you won't have to share your front door with hordes of visitors.'

'I like meeting new people every day,' Louise insisted

'Well, I love that spot where the ferry comes in.' Her mother stopped snipping ends from flower stems and clutched the secateurs to her chest. 'Your father always used to wait there for me when we were courting, and I came over from Edgcumbe.'

'Mum, how can you compare that little strip of water with our wonderful bay?'

'But when you have children ...' Her mother's voice trailed away. They were putting the finishing touches to an arrangement of lilies on a table on the first floor landing. 'The hotel's no place for a family.'

Louise scrunched up the remaining debris from the lilies and bundled it into a newspaper. 'I loved living here when I was a child.'

'*You* did, I know. But Oliver was never happy.' Her mother's eyes took on a dreamy look. 'That's probably why he doesn't come here much.'

This was the moment. Should she confide in her mother the truth of what had happened in London? The real reason why Ollie and Jess stayed away?

She snorted. 'Mum, you know why he doesn't come. He and Dad –'

'Are too stubborn for their own good.'

Louise showered and dressed: black trousers, white shirt. She stood in front of the mirror coiling her hair into a loose bun and folding it on top of her head. As she pushed the last pin into her hair, her mobile bleeped.

'Hi, how's it going?' Matt's words hummed in her ear. 'Any news on your dad?'

'Not since last night. He was comfortable when Mum and I left the hospital.'

'You'd have heard if there'd been any change.' Matt sounded too bright, as if he was determined everything would be all right.

'Mum and I are going to see him this morning.'

'When will you be home?'

Louise stared out of the window at an elderly couple walking arm in arm along The Hoe. 'I'm not sure. I don't want to leave the hotel until Dad's back.'

'The place runs like clockwork.'

'But it needs someone in charge.'

'What about work?' Matt asked.

Louise thought of her three days a week in the offices of Everatt & Johnson, Solicitors. 'They wouldn't expect me to come in,' she said. 'Not with a family emergency.'

'It's lonely here without you.'

She heard the petulance in his voice. It wasn't like him to be selfish. Dad was in hospital, and all he could think –

'Are you still there?' Matt's voice jumped out of the phone.

'Of course, I am, but I'll have to go in a minute.'

'You'll be home tonight though.'

'I'll see how Dad is.'

'I'll come and collect you when I finish work, shall I?'

Louise sighed. Loud enough for Matt to hear, she hoped.

'Come on, love. I'll cook us a nice chicken curry.'

'I'm not sure what time I'll get away,' Louise said, 'so don't go to any trouble.'

'Nothing is too much trouble for my beautiful wife.' Matt laughed. 'You can have a lovely long bath as soon as you get in and wash off the hotel.'

'I've got to go, Matt. I need to make sure the breakfasts go smoothly, and there are guests checking out –'

'You've got staff for that.'

'Dad oversees all of it, and so will I.'

'But you will be home tonight?'

'Tonight,' she heard herself promising. 'As long as Dad's okay.'

Louise looked down at her father. He seemed small and frail in the hospital bed, his skin pale against the yellow cover. His eyes were closed, the lids wrinkled and blue-veined.

She glanced across at her mother on the other side of the bed. 'Are you all right, Mum?'

Her mother nodded, but tears filmed her eyes. 'He seems old,' she said, a note of wonder in her voice.

'He's only sixty-three.'

'But it feels as if our future's been whipped away.' She kissed his forehead. 'Tom, it's Lindy, and Louise is with me.'

Her father's eyes opened, and he smiled. 'Lindy, hello.'

Louise laughed. He sounded so normal, his voice much stronger than she'd expected. 'Hello, Dad. It's good to see you.'

He pulled at his pillow. 'Can you help me sit up?'

'You'd better wait for the nurse,' her mother said. 'You're obviously in pain.'

'Just help me with this wretched pillow.' He wasn't known for his patience, and Louise moved forward to rearrange the bedding.

'How's that, Dad?'

'You shouldn't ignore the pain,' her mother said.

'Never mind that, Lindy, I want to hear what's been happening at the hotel.'

'Everything's fine, Dad. It's not even twenty-four hours since you were there.'

'The hotel needs me. I'll be back at work by the end of the week.'

'We'll see about that.' Her mother's chin jutted forward.

Louise smiled: her father wouldn't listen to her, but he might take notice of his beloved Lindy. Despite the long hours he put in at the hotel, he always gave her tea and the morning papers in bed; loved to spoil her with clothes shopping expeditions; took notice of her advice. A longing for her parents' closeness stabbed at her.

She pushed a chair towards her mother. 'You and Dad have a talk, Mum. I'll get a coffee.'

'I need to give you a list first,' her father said. 'I want Chef to work on the new menus, and there's that big engagement party at the weekend.'

'Will you listen to yourself, Tom?' her mother interrupted. 'This is exactly why you had the attack in the first place.'

'She's right. I can deal with everything.' Louise touched her father's hand. His skin felt clammy.

In the hospital café, she sipped her coffee and jotted down the names of people she needed to phone:

Maeve – the head receptionist would want to know how the boss was doing, and that it was business as usual at the hotel.

Chef – her father needed pacifying on the new menus.

Juliet Phillips – she hadn't confirmed the number of guests for her daughter's engagement party on Saturday.

Felix Everatt – the solicitor Louise worked for would have to get cover for the next few days at least.

Oliver –she had been expecting a call from her brother all morning, but nothing had come.

She retreated to the car park to make the calls. Maeve reported everything was running smoothly at the hotel. She ticked off the other names on her list. The only person she couldn't reach was Oliver. She sent a text: *When are you coming*? A cold wind blew through her jacket, and she shivered as she dropped her mobile into her bag.

When Louise got back to the ward, her father was sitting in a chair, her mother beside him. They were holding hands.

'Dad! What are you doing out of bed?'

He made a face. 'I'm not an invalid, you know.'

Louise turned to her mother. 'Mum, tell him.'

'It's all right. The nurse said it's better for him to be on the move. She'll be back in a while to help him have a shower.'

'And all being well, I can come out tomorrow.' Her father grinned, that wide beam he gave when something went particularly well at the hotel.

'Great. I didn't think it would be so soon.' She turned to her mother. 'But you know once he's out, he'll be back in the thick of it.'

'Don't worry; I've got a plan.'

Louise looked from one to the other. 'What's going on? You two are plotting something.'

'When he comes out, we'll stay at the hotel for a few days till he gets stronger – I've warned him we'll be in the flat and going for walks, *not* working in the hotel – and then I'm taking him right away to convalesce.'

Louise's father laughed. 'You didn't know your mother was such a tyrant did you? See what I've had to put up with all these years?'

'Where will you go?' Louise asked.

'It's a surprise. If I tell him now, he'll come up with all sorts of reasons why –'

'Come on, Lindy. I promise not to say a word.'

'– it's not suitable,' her mother finished as if he'd hadn't spoken.

'That's an excellent idea,' Louise said.

'Get one of those chairs from over there.' Louise's mother pointed to the line stacked against the wall. 'Your father and I want to talk to you.'

There was just room to squeeze her chair between her father's bed and the one next to it. 'So, what's this about?'

'I've got a proposition.'

Her hands went to her neck, fiddling with the ruby on its gold chain Matt had given to her last Christmas. She rubbed her fingers backwards and forwards over the smooth stone.

'As you know, your mother's persuaded me I need to take a break from the hotel.'

'An extended break, Tom,' her mother said quickly.

Her father held up his hands. 'Okay, okay, love. You've already won the battle – I've given in.'

'I don't want you going back on anything, that's all.'

He stroked her cheek. 'Don't worry, Lindy. I've felt off for a few months now, and I haven't got a death wish.'

'Dad!'

'The doc says I need at least three months' recuperation.'

'Longer if I have my way, Tom, but it's a start.'

'Louise, you've worked at the hotel, and you know it as well as anyone.' Her father's face creased in a frown.

'What is it? Shall I call someone?' Her mother was on her feet, poised to rush for a nurse.

'Just a twinge. Obviously, I want to leave the place in competent hands. I appreciate you've got your job at Everatt's, but I'd like you to consider managing the hotel till I get on my feet again.'

'Are you sure? Don't you want to give Oliver another chance?'

Her father stared at the ceiling, as if he was studying the night sky. 'I don't see Oliver anywhere, do you?'

'He phoned last night.' Her mother was fussing with things on the bedside cabinet, positioning and repositioning the beaker of water, her father's glasses case, his newspaper. 'He sounded upset.'

'Not upset enough to visit.' Her father's mouth set in a tight line.

'I've told you, Tom, he's got commitments. He can't just drop everything.'

'I might be dead and he wouldn't know.'

'He does care about you, Dad.'

'That's as maybe. But I can't rely on him to manage the hotel. He's made it clear often enough he's not interested.'

'He needs to grow up a bit, Tom, that's all.' Louise's mother didn't look round; it was obviously difficult for her to admit her beloved Oliver fell short of expectations.

Her father rubbed his hand up and down the wooden arm of his chair, as if he could smooth away thoughts of his son. 'What do you think, Louise? Could you see yourself managing on a temporary basis? Maeve would help you, of course.'

Could she see herself? It was all she'd ever wanted.

'You'll need some time to consider,' her father was saying. 'And you'll have to clear it with Everatt's. Maybe take unpaid leave?'

'And there's Matt.' Her mother had finally stopped fretting over the items on the cabinet and was sitting down. 'You'll need Matt's support.'

Louise pushed her feet hard against the floor, forcing back the urge to skip round the ward. She imagined herself turning a cartwheel and applause breaking out among the patients. Matt's words this morning: *it's lonely here without you* thudded in her mind. He wasn't going to like this development one bit. But she didn't care: she was taking on the hotel whatever he or anyone else might say.

Seven

Ollie let the hot water pound his back, easing the ache in his muscles. He stepped out of the shower and slung a towel round his shoulders. Running a palm across the fogged-up mirror, he peered into the circle of glass: bloodshot eyes, dark circles, stubble. He dried himself and pulled on Jess's robe that was hanging on the back of the door. His hands and arms poked out from the sleeves, and its hem flapped above his knees.

In the kitchen he put the kettle on to boil. He dropped a teabag into a mug and poured in boiling water. The teabag puffed up and floated to the top.

'You're up early.'

The voice made him jump. 'Jess! I was bringing you tea. Give you a bit of a lie-in after last night.'

As her hand grasped the mug, their fingertips grazed each other. 'I wasn't that late.'

'I didn't mean ... Did you have a good time?'

She shrugged. 'Okay. Nothing special.' She took a sip and crossed to the fridge to add more milk.

He studied her face: she looked pale and tired. It probably wasn't the best moment, but ... 'Jess, I know we haven't been getting on very well recently.'

'That's an understatement.'

'It's not all bad. Simone's offered me these extra shifts, and she said my commission will be good this month.'

'That's a drop in the ocean, Ollie.' She put her mug on the worktop and hugged herself, her shoulders hunched. 'I'm stressed with work, looking after Flo, and this place drives me mad. I'd like to move, but how can we save for a deposit?'

'You never said before you didn't like the flat.'

'Well, I don't. You need to pull your weight more.'

'That's not fair, and you know it. I cover the rent. I pay for most of the food, and I spend loads of time with Flo.'

'You could get a proper job.'

A proper job. He felt as if she'd slapped him. 'Where's this coming from? I thought you believed in me.'

'You haven't sold a painting for months.'

He clasped her arms. The rough skin on his fingers caught on the silky material of her nightdress. 'I want us to be friends again, Jess. For Flo's sake as well as ours.'

'Don't drag Flo into this. It's between you and me.'

'But she gets upset when we argue.'

Jess seemed to see him properly for the first time. 'What are you doing in my dressing gown?'

He undid the belt and then remembered he was bollock naked underneath. Too late now. 'Sorry, it was in the bathroom, and I didn't want to disturb you looking for clothes.' He held it out. 'Here, you have it.'

She snatched it free of his hand. 'I'm going to have a shower.'

Ollie enjoyed the trips to or from school with Flo. The short journey gave them some of their closest times together. Walking side by side generated an intimacy it was harder to achieve in the flat. Flo would chatter about her friends, homework, the dream she'd had last night, and if anything was worrying her, it often came out at this time.

But this morning, she lagged behind, whispering to herself. Ollie glanced over his shoulder: her hands were stuffed in her pockets, her head down as if she was searching the pavement for something she'd lost. He ventured a couple of questions, but with little response. They paused at the corner by the newsagent's, and Flo took her rucksack from Ollie and hoisted it onto her shoulders.

'Daddy.' She gazed up at him, and he saw the shine of tears in her eyes.

'What is it, baby?'

A gang of boys heading for the school pushed past them, kicking a tin can from one to the other. It clattered into the gutter, and they ran off laughing.

Ollie stroked Flo's arm, bulky in her anorak. 'What were you going to say?'

'You know what we talked about last night ...'

'The school trip?'

'No.'

'Me and Mummy?'

She nodded. 'You said about getting married again.'

He tucked a stray strand of hair behind her ear.

'Are you going to ask her?'

The memory of Jess's antagonism this morning, dark and blinding like a bat's wing, swooped across Ollie's mind. He forced his mouth into a smile. 'Of course I am. I said so, didn't I?'

'Tonight?'

'Yes, possibly.'

'Shall we ask Lauren's mum if I can stay?'

Ollie took her hand. 'Come on then. Let's find her.'

Ollie arrived at The Serendip an hour early. Angel was up a step ladder hanging a small oil painting, and her head whipped round as he opened the door.

'Ollie, it's you! What are you doing?'

'I do work here.' He screwed up his face. 'Unless you know something I don't.'

'I wasn't expecting you for ages.'

He held out his hand, palm upward and flicked it over. 'New leaf.'

She smiled and turned back to study the painting. It was a perfect scene: a stretch of moorland, the colour of the stippled heather echoed in a smudgy mauve sky. A steely-blue stream snaking across the foreground looked so cold, Ollie's teeth hurt.

He watched Angel place the spirit level on top of the frame and ease the picture up and to the right. He crossed to the small staffroom at the back of the gallery and hung his leather jacket on a hook next to Angel's raincoat. 'Shall I make coffee?' he called.

'Wonderful.'

She was climbing down the ladder when he got back with two mugs. She took one. 'Thanks, I could get used to the new leaf. You did a fantastic job on the stock cupboard as well; I've been putting off tidying that for weeks.'

He felt something uncoiling its grip from round his heart. 'My pleasure. Is everything okay? Simone said you had a family problem.'

Angel flopped onto the sofa. 'Sorry if I dropped you in it yesterday. It was either that or shut up the gallery. '

'I should have had my phone on. What happened?'

'My mum had a fall and was taken to hospital.'

'Oh no! Is she all right?'

'She's fractured her hip.' Angel leant back. 'They operated yesterday evening, so by the time she'd come round and I'd made sure she was settled, I didn't get home until two this morning.'

Ollie sat down next to her and put his hand on hers. 'You should have called me,' he said. 'I could have covered this morning.'

46

She squeezed his hand. 'I know, but I'd rather keep busy. And they said she's better resting today. I'll visit tonight.' She perched on the edge of the sofa, ready to move on, to start work again.

'My dad's had a heart attack.' That was it: the first time he'd said the words out loud.

'When?'

'Yesterday.'

'I'm so sorry. Is it serious?'

He shrugged. 'I don't think so.'

'Are you going down there?'

'Probably.' He felt her watching him.

'I can easily cover your shifts, especially while Mum's in hospital.'

'Thanks, Angel.' He flicked his thumb up and down the handle of his mug, the noise a relentless click. 'I'll see what happens tonight. I might have some good news for them.'

She raised her eyebrows. 'Sounds interesting.'

His cheeks flushed under her gaze. 'It's nothing. I've bought a lottery ticket, that's all.'

'Ollie, you're up to something.' She reached out and took the mug from him. 'Stop making that horrible noise and spill the beans.'

He stood up and fetched the black jewellery box from his jacket pocket. He unfolded the pink tissue paper and held out the box to Angel. The entwined rings lay cocooned inside.

'Ollie! They're lovely. I presume they're for Jess.'

'I'm going to ask her to renew our wedding vows.'

Angel leapt up and flung her arms round him. She was almost as tall as him and her black curly hair tickled his face. Her perfume smelt sharp and unfamiliar. She was bigger altogether than Jess, and her breasts pushed against his chest. He let himself lean into the embrace, and then felt uncomfortable. He shuffled backwards. It was a long time since he'd held another woman in his arms.

'She hasn't said *yes* yet.'

'But she will. It's so romantic.'

'I hope so. We had a blip a few years ago. Separated for a while.' The rawness of Jess and Flo's absence for those few weeks still gnawed at him sometimes in the middle of the night.

'But you got back together?'

He nodded.

'There you are – you've been through the fire and come out the other side.'

He thought of the nightly phone calls: him begging, almost hysterical; Jess, cool, refusing to acknowledge any guilt. And then one night, she'd sent a text: *okay, I'll come back.*

'The other side?' he said now. 'I guess so.'

At Angel's insistence, Ollie left the gallery early and shopped on the way home. Jess had a staff meeting after school, so he had a couple of hours to prepare. He bought her favourites: taramasalata, French bread, steaks, merlot. He hoovered the flat, showered, and arranged the tulips he'd bought in a vase. Jess liked the way they draped themselves over the lip – like dancers' limbs, she always said. By the time he phoned Lauren's house to check on Flo, he'd set the table and put red candles in the holders. When he heard the outside door slam, he pulled down the blind and flicked on the wall lights.

Jess kicked the door shut with her heel, dropped her brief case on the floor and leant back against the door frame, eyes half closed.

He placed his hands on the door on either side of her head. 'Bad day?'

She ducked under his arm. 'You've tidied up. What's with the flowers and candles?' She whirled round to face him. 'Where's Flo, Ollie? What are you up to?'

'It's all fine.'

'Don't muck about.' Her voice was sharp. 'Where's Flo? I thought you were collecting her.'

He put his arms round her. 'It's okay.' He could feel her resistance, but he pulled her close and her hair brushed his cheek.

She pushed him away. 'Ollie, I'm shattered, and I want to know where my daughter is.'

'Lauren's mum invited her to stay the night. Flo was desperate to go and I didn't think you'd mind.' He lifted her fingers to his mouth and kissed them. 'It will give us some time on our own. I'm in charge of cooking.' He tried to ignore her frown. 'Do you want to shower and change, or do you want to dive straight into the bubbly?'

'Bubbly? We can't afford champagne, Ollie.'

'We deserve a treat occasionally, don't we?'

She kissed his cheek. It was weeks since she'd shown him any affection. 'I certainly need one. You won't believe what Old Man Croak's done now.'

Ollie stroked a lock of hair away from her eye. 'Go and have a shower and wash off old Croak's dastardly deeds.'

She laughed. She actually laughed, and relief zipped through him.

When he heard the shower running, he checked the black box tucked into the top drawer of the sideboard: the rings nestled in their pink tissue. She hadn't wanted a wedding ring first time round: 'I don't need a band of gold to tell people I love you, Ollie,' she'd said. This time, it would be different.

In the kitchen, he got out the champagne flutes. They'd bought them from a charity shop to celebrate when they first moved in together – that must have been the night Flo was conceived – and they'd managed not to break them in all those years. He turned on the oven for the chips and washed some salad and arranged it in a bowl. He brushed the steaks with olive oil, and fished around in the bottom of the cupboard for the heavy-bottomed frying pan.

He heard Jess coming out of the bathroom and her feet padding along the corridor to the bedroom. He grabbed the jewellery box from the lounge, and just made it back into the kitchen as the bedroom door opened. Hiding the box in one of the top cupboards, he was poised to pull the champagne cork as Jess came in. She hesitated in the doorway, a tentative smile lifting the corners of her mouth. She was wearing jeans and a purple top the colour of the tulips he'd bought. Her hair was damp and curly from the shower.

The cork flew from the neck of the bottle and shot towards the ceiling. It bounced off and hit Ollie in the back of the neck. Jess laughed. The yellow liquid was already frothing over the top of the bottle, and he reached for a glass. As he watched the bubbles sparkling on the surface, he was conscious of her standing close to him. He breathed in the apricot scent, which carried with it memories of shared late-night showers. She couldn't have always used that gel, but somehow its fruity fragrance captured her.

He felt her fingers on his neck, and he steeled himself: stay calm; pick up the second glass; pour more champagne.

'I'm sorry I laughed,' she said. 'You looked so shocked.'

He rolled his head from side to side. The soft cotton of his collar eased the sting. 'It hurt.' He handed her a glass. 'To us.'

She smiled up at him. 'To us.'

Now? Should he ask her now? The silence felt easy and companionable, not full of spikes as it had been recently.

'Actually, Jess ...'

'It's so quiet ...'

Their voices crashed against each other.

Damn! Why had he spoken at that very second? Typical. He waited, willing her to go on.

'It's lovely and peaceful,' she said, 'but I miss Flo. I ought to phone her.'

'Wait!' Ollie caught at her hand. 'I need to ask you something.'

'You're hurting my wrist.' She pulled her hand free. 'Is it something bad? Something about Flo?'

'Of course not, but I wanted us to have this evening on our own.'

'You've got a funny look on your face. You're up to something.'

He twisted round and reached up to the cupboard with the jewellery box.

'What's that,' she asked.

He turned to face her. 'A present.'

'For me?'

His throat closed up and he didn't trust himself to speak. He handed her the box and watched her open it.

'They're beautiful.' She lifted the rings from the tissue paper and held them in her palm. 'Are they really for me?' She looked up, her green eyes shining.

'Of course. I hope they fit.'

She took them between her thumb and forefinger, and held them poised at the tip of her finger. The fourth finger. But there was something wrong.

'No!' His shout echoed in his head.

'What?' she asked. 'What's the matter?'

'That's the wrong hand. The rings are meant ... well, they're ...' He took them from her. 'They're wedding rings, Jess.'

'I don't understand.'

'Will you marry me again? I want us to renew our vows.'

Eight

Louise paused on the first-floor landing of the grand staircase. She glanced round at the paintings and photos jostling for space on the walls: three-masted schooners crossing the bay, sails brimful of wind; the pier, destroyed in the bombings of the Second World War; a huddle of pilgrims waiting to board the Mayflower down at the Barbican. Her father had been building the collection of Plymouth scenes since he took over the hotel as a young man.

Below her, in the reception hall, the grandfather clock chimed once: eight-thirty. The early morning light from the long window behind her sent a spear of golden yellow across the landing, creeping over the first couple of stairs. Louise clutched the banister and ran her palm backwards and forwards over the smooth mahogany. She'd taken her mother a cup of tea earlier. 'I'll call a meeting and tell the staff, Mum. I won't let you and Dad down.'

It was easy to say, but now with only a flight of stairs between her and the announcement she had to make, her mouth felt dry, and perspiration tickled her armpits. When she came back from London, she had to retrain herself to go down the stairs. She used to go up and down over and over again, like a skier graduating to higher slopes. At first, whenever she stood at the top of the stairs, the treads rushed up to meet her, and the hard wall seemed to smash into her. But gradually, she mastered them without the terror of that night grasping her throat. This morning was the worst time for it to happen again. Gripping the banister, she edged onto the first stair, then the second ...

There was no one behind reception. A couple, a huddle of bags at their feet, stood at the desk clearly waiting to check out. Maeve usually started at quarter to eight; it wasn't like her to be late. Louise glanced round: magazines were scattered across the coffee table in the alcove, and a pile of towels had been left on the armchair. The petals of the flowers decorating the central, circular table drooped brown and limp in their vase. Julie, one of the part-time receptionists, crouched on her knees near the door, helping a man gather up papers that had spilled from his briefcase.

'What's happening?' Louise snapped. 'Where's Maeve? This foyer's a complete mess.'

Julie squatted back on her heels and waited while the man pushed a folder into the briefcase. He smiled. 'That's so kind of you. Thank you.' He turned his smile in Louise's direction. 'I'm a clumsy oaf, and your colleague came to my rescue.' He turned back to Julie. 'It's the little things that count.'

Louise felt a blush spring to her cheeks. *Treat your staff well, and they'll serve you well* was one of her father's mantras. Blunder number one. She'd have to be careful.

'Maeve's gone to see about some crisis in the kitchen.' Julie stood up and looked over Louise's shoulder towards the desk. 'I'd better get back – there's a queue forming.'

'But how come you're here? Aren't you on this evening?'

'Maeve asked me to come in this morning as she expected us to be short-staffed.'

Louise went into the office and shut the door. Maeve's pink cardigan was hanging on the back of her father's swivel chair, the computer was on, and when Louise clicked the mouse, a list of Maeve's priorities for the day appeared on the screen. At the top of the list she'd written: *Meeting with Louise.*

Louise snatched the cardigan from the back of the chair and flung it on the table in the corner. Maeve was her father's right-hand. Louise had watched her in action, notepad poised on her knee to take down his decisions, glass of water ready in case he coughed, anticipating every need even before he knew it himself. She thought of her father's words in the hospital: *Maeve will help you of course.*

You bet she would. You bet. Just like she'd *helped* her out of the events manager's job.

Louise sat down at the computer. She opened a new document and began to type:

> *Maeve – Thanks for agreeing to hold the fort today. My father is doing well and should be out of hospital this afternoon. Perhaps you could order flowers and have someone arrange them in the flat for when my parents get back.*
>
> *I've got to pop out now for a couple of hours, but I'd be grateful if you'd organise for as many staff as possible to be in the lounge at eleven o'clock. I've got some news for them. It might be as well to put a sign outside saying the room will be closed to guests for an hour.*
>
> *Many thanks*
> *Louise*

Propping the sheet of paper on the keyboard, where Maeve couldn't possibly argue that she'd missed it, Louise left the office.

It was months now since she'd visited Freda, the counsellor. The almost daily meetings when she first got back from London had dwindled to weekly, then monthly, until one day, Freda said, 'Shall we leave it that you'll get in touch when you need to?'

Today was that day. It was only Freda's calm voice on the phone, 'I can see you at nine-thirty' that had persuaded her down the stairs.

The paintings on the wall in the waiting room were the same: woodland scenes, paths diverging, the way ahead unseen, unknowable. They always reminded her of Oliver's paintings.

Why didn't he come? She needed his support. Knowing that he'd turned against her because of Eugene was a constant ache. It wasn't fair that he blamed her for everything.

'Louise, would you like to come through?'

She saw Freda's smile, the long floral skirt, her wild frizzy hair, and she wanted to rush towards her, bury herself in Freda's baggy jumper. But she picked up her bag, straightened her back, and forced herself to walk through into the consulting room.

She sat down in the chair under the window. Freda always sat opposite in a red leather bucket chair, a notebook in her lap. She rarely wrote in it, but somehow she remembered every detail of what you said.

'How are you, Louise? Must be over a year since I last saw you.'

'I've been really well, but ...'

Freda waited: that mixture of patience, but intensity and intelligence, in her gaze. 'But? Has something happened?'

'My father's had a heart attack.'

'Sorry to hear that.'

'He's due out of hospital this afternoon.'

'That's good news, but you must have had a shock.'

Louise picked at loose skin on her thumb. 'I thought he was indestructible.'

Freda smiled. 'It takes a long time to realise our parents are as frail and vulnerable as we are.' She waited, letting the silence build.

'The thing is ...'

'The thing is?'

'My mum's taking him away to convalesce, and they've asked me ...' Louise looked towards the green jacket hanging on the back of the door. To the box of tissues on the coffee table.

'Asked you?' Freda's voice was soft.

'To look after the hotel while they're away, and afterwards. Till my dad's better.'

'Do you want to?'

'I love the hotel. I was devastated when I had to leave my job there, and I only moved to London because I couldn't find anything else that gave me the same buzz.'

Helping to set up the arts venue in Islington had seemed a gift at the time. And when Eugene McBride, the new director was appointed, they'd clicked immediately. An Irishman from the west coast, he had a frizz of red hair and a huge laugh. The air around him fizzed with energy, but his soft, brown eyes could exclude the world, so that only you and he existed. She'd introduced him to Oliver and Jess, and he'd arranged for her brother to have some permanent gallery space. It was all perfect until ... until ... it wasn't any more.

She was conscious of Freda's eyes on her. 'Sorry.'

'Take your time. I'm here to listen.'

'Managing the hotel is more than I ever hoped for. But now that I've got the chance, I can't sleep. I've hardly eaten. I've got to tell the staff this morning, and Matt –'

'Louise, slow down.' Freda put her notebook on the floor. 'Take a deep breath, feel it stretching your ribcage ... put your hands there ... that's it, hold the breath, and breathe out. Drop your shoulders. Let your arms dangle. Now, again – a deep breath ...'

As Freda's quiet voice murmured instructions, the scream trapped in Louise's chest subsided.

'Okay, let's go through some of the things you've mentioned. Tell me about Matt.'

'He doesn't like me spending time at the hotel for a start. So, how's he going to react when I tell him I'll be there full-time for the next three months? And he wants to go abroad this summer, and I won't be able to. He wants us to have a baby and ... and ...'

'Let's take one thing at a time. What reasons might Matt have for disliking you being at the hotel?'

'He doesn't enjoy being there, but that shouldn't mean I can't go. I don't stop him going out sailing, or object to the time he spends in the garage on his woodwork.'

'Do you feel threatened by those activities, or the time he spends on them?'

'No, why should I?'

'Could it be because you know he loves you more than any of those things?'

'I'm sure he does.'

'And do you love him more than the hotel?'

Louise stared at Freda. That was ridiculous – of course she did.

'It seems to me, Louise, that the first thing you need to do is talk to Matt. Tell him how you feel, and find out what he feels.'

Louise chewed her lip.

'How does that sound?'

'I can't. We don't have those sorts of conversations.'

'Perhaps it's time to start.' Freda picked up her notebook from the floor. Louise watched her write. She looked up from the page. 'I've got a spare appointment on Friday at two, if you'd like to come along then.'

*

Every available seat was taken in the lounge when Louise arrived. The kitchen staff had squashed together on the window seat, and two of the cleaners were sitting crossed-legged on the floor. The conversation stopped as if someone had flicked a switch when Louise opened the door. She picked her way across the room, and stood in front of the fireplace, a position her father adopted when he had important news to convey. 'Tell them together,' he used to say. 'Stops the rumour mill.'

All the eyes in the room were fixed on her, and she tried to include everyone with her gaze.

'First I'd like to thank you all for coming, and Maeve for organising the meeting at short notice.' She smiled across to one of the sofas where Maeve perched on an arm. 'As you know, my father had a heart attack two days ago.' Tension vibrated in the room. 'My mother and I were desperately worried – as I'm sure you all were – but fortunately, it doesn't seem to have been too severe.' Conversation bubbled up, and she raised her hand. 'All being well, my father will come out of hospital this afternoon and –' Cheers and applause broke out. 'Fantastic news!' one of the chefs shouted. 'Hear, hear!' Voices called out from various parts of the room.

Louise waited until everyone settled down again. 'My parents will be here for a couple of days, and then my mother is taking him away on an extended break.'

'But the hotel –'

'What will happen?'

'Will Maeve ...?'

Snippets emerged from the hubbub.

'I've loved the hotel since I was child ...' Louise's voice cracked, and she took a deep breath. 'And I'm delighted to tell you my parents have asked me to take over the running of the hotel until he's well enough to return.' She felt their surprise rolling towards her like the incoming tide. She fixed her gaze on Phyllis, the housekeeper, someone she knew was fond of her. 'I'm sure I can rely on everyone's support, as we all want the hotel's long-term success. In particular, I'll need Maeve's help, as she has worked so closely with my father over the years.' From the corner of her eye, she could see Maeve's folded arms, her bowed head. She was nearly there; one more burst and she'd done it. 'I'll be away from the hotel the rest of today – obviously I need to organise things at home as well as my job, but from tomorrow, I will be at the helm, and I'll do my utmost to return this place to my parents in as good, if not better, position than it is now. Thank you everyone for listening. Any problems, come and see me.'

Louise smoothed down the skirt of her new green dress and fingered the jade earrings. The day had gone better than she could have imagined: several people had approached her after the meeting to congratulate her; her boss, Julian Everatt, had agreed to her request for leave. 'Of course you must help out – we'll get a temp in,' he said. And best of all, her parents had arrived back from the hospital with her father looking much brighter and stronger.

Matt should be here any minute now. She'd prepared a casserole and the oven had made the kitchen hot. She opened the window onto their small back yard and leant her elbows on the sill. If she tried hard, she could smell the sea. Raised voices erupted from the young couple next door, and their skinny black cat appeared over the top of the fence, slithering down to land on the dustbin and chase across the yard. The dog on the other side barked, and its owner, a muscle-bound man covered in tattoos of snakes, swore at it. Louise slammed the window shut. She could still hear the couple rowing.

'Something smells good!' Matt came up behind her at the oven and put his arms round her. 'What a welcome!'

She hadn't heard the front door, and she swung round. 'Gosh! You scared me.'

He pulled her close, and his lips brushed hers. 'Sorry, just excited to have my wife home.' His mouth was against her ear. 'And don't you look wonderful?' He held her at arm's length. 'That dress is a knockout!'

'I bought it for our anniversary, and tonight's sort of to make up for it.'

Matt shrugged out of his jacket and hung it on the back of the chair. 'I could get used to this.' He pointed to the table. 'Candles, flowers ... and is that a bottle lurking on the worktop?'

'It certainly is.'

He rubbed his palms together. 'Way-hay! It gets better. I presume it's good news on your dad.'

She nodded. 'He came out this afternoon.'

'Great stuff.'

Matt poured them both a glass of wine. She arranged smoked salmon and prawns on plates and topped them with a spoonful of horseradish cream, while he told her about a sailing trip he was planning at the weekend. 'If you don't mind, that is.'

'That's fine with me.' She tossed salad leaves in the lime juice vinaigrette. 'I'll still need to spend time at the hotel. Dad won't be fully up to speed for a while.'

Matt raised his eyebrows, as she placed the plate in front of him. 'This looks great!' He laughed. 'Should I be suspicious? You haven't crashed the car, have you?'

'I told you – it's to make up for our anniversary dinner.' She sat down at the table. 'I need to talk to you, Matt.'

He looked up. 'I knew it! You have crashed the car.'

She sipped some wine. 'It's about the hotel.'

He put down his knife and fork and wiped his mouth on the napkin. 'Go on.'

He had turned the cuffs of his sleeves back, and she

stared at the fine black hairs on his arm. 'I know you're not keen on me spending time there.'

'And there was me thinking this was a celebration for us.'

'It is, but I have to get this out of the way first.'

'If it's not the car, what is it? You're obviously buttering me up for something.' He drained his glass and got up to pour another. His T-shirt had ridden up, and her eyes fixed on the line of skin above the waistband of his jeans. She wondered if the mole in the middle seemed darker.

'Dad's seems well, all things considered ...'

Matt leant against the worktop, his eyes watching her over the rim of his glass.

'But Mum's insisting on taking him away. The doctor says he needs three months' convalescence.'

'Probably a good idea.'

'Do you think so? I wasn't sure at first ... thought he'd be better in familiar surroundings ... but he'd be back in the thick of things within a week if –'

'I presume you're working up to telling me you'll be helping out while your parents are away.'

'Yes ... well ... yes and no.' She saw his frown. 'They've asked me to manage it.'

Matt was silent. She stood up and moved close to him. 'It will mean I won't be here much, but I'll get away as often as I can.'

'What about Wonder Boy?'

'Oliver? There's no sign of him.'

'Bastard!'

'I know it won't be easy.'

'And work? Have you handed your notice in? Jobs aren't two a penny, you know.'

'They were brilliant! They're getting a temp while I'm away.'

'I see. It's all decided.'

'Don't be angry, Matt. This is something I really want to do.'

His face softened into a half smile. 'I'm not angry. If it's important to you ... Oh, I don't know.'

'Talk to him,' Freda had said. 'Find out how he feels.'

'What are you thinking?' She'd never asked Matt such a question before, perhaps afraid of the answer. Afraid he might want more from her than she could give. She'd given everything to Eugene, and –

'It will be a lot of work, and I don't want you to get sick again.'

'I won't. I'm fine now.'

'I worry about you.'

Louise took his face between her hands. The stubble on his cheeks tickled her palms. 'I love you, Matt,' she whispered. 'I do love you.'

Nine

Ollie crawled out of bed and pulled on his jeans and a T-shirt. In the kitchen, he buttered a slice of bread and bit into it, while he waited for the kettle to boil. The box with the rings was on the worktop. He opened it and ran his finger over the rings' interlocked hearts. He'd hoped they'd be on Jess's finger now, but she hadn't said *yes*. Then again, she hadn't said *no*. Where the hell did he stand? He dropped the box into a drawer.

He jumped as arms clasped him round the waist.

Jess grinned up at him. Her cheeks were pink and glowing, her eyes smiling in the way they hadn't done for ages. 'Thanks for last night. I enjoyed it.'

He leaned forward and nuzzled his face against her hair. 'It was good to make love to you again.'

Her head rested on his chest. 'It felt like the old days.'

'We will be all right, won't we?' he murmured.

'Let's give it time.'

'But you do want to renew the vows?'

She didn't answer.

'Look at me, Jess.'

She lifted her head and her eyes met his.

She was as beautiful now as the day he'd first seen her. The tiny indentations of frown lines between her brows, the shadows circling her eyes, the scattering of grey hairs made her all the more precious. He bent his head and brushed his lips against hers. 'I'd do anything not to lose you.'

Her fingers traced the outline of his mouth. 'Let's see how we feel in a few months.'

'I know how I feel.'

She put her hands on his chest, and he felt the tension in her body shift. 'So, waiting won't make any difference.'

Ollie sat on a bench outside Flo's school. A pigeon waddled on the pavement in front of him, searching for titbits between paving slabs, head bobbing on its plump body. He raised his gaze to the school gates. A group of mothers had gathered, circling a pram, their laughter and calls skittering through the air towards him. He'd never forget his first sight of Flo as a squalling, slippery bundle. He and Jess had produced this work of –

'Daddy! Daddy!' Flo darted across the road towards him, rucksack bumping on her back.

He stood up as she reached the bench and flung herself into his arms. 'I've missed you, Daddy.'

He laughed. 'Flo, you weigh a ton. Lauren's mum must have given you bricks to eat.'

She slithered to the ground.

'Did you have a good time?'

'It was cool. We had pizza and watched *Mamma Mia.*'

'You've seen it hundreds of times already.'

'We sang all the songs. *Honey Honey* is ace. Can we go to Greece on holiday?'

'One day maybe.' He sat down on the bench again and pulled her towards him. 'Sweetheart, I need to talk to you.'

She stared at him with those eyes, the same shape and shade as Jess's. 'What did Mummy say when you asked her?' She caught up one of her plaits and stuck the end in her mouth. 'She said *no*, didn't she?'

He eased the hair free of her mouth. 'Why do you say that?'

'You look sad.'

'It's not that. I didn't ask her.'

Her gaze seemed to penetrate his skull, exposing his lie.

'But you said –'

'I know. I know.' He'd wanted to protect her from Jess's doubts, but now it didn't seem such a good idea.

'I told Lauren.'

Ollie groaned inwardly. Lauren would have told her mother, her mother would have ... 'I am going to ask her, but last night wasn't the right time.'

'Why?'

'She was all stressed. She'd had a bad day at school.'

'Flo! The bell's ringing.' Lauren was waving from the other side of the road. 'We're lining up. Come on.'

Flo turned away, her eyes focused on Lauren and school, shutting him out.

'Wait, sweetheart.'

He could sense hesitation flowing down her arm and into her hand. School meant friends, lessons, fun, but she needed to hear something that would remove the desolation from her eyes. 'You know your mum and me have been arguing, don't you?'

She nodded.

'When things have settled down, I'll ask her.'

'Promise?'

He rubbed his nose against hers, a hangover from when she was little, and rubbed noses sealed a bedtime story, an ice cream, a trip to the park. 'I promise. And listen.' He leaned forward. 'This is between you and me. Okay? Don't tell Mummy, or Lauren, or anyone.'

She nodded, and held out her clenched fist. He scrunched his fingers into his palm and fitted his knuckles into the hollows of hers. 'Agreed?'

Flo tapped the back of his fist three times with hers, and then settled it back into place. 'Agreed.'

It was late April, and as Ollie reached the Nag's Head, a cold wind swirled around him, lifting a sheet of newspaper and carrying it away, like a rudderless kite. He pulled his scarf tighter. Jess would be in her classroom by now, a double period of English with her 'A' level students. They were doing *love* she'd said this morning, When they were first together, she'd shown him a poem by Yeats. He remembered the last couple of lines: *I have spread my dreams under your feet/Tread softly because you tread on my dreams.* 'That's beautiful,' he'd told her, and she kissed him. 'We'll always tread softly, won't we?' she said.

But somehow they'd stamped about recklessly, disregarding their fragile dreams. Jess had always believed in him, had loved his paintings. Now she didn't seem to care. His chest tightened as the road curved upwards, and he forced more air into his lungs. Too little exercise and too many fags. He shifted his bag onto the other shoulder.

He arrived at the church. He settled his stool on the opposite side of the road and unloaded his paints, brushes, palette and bottles of water. Pallid sunlight stroked the spire and slanted across the roof. He took out a pencil and sketched in the contours of the church. He added lines to mark the cherry tree on the right. Someone stopped to see what he was doing. He could feel them at his left shoulder and wished they'd go away. Now for some colour on the background. This was always a scary moment. He loaded cobalt blue onto his palette and added yellow, and plenty of water. He swept the wash across the top of the page. Adding more blue to deepen the pigment, he continued the wash down the paper. He rinsed his brush. White clouds tinged with grey scudded across the sky behind the church. He only had a moment to get them down. He wanted to put the paint on while the wash was still wet. He'd bought some coarse handmade paper, and he was enjoying the texture's bite. He blobbed pink onto the branches of the tree to suggest blossom, and darkened the lines of the building to bring it into the foreground.

The clock on the tower began to chime. Ollie stared up at its golden hands and numerals ... nine ... ten ... eleven. He packed up his paints while he waited for the watercolours to dry. It had been good to try something different. He'd been lazy and let things slip recently. Ten to thirty minutes' sketching every morning – that's what his tutor at college had recommended. Ollie tucked his painting between two sheets of card to protect it, and slotted it into his bag. He'd start his new regime tomorrow.

There was no sign of Angel when he pushed open the door of The Serendip, but the ping of the bell brought her scurrying from the stock cupboard. 'Thank God, it's you, Ollie.'

He laughed. 'Who were you expecting? The dreaded Simone?'

She shook her head. 'I've had a busy morning. More customers in a couple of hours than we usually have in as many days.'

'That's good, isn't it?' Ollie ran his finger down the line of sales. 'Hey, that ghastly abstract's gone! If I had to look at that another day –' He jumped when Angel snapped the book shut on his fingers. He raised his eyebrows at her. 'What's up? Surely you're as glad to see the back of that one as I am.'

'Yeah, there's lots of good news.' She picked up the book and held it against her chest. 'But I want to hear yours first.'

'Mine? What do you mean?'

'What happened last night with Jess?'

The positive feelings the watercolour had generated gushed out of Ollie like a deflating balloon.

'Don't keep me in suspense! What did she say?'

'She didn't –'

'Don't tell me she said *no*?'

He shook his head.

'What then?'

'Let's just say the jury's still out.'

Angel leant forward, her elbows on the desk, her gaze boring into him.

'You're wasted here,' he said. 'You'd better get down to MI5 and offer your interrogation services.'

'You can't blame me for wanting to know. My romantic life is as barren as the tundra.'

Ollie crossed to the sofa. 'She wants to wait. See how we get on over the next few weeks, months ... I don't know ...'

'I'm sorry, Ollie. I shouldn't have probed.'

'You weren't to know.'

Angel held up the book she was clutching. 'But I have got news that will cheer you up.'

'I can't wait.'

She opened the book and placed it on his lap.

'First you don't want me to look. Now you do.'

'Check today's sales.'

His eyes slid down the list of names: Jenny Reed: *Dawn Chorus* oils; Phil Hazelhurst: *The Painter's Muse* acrylic; Frank Goodwin: *It's a Cat's Life* charcoal sketches; Oliver Anderson – He shot upright. 'It's one of mine! You've sold one of mine. Which one?'

'Have another look.'

Oliver Anderson: *Parting of the Ways* watercolours I, II, III and IV. He slammed the book shut and ran to the side gallery. It was true. There were his paintings, the red circle on all four confirming the sales. He let out a yell.

Angel appeared beside him. 'Isn't it great? This woman

fell totally in love with them. She's going to put them in the dining room in her house in Sussex, and she wants more of yours for her London flat!'

Ollie punched the air with his fist. He caught hold of Angel and waltzed her round the gallery, bumping into the desk and knocking over a chair. Her breath was hot against his cheek, her hair whipping across his face with every turn. He fell onto the sofa, pulling her down with him.

'You're mad, Ollie. Totally mad.'

'I know.'

'What will you do with the money?'

'You're joking, aren't you?' He sat up, his excitement dashed. 'Any extra money I make goes straight into the household pot.'

'But if you could spend it how you liked – what would you do?'

'That's easy. I'd be on the next plane to Venice.'

'Hey, that's my dream too.' Angel fixed her brown eyes on him. 'I did my dissertation on Veronese, and I've always wanted to go.'

'John Singer Sargent's paintings of Venice are unbeliev-able. If I could paint light like that …' He fished his mobile from his pocket. 'There's a call I need to make.'

'That sale has galvanised you.'

'I'm going outside, but I'll make it quick.' As he stepped out on to the pavement, the cold wind struck through his T-shirt. He scrolled down the names in his phone until he found *Dad*.

'Oliver, it's you.' It was his mother's voice.

'Mum, hi.'

'It's good to hear from you.'

'I was expecting Dad ... how is he?' He pushed the phone harder against his ear. 'He is okay, isn't he?'

'He's fine, love, but he's very tired.' *Very tired* – it was what she always used to say to him after she'd read him a bedtime story, pulling the covers tight to his chin: 'Off to sleep now, you're very tired.'

'Can I speak to him?'

'He's having a rest. We went out for a short walk earlier, and it took it out of him.'

'Is it all right? Should he be out walking?' Ollie noticed a shadow on the pavement in front of him. He looked up. A Japanese man held out a map; a woman and two young girls hovered behind him. Usually Ollie liked to help tourists, but now ... 'Sorry, Mum. What did you say? Someone was asking me for directions.'

'The doctors said he needed gentle exercise. We only took a few turns along The Hoe.'

'Listen, Mum, I'm coming down at the weekend. Sorry I haven't been before but –'

'Oh dear, we're going away. Your father needs a complete break: he's already worrying about the hotel.'

Ollie leant against the wall. Just as he'd worked himself up to visit. 'Where are you going?'

She laughed. 'It's a secret. Tom's pestering me to tell him, but my lips are sealed.'

He knew it was no good trying to persuade her. No matter how much you wheedled, she was made of iron when it came to secrets.

'How long are you going for?'

'A month.'

'Who's looking after the hotel?'

'Well, Maeve will be here ... and Louise is going to help.'

A longing to see his parents washed over him. Why had he cut himself off in this stupid way? He should have gone straight down there when he first heard about his father.

'Mum, I've sold four paintings.'

'Love, that's wonderful! I'm so pleased for you. I'll tell

your father ... that's him calling now. I'll have to go. Love you.'

'I'll come down when –'

The phone beeped once and then went dead. He squeezed it until his nails dug into his palms.

Ten

L ouise leant back in the chair. 'That curry was delicious.'
Matt cleared the plates away. 'All part of the service, my lady.'

'You were right – I needed a night off.' She yawned and stretched upwards, trying to ease the ache in her spine. 'Thanks for persuading me.'

'It was good to see you laugh.' He was stacking the dishwasher. 'You're so serious these days.'

'I suppose it has been full on.'

He straightened up. 'Let me help relax you some more.' He turned out the light, so that only the glow from the candle on the table lit the room. He stood behind her chair, and caught hold of her top. He lifted it over her head and unhooked her bra. The wisp of silky material fell into her lap. His hands on her shoulders were warm. His thumbs circled outwards from the top of her spine towards her left shoulder, back again and over to the right. She stared at the candle's flickering reflection on the wall. His thumb pressed into the knots of pain and she imagined muscle cells untangling, sliding free of their snarled braid. She swivelled round in the chair and he lowered his head to hers. His tongue slipped into her mouth. He knelt in front of her and unzipped her trousers, his eyes fixed on hers. She lifted her hips and he eased the trousers down her legs and over her feet. He teased her pants to one side, and she caught her breath as his fingers found her. Her mind pulled free of the hotel, like a boat slipping its moorings. She let herself float, no demands, no phone calls, no responsibility. A car pulled up in the narrow street outside, and her gaze followed its headlights swooping over the blind in the darkened room. His fingers probed deeper. Car doors slammed. Voices called *good night, good night*. Then silence. And the tingling began, growing and swelling, spiralling upwards and across her belly and spreading down into her thighs.

Matt was standing at the cooker. He looked over his shoulder and winked. 'Morning! How does scrambled eggs on toast sound?' He banged two slices of bread into the toaster. Louise imagined the soft gooey texture of scrambled eggs and her throat constricted.

He put the plate on the table and twirled the tea cloth above his head. 'Tea or coffee?'

She pulled out a chair. 'Coffee will be great.'

He lifted the cafetière from the cupboard and reached for a packet of fresh coffee.

'Just instant, Matt. I'm late as it is.' She picked up her knife and fork and cut off a corner of toast, pushing egg onto it.

He plonked a mug beside her. 'Blimey, Louise, that's not going to keep a bird alive.'

She forced the egg past the lump in her throat. 'You know I'm not good with breakfast.'

'You've lost weight since you've been running round that hotel.'

She sipped her coffee and gulped down another mouthful of egg. 'That was lovely. Thank you.'

'But you've left loads.'

'Sorry.' She stood up and grabbed her handbag from the chair.

He stepped towards her and clasped his arms round her waist. 'Last night was great.'

In the distance, a clock began chiming. She counted: seven. 'It *was* lovely, but I must go.'

'When are you expecting your mum and dad?'

'Sometime this afternoon.' She unhooked her jacket from the back of the door. 'Why don't we have dinner at the hotel tonight? They can tell us about their trip.'

He took the jacket from her grasp and held it while she eased her arms into the sleeves. 'I'd rather spend the evening here at home.' He sighed the words into her ear. 'Just the two of us.'

'I'll phone, Matt, when I find out what's happening.'

'But you will be home, now your dad's back?'

She kissed his cheek. 'I'll let you know.'

Mike, the night porter, was hovering by the door when she arrived in reception.

'I know, Mike,' she said before he could protest. 'I'm late.'

'The missus is working today, so I need to take the kids to school.'

'Sorry to hold you up.' Mike lived in Plympton and it could take ages to get across Plymouth at this time of day. 'Has it been a quiet night?'

'Thought I might have to get an ambulance for the old boy in room sixteen.'

'What happened?'

He crossed the foyer to the desk, and picked up the incident book, pointing to the last entry. 'He had the worst nose bleed ever. Didn't help his wife was panicking.'

'What did you do?'

'Phoned the out-of-hours people and followed their

instructions. It's all detailed in the book. The room and bedding will need a good sort out. There was enough blood to –'

'I'll let Phyllis know,' Louise said. 'Thanks for dealing with it. Get off home, and I'll see you tonight.'

'Is it today the governor's back from his holiday?'

'Yes, but I doubt he'll rush straight into things. Mum will make sure of that.'

'It will be nice to see him fit and well again after what he went through,' Mike said.

By the time Maeve arrived to take over the desk, Louise had checked out several guests, dealt with a complaint about a faulty radiator, made sure Mr Evans in room sixteen was better, and moved him and his wife to another room. She was relieved to see Maeve: a headache had gathered over her right eyebrow and was advancing down the side of her face.

She sat in the window seat of the sitting room, which looked out onto The Hoe, and began her list: (1) See Chef about special welcome home meal for Mum and Dad (2) Check their flat and arrange fresh flowers (3) Ring Oliver (4) Discuss bookings with Maeve.

Chef's voice reverberated around the corridor as Louise made her way to the kitchen. 'That purée won't do!' he screamed at the new commis chef. 'It tastes like washing up water.' He was usually mild-mannered and she'd never heard him raise his voice before.

'Chef, the guests will hear you.'

He threw a roasting tin across the room. It clattered to the floor. 'I don't give a fuck! Get that man out of my kitchen.' He gesticulated with a carving knife.

Pete, the commis chef, backed away. 'Sorry. I'm really sorry.'

'Pete, wait outside my office,' Louise said. 'I'm sure we can sort this out.'

He sidled out of the kitchen, his eyes fixed on the carving knife Chef was clutching.

As soon as he'd gone, Chef turned back to the joint of lamb he was basting.

'Can we talk about this, Chef?'

He didn't look round. 'He's a total incompetent that man.' He spooned juices over the meat. 'If he comes back, I go.'

The kitchen was suddenly still, as if the ultimatum had cast a spell. Louise sensed them all waiting for her to react. She glanced at Chef's face, at the grim set of his mouth, his eyebrows that seemed to be working independently. He'd arrived about five years ago, trailing Michelin stars in his wake, a feather in her father's cap.

'Chef, can you manage for today if I send Pete home. We'll get a temp from the agency for tomorrow, and then look for someone more permanent.' She waited, but he didn't answer. 'You'll have the main say about who we take on.'

The change in the atmosphere was tangible.

'No problem, Miss Louise.' Chef's voice was his usual undertone. 'Oh, and it's boeuf bourguignon on the menu tonight, in case you were wondering. Your father's favourite.' He gave a broad wink.

Louise walked back to the office, her heart pounding. This was a high risk game. Had she just won or lost a round?

There was no sign of Pete outside her door, but Maeve was at the desk.

'Have you seen, Pete?' Louise asked.

Maeve was staring into a small mirror, reapplying her lipstick. 'Who?'

'The commis chef you got from the agency.'

'No.'

Louise turned away and then swung back. 'Actually, Maeve, as you're free at the moment, I'd like a word.'

Maeve dropped the mirror into her bag and folded her arms. 'What is it?'

'I was checking reservations this morning.' Louise paused, determined not to be the first one to look away. 'We don't seem to have much in the book.'

'It is quiet.'

'But it's the beginning of June.' Louise tapped her pen on the page – only half the rooms were booked for next weekend. 'We should be really busy.'

'You'd think so.' Maeve screwed up her nose.

'I'd like you to investigate setting up an online booking system. I've been reading about it. Apparently it co-ordinates all the hotel functions like bookings, sales and marketing.'

Maeve turned over pages in the reservations book, her nails a vivid red against the white paper. 'Ours has always seemed efficient to me.'

Conscious of her own neglected nails, Louise slid her hand behind her book. 'But so many people book online nowadays. What's stopping us setting that up?'

Maeve fussed with the collar of her blouse. 'Your father.'

'Dad? Why?'

'I don't like to criticise him, Louise. Especially when he's been so poorly.'

'I won't tell him. But I'd like to be in the picture.'

'He believes personal interaction between guests and staff is the key to success.'

'Of course, but –'

'He says there's nothing worse than arriving at a hotel and being met by banks of computers, and staff with their eyes focused on screens.'

'But the way it's going, we soon won't have guests arriving.'

Maeve raised an already finely-arched eyebrow and turned away when the phone started ringing.

Louise had ordered an arrangement of roses and gypsophila for her parents' flat, and she stood back from the table under the window to admire them. The pink blooms injected life into the room.

She checked the fridge in the tiny kitchen for the basics she'd asked Chef to provide, and found the fruit bowl on the worktop laden with apples, oranges and bananas. She peeled back the skin from a banana and took a bite. What to do about Oliver?

In the first few days after her father's heart attack, she'd phoned her brother every day. *Yes, he'd be down. He'd spoken to Mum. Yes, of course he cared about Dad – but things were difficult.* Since they'd been away, she hadn't bothered. But now, she took out her mobile and clicked on his name.

To her amazement, he answered straight away. 'Hi, Loulou. I was going to phone you.'

Oh, yes? Why did he always say that when it was obvious nothing had been further from his mind?

'Have you heard from Mum and Dad?' he asked. 'They're due back today, aren't they?'

'How do you know?'

'I've rung them while they've been away.'

Louise's hand tightened round the banana. It oozed out of the skin and smeared itself across her hand. Talk about the prodigal son. He'd be down here the minute they were back and have them eating out of his hand.

'They said you've been doing a great job.'

'It's been a lot of work, and poor Matt has had to fend for himself.' Louise dropped the banana onto the worktop and crossed to the sink. She held her hand under the running water and watched it sluice away blobs of banana.

'I've promised them I'll come at the weekend,' Oliver was saying.

Louise wiped her hand across the towel. '*This* weekend? You mean tomorrow?'

'I don't know yet if it will be tomorrow or Sunday. Need to sort it with Jess. We've been ... me and Jess ... we've been having some problems.'

That would be right. Problems followed Jess like a bad smell.

'Are you coming on your own?' She felt sick at the thought of seeing Jess again.

'If Jess can come, it might be a chance to put the past behind us.'

'Does that mean you don't blame me any more?'

'I don't know,' he said. 'We were all to blame in a way.'

'How can you say that?' Louise heard herself screeching. 'I've never understood why you were angry with me.'

'Easier than blaming Jess, I guess.'

'I've got to go, Oliver. I've got loads to do.'

She slumped onto a chair and eased off her shoes. Images of Eugene swirled in her mind, as vivid as if it had all happened yesterday. He used to joke that with his red hair, brown eyes and freckled skin, he was an Irishman straight from central casting, but he was unlike anyone she'd ever known. Being with him made her stronger, cleverer, more beautiful. And the tenderness in his eyes spun a web, which pulled her ever closer to him. Until the web snapped and the world went dark.

Matt had made her feel safe again when she came back to Plymouth, but running the hotel had lifted the dark-ness completely. She'd found where she wanted to be. She couldn't go back to the office job waiting for her at Everatt & Johnson, evenings watching TV with Matt, coffee mornings with Emily. She wouldn't.

She was woken by a vibration against her chest. She opened her eyes. The sun was hot on her face. She stretched her legs and felt the pain of cramped muscles. Her hands hurt where she'd been clenching them under her chin. She straightened her fingers and realised she was clutching her mobile. It had gone silent but as she stared at it, it started up again.

'Maeve.' Louise tried to make her voice bright, but her tongue felt too big for her mouth. She hated falling asleep in the daytime. 'Is everything okay? I'm getting the flat ready for Mum and Dad.'

'They're back!'

'Back?' Louise sat up. 'What time is it?'

'Three. They caught an earlier train. I've arranged tea in the sitting room for them.'

'I'll be down in two minutes.'

Louise pushed herself up from the sofa. She couldn't recall going to sit on it, let alone lying down and falling asleep. But the dream clotting her mind felt real enough: the new computer system installed, a barrage of screens sprawling over the reception desk, and guests arriving in tens, hundreds, thousands, banging on the doors and windows, jammed into the foyer, screaming for rooms.

Eleven

Ollie shuffled into the living room in his dressing gown. Jess and Flo were at the table doing a jigsaw. He'd only managed snatches of sleep until about five o' clock when he'd finally drifted off. He slumped onto the sofa and peered at the time on his mobile through bleary eyes: 10.05. Looked like the trip to Plymouth was off today.

'What's the plan?' he asked eventually, when it seemed the two of them might mutter indefinitely about corners, and edge pieces and too much sky.

'What do you mean *plan*?' Jess didn't look round.

'You know – plan. Have you two got anything planned for today?'

'Flo's got her dance class this morning. And I thought you might take her swimming this afternoon, so I can get my marking done.'

Flo twisted round in the chair. She had green stuff on her eyes. 'Can we, Daddy? I want to show you my dive.'

'What dance class?'

'It's a new one.'

Why were there always things going on that he didn't know about? 'Can't she start next week? I thought we might have a day out somewhere.'

Jess continued sorting pieces of the jigsaw, but Flo shook her head. 'I've got a new leotard specially.'

'Well, do you have to mark today, Jess?' Ollie asked. 'We could still go out this afternoon, and it is the weekend.'

'Teachers don't get weekends, or hadn't you noticed?'

Flo pulled a face at him and turned back to the jigsaw.

'Perhaps if you didn't squander money on wine, I wouldn't have to work so hard.'

'Okay. No need to snap.' Ollie wondered how the back of Jess's head managed to convey so much irritation. 'I sold some paintings. I thought you might want to celebrate with me.'

She jumped up, scattering pieces of jigsaw. 'You won't get the money for those paintings for ages yet, and by the time the gallery takes their cut ...'

'Mummy, don't cry.' Flo wrapped her arms round Jess's waist.

For a few seconds Ollie was transfixed by the neatly-braided plait of blonde hair hanging down Flo's back in the valley between her shoulder blades, and then the sound of Jess weeping reached his brain. He was up and across the room, his arms cuddling both of them close to him.

'Ssh. Ssh,' he crooned. When the spasm eased, he led them to sit on the sofa. He put his arm round Jess's shoulder and pulled Flo onto his lap. She stuck her thumb in her mouth. The green stuff on her eyes had smudged onto her forehead.

He eased Jess's hands away from her face and passed her a tissue from the box on the arm of the sofa. 'What's brought this on?'

'I don't know. I'm so tired and stressed.' She scrubbed at her face with the tissue. 'We've got Ofsted in two weeks, and the paperwork is horrendous.'

'I'll help you, Mummy.'

Jess stroked Flo's cheek. 'I know you will, baby, but this is something I've got to do myself.'

'Can I make a suggestion?' He hoped Jess couldn't feel

his heart thudding. He wanted to make this come out as if it was the most casual thing in the world. 'A change of scene would do you good. Do us all good. How about I take Flo to dancing and swimming today, while you do your work, and tomorrow we all go to Plymouth.'

'Tomorrow?' Jess pulled free of his arm. 'Are you crazy? I've got so much on and –'

'We can see Mum and Dad, and the sea air will fill us with energy.'

'When you came back from Plymouth the last time, you said you hated your dad and you'd never go again.'

'Doesn't do any good to hang on to bad feeling.'

Jess eyed him, suspicion radiating from her. 'Why now?'

'Family day out.'

'Will Louise be there?'

'Yes, but –'

'Then I'll be as welcome as a wasp at a picnic.'

'Come on, Mummy, please say yes.' Flo jumped up and down on Ollie's lap.

'You go, Ollie,' Jess said. 'I've agreed to go to the head of department's barbecue. He's got a daughter Flo's age.'

'Can't you cancel?'

'It's been arranged for weeks.'

'You can come with us.' Flo looked at Jess. 'Daddy is invited, isn't he?'

'Of course he is. But I didn't think teacher talk at barbecues was his sort of thing.'

'Please, Daddy, say you'll come. Then we can still have a day out together.' She clasped his face in her hands and planted a kiss on his nose.

'Okay. Barbecue it is then.'

Ollie saw Flo into the dance class. 'Have fun, sweetheart. I'll wait outside.' She waved as she skipped off with a couple of her friends from school. He settled on a bench across the road and pulled his sketch pad from his bag. His eyes rested on the tramp sitting on a bench a few feet away. Shaggy white hair reached to his shoulders, and his knobbly hands clasped the top of a stick. Ollie rummaged in his bag for the packet of charcoal; he'd just bought a new set of willow. Holding a piece of rubber putty in his left hand to keep it warm, he drew the shape of the old man's head. The left side of his face was in shadow, and Ollie worked in the charcoal with his fingers to get some shading.

'Hi, there. Long time no see.'

The voice was close. He glanced round and found Belinda, a friend of Jess's, had joined him on the bench. Despite an overcast sky, she wore huge sunglasses.

'Hi,' he said, returning his gaze to the sketch, hand poised to resume drawing.

'Rosie started the class last week, and she thought it was brilliant,' Belinda said. 'I phoned Jess and told her it would be great for Flo.'

'Right.'

'Is everything okay with Jess?'

The piece of charcoal in Ollie's fingers snapped in half. He put the sketch pad on the bench beside him and turned to face her. She'd pushed the sunglasses up on top of her head and was watching him through her fringe of false eye-lashes.

'Jess is fine,' he said. 'Getting her marking done this morning, so that we can enjoy the rest of the weekend.'

Belinda smiled, revealing some jewel thing on her front tooth. 'I said that to her. I said "Listen, honey, you need more time together, and everything will be cool."'

The old man on the bench hauled himself to his feet and shuffled away. His coat was tied round the middle with string, and the sole of one of his boots flapped with every step. Ollie turned back to Belinda. 'You've obviously got your wires crossed. Everything's already cool.'

'It sure didn't seem so when I had coffee with Jess the other day.'

'Why?'

Belinda twisted the huge diamond that glittered next to her wedding ring and resettled it. 'I don't like to see my friends cry.'

Ollie gulped down all the replies that leapt to his lips. If she thought he was going to give her the satisfaction –

The sound of his mobile came from his bag. He glanced down and then away again as if it was nothing to do with him.

'Don't mind me,' Belinda said, 'if you want to get that.'

He clamped his hands between his knees to stop him reaching for the phone. It might be Jess ... perhaps she'd changed her mind about tomorrow. The phone stopped. He glanced across the road: must be nearly time for Flo to come out. An incoming text buzzed.

'You'd better check that,' Belinda said.

Ollie stood up and swung his bag onto his shoulder. 'Yeah. Must go. See you around.' He strode away. Even if she reported him to Jess, he couldn't stand the witch for another second.

He leant against a wall and pulled his mobile from his bag. He clicked on the text: *Haven't heard from you about today, Oliver, so presuming you'll be down tomorrow. Do bring Jess and Flo. Mum x*

Ollie was in the bathroom the next morning when he decided he couldn't face the barbecue. And Jess didn't seem to care if he went or not. He'd bought roses for her on the way back from the dance class, taken Flo swimming, vacuumed the flat, ordered Chinese take-away for them in the evening, and it was as much as she could do to kiss him goodnight.

He climbed into bed, and pulled the duvet up to his chin, but he couldn't get warm. He lay on his back and stared up at the ceiling. Years ago, they'd bought stars that glowed in the dark and stuck them up there. After they'd switched the light out, they used to lie, hand in hand, watching the stars and whispering, so as not to wake baby Flo in her cradle. There were twenty stars, and they took turns to share their dreams. Sometimes they were small: *Please let Flo sleep through the night*; other times big: *I want to have an exhibition at the Royal Academy;* and once Jess had murmured: *I hope we grow old together*. Most of the stars had fallen down over the years, but two clung on. Ollie fixed his gaze on each of them in turn: *Please let Jess still love me* and *Make my dad well.*

The door banged open and Flo bounced into the room. She flung herself onto the bed, and sat cross-legged, her eyes on Ollie's face. 'Mum says we're going soon.'

'What's that on your eyes?' he asked. The green stuff was back again.

'Eye shadow. Mummy said I can.'

'Did she?'

'We heard you in the bathroom.' Flo manoeuvred herself closer. 'How come you're back in bed?'

'I'm not feeling that good,' he said.

'Shall I get the thermometer?'

'No, I've got a bad stomach, that's all.' Which wasn't a lie. Whenever he thought of his parents waiting for him to arrive, pain radiated through his body.

'I'll tell Mummy.' Flo jumped off the bed and disappeared from the room. He heard her voice in the kitchen and the murmur of Jess's.

He felt round for his phone on the bedside table. *Sorry, not going to be able to make it this weekend after all. Picked up some bug – puking my guts up. Hope you're okay.'* He scrolled down to his mother's name and sent the text before he got cold feet.

The slam of the front door woke him. He listened to the silence of the flat. Surely they hadn't gone without saying anything? He jumped out of bed and rushed to the window in the living room. Opening it wide, he leant out. He could see them at the end of the road, tiny figures about to turn the corner. He shut the window and slid down the wall until he reached the floor.

He woke again, still slumped on the floor, to the noise of a text. The message was from Dan: *Get down here now. I'm a pint ahead.*

Dan ordered two more lagers. 'Thanks for coming, mate. Didn't think you would.' He was wearing a canary-yellow shirt and black and white checked trousers.

In his blue T-shirt and jeans, Ollie felt old and staid. He sipped his drink. 'What's the occasion?'

Dan shuffled his feet in an awkward little tap dance. 'You won't believe it, man.'

Ollie laughed. 'Try me.'

'Me and the guys have only gone and got a recording contract.' Dan grinned, showing the gap between his two front teeth, and Ollie was back to the first day at college when they'd met.

He lifted his glass to Dan's. 'That's amazing. How come?'

'We made a demo tape, sent it off to Decko, expecting zilch as usual, and they asked us to go in to see them.'

'What happens now?'

'We're writing new songs like crazy. We start in the studio next month.'

Ollie finished his drink. 'I'm chuffed for you. I really am.' He pointed at Dan's glass. 'Another?'

'Is the pope a Catholic?'

'I take it that's a *yes*.' Ollie signalled to the barman. 'A pint, please.'

'What about you?' Dan asked. 'I thought we were going to make a night of it.'

'I'll sit this one out.'

'Getting sensible in your old age, man.' Dan twirled Ollie's ponytail in the air and then draped it over his top lip. 'What do you think? Fu Manchu?' He curled one end. 'What about Salvador Dali?'

'You're an idiot!'

'An idiot with a recording contract, don't forget.'

'As if you'd let me.'

'So, what's happening, man?'

'In a word – shit-all.'

'Strictly speaking that's two words, Ollie m'boy. I take it things aren't good.'

'You take it correctly. Jess and me ...' He stopped; he'd never said anything bad about Jess to anyone. Except ... no ... he wasn't going to go there.

'Not you and the wondrous Jess. I thought you were dead certs for the old golden anniversary.'

'We are. We are.' The urge to keep repeating *we are ... we are* pulsed through Ollie. 'It's temporary.'

'Whatever you say, mate.' For all Dan's wildness and crazy chat, he was sensitive about when to ask and when not to. 'How about painting? Mum said you haven't been round much lately. She's got a real soft spot for you.'

Ollie had got rid of his studio and was renting Dan's mother's back room to paint.

'The gallery sold four of mine last week,' he said.

'No way? That's ace!'

'And the woman who bought them wants more.'

Dan clamped his hands on Ollie's shoulders. He pulled

him closer, and planted a sloppy kiss on his cheek. 'There you are. Proud of you, I am!'

Ollie shoved him away. 'Get off me!'

As he let himself into Dan's mum's house, he heard the television blaring as always. He knocked on the lounge door – three short taps – to let her know he was there and went upstairs. The drink with Dan had spurred him on to start the painting that had been building in his mind for days.

The evening wasn't an ideal time to work, but he'd had a specialist florescent tube fitted, which gave out a more natural light. He was hit as always by the smell – a strange concoction of paint and disinfectant. Dan's mum was a ferocious cleaner, and although she stayed out of his room, an aroma of bleach pervaded the house. He pinned paper to his easel: a rough, heavyweight sheet, as he wanted this to be bigger than his usual work. He mixed a greyish wash on his palette, and his hand hovered over the paper. It was a moment he hated: the blank sheet, the fear that the picture in his mind wouldn't translate to the page.

He rested the brush on the palette and stood back. It didn't help that he was surrounded by evidence of his failures. Piles of half-finished paintings were strewn across the small single bed, and propped up against the walls. Discarded drawings were stacked in a corner. He promised himself a clear-out once he'd got this painting done. For once, he had no sketches, no photos to work from: the scene was in his psyche. He put the palette down on the low table, crowded with used coffee mugs, drawings, a book on Hockney. Pulling his phone from his pocket, he pressed on Jess's name: *Need to do some painting. Back soon. Hope barbecue was fun. O xx.*

Okay, he couldn't put the moment off any longer. A grey wash all over the paper. He rinsed his brush, and loaded ultramarine onto the palette, mixing in a little rose for the warmish tinge he wanted. He added a spot of white and stroked the paint across the top, scoring lines in the wet paint with the end of his brush to suggest shadows.

He heard Dan's mother climbing the stairs and shuffling across the landing.

'Night, Ollie. Don't work too late.'

'I won't, Mrs D,' he called. He rolled his shoulders; the tension was already building in his neck. And he needed to get this painting right: it was for his dad.

Twelve

After Matt left for work, Louise sat at the kitchen table and poured herself a cup of freshly-brewed coffee. She'd worked round the clock at the weekend, determined her parents should see how smoothly everything had run in their absence, and she planned to have today off. Tomorrow she'd be back in the saddle – it would be a while before her father found his feet. She'd had a shock when they arrived on Friday.

It had been quiet in the sitting room at that time in the afternoon. Her mother poured the tea and they settled in armchairs tucked away in an alcove.

'What's been happening?' her father asked. 'Any dramas while we've been away?'

'For heaven's sake, Tom! We've only this minute stepped over the threshold. I told you this would be happen.'

Her father flapped his hands about as if he could waft away his wife's voice. His bony wrists stuck out from his sleeves.

'Nothing to report here,' she said. 'I want to know about your trip. Where did you go? You've been very cagey.' She glanced from one to the other. Her mother, perched on the edge of her chair, looked tanned and rested; being away from the hotel had obviously done her good. Her father, on the other hand, sat curled against the back of the armchair as if he might disappear into it. His skin was pallid, and there didn't seem to be enough of it to cover his cheekbones.

'We spent the first week with Tom's sister in Derbyshire, and that was lovely.'

'Apart from having two of you fussing over me instead of one!'

'Jane waited on us hand and foot. We walked every day, and Mark drove us to such interesting places. It was good to see other things after spending all our time in Plymouth, wasn't it, Tom?'

'If you say so. I don't understand how people live without even a whiff of the sea.'

'Take no notice of him, Louise. Says he loves the sea, but he grumbled all the time on the ship.'

'What ship?'

'My darling Lindy has known me for more than forty years, and she still thought I might enjoy a cruise.'

Louise's mother raised her eyes towards the ceiling. 'If you'd been on land, you'd have been rushing round like a Jack Russell. It was the only way to keep you quiet.'

Her father clamped his palm to his head. 'Imprisoned more like.'

Louise stared at the raised blue veins on the back of his hand. 'You look pale, Dad.'

'That's the travelling. If your mother hadn't made me go off on some –'

'You might as well tell her, Tom. You know what we agreed.'

'Tell me what? What's happened?'

'Tom wasn't well while we were away.' Her mother's voice was calm, but Louise detected a tremor below the surface.

'I thought there was something,' she said.

'He had a couple of scares while we were on the ship. Nothing as bad as that time here, and the ship's doctor was brilliant, but we had to get off at Gibraltar. Your dad spent a couple of days in hospital and he's had another stent fitted.'

'Oh, that's terrible, especially in a strange place.'

'The hospital was excellent.'

'Why didn't you let me know?'

Her mother shrugged. 'What good would it have done? We didn't want to worry you.'

The phone jolted her out of her thoughts: 'Louise, are you busy this morning?' Her mother's voice was hesitant.

'Mum, what is it?'

'Nothing to worry about. Dad and I would like to have a chat, that's all.'

'Has Oliver arrived at last?'

'No, he sent a text on Sunday to say he was ill and couldn't make it ... just a minute ...' Louise heard the clunk of the receiver being put down, a door closing, and then her mother's voice again. '... Sorry about that. I didn't want your father to hear. He's pretty cut up about it. I warned him not to get his hopes up.'

'I don't understand Oliver.'

'Never mind that. I know you're having a day off today, but we would like the chance to talk to you.'

'I can come in this afternoon.'

'That's perfect.'

'Sit down, Louise.' Her father was sitting in an armchair in the main lounge. 'We need to discuss some things.'

She stooped and planted a kiss on his head – even his hair seemed whiter and thinner. She settled back in a chair. 'How are you feeling today?'

'Better for being home.'

'Now, Tom –'

'I was responding to the question, Lindy.'

Her mother shot him a look. 'Don't try to wriggle out of it. We've asked Louise here to sort out what happens next.'

Louise looked from one to the other. What were they up to?

'As we told you when we got back on Friday, your father had a couple of health scares when we were on the boat.'

'It was nothing much.'

'Tom! Let me speak.' Her mother could be steely when she wanted to. 'After he came out of hospital in Gibraltar, we stayed in a lovely little guest house until he was well enough to travel. When we got back to England, we went to a hotel in Cornwall run by a friend of your dad's.'

'And a very nice place it is too. I picked up a few ideas while we were there.'

'Tom! Don't you dare go back on our agreement.'

'I've got no intention of doing so, my darling. I know my limitations.'

'Just so long we're on the same hymn sheet.'

'Singing from the same hymn book I think you'll find.'

'Dad!'

'Tom and I have done a lot of heart-searching in the last few weeks,' her mother said. 'And we've decided to move out of the hotel.'

'Move out? Where will you go?'

'Miles from here if I had my way, but your dad won't hear of it.'

'We're born and bred here, Lindy. This sea is in our blood.' Her father stood up and straightened his shoulders. 'Okay, enough beating about the bush ...' He clasped his hands behind his back and positioned himself in front of the fireplace. Louise's eyes went to the portrait on the wall behind him, to the whiskered face of the first owner of the hotel. Whether he realised it or not, her father had emulated old Jasper Anderson's stance.

'Much as it pains me, I recognise I'm a sick man and can't carry on at the hotel any more. It's not fair to any of us, and it's not fair to this grand old place that we all love so much.'

'But Dad –'

'No.' He held up his hand. 'This is hard enough without interruptions. I've decided to hand over the management of the hotel.'

She kept her eyes fixed on the portrait above her father. It was said the old boy's wealth had come from the slave trade and meeting his gimlet gaze, Louise could believe it.

'Lindy and I have already begun negotiations to buy an apartment in the block next door.'

'But you always said ...' Her father had fought the new block every step of the way when it was first proposed.

'We've seen photos of it; it's a fair price, and if we like it when we view it tomorrow, we'll put in an offer.'

'Mum, are you sure about this?'

'Listen to the rest.'

'As we know, The Plymouth Hotel has been in the Anderson family for generations. Now it might be old-fashioned these days, but you both realise my dearest wish has been to pass it on to Oliver, so that I could teach him all I know, as my father taught me. Up until now, he's made it clear he's not interested in taking the hotel on.'

'I'm sure –'

'But that was ...' Her father continued as if she hadn't spoken. '... that was when he was going to have to work under me, to do as he was told.' His mouth lifted in a sort of smile. 'Looking back, that could never have worked.'

'Get on with it, Tom.'

'You've done a wonderful job looking after the hotel, Louise, while we've been away.'

'I'm glad you think so. I've tried to keep everything running smoothly.'

'And we can't thank you enough for stepping into the breach.'

'But? There's a *but* coming here, isn't there?' Louise asked.

'Obviously when we asked you, it was only going to be for a short time.' Her father rocked backwards on his heels. 'Now, that it's permanent, it's time to reconsider. You've got your job at Everatts. You and Matt will want to start a family.'

'What are you saying, Dad?'

'What your father's getting at, Louise – in his usual long-winded way – is that he thinks it's only fair to give Oliver another bite of the cherry.'

Her parents looked at her expectantly, but Louise's mouth was dry, and she struggled to swallow.

'We'd love you to carry on until we get the yay or nay from Oliver,' her mother said. 'And he'd need you to show him the ropes as well.'

Louise stood up. 'I don't understand how you can consider it. He didn't even turn up this weekend when he promised to come.'

'He sent a text; he wasn't well.'

'Oh, that's all right then.' Louise felt colour flood her face. How dare they treat her like this?

'I know the uncertainty's hard on you.'

'You obviously understand nothing about how I feel.'

'Come on, Louise, love.' Her mother held out her hand. 'You know how much it would mean to your dad to see Oliver installed here.'

'I can see it's a bit of a shock for you. We've been mulling it over for a while, but we have rather sprung it on you.' Her father rubbed his hands together. 'Don't think we're not grateful for all you've done. But I owe it to the Anderson name, and the promise I made my father, to give Oliver one more opportunity.'

Thirteen

Ollie was buoyed up by thoughts of his dad's painting. He pushed the duvet to one side and sat up. A shaft of sunshine lit up the room. He had a feeling – a scary shiver in the pit of his stomach – it might be the best thing he'd done. The grandeur of the hotel, its elegant Georgian lines held within the cradle of The Hoe, sea shimmering around the edges. He couldn't wait to get back to Dan's mum's to see it in daylight.

He was whistling as he went down the hall towards the lounge. Jess and Flo must have been really quiet this morning. He hadn't heard any of the usual gearing-up for the day noises. He pushed open the door.

Jess sat on the sofa, a magazine on her lap. She never had days off school if she could help it.

'What's up?' He was still hacked-off she'd gone to the barbecue without saying goodbye.

'Sit down, Ollie,' she said.

He crossed over to the sofa and lowered himself to sit beside her. The scent of her shower gel wafted across to him. He looked down at his boxers and T-shirt, feeling grubby and messy in comparison.

'Not here,' she snapped. 'Go and sit at the table.'

'I'm not one of your pupils.' He settled a cushion behind

his back. 'What's wrong with the sofa? There's room for both of us.'

'I don't want you near me.'

He jerked to his feet. What the fuck was going on? 'Where's Flo?' he asked.

'At school. Where I should be.'

'Why aren't you?'

'I've been waiting to talk to you.'

Talk. That sounded ominous. 'Right. Shall I make us some tea first?'

She flung the magazine onto the floor. 'I don't want tea.'

He went over to the table and perched on a chair. He stared across the gulf between him and Jess. Her hair was loose round her shoulders, framing her face. He loved the way she looked, had done from the first minute he saw her walking through the park. She'd stopped beside his easel.

'It's brilliant the way you've captured the sunlight touching the surface of the lake.' Her voice was soft and breathy, tiny bursts of sound bouncing round him.

'Thank you.' He smiled at her. 'Do you paint?'

She shook her head, her hair falling across her brow. 'I wish I had the talent.'

He'd made sure he was at the same spot beside the lake the next day, and the day after. It had been a week before he saw her again, but he was ready. He plucked up courage and invited her for a coffee.

'I'm leaving you, Ollie,' she said now, and the image suffusing his mind – the lake, the hanging willow tree, the sensation of warmth on his skin as she stood next to him – shattered, as if she'd fired a gun into the scene.

He flexed the muscles in his thighs, crushing his hands against the chair.

'You see, this is the trouble.' Jess got up and crossed to the door.

She was going – just like that. After that last time, he'd always known she would one day.

'For Christ's sake, say something!' She turned back and began pacing the floor.

He counted: from the door to the television, television to door, twelve paces one way, twelve back.

'This is typical of you. I tell you I'm leaving, and all you can do is sit there!'

'You can't go,' he said. 'I love you. There's only you –'

'You've got a funny way of showing love.' Jess resumed her position on the sofa.

He got to his feet and stepped towards her.

'Don't come any closer.'

He stopped abruptly, as if he was playing some stupid game of *What's the Time, Mr Wolf?* 'Please, Jess. We've had ten good years together.'

'Eleven.'

'What?'

'It's eleven years since we met. You can't even get that right.'

'Eleven, then. We can't throw all that away. We can make this work.'

'*We?*' Jess's tone was arctic. 'We've never made it work. It's always me, Ollie. *I've* made it work. I earn the money. I look after Flo. I shop, cook, clean, but you – you're an artist. And nothing can interfere with that.'

Ollie stood in the middle of the floor, arrested in mid-stride, exposed in his boxers and T-shirt. 'I thought you supported me. I thought you believed in my painting.'

'I did, and I still do. But I can't live like this any more. I work like mad at a job I don't like. I'm always worried about money. The responsibility for Flo falls to me.'

'I took her to dance class on Saturday, and I wanted a day out together yesterday, but you –'

'I what?'

'I thought we were going to try. The night I asked you to renew our vows, you said we'd try. But you don't want it to be right, do you?'

Jess picked up the discarded magazine from the floor and flicked through the pages.

'You keep telling me how irresponsible I am, but not everything's my fault is it?'

Her head jerked back. 'So, you're dragging all that up again, are you?'

'Well, it happened, didn't it?'

The magazine was still open in her hands as if she was going to read him some juicy gossip, or show him a dress she liked. But her eyes had narrowed and her mouth was drawn in a thin line. 'Have a go at me. Maybe I deserve it, but don't try blaming me because you've let your father down big time.'

The accusation caught Ollie like a blow to the solar plexus. 'What's the old man got to do with it?' he demanded.

'Your mother phoned me last night.'

What the hell? They were all closing in on him, like baying wolves.

'Why didn't you tell me your dad's had a heart attack?'

Ollie slumped onto the chair, covering his face with his hands. 'I tried to. The night I got the phone call. But you were in a mood. You said you didn't want to hear any more about my father.'

'Why would that stop you going to see him?'

He forced his hands away from his face. 'I wanted to go yesterday, but you had this barbecue thing.'

'Why didn't you go when it first happened?'

'You know how things have been here, Jess. I was waiting till we'd made up.'

'No. No. No.'

'What? What have I said now?'

'You always do this. Offload the blame onto me – or

anyone as long as it's not you.' Jess's hands balled into fists.

'Okay, I'm a rubbish son.' He scratched at a mark on the table – glue or something from one of Flo's projects. 'I've disappointed them.'

'Disappointed?' Jess shook her head. 'They waited for you all weekend.'

'They knew I couldn't come. I texted them on Sunday morning.'

'You've got no idea, have you?'

'I'll go down there tomorrow.'

'And one quick trip will put it all right, will it?'

'I thought that's what you wanted?'

Jess laughed. A harsh sound, he'd never heard from her before. 'What *I* wanted? This is between you and your mum and dad,' she said. 'I know, and you know – although you pretend you don't – how much he wanted you to take on the hotel. You've broken his heart.'

Ollie felt blood rush to his face. 'You know nothing about him,' he snapped. 'You haven't even seen him for years.'

'I wouldn't have been welcome there, would I?'

'And whose fault is that?'

'You could have taken Flo. How could you stop her seeing her own grandparents?'

'Don't try to pin all of this on me. I wasn't the one who fucked someone else.'

'Oh, how noble of you! I suppose in your view, you don't screw up all the good things in your life. You don't destroy the relationships closest to you, scattering people you supposedly love along the way.' She stood up, dropping the magazine onto the sofa. 'We'll be staying at Mum and Dad's until I can find somewhere. I've only packed enough to keep us going, so I'll have to come back to get the rest of our stuff.'

Packed? Ollie's gaze swivelled round to the suitcase and rucksack by the door. Where had they appeared from? He stared at the pink rucksack. Flo had chosen it specially when she had her first overnight trip camping with the Brownies. 'You're not taking Flo.' He strode to the door and snatched up the rucksack. He remembered the day they'd bought it. 'That one, Daddy,' she'd squealed. 'The pink one.'

'Flo is coming with me.'

'I'm her father, and I say she's not.'

'She's coming with me. Who else would look after her?'

Ollie's head shot up like a fox scenting danger. 'I would. She's my daughter. I'll look after her.'

Jessie snorted. 'You can't even take care of yourself, let alone a ten-year old child.'

'You're not taking Flo.' He couldn't stop himself saying the words. 'You're not taking Flo.'

'Give me the rucksack, Ollie.'

He backed away. 'No, you can't have it.' He clutched it to him, as if his daughter was nestling inside.

'Let me have it.' She caught hold of the straps. 'The taxi will be here in a minute.'

'I won't let you take Flo.'

'Come on.' Jess's voice was gentler now, crooning almost.

He felt her grip on the rucksack tighten. It was slipping from his grasp. 'You can't have it.'

'This is ridiculous. Give it to me.'

Without realising he was going to, Ollie released his hold. His legs didn't feel strong enough to support him. 'Tell Flo I love her,' he said. 'I'll phone her tonight.'

'It's better you don't. Let her get used to the new situation.'

Jess's mobile bleeped, and she checked the screen.

'Ignore it.' Ollie said. 'What's more important – Flo's future, or some poxy call?'

'It's the taxi.'

'So, I've had my allocated time, have I?' He collapsed back on the sofa. He could feel Jess waiting for him say something. To tell her it was all right. He was a bastard, and he didn't blame her for leaving. 'You won't get away with this,' he shouted.

He listened to her footsteps on the stairs, heard the case bang against the wall. The door to the street opened, and he heard the taxi driver's voice. He got up and went to the window. He stared down at the car parked across the road, at the driver carrying the suitcase, at Jess, loaded down with the rucksack, her laptop, her bag for school. They sorted the luggage into the boot and climbed into the taxi. The slam of the door echoed round the narrow street.

Fourteen

Louise blew her fringe from her forehead. Sweat trickled between her breasts.

'This office is sweltering.' Maeve's face was flushed and a circle of perspiration dampened her shirt under her arms. 'Shall I get another fan? There are more in the store room.'

Louise glanced down at the list of items she wanted to discuss. 'Let's leave it. I'd like to get on to the new computer system. I've done some research and I think it's essential.' She crossed her fingers behind her back. If she said it with enough confidence, Maeve would have no reason to question her decision. On no account must she find out Louise's role might be temporary. That any day the phone call could come and Oliver would sweep in to claim his inheritance. Louise's insides churned. She'd hardly slept since her parents dropped their bombshell.

'Bookings are down, I must admit, but the restaurant is busy,' Maeve said. 'In fact, I've asked the agency for two more waiting staff.'

'I would have liked you to run that by me first.'

Maeve shrugged. 'Up to you, but your father likes me dealing with staff for the restaurant and the chambermaids. It removes at least one worry from his shoulders.'

Louise drew lines under item two on her list. 'We need to think about allocation of responsibility. I know your job title is head receptionist, but in practice, you've been Dad's right hand.'

'I think we share quite a special relationship.' Maeve smoothed back her hair, her red nails vibrant against her dark waves.

Louise stared at her. Her manner was almost coquettish. 'The trouble is, I think reception has been neglected, Maeve. There's often no one at the desk; there are queues when people are checking out –'

'Are you criticising my work?'

'No, but I think my father's reliance on you in the office has had repercussions for reception.'

Louise watched Maeve pulling at her lower lip. 'Have I said something wrong, Maeve?'

'I work very hard. You ask your father.'

Louise rubbed her fingers over the ruby at her neck. 'You're missing my point. Everyone works really hard, and I think we need to employ another member of staff.'

Maeve was doodling on her notepad and didn't look up.

Louise ploughed on. 'I'm going to advertise for someone who can help me part-time in the office and act as relief receptionist. That should free up some time for you to get on top of reception.'

'Whatever you say.'

'Okay, now can we get back to the question of a new computerised system for bookings, online reservations etc?'

Maeve frowned. 'I don't think you should go ahead with that.'

'I disagree. It's vital we co-ordinate all the hotel's functions.'

'Like I said before, your dad isn't keen.' Maeve turned over a page on her notepad and started a new set of doodles, a series of interlocking circles. 'And I'd hate him to be even more upset.'

'Why do you say *even more upset*? What's wrong with him?'

'I know his health demanded he take extended leave, but I don't like seeing him so sad.' The circles grew more complicated.

'He and Mum are quite contented,' Louise said firmly. 'Their new apartment is beautiful.'

'But he hasn't been back since they moved out. He can't bear to see the hotel now he's not in charge.'

Louise picked up her glass of orange. The ice-cold liquid sent a wave of pain through her teeth.

'That's not why he's staying away.'

'Why then?'

'He wants to give me a chance to manage the hotel, without him breathing down my neck.' Louise banged the empty glass on the desk.

Maeve nodded. 'That's the sort of man he is. Generous to a fault.'

Louise couldn't identify how this praise managed to contain a slight to her, but it brought back the sly digs she'd had to tolerate from Maeve when she worked at the hotel before. 'The fact is my father has given me responsibility to make any changes which are in the hotel's best interest. And my research suggests we can't afford to delay on the computer system.'

'The hotel was almost full last week, Louise.'

'But one week is not enough. Sometimes we're reaching only fifty per cent occupation.'

Maeve shrugged. 'Obviously you call the shots at the moment.'

'That's right.' Louise's finger hovered over item three on her list: *hotel upgrade*. 'Once the computer system is installed, I'd like to embark on a makeover programme. Some of the rooms are looking shabby.'

Maeve's eyeliner had smudged in the heat, and Louise saw the blackened eyes turn in her direction.

106

'I've got an idea for a theme,' she said. 'Plymouth is a city full of history, so I thought we'd call on other historical places: perhaps have a Florentine room, and an Egyptian one; maybe something South American.'

'Sounds expensive,' Maeve pronounced.

'I've got a meeting with the accountant next week. We'll take it gradually. Try to get a magazine to sponsor us with a view to a photo shoot of work in progress and the finished product.'

Louise was surprised to see a smile spread across Maeve's face.

'That's a great idea,' she said. 'I'd love to work with you on that.'

'Excellent. I'll research some interior designers; perhaps send off a few emails. That's all for now, Maeve.'

There was a noise at the door.

'Hi, Sadie. Everything okay?'

Sadie, one of the cleaners, dangled an item made of flimsy material between her thumb and forefinger. 'We found these in the Armada room this morning when we were making up the bed.' The Armada was one of their most expensive, with a four-poster bed, and views on to The Hoe.

Louise stretched out her hand. 'Pyjamas,' she said. They were cream and silky, and as she dropped them on to the desk, a musky scent wafted into the room. 'They certainly aren't a cheap pair from Marks.' She laughed. 'People will leave their false teeth behind next.'

Sadie still hovered in the doorway. 'Miss Louise ....'

'Is there something else?'

'The other cleaners and me ... well, we've heard ... about money going missing.'

Louise looked up from the pyjamas. 'Where did you hear that?'

'Jane, one of the others, was there when Maeve was talking to Phyllis about it.'

'Close the door, Sadie, please.' It was true that there had been an incident of money apparently going missing – the third occurrence in fact – but the guest had decided he must have mistaken how much he left in the drawer.

'It wasn't me what took the money, Miss Louise.' Sadie was clutching the door knob as if she couldn't wait to escape.

'I don't think for one minute it was you, Sadie, but if you do know anything ...'

'I'm really sorry, Miss Louise, but ...'

'But?' Louise hoped she sounded encouraging. 'Anything you tell me is completely confidential.'

'It's probably nothing, but me and Jane cleaned the room where the last lot of money went missing.' Sadie scrunched the tissue she was holding into a ball. 'There was a watch on the bedside table, and Jane slipped it into the drawer while she dusted. I remember her saying "There's two £50 notes in there", cos I said "Shut that drawer. You know we're not allowed to look in them".'

'And what happened then?'

'After we'd finished the room, Phyllis went in to check it, and then the man came back and complained some of his money had been stolen.'

'He told you that?'

'We were in the corridor outside and we heard him shouting at Phyllis that he'd left two fifties but now there was only one.'

'And no one other than Phyllis went in the room?'

'Not between us leaving and the man coming back.'

A shiver ran through Louise. 'But that man decided he couldn't have left the amount he thought in the drawer.'

'But he did. Me and Jane saw it there.'

'What are you saying, Sadie?'

'I don't want to get anyone into trouble, but next time me

or Jane might get the blame ... or one of the others, and ...'

'And?'

'It's Phyllis. It must be.'

Louise crossed The Hoe that evening breathing in the breeze that came off the sea. The sun that had glittered fiercely all day had yielded to blowsy clouds streaked with pink slivers of dying light. Sailing boats straggled along the bay like reluctant children after a day out. One of the big continental ferries drove through the waves, dwarfing the yachts.

On the way back to the hotel to collect her car, she glanced up at the apartment block next door. Her eyes sought out the lights on the third floor. Her parents had moved in a week ago, and since then she'd kept well away. Before they left the hotel, she could hardly bring herself to speak to them. A figure appeared at the window, and pulled the curtains. Why couldn't they see how they'd humiliated her with their offer to Oliver?

Louise sat down on the sofa next to Matt. He was watching television, beer in hand. She put her arm round him and kissed his cheek. 'You smell nice.'

'Freshly shaved and showered for you.'

'Sorry I'm late.' It was the same mantra she trotted out each time she got home.

He grinned. 'You said seven-thirty, so I figured nine at the earliest.'

'You seem happy. Has your lottery ticket won or something?'

'Better than that!' Matt rubbed his hands together. 'I've got the brochures for the holiday. Thought we could go through them in bed.'

'Oh Matt, I've had a hell of a day.'

'You can relax now you're home.' Matt reached down

and pulled off her shoes. 'How does a glass of chilled white sound?'

'Wonderful.'

She closed her eyes and was drifting off to sleep when Matt came back. 'Here you go.'

She forced herself awake. Matt had pulled up a small table and the glass was sitting at her right hand.

'Have you eaten? Because I can easily heat –'

'No, it's fine. I grabbed something from the hotel kitchen earlier.'

'You need to eat properly.'

'Matt, don't go on. It's lovely to be home. It's been non-stop at the hotel.'

Furrows creased his brow. 'You don't have to work there. You had a perfectly good job at the solicitor's.'

He flicked the television off.

She tried to think of something to fill the silence. 'Have you had a good day?'

'Usual.'

Guilt spurted through her as she realised it was weeks since she'd asked him. 'Are you busy at the moment?'

'Busy, not busy – it's a job. Pays the bills, and more importantly ...' He patted her thigh. '... buys the holiday!'

'Matt, about the holiday.'

'Greek island or the Canaries? What do you think?' He drained his glass and held it up. 'Another?'

She shook her head. 'I need to talk to you.'

'Oh, blimey!' He stood up. 'I definitely need another beer.'

She followed him into the kitchen.

Matt took a can from the fridge.

She sat down at the table, staring at the angle of his head, at the set of his shoulders. 'Let's clear the air, Matt. We have to be honest with each other.'

He pulled a chair towards him and hooked his leg over it. 'What do you want to say?'

'Will you hear me out? Not jump in before I have a chance to explain.'

He put his elbows on the table and planted his chin in his hands. 'You make it sound as if I'm some sort of monster.'

'That's not what I meant. But you haven't made a secret of the fact you don't like me working at the hotel.'

'I've no problem with you *working* there. It's living, breathing, being consumed by the place that gets me. I'm nothing but a hotel widower and I didn't buy into this when we got married.' He sat back and clasped his hands on the table in front of him. 'I'm counting the days till you finish.'

Louise focused on the curtains. Behind them, the window was open, and the cotton material moved as if some ghostly hand had ruffled it. This was her chance, the moment when she might be able to get Matt's support. But she had to be strong. She couldn't even hint that Oliver was still her parents' first choice.

'I've always loved the hotel, ever since I was a little girl. I used to stand behind reception on a stool and fill in the names of imaginary guests in the book. Dad got irritated sometimes.' She kept her eyes on the swaying curtains as if the breeze lifting them could inspire her with the right words. 'The other girls at school used to want to be ... I don't know ... ballet dancers or nurses, but all I ever wanted was to run a hotel. It's like a magical world where anything is possible. The arrivals and departures, the constant swirl of people filling the place with energy. It was a dream come true when Dad offered me the events manager job.'

She glanced at Matt. His eyes were closed: he was listening, taking in what she was saying, perhaps even being convinced.

'Okay, I get it,' he said.

'You mean you don't mind if I take it on while Dad recovers?'

'I can see how much you love the place. Don't understand

it myself, but your dad's a good bloke, and if you looking after it while he convalesces is going to help him get better, then I'll go along with it for a while.' Matt leaned back in his chair and grinned. He clearly expected applause and kisses.

'When you say a while, Matt ...' Louise kept her voice measured. '... how long are you thinking?'

'When do the docs expect your dad to be up to full strength?'

Thoughts careered across Louise's mind: he was agreeing; they could stop these awful rows. But she hadn't even told him her parents had moved out of the hotel. And if he heard even a whisper that they were offering the hotel to Oliver again.

'They said three months in the first place, but that was before the attacks he had while they were away. He's still very weak. It will mean a holiday is out this year.' Might as well clear the ground on that one.

He shrugged. 'We'll make it a bumper one next year.'

'Are you sure?'

He spread his hands palm down on the table. 'Okay, here's the deal: six months to get your dad on his feet. Then we try for a baby.' He looked across at her. 'Agreed?'

'Agreed,' she whispered. 'Agreed.'

Fifteen

Ollie flung his paintbrush across the room. It hit the window and bounced to the floor. He leant his forehead against the glass, and stared at the scar of red paint until it merged with the roses in the gardens at the back of the flats. When Flo was little, she used to drag a chair across to the window and point at the red petals on the ground. 'Poor flower hurt hisself,' she'd say.

He pulled his earphones out and chucked the ipod onto the bed. Jeff Buckley was one of his favourite singers to listen to when he was painting, but today his plaintive cry to his father in *What Will You Say* splintered his heart.

He made for the door, Flo's dressing gown, which still hung on its hook, brushing against his cheek. In the kitchen, he flipped the switch on the kettle and reached into the cupboard for a mug. He picked up his mobile from the worktop and scrolled down till he found his mother's email. He'd reread it endless times: *We've decided to retire ... one final offer ... it would be yours outright.* His hand tightened round the phone. Perhaps this was a sign. A way to salvage something from the whole mess.

He was about to click off when the screen lit up: Jess. She hadn't rung since she'd left. She'd been back to the flat once when he was out, collecting more stuff, and she'd left her keys on the table. They'd spoken only when he phoned, asking to see Flo, but her response was always the same: *Give it time. Let her settle.*

He pressed *answer*.

'Ollie, at last. I was about to give up.' Jess's voice was bright, that hint of laughter singing in his ear.

'Is everything okay?' he asked. What a stupid thing to say. Of course, everything wasn't okay. Nothing would be okay ever again.

'Fine. It's all fine, but Flo –'

'Flo?' He slammed the mug down on the worktop. 'What's wrong with her?'

'Nothing. Why should there be?'

'When can I see her? You can't stop me indefinitely.'

'Don't be so melodramatic.' Irritation had taken over from the laughter in Jess's voice. 'This is not all about you. She needed time to adjust.'

'Three weeks. It's been three weeks now. And all you've allowed is one fucking phone call.'

'And look what happened then – it took me ages to console her.'

'You don't think she might have cried because she's missing her dad?'

'I didn't phone up to bicker.'

'Well, you didn't ring to say you've made a terrible mistake and you want to come back.'

'You know we've gone too far for that.'

Oh, did he? Actually, he knew nothing. He'd thought, despite everything, they loved each other, and all the time –

'The thing is, Flo and I were talking last night, and she's promised me she won't make a fuss when she has to say goodbye to you.'

Ollie suppressed a whoop of joy, 'You mean I can see her?'

'Can you pick her up from school?'

114

He glanced at the clock on the cooker. Half an hour to shave and shower – recently he'd only bothered on his days in the gallery. 'I'll be there, Jess. She can stay overnight if she likes.'

'I was hoping you'd say that. She's still got some things at the flat, hasn't she?' Jess sounded business-like, as if now she'd got his agreement, she couldn't wait to get off the phone. 'Oh, she won't be expecting you.'

'How about meeting for coffee next week? Would be great –' The phone burbled in Ollie's ear: Jess had gone.

Ollie scoured the school playground, eyes darting over the girls with blonde hair who passed him ... at last ... Flo ... walking on her own, rucksack on her back, scuffing her feet.

'Flo! Flo! Over here.'

She looked up and saw him. He'd daydreamed these last few weeks about what it would be like when he saw her again: he'd lift her up and swing her round; they'd shout and jump up and down.

Now, she was beside him. 'Hello, Daddy.'

He leaned forward to hug her, but something in her face stopped him: a question, a wariness in her eyes he didn't remember. He eased the rucksack off her shoulders. 'This weighs a ton. Let me carry it for you.'

'Where's Grandad?'

'I don't know. Mummy asked me to collect you.' Ollie was itching to take hold of her hand, or to place an arm round her shoulder. They passed through the school gates to the road. It was a fifteen-minute walk back to the flat. 'How was today?' he asked.

'I failed the maths test.' Flo kept her head down, kicking stones and bits of rubbish.

'Bad luck. I was never any good at maths.'

'But Miss Jones says I *am* good. I've never failed a test before.'

'It must have been hard. How many others failed?'

'No one. Not my friends anyway. Lauren and Mandy laughed at me.'

Ollie didn't know what to do or say. He'd never had to worry before; his relationship with Flo was as easy as breathing, but now, he felt awkward and tongue-tied.

'How long am I staying?' she asked as they turned into the main road.

'Till tomorrow.' He shifted the rucksack to his other shoulder, his mind ranging over the empty cupboards and fridge at the flat. 'How do you fancy McDonald's for tea?'

'Mummy doesn't like me going there.'

'I'm sure she won't mind – just this once.'

'Can we go home first?'

Home! She called it home. 'Yeah, let's dump this rucksack, and you can get changed if you want. You've got a few clothes in the wardrobe.'

'Is Panda still there?'

Ollie glanced down at Flo's bent head, her gaze seemingly glued to the pavement. He remembered seeing the pulse beating in that soft part of her scalp when she was a baby. Could still recall his panic. 'You bet he is. He's sitting on your bed waiting for you.' The lights changed and they crossed the road. A few minutes and they'd be there. 'I told him before I left that you were coming, and do you know what he said?'

'Panda's not real, Daddy.'

'Well, no ... of course he's not ... but –' He caught the look she cast at him and clamped his mouth shut. They stopped at the front door and he pulled out his key. 'I need to warn you,' he said, 'your bedroom's a bit untidy.'

Flo shrugged. 'I don't mind.'

Ollie went into the kitchen and put the kettle on. He called out, 'Fancy cheese on toast, Flo? Just to tide you over.' She was always ravenous when she came in from school.

'I'm not hungry.' She'd gone straight to her bedroom and shut the door.

He tapped at it. 'Can I come in?'

She didn't answer, and he peered inside. She was sitting on the bed, Panda cuddled in her arms. Silent tears streamed down her cheeks. In two paces he was beside her and on his knees by the bed. He clasped his arms round her, squeezing Panda between them. 'Flo, my baby. I love you, Flo.' Panda's fur tickled his cheek. 'What's wrong? Why are you crying?'

She pulled away from him and gestured round the room. 'There's mess everywhere! You've made my room a complete mess.'

He sat next to her on the bed. Taking in the room through her eyes, he was assaulted by the debris of discarded sketch pads, tubes of paint, brushes. 'Sorry, Flo. I know it's bad.'

'But why are you painting in here?' She started to cry again.

'It didn't seem worth paying rent for the room at Dan's mum's now there's only me in the flat.'

'But it's mine.'

'I know, and I felt closer to you being able to imagine you, doing your homework, reading –' He looked up and caught a glimpse of the half-finished painting on the easel. 'Not that it's done me much good. Everything I've painted since you and Mum went has been rubbish.'

His comment appeared to reach through her misery. She climbed off the bed and crossed to the easel. 'Where's this?'

'Trafalgar Square.' He stood beside her, his arm round her shoulder. 'I thought it was about time I tried new places.' He didn't tell her he'd gone to Hampstead Heath once after she and Jess left, but memories of being there with her had swamped him. His palm had prickled as he tried not to curl his fingers round her imagined hand.

'I like the sky – looks as if it's on fire.'

'Yeah, I'm pleased with that, and the way the London bus echoes its colour, but it's the people in the foreground that aren't working.' As soon as he'd seen the man with his small daughter nestling in the crook of his elbow that day, he'd wanted to paint them. But the man's arm looked as if it was broken rather than cradling his child. And the little girl appeared set on escape from the embrace.

Ollie was thinking how he might be able to scratch in a new line to raise the angle of the man's elbow, when he felt Flo pull away. He whirled round to see her curled into a ball on the bed.

'I've been thinking about my room all the time.' Her voice was muffled by her tears and he knelt down and put his face close to hers on the pillow. 'Mum and I have to share at Nana's and I don't like it. I thought this was mine and you've ruined it with all this ... stuff!' Flo was pulling at Panda's fur, a tuft clutched between her fingers.

He'd never felt so ashamed. 'I'll clear up. I promise to get everything out of here.'

'But where am I going to sleep tonight? The bed's covered with paper and paints.'

'Okay, I tell you what.' Ollie jumped up. 'How about we tackle it now? Together. And then McDonald's will be our reward.'

Flo sat up. She placed Panda carefully on the pillow. 'I'll get changed first.'

He wanted to pick her up and shower her with kisses. He wanted to shout *Thank you! Thank you!* She was smiling – she was his beautiful daughter again. But she was already opening her wardrobe and pulling out a pair of jeans. 'These are my favourites. I can't believe Mummy didn't pack them.'

A memory of Jess's words on that last morning flashed into his mind: *You screw up all the good things in your life.* He gripped the door handle, watching his knuckles turn white. He could do this. He wasn't going to screw up his relationship with Flo whatever happened. 'I'll make that tea, shall I? And then we'll get started.'

Ollie decided once Flo saw the gooey cheese melting into the toast, she wouldn't be able to resist. They'd eat it in her bedroom, like the picnics they used to have when she was little and it was too wet to go out.

He carried the tray into her room. She was sitting on the bed reading. She'd put the jeans on but was still wearing her school shirt.

He placed the tray on the floor. 'Grub's up.'

Flo's eyes remained fixed on the book in her hands.

'What are you reading?'

She looked up at him, and her expression was one he couldn't fathom. 'It's something you wrote at school.'

He recognised the green cover of an old exercise book he'd used for compositions. Since he'd been on his own he'd ridden a tortuous helter-skelter of questions: how the fuck had he reached the grand old age of thirty-nine saddled with the detritus of broken relationships and dreams? He'd been poring over photos and books searching for answers.

'You wrote this when you were only eleven.' Flo's finger was poised over a line in the book. 'It's called *Myself in Ten Years*. You've written: *I will own a big hotel on The Hoe in Plymouth. My granddad, who had the same name as me, gave it to my dad, and my dad will give it to me, and I'll be very important because I have to tell everyone what to do.*'

Ollie stared out of the window into the gardens. The building had been a convent before it was turned into flats and the open space at the back had been retained. It was one of the reasons they'd chosen the flat. But now he imagined figures of nuns scurrying along its paths like giant crows.

'Are you okay, Daddy?' He felt Flo's arms slip round his waist. 'I didn't mean to upset you.'

'Don't worry. I'm fine.'

'Are you crying?'

He shook his head. 'I'm upset because my dad's not well.'

'Grandpa in Plymouth?'

'Yeah. He's okay, just something with his heart.'

'Have you been to see him?'

Ollie didn't answer, but she must have been able to tell from his face.

'Daddy! You should go.'

'I know. I know.'

'I'd come and see you if you were ill.'

'I know you would, but it's complicated.'

'I'll come with you. I haven't seen Granny and Grandpa for ages. They gave me Panda when I was born, didn't they?'

Ollie nodded.

'It must be fun to live in a hotel.' Flo skipped over to the tray and picked up a slice of toast. 'Mm, it's nice when it's gone cold.'

Ollie remembered what it was like when he was a child – his parents always busy, people everywhere, vast rooms and none of them his. 'I didn't enjoy it much.'

'Mummy and I are going to stay in a hotel soon,' Flo said.

'Are you? How come?'

'Genie's taking us.'

'Genie?' Adrenaline surged through Ollie's limbs, as a premonition hit him. 'Who's Genie?

'Mummy's friend.' Flo put the crust on the plate and picked up another slice of toast. 'I don't think that's his real name, but that's what Mummy calls him.'

Next day, Ollie was in the back room when the door of the gallery opened. He peered out and took in the figure studying the painting he'd left propped against the front desk: Angel.

He stepped out from his hiding place. 'I thought you were spending the day with your mother.'

'I've only popped in. Left my phone here.' She moved to the desk and pulled her mobile from the drawer. 'Can't believe I forgot it.'

The thought she might leave, that he might be alone again with the unremitting ache in his belly, filled him with panic. 'No, please stay.' He was about to grip her hand when he saw the way she was staring at him. 'I mean ... if you can hang on ...'

'What's wrong, Ollie?'

He sat on the sofa and leant forward with his head between his knees.

He became conscious of a cool hand on his back, Angel's voice in his ear: 'Take some deep breaths.' He did as he was told and the flutterings in his chest subsided.

'Are you feeling better?'

He nodded.

'I'm not going until I know you're all right.'

'Have you got a magic wand?' he asked.

'Don't talk in riddles, Ollie.'

'Nothing else will patch things up with Jess.'

'But I thought ... aren't you seeing how things go before you renew your vows?'

'We were. But she's left and taken Flo.'

'Oh, no. When?' Angel sat down next to him on the sofa and eased open his clenched fists. She ran her finger over the indentations his nails had left in the palms.

'A few weeks ago.'

'Why on earth didn't you tell me?'

'Because I knew you'd be nice to me, like you are now, and I'd end up blubbing all over you.'

Angel put her arm round his shoulder. 'I'm so sorry. I know how much you love her.'

'It's not only that. I've just found out she's met someone.'

'My God! Already?'

Already ... pain he'd already lived through ... already ... before ...

'Do you want to talk about it?'

The notion of 'it' opened up a kaleidoscope of images: Jess's naked limbs entwined with thighs gigantic as tree trunks; the little o her mouth made just before she came. Jesus Christ, he'd kill that bastard if he ever saw him again.

Sixteen

Memories spooled through Ollie's mind on a continuous loop, sensations of sound, colour, touch, like the most extravagant 4-D film. He'd replayed that evening so many times in the months that followed, willing the reel of images to sputter to a stop like the film sometimes did in the indie cinema he and Jess used to go to. But instead frame succeeded frame, images burrowing into his head. Had that night been the first chink of betrayal? The first crossing of a line that opened up the way for other hurts? Suppose the seeds of Jess's decision had been planted at that moment in the past, roots snaking their way unseen through the dark, silent ground, only to burst into the light with a triumphant *Ta dah!* 'I'm leaving you,' Jess said. A bolt from the blue. Or was it?

He is reading Flo a story, her warm body tucked inside his arm. Jess appears in the doorway of Flo's room in a floaty, blue dress he hasn't seen before, the swell of her breasts just visible, perfume swirling around her. Flo says: 'You look lovely, Mummy.'

And Jess laughs: that infectious sound, bubbling in her throat, bursting from her lips, so that he laughs too, and Flo, looking from one to the other, joins in. Jess is happy, excited to be going out. Money is tight, and babysitters cost. But since Louise moved to London and met her new boyfriend, they've joined them for a drink, or a meal, especially if Ollie has sold a painting. Louise's bloke is generous, not only with his cash, but letting Ollie have gallery space. 'A poor show if we can't help the artist in his garret,' he often says, his paw of a hand thumping Ollie on the back.

And he's good for a laugh as well. A bellow of sound, his head thrown back, his red hair jumping with the movement. Some of Louise's boyfriends have been dire. There was one back in Plymouth – Matt, or something, his name was. He used to sit in the corner of the pub, nursing a pint, afraid to open his mouth. 'He's shy,' Louise would say, 'but he's really kind.' And then she came to London and met Eugene – a different kettle of fish altogether.

Louise and Eugene are already at the pub when they arrive. The babysitter was late, and at the last minute Flo kicked up a fuss. Ollie expected Jess to cancel, but she lay on the bed and sang lullabies until Flo drifted off to sleep.

The place is packed, and Ollie weaves his way through the crowd, his hand clutching Jess's. Louise is waving: 'Over here. We've got a table.'

He kisses her on the cheek and submits to Eugene pumping his hand. He squeezes into a seat in the corner, giving the thumbs-up to the pint of beer in front of him. He watches as Eugene greets Jess: she almost disappears inside the bear hug. Someone knocks his elbow and liquid slops from his glass onto the table. He attempts to mop it up with a beer mat, and when he looks back, Jess is sitting down, smiling.

The noise in the pub buffets Ollie. Louise tells some long, complicated story, but he only catches occasional words.

She's laughing, gesticulating, and then she reaches over and kisses Eugene on the mouth.

'Ollie, are you with us tonight?' Jess pats his knee. 'Eugene's asking about your painting.'

'Oh great, yeah, yeah,' he says. 'It's fine.'

'Last time we met, you were on a high the height of Everest, so you were,' Eugene says. 'You were after winning that competition.'

Ollie nods. 'The park project,' he says, as if competition wins are two a penny.

'We saw the photo of you all in the paper at the unveiling ceremony,' Louise says.

Ollie loved posing for the photos with an arm round Jess and Flo – they both had new dresses for the event and looked beautiful. They were there to celebrate the opening of the Waterlow Park Centre. The house and garden had fallen into disrepair until the local council restored them and held a competition to select paintings for the newly-established Centre. Ollie submitted a series of watercolours featuring the same scene at different times of day, from sunrise to sunset. He worked on the paintings over three months, often abandoning one and starting from scratch when this or that detail wasn't right. By the time the closing date for the competition arrived, he was exhausted. And although he knew he'd produced some of his best work, he couldn't believe it when he made the shortlist of five. He was interviewed by the three judges and announced the winner.

'What are you working on now?' Eugene asks. 'You'll be capitalising on the win.'

'Nothing.' Jess drains her glass. 'Ollie hasn't picked up a paint brush since.'

'I worked hard for the competition,' he says. 'I need some down time before I decide what direction to take next.'

'Hey man, you ever thought about the long hours we all work?' Eugene asks.

'That's different,' Jess says. 'Ollie's painting is on a higher plane.'

Ollie recoils as if Jess has slapped him. Perhaps she has – his cheeks feel on fire. He fixes his eyes on her, but she's studying the bottom of her glass and doesn't look up. What's she playing at? *He hasn't picked up a paintbrush since.* The words beat a tattoo in his brain.

He wants to propel Jess from the bar with a curt *We're going now*, but instead he drains his glass and fishes in his wallet for some notes. 'My round.' He holds them out to Eugene. 'If you don't mind doing the honours. I'm wedged into this corner.'

Eugene waves the money away. 'My treat.'

Ollie's arm hangs in mid-air, the notes caught between his middle and forefinger. Then he shoves the money into his jacket pocket.

'Have you spoken to Mum and Dad recently?' Louise throws the question into the hole the last few minutes have exposed.

'Not for ages. You?'

'We're going down at the weekend. I want to introduce Eugene to them.'

Ollie has a momentary picture of Eugene towering over his father, of the Irishman striding through the rooms of the hotel, his exuberance charming everyone in sight, his father trailing in his wake.

'It's serious then?' Jess asks.

'I hope so.' Louise strokes her stomach.

'You mean ...?' Jess nods her head in Eugene's direction. 'Is he pleased?'

'He doesn't know. No one does.' Louise's reply comes quickly. 'I didn't mean to tell you two.'

'Congratulations, Loulou!' He leans across the table and kisses her cheek. 'Fancy my little sis up the duff.'

'Ollie!' Jess frowns at him. 'That's not a very nice way to say it.'

He shrugs. 'It was meant to be affectionate.'

'It's brilliant news, Louise,' Jess says. 'How far are you?'

'Only just taken the test. That's why I don't want anyone to know yet.'

'But you'll tell Eugene? He'll be thrilled.'

'Ssh! He's coming back.' She draws her finger across her lips. 'Keep it zipped in the meantime. And that includes you, Ollie.'

Eugene arrives at the table with a tray of drinks. 'Here you go, me little chicks.' Instead of resuming his seat next to Louise, he squeezes onto the bench beside Jess. 'Let's all move round one,' he says. 'Not going to keep this woman to yourself all evening, are you?'

Ollie feels himself being forced off his end of the bench. A look of panic flashes across Louise's eyes as they meet his, and he slides onto the seat on her side of the table. He lifts his glass to hers. 'Here's to the future.'

He drifts off from the conversation. He catches the occasional comment – Jess complaining about school, Louise and Eugene discussing the festival they're planning – while his mind focuses on the next day's work. He's ready to start something new, and if only they'd met Louise and Eugene a few days later, the conversation might have been different. If he's honest, there's a grain of truth in Jess's scathing remark: he has rested on his laurels since the win. He's allowed himself to believe he's made it. Galleries will come knocking, offer him exhibitions; big buyers will be sniffing around. But as yet new offers haven't flooded in.

'Ollie! Ollie!' Jess is tapping his hand across the table. 'You haven't said a word for ages, and it's definitely your round this time.'

Ollie opens his eyes; the faces of the other three staring at him are a shock.

'The round, Ollie.' Jess points to the empty glasses. 'It's your turn, or shall I get them?'

'Don't be worrying.' Eugene is half way out of his seat. 'I'll go again.'

'No!' Ollie's shout sounds too loud even to his ears. 'If you can let me out, Louise.' She stands up and he slides across the bench. 'Same again for everyone?' They nod.

It takes forever to be served, and Louise is sitting at the table on her own when he returns with the tray of drinks. 'Where are the others?'

'Jess went to the toilet, and Eugene's gone outside – phone calls, he said.'

Ollie places orange juice in front of Louise, and sips his lager. 'No offence, Louise, but I'll rejoin Jess's side of the table now.'

'Suits me.' She grins at him. 'Lover? Brother? I'll go for the lover next to me if it's all the same to you!'

'Seriously, I'm glad to get a minute on our own.' He sits down opposite her. 'Great news about the baby.'

'It's early days ... Make sure you don't tell Mum and Dad. Nor Eugene.' She glances round. 'Especially Eugene.'

'He'll be chuffed, won't he? I know I was with Flo.'

She shrugs. 'He's unpredictable. A free spirit.'

'He'd better not mess my sister around, that's all.'

Louise laughs. 'No good playing the hard man. It doesn't suit you!'

He looks round. 'Wonder where the other two have got to?'

'Eugene's probably talking to his mum. He phones her nearly every day.'

'Didn't have him down as a mummy's boy.'

'I think it's sweet.'

'I'll check Jess is okay. Hope she hasn't overdone the vino.'

'Don't be long,' Louise tells him. 'Not much fun sitting here on my own.'

'Better tell the boyfriend, not me.'

Wood panelling covers the walls in the corridor to the toilets making it dark after the brightness of the bar. A watercolour catches Ollie's eye, and he pauses to study it. It's a lovely, little seascape – a tumult of slate grey waves erupting into a foaming fountain in the middle of the scene. He leans back, enjoying the way the spurting water appears to reach up to the white of the clouds. Watercolour is the perfect medium for seascapes. He's been hooked on trees for so long, he's almost forgotten how exciting it is to try to capture the sea.

A noise at the end of the corridor makes him look round. In the dim light, he's not sure what he sees. Arms, a bent head, a flash of red. It's not. It can't be.

'Jess?' He moves towards the figure. 'Is it you, Jess?'

There's a soft hiss as a door closes. Jess emerges from the gloom. 'Ollie, you okay?'

'I was wondering the same about you. You've been gone ages.'

She takes his hand. Her palm is hot and clammy. 'Sorry, bit of a tummy upset.' She pushes her hair back from her face, and he glimpses a red mark on her neck. 'Don't think I'll have any more wine,' she says.

He reaches for her other hand and pulls her towards him. He squeezes her against him.

'Ollie, you're hurting me.' Her voice is muffled. 'Let me go.' She reaches behind her and grips his arms, peeling them away. Stepping back from his embrace, she clutches his wrists to keep him at a distance. Her eyes flit across his face. 'What's going on?'

'You tell me, Jess.' His chest is tight; his lungs feel starved. 'What were you doing?'

Seventeen

L ouise hesitated outside her parents' apartment. Guilt had forced her here. She'd barely seen them since their disagreement and was curt whenever her mother phoned. But she'd lain awake in the night worrying about them.

She raised her hand to knock, but then she heard the low rumble of her father's voice, followed by a woman's laugh. She rested her ear against the door. It was: she was sure of it. She took the key they'd given her for emergencies from her bag and inserted it into the lock. Pushing the door open, she stepped inside.

Just as she thought. Maeve. Sitting over by the window, her chair pulled close to Louise's father, her head inclined to his.

Louise pulled herself up straight. 'I thought you were supposed to be on duty, Maeve.'

They swung round, surprise etched across her father's face, Maeve's red lips open in a circle of astonishment.

'Who's looking after reception?' Louise kept her voice low and cold.

Maeve fussed with the charm bracelet on her wrist. 'Julie said she'd manage for an hour or so while I popped over here.'

'Julie's not there to cover for you while you make social calls.'

'Now don't be like that, Louise, love.' Her father gripped the arms of his chair and pushed himself to his feet. 'Your mother was tired and wanted a nap. I asked Maeve to come over and keep me company.'

Maeve smiled. 'That's right. Your dad was just saying they haven't seen you for ages.'

Louise glared at Maeve. 'Well. I'm here now. You can get back to work.'

'You'd better go, Maeve. Do as she says.'

Maeve stood up. 'Lovely to see you, Tom.' She kissed his cheek. 'You take care of yourself.' She pushed past Louise and the door clicked behind her.

Louise went into the kitchen to make tea. She banged mugs on the tray and slammed the fridge door shut. She breathed slowly in and out, as Freda had taught her. Stay calm. She had to stay calm.

'I thought I heard voices.'

Louise jumped. 'Mum, I thought you were asleep.'

'I was only dozing.' Her mother gave her a hug. 'I'm so pleased you've come. I thought you were cross with us.'

'I am, Mum, but I wanted to make sure you were all right. I wasn't expecting Maeve to be here.'

Her mother shrugged. 'She keeps your dad up to date with hotel gossip.'

'What gossip? There isn't any gossip.'

'Oh, you know what people are like.' Her mother gave her a nudge. 'You go and have a sit down while you can. I'll bring the tea in.'

Her father's eyes were closed, his head resting against the back of the chair. Louise sat on the foot rest. 'Dad.'

His eyes shot open.

'I'd like to talk to you about Maeve.'

He pulled himself upright. 'Go on.'

'I don't like her coming here all the time.'

He slapped his forehead. 'What, I'm not allowed visitors now? You're worse than your mother.'

'You know I don't mean that.' She swallowed. 'But she tries to undermine me all the time, and your cosy chats are helping to fuel that.'

Her mother came in with the tray. 'What cosy chats?'

'It doesn't matter, Lindy. Nothing important.' Her father waved his hand dismissively.

Louise caught the furious look her mother shot at him.

'Have it your own way.' She put the tray on the coffee table. 'I've brought freshly squeezed orange for you, Tom. Would you like water as well to take your tablets?'

'Don't fuss, Lindy. Juice is fine.'

'See what I have to put up with?' She positioned a small table with the drink and the uncapped tablet bottle near his right hand.

'It's bad enough being an invalid without constant reminders.'

'I give up.' Her mother handed Louise a mug and thumped down onto the sofa.

Louise glanced at each her parents. She'd never seen them so short with each other. 'Shall I open the door to the balcony,' she asked. 'It's stuffy.'

'See, Tom,' her mother snapped. 'I keep telling you it's too hot in here and we need to get out.'

'Well, I'm cold. And what's the point of going out for the sake of it?' He held a tablet poised on the end of his tongue and swallowed it back with some juice. He shuddered. 'Why they have to give it that horrible taste, I've no idea.'

'Louise doesn't want to listen to us squabbling, Tom.' Her mother sipped her tea. 'No wonder she hasn't been over to see us. How are you, my lovely?'

'Busy. There's a lot going on.'

'Maeve said something about money going missing,' her father said.

'Oh, did she?' Damn the woman. She'd had no intention of telling her parents. 'It's nothing, really. You don't need to worry about it.'

'Money going missing doesn't sound like nothing to me,' he said.

'Perhaps your father will be able to advise you, Louise.'

Oh, God, this was a nightmare. She shouldn't have come.

'Tell us what's been happening, love. A trouble shared and all that.'

'She's trying to, Lindy.' Her father tapped a rapid, staccato beat on the wooden arm of the chair. 'If only you'd give her a chance.'

'Okay, yes, money's gone missing,' she said.

'From where? I always kept the petty cash locked away in the office, and the bar –'

'This is money from guests' rooms, Dad.'

'Every room has a safe, and you should –'

'You can't force people to put their money in a safe,' Louise snapped.

'How many times has it happened?' her mother asked.

'Four – as far as I know.'

'As far as you know!' Her father's rapping on the arm of the chair increased in speed. 'You have to keep on top of things, or staff and guests will run rings round you.'

'She's not stupid, Tom. Could it be another guest?'

'Unlikely, given it's happened on several separate occasions.'

'One thing for certain ...' Her mother collected the mugs and picked up the tray. 'It won't be any of the cleaners; I interviewed every one of them myself.'

'You need to get to the bottom of it, and sharpish.' Her father rested his elbows on his knees. 'The last thing we want is the hotel getting a bad name.'

'I know that, Dad. It's deciding the best way to handle it.'

'There's an easy answer to that. Ask Phyllis. There's not much goes on she doesn't hear about.'

'The problem is one of the cleaners has accused Phyllis.'

'Never!' Her mother put the tray down again and resumed her seat.

'I'd trust Phyllis with my last penny.' Her father glared at Louise as if she was the one who'd been caught stealing.

'But I can't ignore the accusation.'

'Have a meeting. Your father swears by meetings.'

'Absolutely right, Lindy.' He smiled across at her mother. 'I always say: *Whatever the issue, get it out in the open.*'

'I don't think a meeting is the answer in this case,' Louise said.

Her father rubbed his hands together, clearly relishing engaging with hotel business again. 'Get them together, love. Kill the tittle-tattle.'

Louise stood up and crossed to the window. Sunlight glittered on the waves. 'This is a fabulous view.'

'That doesn't mean you need to sit there watching it all the time, Tom. It won't go away.' Her mother picked up the tray and went out to the kitchen.

Louise crouched beside her father's chair. She took his hand. The skin felt dry and papery. 'I was wondering if you've heard –'

'I miss the hotel, Louise.' His grip on her hand tightened.

She'd lost her chance. She could hardly mention Oliver now.

'How about you come over and see everyone? The staff would love it.'

He shook his head. 'Not while I'm like this.'

'But you do need to walk more, Dad, to build up your strength.'

He let go of her hand and lay back against the chair. His face looked grey and drawn. 'I'll see how I feel.'

Louise kissed his forehead. 'I need to get back now, Dad. Bye.'

At the door to the apartment, she hugged her mother.

She'd lost weight since the heart attack, and grey roots showed in her hair. She'd always been proud of its rich chestnut colour.

'Mum, have you heard from Oliver about your offer?'

'I've emailed and phoned him, but you know what he's like.'

Louise shoved her bag onto her shoulder. 'I'm in limbo. I'm managing the hotel, but only until Oliver deigns to reply. It's ... well, it's difficult.'

'We have to be patient, Louise. I don't want your father upset.'

'And suppose Oliver says yes – he'll take the hotel on – what then? Where does that leave me?'

Her mother stroked Louise's hair back from her forehead. 'Oliver knows nothing about running a hotel. He'll need help.'

Louise pulled away and snatched open the door. 'You don't understand? I don't want to *help*.'

'Lindy, are you there?' Her father's call reached them from the lounge.

'Be there in a minute, Tom.' She turned back to Louise, her face creased in a frown.

'Lindy, I want –'

Her mother pulled the door to, cutting off her father's voice.

'I've got to go.' Louise took several paces along the corridor. She jabbed at the button on the lift. 'But tell Dad – I need to know one way or the other.'

Louise strode across The Hoe and ran down the steps, almost stumbling as she reached the road. She leant against the rail, her fingers drumming an angry beat on it. The outline of a ferry, ploughing its way westward across the bay, its foaming wake flaring behind it, grew indistinct as tears filled her eyes. She was an idiot. Everyone seemed to think she was some gullible fool. No backbone, a teacher had said once. They were all the same: her father, Oliver, Eugene. Only Matt cared about her, but that was the other extreme, as if she was a wounded bird to be watched over and protected.

She pulled her phone from her pocket and clicked on Oliver's number. She tracked the progress of the ferry while she counted the number of rings. It was disappearing round the headland when Oliver finally answered.

'Hi, Louise.' His voice sounded groggy with sleep. 'Everything okay?'

'Not exactly, no.'

'What's up? Not bad news? I'm up to my neck in crap as it is.'

Louise waited. Why should she sympathise with the crappiness of his life?

'I rang Mum yesterday.' He let out a loud yawn. 'She said Dad was doing well.'

Oh, did she? She'd kept that quiet, hadn't she? No, not quiet, deliberately hidden.

'Did she ask you about the hotel?' Her heartbeat thudded in time with her fingers on the rail. *Ba dum. Ba dum. Ba dum.* 'You got Mum's email about them retiring?'

'Yeah, that's a turn up for the books, isn't it?'

'What are you going to do?'

'About?'

A scream swelled in her throat. 'The hotel, of course! You must have discussed it when you rang.'

She heard some crashing about.

'Christ, Louise, if you knew what I was coping with.'

'I don't care. I need an answer. Are you taking on the hotel or not?'

'I don't know.' The crashing intensified as if he was smashing crockery or something. 'What's the rush?'

There was a shriek from below her. Some youths were wrestling on the rocks that stretched out into the sea. They were pulling one boy's arms, forcing him into the water.

'The rush is because my life is on hold, Oliver. I need you to tell them as soon as possible.'

Back at the hotel, she stopped at the desk. The new assistant manager and part-time receptionist was on duty. 'I'll be in my office, Katie, if you can ask Phyllis to come and see me.'

'I'll go and look for her.' Katie checked the book on the desk. 'Oh, and you've got a visitor. I've given him coffee in the lounge. Said you'd be with him shortly.'

'Did you get his name?'

'Seb Flanders.'

'Doesn't mean anything. What does he want?'

'He wouldn't say.'

'Ask Phyllis to come in half an hour. I'd better see him first.'

Katie smiled. 'He's very good looking"

Louise hesitated in the doorway to the guests' lounge, sidetracked by the huge vase of blue hydrangeas on the oak sideboard. Her mother had always looked after the flowers, and it was a job Louise wanted to keep as hers. She'd made that clear to Maeve when they'd discussed allocation of responsibilities.

A cough dragged her attention back to the room. A thatch of blond hair sticking up above the chintz armchair was all that was visible of her visitor. She moved closer. 'Mr Flanders?'

The figure in the chair uncoiled his legs and turned to face her. 'Seb Flanders. Please call me Seb.' His voice was deep and rich, at odds with his slight frame and long, thin face.

She held out her hand. 'Pleased to meet you ... Seb.'

His warm grip enclosed hers. 'And you. I'm delighted.'

'I'm sorry to keep you waiting,' she said, 'but if you'd let me know you were coming ...'

'Apologies for that, but I was in the area, and after your invitation –'

'What invitation?'

'In your letter. You said to call in and say hello.'

'My letter?'

'Yes, you wrote to me.'

'I did?' She was conscious of his eyes appraising her. They were dark blue, the colour of the sea almost.

'I decided a reply in person would be better than an email.'

Louise racked her brains: Seb Flanders. Seb Flanders? The name didn't ring any bells.

He was smiling. 'I'll put you out of your misery. I'm the owner of Dream Designs. You said you were looking to revamp the hotel.'

'I'm really sorry, but I think you've made a mistake.'

'No, you definitely sent a letter.' He bent over, searching through a sheaf of papers in his bag. 'Here we are.' He held out a sheet of A4 and she took it from him, scanning the page. It was the hotel's letterhead ... *interested in ... redesign ... outdated ...* Her eyes moved to the close: *Yours sincerely* and, yes, her name printed underneath, but the signature? She studied it: it was similar to hers, she had to admit, but the *s* was different, and the dot above the *i* was bigger and more rounded.

She handed back the sheet of paper. 'Oh yes. I remember now.' She wasn't going to admit she couldn't control what went on in the hotel. 'I sent off exploratory letters.'

'I like to get a feel for a place before I do any designs, even provisional ones,' he said. 'This is certainly a beautiful building which any designer would love to work with.'

He was wearing a black T-shirt, and the fine hairs on his

tanned forearm drew her gaze. Compliments for the hotel were bound to get her onside. But what the hell what she was thinking of? She was only a temporary manager with no right to instigate anything. 'I'm afraid you've had a wasted journey. I sent out several enquiry letters. Very much the beginning of the process.' She looked past his shoulder to the coffee table where she could see drawings, swatches of material, paint charts. 'I'm sorry if you got the wrong idea.'

A smile lit up his face again as his eyes followed hers. 'If you'd let me show you.'

She wanted to keep the smile there, to feel it warm her skin. It wouldn't do any harm to take a look. But Oliver's face loomed across her mind.

'I'll keep your name on file, Seb. When I decide to go ahead, I'll be in touch.'

He gathered up the drawings and material and piled them into his bag. 'I'm sorry you don't feel able to glance through my ideas.'

She looked down at the floor and her gaze settled on his brown brogues.

Louise sat at her desk and waited. Phyllis had been at the hotel for as long as she could remember. When Louise was young, she'd often helped her tidy the laundry room. The smell of clean linen reminded her of the sea. She'd run her hand over the pristine sheets and wonder how they could be so smooth.

'Now, don't you be making a mess of those sheets,' Phyllis used to scold. But Louise knew she had a soft spot for her really. She'd never had *little uns* – as she called them – of her own: 'The hotel and my George is the only children I need,' she would say.

There was a tap at the door, and Phyllis poked her head round. 'You wanted to see me, Miss Louise.'

'Yes, come in.' Louise indicated the chair adjacent to hers. 'Do sit down.'

Phyllis ventured into the room, but hovered inside the door. 'I'd prefer to stand, if you don't mind.'

Louise looked up at her lined face, at her grey bun, wisps of hair straggling free, at her hands clenched in front of her, a bony ridge of white across her knuckles. 'It will be easier to talk if you sit down.'

Phyllis sat on the edge of the chair. 'How's your dad doing? I miss seeing him about the place.' A thin whistle accompanied her words.

'Dad's fine, thank you. But there's something I need to talk to you about.'

Phyllis clapped her hands to her cheeks. 'It's that woman in fifteen, isn't it? She said the pillows were hard, but –'

'It's not about the pillows.' God, she'd never get it over with at this rate. 'I'm afraid we've received several complaints.'

Phyllis drew a hand over her face as if she was removing an imaginary spider's web. 'The rooms are spotless, Miss Louise. I check them over meself when the girls have finished.'

'There's no problem with the rooms. Apart from money apparently going missing.' Louise waited. 'Is there anything you'd like to tell me?'

She bent down and switched on the fan at her feet. Its gentle whirring eased the silence.

Phyllis stared at her lap.

'There is something I need to tell you,' Louise said.

'I hope it won't take long because I've still got to do refills of the toiletries on the top floor.'

Right, no point delaying any longer. 'This is not an easy thing for me to say, but there's been an accusation that you took the money that's gone missing.'

Phyllis flung her head back as if Louise had slapped her. 'I ain't done nothing. Who's accused me?'

'That's not really the point. I need to ask you – have you taken money from guests' rooms?'

'Nope.'

Louise was desperate to say *Okay. Fine.* Then Phyllis could go and finish her jobs, and they could put this horribleness behind them. But her instinct told her Phyllis's bluster was covering something up. 'Is everything all right at home?'

'Why shouldn't it be?'

'It's just you seem rather tense.'

'It's all fine.'

'I'm sorry to push it, Phyllis, but I'm going to ask you again – do you know anything about money going missing from rooms?'

'I've said, haven't I?'

Louise kept her eyes on the housekeeper's face and detected a tiny movement of her lips, a downward pull at each corner. Guilt, she was sure. For a few seconds her mind slipped to that linen cupboard: *Don't you be making a mess of them sheets.* 'Have you got any holiday due?'

'No.'

Louise clicked on the computer as if she was checking something, although only the icons on the desktop were showing. 'It says here you're owed holiday.'

'I've had me holiday.' Phyllis's voice quavered.

'You're due another fortnight.' Louise kept her eyes on the screen. She was only delaying the inevitable, but inspiration as to how to deal with this might strike her in the meantime. 'I think it would be just as well if you started your holiday tomorrow.' She made herself look at Phyllis. If she argued about the holiday, it would be a sign she was innocent. If not ...

Phyllis stood up. 'Whatever you say. Some people can't wait to stab you in the back.'

'Perhaps we could have a coffee in town,' Louise said. 'In a few days' time.'

Phyllis pushed the chair away from her. It scraped on the tiles. 'I don't drink coffee,' she said.

Eighteen

Ollie stared into the froth of his cappuccino. Jess was late. He'd suggested meeting in the coffee shop round the corner from her school to make it easier for her, but she wasn't going to come. She'd probably never intended –

'Hello, Ollie.'

Her voice startled him. She leant forward and kissed his cheek, and he smelt a sharp lemony scent, not one he remembered. She hung her bag, the multi-coloured leather one he'd bought her last Christmas, over the chair and sat down opposite him.

'Coffee?' he asked.

She shook her head and indicated the glass the waitress had placed on the table. 'Water is fine.'

He forced himself to look at her. Her hair was piled on top of her head, her eyes ringed with black eyeliner, and her makeup looked thicker than she used to wear. A spot reddened her chin, and dark circles shadowed her eyes. She looked the same, and yet infinitely different. It made him want to cry.

'How are you, Ollie?' she asked.

He shrugged.

'Painting?'

'A bit. And you? How are you?'

'I'm fine.' She took her phone from her bag, and put it on the table. They used to laugh about couples who spent all their time on their mobiles instead of talking to each other. 'In case my head of department wants me. I'm supposed to be working in the library.' She didn't meet his eyes. 'I haven't got long. You said you needed to talk.'

Ollie focused on the spilt sugar grains on the table. 'How are you getting on?'

She flicked her middle finger against her thumb. 'You said you had something important to ask me.' She was wearing pink nail polish. He'd never seen her with colour on her nails before.

'Come on, Ollie, what is it? I've got to get back to work.'

'Flo said you've met someone.'

Colour flooded her face. 'What's it to you?'

'She said he was taking you both to stay in a hotel. If my daughter's involved, it's got everything to do with me.' He'd rehearsed that in front of the mirror this morning.

'Okay, then, yes, I've met someone.'

'Who is he?'

She folded her arms and sat back against the chair. 'That's definitely nothing to do with you.'

'When you say you've met someone ... is this a new someone or a someone you already knew?'

Jess reached behind her to unhook her bag from the chair. 'Was there anything else? I need to go.'

'We're not even divorced yet.'

'It's not me holding things up.'

Ollie pictured the pile of unopened post on the table in the flat. There was one with a solicitor's stamp on the envelope. He'd sort of guessed its contents. 'You've started proceedings?'

'There's no point waiting.'

'On what grounds?'

'Unreasonable behaviour.'

'What? Whose?'

'Don't be stupid. Yours, of course.'

'But I love you ... it was a rough patch.'

'I'm sorry, but it's over.'

'Flo mentioned a name ... Genie ...' He swallowed. 'Is that ... is it who I think it is?'

She rested her hands on her bag, fingers interlocked. There were indentations where her nails were digging into her knuckles. 'If you mean Eugene,' she said, 'yes, it's him.'

He'd wanted to know. It was always better to know than to wonder. Suspicion corroded your insides and ate them away. But now she'd said it: the nightmare was true. 'You haven't been seeing him since ... you don't mean that ...'

'No, I'm not that much of a bitch. He got in touch a while back, said he'd like to meet up ... for old times' sake and well ...' She shrugged. 'You can guess the rest.'

'You're making a big mistake.'

'Oh? How come you're suddenly the fountain of all wisdom?'

'You know what he did to Louise, don't you?'

'It was an accident. He's told me how sad he was about all that.'

'He caused it, Jess. It was his fault.'

'If you hadn't gone over there, chasing after him.'

He laughed. He couldn't help it. The thought of the two of them justifying it all to themselves, reordering the past, so that it was bearable. He might have lots of faults but at least he was honest with himself.

'I don't know what you find so funny.'

'You can pretend as much as you like, but we both know what happened, don't we?'

She stood up. 'I've got to go.'

'Stay a bit longer. There's something I want to ask you.'

She glanced at the clock and sat down. 'Okay, but make it quick.'

'Mum and Dad have made me an offer about the hotel.'

She slapped her hand on the table. 'Not this again. How many times have we discussed it already? Besides it's nothing to do with me now.'

'Hear me out, please.'

'I've got a meeting in twenty minutes.'

Ollie cleared his throat. He could do this. 'Mum and Dad are retiring. Giving up the hotel altogether, and they've offered it to me.'

She clicked the catch on her bag open and shut. Open and shut. 'What's new? You're not interested in the hotel.'

'Dad never talked about retiring before. I was going to be working with him, under his control.' Ollie dug the spoon into the sugar bowl. 'That would have been a disaster.'

'And you're considering it?'

'Yes.'

'So much for your commitment to Flo, if you're down in Plymouth.' Her mobile bleeped, and she checked the screen. 'My head of department wondering where I am.'

'That's the point, Jess. What about if we were to make a fresh start in Plymouth, the three of us?' The blood throbbed in his ears. 'Get away from everything. We'd have money. You could give up teaching. Flo would love living by the sea.' He gazed up at her. 'What do you say?'

'Sorry, Ollie.' Her eyes raked his face. 'It's too late.'

He jumped up and faced her across the table. 'Just tell me one thing.'

'What?'

'Why?'

'For God's sake! *Why?* You're talking in riddles now.' She turned away, and he caught her arm.

'Why him? Why does it have to be him of all people?'

She pushed his hand from her arm. 'You really want to know?'

'I asked, didn't I?'

'Eugene's exciting. He's dangerous – you never know what he'll do next.'

'Sounds like a character from some trashy romance.'

'Okay, mock it, but he makes me feel alive.'

'And I don't?'

She swatted a fly that had landed on her hand.

'And I don't?'

'No, Ollie. You don't.'

He ran. Blindly. He swerved across roads. Cars honked their horns. Cyclists swore at him. By the time he reached the gallery, he barely had the energy to open the door and fall up the step. Above him the bell jangled.

'What the –?' a voice exclaimed. Hands grasped his shoulders. 'Ollie! Ollie!' The voice – Angel's – was next to his ear.

He closed his eyes. The world dissolved in that black space. No Jess. No Flo. Best of all, no Eugene.

'Ollie, a customer might come in.'

He groaned.

'Are you hurt? Tell me where it hurts.'

Everywhere. His skin prickled as if hundreds of needles were jabbing him.

'Come on, Ollie. Get up.'

He struggled to his feet and into the store room at the back of the gallery. He slumped into the chair and took the glass of water Angel held out. He drank it back in one go.

'Angel, you're a lifesaver. Thank you.'

'What happened? I thought you'd been drinking, but you haven't, have you?'

He shook his head. 'I met Jess.'

'Good. You needed to thrash things out.'

'No, not good. She is with that arsehole I told you about.'

'At least you know. You can start to rebuild –'

'No!' He rammed his fists against his eyes. 'When I think he sees my baby more than I do.'

'Stop it. This isn't doing you any good.' She smoothed out his fingers, one by one. Her hands were cool, soothing. They cupped his face, forcing him to look at her. Hazel eyes. Lighter flecks glinting in them.

'Flo is your daughter. She loves you. Whoever this man is, he's not her daddy and never will be – unless you let him.' Her fingers wiped away his tears. 'You can't go to pieces like this.'

Her face was close, her breath warm against his skin. He touched her lips with his. They were soft. Quiescent. They opened. Her tongue found his. Sweetness ...

'Well, this is a pretty scene.'

The voice sliced their mouths apart. Angel rocked back on her heels. Ollie followed her gaze to the doorway. A man stood there. A man ... Christ, he'd know those red braces, that beard, anywhere.

Angel recovered first. She got to her feet and held out her hand. 'I'm Angel, the gallery manager. Can I help? What sort of work are you interested in?'

'My dear, I'm not here to buy.'

That voice. Sneering. Dismissive. Ollie stood up. 'What are you doing here?'

Angel looked from one to the other. 'You two know each other?'

'Indeed we do. I'm Guy Norton, the new owner of The Serendip.' He stroked the hideous goatee beard. 'Not that it will be called that for much longer.'

Nineteen

Louise came downstairs as the grandfather clock chimed nine.

Maeve was at the desk. 'I wondered if we'd see you today,' she said as the last bong died away.

'I had some calls to make. I knew you were on reception this morning, so everything would run smoothly.' Louise pulled the duty book towards her, but none of the writing registered as words. Her mind was still awry from the row she'd had with Matt on the phone:

We agreed six months ...

Yes, but I expected you to come home occasionally in that time ...

It's full on, Matt. Why don't you move in here temporarily? ...

Being cooped up in that place would drive me mad ...

'Oh, and while we're talking, Maeve, I wanted to ask you about Seb Flanders.'

'Who?' Maeve shifted the pot of pens on the desk from right to left and back again.

'Seb Flanders. He's an interior designer. I think you know of him.'

'I don't believe I do.'

Louise kept her gaze on Maeve's face. 'He came to see me last week. He had a letter, apparently from me.'

'I don't know what you're getting at.'

'I hadn't sent it.'

Maeve's eyelashes batted furiously. 'Oh yes, I remember now. I sent out a few on spec.'

A guest was sitting on the sofa reading the newspaper at the other end of the foyer, and Louise kept her voice low. 'I'd be grateful if you'd consult me before you do anything like that again, Maeve. I'm not happy about my signature being used without my knowledge.'

Maeve chewed the end of her pen. 'I often sent out letters using your dad's.'

'I appreciate the change of management is an adjustment for you. But from now on, what I say goes.'

'Until your brother makes up his mind.'

The words were muttered, but Louise was pretty sure she'd heard them correctly. 'As things stand, Maeve, I'm managing the hotel.' She wasn't imagining it – a nerve twitched in Maeve's eye. 'I'd like you to remember that.'

'Fine with me.'

'Good, I'm glad we've cleared that up.'

Louise checked emails, made some notes for a meeting about a conference at the hotel next month, and phoned the Visitor Information Centre for more free maps and guides. It was no good. For every minute of focus, she spent five doodling on her notepad. She grabbed her bag, locked her office and headed for her parents' apartment.

She tapped at the door, and her mother answered. She put her finger to her lips. 'Tom's gone back to sleep.'

Louise followed her into the room. A writing pad was open on the dining table.

'This is a nice surprise,' her mother said. 'Coffee or tea?'

'Mum, I need to talk to you and Dad.'

'What about?'

'Oliver.'

'I thought so. After what you said last week.' They sat down at the table, and her mother picked up the biro and drew on the pad, a seagull in mid-flight, its wingspan huge. 'I told Tom you needed an answer.'

'I've tried to be patient, but Maeve is driving me mad.'

Her mother nodded. 'You make some tea. I'll get your father up.'

Louise went into the kitchen and boiled the kettle. She put cups and saucers on the tray and carried them to the table. Her father, wrapped in his dressing gown, was sitting in his chair by the window. His eyes were closed.

'He's not feeling so good today,' her mother whispered. She took a cup from the tray and carried it over. 'Here you are, Tom. Louise has made us tea.'

He opened his eyes and raised his hand in a sort of salute.

'What's up?' Louise asked. 'Should you call the doctor?'

He shook his head. 'Bad night, that's all. Your mother was snoring.'

'Tom, how dare you?' She tapped his arm. 'If there was a snoring competition ...'

'I know, I know.' He grinned, a glimpse of his old self emerging. 'What can we do for you, Louise? Lindy says it's important and I had to get up.'

Louise sat down on the footstool next to his chair. The sun slanted in through the side window and lit up his head. She hadn't noticed his hair had grown so thin. Her mother was at the table, her head resting in her hands.

Louise patted the other armchair. 'Come and sit here, Mum. I want to say this to both of you.' Her mother's closeness might make the conversation easier, but it was her father who held all the cards on the hotel's future.

'How long are you going to wait for Oliver's reply?'

'About the hotel you mean?' Despite the heat in the room, her father pulled his dressing gown tighter.

'Yes, the hotel.' Louise cupped her hands round her knees, willing herself not to rock backwards and forwards. 'I need to know where I stand.'

'You're the manager, responsible for the day-to-day running of the hotel.'

'Day-to-day? So, no major decisions then?'

'I guess not.'

'Don't you see how impossible that makes my position, Dad? I'm okay on a temporary basis. But anything more permanent needs Oliver, the son and heir. Maeve reminded me of that again only this morning.'

Her father's eyebrows shot up. 'What's Maeve got to do with it?'

'I told you about her before. She's always looking for ways to put me down, and all this uncertainty is fuelling that. Your involvement with her makes her think she's invincible.'

'Involvement? What are you talking about?'

'All the time she spends here gives her –'

'You've got my full support, Louise. I'll make sure Maeve understands that.'

'Perhaps we have taken you for granted,' her mother broke in. 'But I'm sure it won't be long till we hear from Oliver. We don't want to rush him.'

'No, it wouldn't do to upset Golden Boy, would it?'

The atmosphere in the room was suddenly thick and heavy. It sat on Louise's skin, filled her nose and throat, so she couldn't breathe. If only she could shrug her shoulders, laugh, *oh I didn't really mean that*, everything would be all right. Her parents' shocked expressions would disappear. But she couldn't; she was too far in now.

'You don't get it, do you?' she said. 'You've always been too besotted with Oliver to think about me, Mum. And all you've ever wanted, Dad, was for him to take on the hotel.'

'I don't think that's fair, Louise. Your father worshipped his little princess.'

'*A little princess*. A trophy. That's all I was ever supposed to be.' Louise jumped up and made for the door. 'Not a grown up woman with talent and opinions of my own.' She gripped the handle, her forehead pressed against the hard oak. Her father's breathing filled the silence.

'Louise, my lovely, where's all this coming from?' Her mother's voice sounded old and tired.

Louise swung round. 'I'm the one who's got the passion for the hotel, the skills to run it. But we have to maintain this nonsense of father to son.'

'I had no idea you felt like this,' her mother said. 'You've never said.'

'Well, I don't, do I?' Louise's palms were slick with sweat. 'Just because I try to keep the peace ...'

'You're right, girl. I've been chasing this dream of Oliver inheriting the hotel since he was born.' Her father's eyebrows were clenched in a deep V and the lines running from his nose to his mouth looked as if they'd been chiselled into place. 'It's about time I saw sense.'

'Tom, do you know what you're saying?'

He thumped the arm of the chair. 'I've got a heart problem, Lindy. I haven't gone doolally.'

Louise darted over and squatted next to his chair. 'Do you mean it, Dad?'

'I've been a fool.' He hauled himself to his feet. 'You've shown how capable you are. The hotel couldn't be in better hands.'

She reached up and kissed his cheek. 'You don't know what that means to me.'

'We'd better tell Oliver,' her mother said. 'I sent him that email.'

'No.' Her father's hand sliced through the air.

'It's only right to let him know.'

'He's had his chance, Lindy. He'd rather play with his paints.' Her father squeezed Louise's hand. 'I'm pleased to

hear you stand up for yourself. We'll get the paperwork
drawn up and have the solicitor over as soon as possible.'

Twenty

Matt grumbled all that weekend, and he was still grumbling as they drove to Louise's parents on Sunday evening. 'I don't know why I have to show up. It's you they want to see.' He fiddled with the car radio, and some heavy metal music boomed into the car.

She leaned forward to turn it down. 'Mum specifically said to invite you.' She'd offered to drive, the thought of him morosely nursing an orange juice all evening adding to her jitteriness. 'You haven't seen them for ages. You'll love their new apartment.'

'I don't know why they moved out.' He was doing that jiggling thing with his right leg.

'Mum insisted they had some space, so that Dad couldn't rush round 24/7.'

'Like you are, you mean.'

'Don't start that, Matt. Not now.' She slowed as they approached a roundabout. The road was clear and she pulled forward. 'Let's have a nice evening.'

'Why do I have to visit when your brother hasn't been?'

Her fingers tightened on the steering wheel. 'Why are you measuring yourself against Oliver?'

'I don't see why he gets off scot-free, while you're working your arse off.'

There was a parking space at the top of Elliot Street and Louise pulled in. She turned off the engine. 'I love running the hotel, Matt, you know that.'

He slapped his palm against the door. 'And there was I thinking you loved me.'

'I do love you, but I can love my job as well.'

Her father opened the door. 'Come on in. Come on in.' A smile lit up his face. 'Your mother's in the kitchen.'

Louise kissed him. 'You sound upbeat, Dad.'

'I've been looking forward to some company.' He shook Matt's hand. 'Good to see you. Don't stand there at the door – come in.'

Matt glanced round. 'Nice place.'

'We like it.' Her father waved his arm towards the window. 'And that view is priceless.'

They stood, awkwardly, in the middle of the room. From the kitchen came the clatter of pans.

'I'm sorry to hear about your heart attack, Tom.'

Louise flashed a smile at Matt: he was obviously making an effort.

'Water under the bridge now. The consultant says I'm doing well. What can I get you to drink?' He winked. 'I've got a rather fine malt I think you'll like.'

'It's lovely to see you up and about, Dad,' Louise said, 'but don't overdo things, just because of us.'

'You being here is doing me a power of good.' He crossed to the sideboard where a circle of bottles stood. He poured a whisky and brought it over to Matt. 'What about you, Louise?'

'A glass of wine with the meal will be lovely. Do you think Mum's okay in the kitchen? It's gone very quiet.'

'You two stay here and enjoy the view. I'll see how she's getting on.'

Louise moved to the window. Wrapped in its horseshoe of limestone cliffs, the expanse of water glistened. Shadows scudded across its surface as occasional clouds played with the evening sunshine.

Matt's arm slipped round her waist. 'Your dad looks great.' His whisper tickled her ear. 'At this rate, I'll soon get my wife back.'

She kept her eyes fixed on The Hoe, crowded with early evening strollers. Two dogs approached each other, their owners pulling on their leashes to hold them back. The spiky-haired terrier leapt up at the collie, circling and biting at its tail.

'Here we are: dinner's ready.' Louise's mother placed a serving dish on the table.

'That looks wonderful, Mum.' Louise took in the slices of beef, surrounded by golden-topped potatoes, mounds of Yorkshire pudding. 'Why don't my roasties look like yours?'

Her mother smiled, her cheeks pink, her hair dishevelled from the steam in the kitchen. 'I'm sure they do.' She kissed Matt's cheek. 'Lovely to see you again. I've been so looking forward to tonight.'

Louise wiped her mouth on her napkin. 'That was wonderful, Mum. Thank you.'

'What did you call the dessert?' Matt asked. 'Strawberry something?'

'Strawberry roulade. It's Tom's favourite.' Her mother cleared away the plates. 'Although that was a special treat. Don't go thinking you can have pudding every day, Tom.'

'For heaven's sake, Lindy, can't I have one night off from worrying about my health?' He turned to Matt and Louise. 'Now, what about another drink before we get down to business?'

For weeks Louise had pretended to ignore the calendar

in the kitchen at home, the red line Matt drew through each day, the gold star he'd stuck on 30th November, the day their agreed time ran out. His words jumped out at her: *six months to get your dad on his feet. Then we'll try for a baby.* It was August, almost half way through.

Her father was standing over by the drinks. 'Another whisky, Matt?'

Louise wanted to suggest they all had coffee, but Matt was already agreeing.

'And you, Louise? Another glass?' Her father held up the bottle. 'We'll need a toast.'

She covered her glass. 'No, no, I'm driving.'

'We could have a taxi.'

Was it her imagination, or was Matt slurring his words? 'I've got an early start in the morning,' she said.

The table was cleared and Louise's parents were in the kitchen. Matt pulled her close to him and kissed her.

'Great evening. Better than I expected,' he said. 'And nice drop of malt.'

The woody taste of the whisky stung her lips. 'We won't stay too late, will we?' she whispered.

He was studying his glass, holding it up to the light and twisting it.

'Matt, let's go soon.' She ran her hand up and down his thigh. 'I've got to be at the hotel at seven tomorrow.'

He downed some more whisky and grinned at her. 'Not for much longer though. Your dad will on the case again soon, and you don't even need to go back to Everatt & Johnson if you don't want to.'

'You mean not have a job?'

'Yeah. Why not?'

'What would I do all day?'

He stroked her cheek. 'I love you. Let me look after you.'

'You do look after me, but I don't need cosseting as if I'm some rare creature.'

'You are one to me.'

'Oh, Matt, don't be soppy.'

His touch on her skin was gentle, his finger stroking her cheek. 'You were broken when you came to me.'

'But I'm fine now, and you helped me get better.'

'Louise, I can see what running the hotel is doing to you, and I won't let you get in the same state again.'

She caught his wrist and held his hand away from her face. 'It was completely different then. You know what I went through in London. You can't compare that with a job.'

'Here's the coffee.' Her mother came in carrying a tray, and her father followed, a red folder under his arm.

'I presume Louise has brought you up to speed with our discussions, Matt.' He slid some sheets of paper across the table. 'This is the key document. We need to have my solicitor present for the actual signing, but I thought we'd run through it first.'

Matt picked up the first sheet.

She opened her mouth to speak. Her lips were poised, ready to shape the sounds. To make words. To make him understand. An image of her hand on Matt's arm floated past her. Blue veins striping the back. Gold wedding ring. Neglected nails. But her hand wouldn't move. The window swerved to the ceiling. Patterns of light circling above her head. An arm round her shoulder. Voices in her ear.

'Louise. Louise, love. Are you okay?'

The window righted itself. Her mother was leaning over her. 'You've gone as white as a sheet.'

'Just a dizzy spell, Mum.'

'Do you want to lie down? Dad can explain things to Matt.'

'No, no. I'm fine.' She needed to be there to steer the conversation. 'Why don't we leave this until another time, Dad? Matt doesn't want to hear all this stuff.'

He shot a look in her direction. 'On the contrary. I do want to hear.'

'Give it a quick once-over, Matt,' her father said. 'I think you'll find it's all in order. The legal boys have been through it with a fine toothcomb.'

'I'm not sure I understand.'

'It's all the legalese they insist on using.' Her father took the paper from Matt's hand and fixed his glasses on the end of his nose. 'Here, I'll read it and try and explain: "I, Tom Anderson, referred to as OWNER, herewith unconditionally assign all of my right, title and interest in an expectancy of the estate of THE PLYMOUTH HOTEL to Louise Bradbury (nee Anderson), referred to as ASSIGNEE, under the terms and conditions stated herein. I –"'

'What's this all about?' Matt gripped the back of the chair. 'Why is the hotel being signed over to you, Louise?'

'Oh, don't worry.' Her father put his hand on Matt's shoulder. 'As Louise's husband, you share in the ownership, even if you're not working at the hotel.'

'Of course it would be a huge help to Louise if you decided to come on board fully,' her mother said.

'Exactly. I couldn't have managed without Lindy by my side.' Louise's father blew a kiss at her mother.

Sweat ran down Louise's back. This was turning into a nightmare.

'Anything you'd like to tell me about?' Matt's eyes bored into her.

There was nothing for it but to come clean. 'Dad is making over the hotel to me.'

'For how long?'

'It's permanent,' her father said. 'The hotel will be Louise's. And yours, of course.'

'We agreed six months, Louise.'

'I should have told you, but I was worried what you'd say.'

'Worried what I'd say!' Matt gave a dry laugh. 'So, you've been plotting all this behind my back?'

'It wasn't like that. But you were so against me managing the hotel, and I didn't know ...' She didn't know what? How he'd react? How angry he'd be? No, she'd known all right.

Matt caught hold of her wrist. The thin skin wrinkled under his grip. 'You conned me into thinking you were at the hotel on a temporary basis.'

'But it was temporary until recently. Mum, Dad, tell him.'

Matt grabbed the sheet of paper from her father and flicked it in her face. 'I'm sorry to spoil your lovely evening, Mr and Mrs Anderson. But I had no idea I was being dragged along to take part in this farce.'

'Matt, it's not like that.' Louise's mother retrieved the paper. She smoothed it out. 'We wanted to see you. And Tom and I ... well ... we didn't know Louise hadn't told you.'

Louise glanced across at her father. He was slumped over the table, his head in his hands. 'Let's go home. We can talk about things there.' She went round to Matt's side of the table. 'I should have explained before. But I'm sure we can –'

He pulled away from her 'Don't touch me. I'm getting out of here.'

'Wait.' She scrabbled under the table for her bag. 'I'm coming with you.'

He strode to the door and flung it open.

Louise's father groaned, and she turned to him. 'Dad, are you all right?'

'I'll look after your father,' her mother said. 'You go with Matt.'

She ran to the door. The corridor was empty, and there was no sign of Matt.

*

Louise stepped out of the lift. Matt wasn't in the entrance hall. She jabbed her finger at the security panel and the doors slid open. She ran down the path and pulled open the gate onto Cliff Road. He was still nowhere to be seen. Her chest was tight when she reached the car. He wasn't there. Dragging her phone from her bag, she clicked on his name: straight to voicemail. 'Matt, please let's talk. We can deal with this. I'm sorry ... I should have told you. But we can make it all right. Matt ... I love you.'

She leant against the car, a stitch needling her side.

Her mobile rang. Her fingers fumbled with the keys. *Accept.* Quick. Press *Accept.* 'Matt, where are you?'

'It doesn't matter.' His voice rasped against her ear.

'Let's go home. I can explain.'

'I'm not coming home.'

'What do you mean? Where are you going?'

'I don't know. I need to think.'

'Come home, please.' She waited. 'Matt?' The phone line was dead.

Twenty-one

A woman and her little boy sat opposite Ollie and Flo on the train journey to Plymouth. They played games and coloured in pictures together. After a while, the boy pulled his teddy close and fell asleep against his mother's shoulder. His thumb fell from his mouth, but even in sleep he managed to hang on to teddy. Ollie glanced down at Flo beside him. She was watching the little boy too, but she smiled up at Ollie, when she felt his gaze on her, patting her bag where Panda was nestling. 'Granny and Grandpa will expect me to bring him,' she'd said when they were getting ready that morning.

The taxi dropped them off at the end of Citadel Street, and they walked the last stretch to the hotel. Now the time was almost here, his mouth felt dry at the thought of seeing his dad again. 'Are you nervous?' Flo had asked him on the train. Nervous? He didn't know how to unravel the knot twisting his stomach. It was all over for him and Jess, but his parents' offer might be just the kick up the butt he needed. He couldn't paint stuck in that poky flat, paralysed with misery, and he was tired of being at war with his dad.

*

It was drizzling as they reached The Hoe, and rain clung to his skin and settled on his hair. He pulled up the hood of Flo's anorak, and lifted the rucksack from his shoulder, clutching it in his arms. He looked out over Plymouth Sound. White sails bobbed on the choppy sea; a ferry was forging across the bay, but the Breakwater, Drake's Island, Mount Batten were all shrouded in mist.

'Shame we can't see much today, Flo,' he said. 'It's a fabulous view. This is where I learnt to paint.'

'I like the smell of the sea.'

He breathed in. 'Ozone.'

'Better than stinky old London.'

Ollie pushed open the door of the hotel and crossed the foyer to the desk. Dad was usually here or not far away, but today there was a woman behind it. She had her back to him. He studied her blonde hair, and her bottom, shapely in a tight black skirt. He tapped the desk and she turned round.

'Maeve!' She used to help his father, but now she looked more as if she owned the place.

'Oliver? Is it really you?'

She rushed out from behind the desk and flung her arms round him. Her hair tickled his cheek, and he caught the smell of peppermints on her breath as she giggled. She leaned back and studied his face. 'How handsome you've become. You've obviously inherited the Anderson good looks.'

He moved to extricate himself from her embrace. She never used to like him much. She'd tackled him one day: 'You know your father's a lovely man. You'd do well to follow in his footsteps.'

164

But now she was beaming, looking from Ollie to Flo. 'And this must be your beautiful daughter.' She swooped down and kissed Flo. 'Your grandpa is going to be thrilled to see you.'

Flo glanced at Ollie. Her cheeks were pink.

'This is Maeve, Flo,' he said. 'Do you remember her?'

She shook her head, but stuck her hand out. 'Hello.'

'And where's your mum?' Maeve glanced towards the door. 'You haven't left her in London have you?'

His eyes skimmed Flo's trying to flash a warning, but she didn't notice. 'Mummy's at home –'

'Jess couldn't come today,' he cut in quickly.

'That's a shame.' Maeve caught hold of Ollie's anorak. 'You're soaked. And you, Flo.' She pulled at the sleeve. 'Let me have these wet things. I'll hang them on the coat stand to dry off.'

Ollie and Flo shrugged off their anoraks. 'Is Dad around?' he asked.

Maeve's eyes narrowed. 'You mean you don't know?'

'Know what?'

The phone rang and she dumped the anoraks on a chair as she reached for it. Ollie took in the brash-red nails, the glossy lips, as she spoke into the receiver: 'The Plymouth Hotel ... a double room? ... and how many nights? ...' She gave a simpering smile he was sure was for his benefit.

He turned away, trying to block out the voice. Everything looked the same: leather armchairs, flowers on the oak chest, newspapers on the coffee table. It was comfortable enough, but definitely in need of an update. He'd start by –'

'Your parents have moved out of the hotel.' Maeve's voice scratched at his ear.

He turned to face her. 'I know, but I presume they're still here some of the time.'

His father had complained every step of the way about the new apartment block next door: during planning, during the building, while the apartments were being sold. The noise, the dirt, the pollution, the loss of tranquillity … on and on … every phone call, every visit dominated by some new outrage. And now he'd bought one of the damned things.

'They haven't been here since they moved. Your father's too poorly to work.'

'Hey, Daddy, come and look at this,' Flo called from the landing.

'Be there in a minute,' he said.

'I'll ring them and say you'll be round.' Maeve held the telephone to her ear. 'What time are they expecting you?'

'They're not. I wanted to surprise them.'

Maeve dropped the receiver into its rest. 'You'll give your father another heart attack.'

'It will be fine,' Ollie said. 'Besides I want to show Flo round first. Have her meet a few people.'

'Oh, who?'

It was nothing to do with her, but there was no point antagonising her if they were going to work together. 'Phyllis, for a start. I'm sure she'd love to see Flo.'

'Phyllis is on gardening leave.'

'Gardening leave? How come?'

'Some difficulty with your sister, I think.' Maeve leant forward on the desk and Ollie found himself staring into her cleavage. 'I'm sure you'd manage things much better.' She smiled up at him.

Christ, he had to get away from her. She was poison. A memory flashed across his mind: coming home from school early when a cricket match was cancelled, his mother curled up in her bedroom, her eyes red:

What's up, Mum?

It's nothing. Just a misunderstanding with Maeve.

He moved away from the desk and ran up the stairs two at a time, his rucksack banging against his hip. 'What did you want to show me, Flo?' He stood behind her, his hands on her shoulders. Her bones felt sharp and brittle. Had she lost weight, and he hadn't noticed?

'Look at this picture of the Mayflower Steps.' She was studying the paintings on the landing. 'We've been doing the Pilgrim Fathers at school.'

'We can go and have a look at the steps if you like,' he said.

'Oh, cool. Wait till I tell Mr Jarvis I've seen them.'

'I'm not sure it's the actual steps.'

'That's okay. I can imagine.'

She put her hand in his. 'Those flowers remind me of Mummy. I wish she was here.'

'I know, sweetheart. So do I.' He stared at the huge display of yellow and gold lilies on the table under the landing window.

'Do you remember when Mummy and me grew a sunflower in a pot?'

He laughed. 'You mean the one that wouldn't stop growing?'

'Mummy said it was like Jack and the Beanstalk.'

The clock in the foyer started to chime. Its sonorous notes had struck at so many key moments in his life: the morning he opened the letter offering him a place at art school; when a row with his father had erupted in front of a group of guests; his last visit, his mother in tears as he left. Bong... bong... bong... The echo died away.

'Come on, Daddy, what are you waiting for?' Flo was leaning over the balustrade on the next floor, and he chased up the stairs.

She opened the fire door which led on to one of the hotel corridors. 'Look at all those doors.'

His gaze slid along them. 'Eight on each side on this floor,' he recalled. 'Sea view or the city's rooftops. Forty-eight rooms in total.' The pride in his voice surprised him. What credit could he take for any of them?

Just then, the door closest to them opened and one

of the cleaners came out. Her face broke into a smile. 'It's Oliver, isn't it?'

Ollie looked closer. 'Joy! I didn't recognise you.'

She laughed. 'That would be all the wrinkles and grey hair.'

Joy had come to work at the hotel when he was about twelve, and she used to insist on cleaning and polishing his rugby boots. In return, he would fill up the trolley with new toiletries.

'How lovely to see you again. Are you staying long?'

'A couple of days. Flo's school has teacher training.'

Joy's eyes went to Flo. 'This is your daughter?'

It wasn't a surprise people didn't recognise her. The rows with his father had become so toxic, he'd come down on his own for the last few years on the rare occasions he made the trip. He even had to make an excuse for Louise's wedding, when she'd told him Jess wasn't welcome. He wondered if she and Matt had dumped the painting he'd sent them.

Joy smiled at Flo. 'You're beautiful, my darling.' She laughed. 'No offence, Oliver, but I presume she takes after her mum.'

'She's the image of her.'

Flo wrinkled her nose. 'Her eyes are greener than mine.'

'I'd better get on,' Joy said. 'We're short-staffed, and I'm in charge.'

'Maeve said Phyllis was on gardening leave. What's that about?'

'Some trouble.' Red flared in Joy's cheeks. 'You'll have to ask your sister.'

In the kitchen the staff pounced on Flo. Chef left the meat he was slicing and gave a little bow. 'Welcome. We don't have many visits from young ladies here.'

Antonio, a volatile Italian with a pencil-thin, black

moustache, who'd been the pastry chef for a long as Ollie could remember, dropped the dough he was kneading as soon as he saw them. He caught Flo up in a bear hug. '*La bambina bellissima!*' He planted kisses on both her cheeks.

She made a face at Ollie over Antonio's shoulder.

'Hi Tony! Good to see you!' Ollie lifted Flo from his arms and set her on the floor again.

'Hey man! How you get such a beautiful *bambina*?' Antonio's accent remained as thick as ever.

Ollie winked. 'Marry the right *mama!*'

'Tom's waiting for you in the guest lounge,' Maeve said when they got back to reception.

'But I told you we wanted to surprise them.' Ollie glared at her. Why did she have to interfere? The last time he'd been down, they'd had a bust-up in the lounge, his father jabbing his finger repeatedly towards the portrait above the fireplace. 'Jasper Anderson must be turning in his grave. He wouldn't have put up with this ... this ... insubordination from his son.' If he hadn't been so angry, Ollie would have laughed. Insubordination made him sound like a rebellious private facing the sergeant major.

He caught hold of Flo's hand and made for the double doors which stood open into the lounge. The top of his father's head was visible above the high-backed sofa, the hair wispy and white instead of the thick, iron-grey it used to be.

Flo pulled on his hand.

He looked down. 'What is it?'

'I'm scared, Daddy.'

He bent down so that his face was level with hers. 'There's nothing to be scared of.'

'Grandpa might be cross with us.'

'Me, perhaps, sweetheart, but not you.'

'But suppose he shouts at you?'

God, he'd obviously told her too much about the rows with his father. 'I'll hardly get a look in once he sets eyes on you.'

'But you will show him what you wrote in your book?'

'Of course. That's why we're here, isn't it?' He glanced over his shoulder. Just as he thought – Maeve was staring at them from behind the desk.

He eased a strand of chewed hair from between Flo's lips. 'Let's go in.'

His father was standing now in his favourite position in front of the fireplace under his ancestor's painting. His hands were clasped behind his back as usual, but in other ways, he was transformed. His face was a waxy yellow and he'd lost an enormous amount of weight. His shirt was baggy and tucked into his loose trousers with an over-sized brown leather belt.

'Hello, Dad.' Ollie stepped forward.

His father turned his head, but he didn't speak, didn't smile. Flo dragged on Ollie's arm, but he pulled away moving towards his father. 'Good to see you, Dad.'

'Is it?' His father shuffled back to the sofa.

Ollie sat down next to him, clasping Flo on his knee.

'Where's Mum?'

'Gone shopping. You were the last person we expected to see.'

Ollie took a deep breath. 'I know I should have come before. But we didn't exactly part on good terms in London, did we?'

'You do realise I've had a heart attack since then?'

'I'm sorry, Dad, I should have asked straight away – how are you?'

'Much as you see.'

'I've planned to come so many times, but things have been ... tricky.' His father didn't meet his eyes. This wasn't going to be easy, but there was no going back now. He'd show Dad his exercise book. Tell him that he was going to accept his offer. He would take on the hotel.

'This is Flo, Dad. Do you remember her?'

His father's gaze swept over Flo. 'My granddaughter? Of course I do.' He smiled, his cheeks wrinkling into dry creases. 'How about a kiss for your grandpa?'

Ollie felt her hesitation, her legs swinging, heels ramming into his shins. 'Perhaps when she gets more used to you, Dad. She –' But Flo had already slipped off his lap and planted a kiss on his father's cheek. He rested his hand lightly on her head and Ollie saw the tears brimming on his lower lids.

Flo plonked herself on the sofa between them. 'Go on Daddy.'

He reached for his rucksack, but his father had picked up the newspaper from the coffee table and turned the page.

'Shall I get Maeve to bring some tea or coffee?' Ollie asked.

'Not allowed caffeine any more.'

'Oh, right.' Ollie glanced up at the Jasper Anderson portrait. The face was as stern and unyielding as ever, as if it was hewn from granite. 'What time will Mum be back?'

'I don't know. I sent her a text to say you'd shown up at last.'

'What's the new apartment like? Must make a change from the poky flat upstairs.'

'Your mother insisted we move out.' His father stared into the distance. Seeing what? The hotel full of guests, laughter, music? The huge fire that blazed in here every winter? His son behind the desk, charming and soothing weary guests? 'And she was right – I couldn't cope any more.'

'So Maeve and Louise are covering temporarily?'

'Maeve is still the receptionist. Louise is managing the hotel.'

'Oh, she's looking after it for you?'

'No, Oliver. It's hers, or it will be.'

'Hers? But you and Mum have offered it to me.'

His father flicked through the newspaper. The rustling was unbearably loud. 'You didn't reply. Your mum emailed and phoned, but there comes a time –'

'It was a big decision, Dad. I needed to be sure.'

'You could have told us that. The hotel can't wait around indefinitely while you weigh up the options.'

Flo tapped Ollie's hand and her eyes darted towards the rucksack by his feet.

He took out the exercise book. 'Dad, I want you to listen to this. I wrote it when I was at school: *Myself in Ten Years.*' He hesitated, but his father's eyes remained fixed on the paper.

'Go on,' Flo whispered.

'*When I am twenty-one, I will be the owner of a big hotel on Plymouth Hoe. It is the grandest, smartest hotel in Devon, in England, in Europe, in the whole wide world ...*'

He stopped again, and Flo nudged his elbow.

'*I will have a big party and invite Michael Jackson, the A team, the Queen, the Prime Minister ...* You see, Dad. It was meant to be.'

His father flung the newspaper away from him. The sheets fluttered to the floor. 'You're telling me that? It's what I believed from the moment you were born. I had a son who would inherit.' He shook his head and folded his arms. 'You had other ideas.'

Ollie didn't dare look at Flo. He closed the book. 'So what now?'

'Luckily Louise loves the hotel as much as I do.'

'You've really given it to her instead of me?' He took out his phone and scrolled through his mother's emails. 'Look – *one final offer ... yours outright.*' He held out the mobile.

His father ignored it. 'You don't want it, Oliver.'

'Things are different now. I was coming round to the idea.'

Beads of sweat lined his father's top lip. He didn't answer.

Ollie paced the room, chafing at his father's silence. 'Dad, is it all wrapped up legally?'

'More or less. Just a few documents to sign.'

'Then, there's still a chance for me?'

'You've had your chances. How many do you need?'

'I didn't realise ...'

'I told you I was finding things difficult. That day we met in London – I'd come up privately to see a specialist.'

'Why didn't you tell me then you were ill?'

'I didn't want you to come out of pity. But it's irrelevant: you told me in no uncertain terms that you weren't interested.'

From the corner of his eye, Ollie caught sight of Flo pressed into a corner of the sofa. She was clutching a cushion to her chest. He had to bring this to an end. 'But you gave me another chance. Mum's email. She said –'

'I know what she wrote in the email,' his father snapped. 'But it's too late. I've promised Louise.'

'She'll understand. She knows you always wanted it for me. Oliver Anderson. Tom Anderson. Oliver Anderson: an unbroken line.' He saw doubt in his father's face. He was weakening.' I'll make sure she has a job here. Matt, too, if he wants it.'

'It's you.'

Ollie's head jerked round at the voice. Louise was standing in the doorway, her hands on her hips. Spots of colour stained her cheeks. 'What do you want?'

'Hello, LouLou. I've come to see Mum and Dad.'

'Where is Mum?' Louise's stance didn't soften.

'She's shopping. Should be back soon.'

Louise came into the room and noticed Flo. 'Hello, Flo. Maeve said you were here.' She perched on the arm of the sofa. 'It's lovely to see you, and looking so grown up too.' She smiled at Flo, but when she turned to Ollie, the angry glare back in her eyes. 'Where's Jess?'

'Mummy had to go to work,' Flo said.

'Is this a flying visit?' Louise asked.

Her tone was suspicious, and Ollie couldn't bring himself to say he and Flo planned to spend a couple of days in Plymouth. 'Well, we could stay overnight, if it's not inconvenient, couldn't we, Flo?'

'We've brought our pyjamas.'

'Your brother's been trying to persuade me to hand over the hotel to him.'

'Hey, steady on, Dad.' Ollie clenched and unclenched his fists. If only his mother would come – she'd be on his side. 'You always said you wanted me to have the hotel. And what about Mum's email?'

Louise jumped up. 'Dad, tell him. You and Mum have given it to me, haven't you?'

Ollie saw Flo shrink further into the corner of the sofa, her legs curled underneath her.

His father pushed himself upright and returned to his spot in front of the fireplace. Ollie's heart constricted: the stooped shoulders, baggy cardigan, gaunt face emphasised the contrast with the man he had been. He couldn't die. All this uncertainty about the hotel had set back his recovery, but Ollie would make it up to him. Give him the peace of mind he needed.

'Go on, Dad. Tell him.' Louise's hair had come loose from its clasp and strands hung round her face. 'You already had the papers drawn up when Matt and I came for dinner.'

His father's forehead wrinkled. 'Your mother and I are concerned about Matt's attitude, Louise. He was pretty angry the other night.'

The skin on Louise's neck was stained red. 'Matt's attitude has got nothing to do with it.'

His father shook his head. 'It's a tough job without your partner's support, love. Believe me, I couldn't have managed without your mother beside me every step of the way.'

'But I'm the one who's running the place, making the decisions. At least I am if Maeve would stop interfering, which she's still doing, although you said you'd stop her, Dad.'

Ollie's gaze shot between his father and his sister. Where had that come from?

'And what about you, Oliver?' Louise took a couple of paces towards him.

'Me? What about me?'

'Have you got a supportive partner?'

There was no sign of the timid sister he'd known in London. The sister scared to blink in case Eugene disapproved of blinking. If she'd stood up to him, he might not have ... he and Jess might not have ...

'Jess believes in me as a painter, but she'll be down here like a shot if we get it sorted out.'

'Only if it suits her. Don't forget I know what Jess is capable of.'

Her words punched Ollie in the stomach. Christ, she wasn't going to blurt it all out, was she?

'I can't see Jess willing to give up her precious career and trail down here after you.'

Ollie felt Flo's hand curl round his. She'd crept from the sofa to stand beside him. He couldn't let her hear any more. He'd thought he could trust Louise on this. She'd told their parents Eugene had had an affair, but she'd promised Jess's role in the whole thing would remain a secret.

'Okay, we're obviously not welcome here.' He slipped his hand free of Flo's and crossed the room to his father who had slumped back onto the sofa. He bent down and kissed the top of his father's head. It was the first time he'd kissed him for years. 'I'm sorry, Dad,' he said. 'I can see I've left it too late.' Tears filled his eyes.

His father's head was bowed. A soft whimpering sound escaped from him.

Ollie lifted his rucksack onto his shoulder, and held out his hand to Flo. 'Come on, sweetheart. I think we should go.'

Flo stared up at him, her eyes wide. 'What about Granny? I want to see her.'

'I know you do. So do I, but we'll have to arrange something else. We need to go now.'

She picked up her bag without a word. Ollie glanced round. Would he ever see this room again? His father remained motionless on the sofa. Louise had moved to stand beneath Jasper Anderson's portrait.

'We'll go then,' he said.

No one answered.

Ollie paused on The Hoe to look out across the Sound, but had to sidestep when a skateboarder almost crashed into them. An elderly woman shook her head as she passed: 'Men! They never grow up.'

He and Flo climbed down the steps to the road and crossed over. He tried to take Flo's hand, but she pulled it away. 'I'm sorry, baby,' he said. 'It didn't work out as I planned.'

They leant on the railing, and he gazed down into the lido, the saltwater pool he and his friends had lived in during summer holidays. He'd always imagined he would teach Flo to swim here one day.

'Better make a move.' He set off towards the Barbican, the rucksack dragging on his shoulder. He'd packed his sketchpad and paints as well as clothes. He heard Flo's footsteps behind him, her trainers squeaking against the wet pavement. If only he could think of something to say, something to break this horrible silence. Perhaps he should check them into another hotel. Try again with his parents tomorrow.

The rain ran down his face and into his collar. Through the drops, he saw the little ferry set out for Mount Batten. Before he left Plymouth to live in London, he used to set up his easel on the end of the quay and paint: pages filled with sunlight fingering the surface of the water; ballooning waves on a windy day; the gun-metal grey of sea merging into sky in winter.

'This is it, Flo,' Ollie said, as they arrived at the Mayflower Steps. 'It's always seemed a magical place to me. The Pilgrim Fathers had already set sail once, thinking they'd said good-bye to England forever, but bad weather forced them back onto land here.'

'Mr Jarvis told us that.'

'I wonder what went through their minds, as they waited for the storm to stop. Imagine them arguing about whether to risk setting out again:

It's too dangerous.

We have to go.

Let's stay put and make a life here.

We need a new life …'

He waited, but she kept her head turned away from him. What mad idea had made him think he could come down here and make everything all right again? He pulled the rucksack from his shoulder and undid the straps. He took out the exercise book and opened it at the page. *Myself in Ten Years.* Splodges of rain fell on the black ink, drowning some of the letters. He held the book out until the ink had crawled and spattered its way down the page. With a twist of his wrist, he flung it as far as he could.

'What did you do that for?' Flo demanded.

'No point keeping it now.'

The book bobbed on the surface for a few minutes, and then disappeared into the water.

He stared at the waves, pushing and pulling against each other, until the rain and the sea blurred.

He turned away. They needed to decide: spend the night here or go back to London. 'Flo ...'

She wasn't there. She'd been beside him when he threw the book into the sea, but she'd gone. He scanned the area, checking the landing stage and the bridge over to the aquarium. She couldn't have gone far. He raced up Quay Road, heart pounding, eyes searching for the pink rucksack. There! There, she was ahead of him. He slowed to a walk. Thank God she was safe.

He was soaked through now. Lifting the rucksack back onto his shoulder, he followed Flo's small figure up the road. His exercise book had gone, but, somehow, the rucksack felt heavier.

Twenty-two

Louise clicked on the bedside light. She sat up and hugged her knees to her chest. Matt's side of the bed yawned, wide and empty. Where the hell was he? She'd sent him any number of texts and rung his mobile over and over again. His friends hadn't seen him, although a work colleague said he'd phoned in sick on Monday morning.

She was supposed to be on duty at the hotel tonight, but swapped to be at the house in case he turned up. Besides she'd needed to get out after the Oliver fiasco. Maeve had fussed over her father, insisted on walking him back to the apartment, and she'd locked her office and left. She'd put her heart and soul into managing the hotel, but that didn't seem to count for much. She might have won yesterday's round, but if Oliver hadn't had Flo with him, he wouldn't have backed down so easily.

She pulled her notebook towards her. At item number four, she stopped: Matt's name was written over and over again down the right hand side of the page. It was her writing, and there was a circle of kisses round the name each time. But they could just as easily have been crosses.

By six in the morning she was showered and dressed. Dragging off the duvet cover, she flung it and the sheet and pillowcases into the washing machine. She searched through the airing cupboard, selecting clean linen. She put the blue-striped sheets, Matt's favourite, on the bed, and kicking off her shoes, lay down on his side. It was strange seeing the room from this angle: the same window, with the lacy curtains she'd chosen, Oliver's painting of The Hoe on the wall opposite, the chest of drawers with her underwear and T-shirts. Matt might have chosen the house, but her stamp was on every bit of this room. She twisted her head towards the framed photo on his bedside table: their wedding day. She ran her fingers over their faces. The press of a button freezing the moment: him in his dark suit, her with her long cream dress, a garland of pearls pinned to her hair. He was smiling at the camera, his right hand holding hers, his left arm round her waist.

She stood up. Her hand lingered on the cotton pillowcase, smoothing its wrinkles, circling the cornflower embroidered in the corner. 'Where are you, Matt?' The words hung in the room, vibrating against the silence.

The foyer was quiet when Louise arrived.

'Morning, Katie. How was your night?' Katie was proving easy to work with, efficient, always in a good mood. She'd readily accepted Louise's request to take on her overnight duty.

'Quiet,' she said now. 'I even managed a few hours' sleep.'

'That's good.' Louise studied her, looking wide awake and fresh-faced, so different from her own reflection: puffy eyes, pasty skin. 'If you can hang on for a while,' she said, 'I need to get a few things sorted, and then I'll take over until Maeve gets here.'

'That's fine with me. Oh, there is one thing ...'

'What is it?'

'I hope you don't think I'm being forward, new girl and all that –'

'No, fire away.'

'I wondered why we don't have an online facility.'

'Has someone said something?'

'A few guests have mentioned they prefer to book online – that's all.'

'It's in the pipeline,' Louise said.

'Oh good. Only I suggested it to Maeve, and she said it wasn't hotel policy.'

'I see. Probably best to leave it to me to discuss with Maeve.'

'Of course. I'm sorry if I've spoken out of turn.' The frown on Katie's face changed to a smile. 'You might get a surprise when you go into the office.'

'Why? What's happened?'

'Don't look worried. It's a nice surprise.'

The scent hit Louise as soon as she opened the door. A vase of white roses stood on the coffee table. She moved closer, the musky fragrance filling her nose. They must be from Matt. He was sorry he'd bolted off like that. He'd be home tonight. She brushed her thumb over one of the creamy-white flowers and felt its velvety smoothness. An envelope was propped on the computer. She tore it open and pulled out the white card, crammed with bold, black writing: *I didn't mean to intrude. I genuinely thought you had invited me to the hotel. I'll be in Plymouth again soon – perhaps we can meet for a drink. Sincerely Seb Flanders.*

Louise stared at the roses, their petals tightly packed in a pattern of concentric circles, and tapped the card against her chin. Seb Flanders. A picture of blond hair, sea-blue eyes flashed across her mind. He'd been wearing brown brogues. She didn't know why, but they'd stayed in her mind. She dropped the card into one of the desk drawers and sat down at the computer.

*

She'd caught up with emails from the previous day when the phone rang. 'Hello, Mum. You're up early.'

'I've hardly slept.'

'No, nor me.'

'I can't believe Oliver came and left without seeing me. And little Flo too.' Her mother's voice had a catch in it.

'It wasn't very nice, You wouldn't have wanted to be there.'

'But I'd never have let him take Flo off in the pouring rain. You and your father should be ashamed.'

'I don't know about Dad, but I feel bad. Poor little mite looked terrified.' Louise glanced over her shoulder. Guests were milling round in the foyer, on their way to breakfast, settling their bills. 'The whole thing escalated really quickly. And then Oliver went off.'

'I can't tell you how heartbroken I am.'

'I'm sorry, Mum. I don't know what to say.'

Her mother drew in her breath as if she was biting back a reply. 'Anyway, Tom asked me to ring you first thing: the solicitor's coming over today to witness the signatures.'

'Today?' Louise massaged the pain at the top of her spine. 'So, why did Oliver say you and Dad have offered the hotel to him?'

'We told you about that – it was weeks ago.'

'But then you decided: it would be mine. Dad was definite, but he seemed to be backtracking yesterday.'

'You know how important the father to son thing has always been for him.'

'So Oliver can turn up unannounced. Crook his finger –'

'Let it go, Louise. It's you we want. Why do you think your father got out the papers the other night after dinner?'

Louise swallowed. She was kicking up all this fuss about Oliver, but she wasn't exactly telling her parents the truth, was she? 'Okay, Mum. What time do you want me?'

'Just one thing ... Tom's a bit worried about Matt. Is

everything's all right now? I presume you've had a chance to thrash it out.'

'Em ... Matt's ... well, Matt's ...'

'Is he still being difficult?'

The words on the computer screen blurred.

'Come on. I know that tremor in your voice.'

Louise had the sensation of being sucked down a hole. Warm arms held her. The smell of her mother. The tickle of hair against her cheek. The softness of her voice.

'Matt ...'

'What's he done?'

'He's disappeared.'

'What are you talking about?'

'He went off on Sunday evening and he hasn't come home.'

'Good grief! Have you spoken to him?'

'Not since Sunday. He said he needed time to think. Mum, I don't know what to do.'

'I'm coming over. Give me an hour to get your dad up and showered. We'll talk then.'

'What about the solicitor?'

'We'll postpone it. A couple more days won't hurt.'

'Don't tell Dad.'

'Leave your father to me, Louise.'

When Louise went up to the flat, her mother was in the kitchen, a pot of coffee on the table, two mugs, a plate of chocolate biscuits. A vase of bright red dahlias stood beside them.

She kissed her mother. 'Thanks for coming. Is Dad all right?'

'He's got the newspaper and crossword; he'll be fine for an hour or two.' Her mother sat down at the table and poured coffee. 'He's even agreed to come shopping for new trousers this afternoon.'

Louise sat down. She sipped her coffee, its bitter warmth spreading through her chest. 'Was he cross about putting off the solicitor?'

'I told him you had a hectic couple of days. You know Tom – the hotel will always come first.' Her mother pushed the plate towards her. 'But tell me about Matt.'

Louise bit into a biscuit. She stared at a photo of Oliver and her which still hung on the wall: two dark haired children, faces and legs tanned from the summer sun, arms round each other, squinting into the camera. And her white sandals. She'd loved those sandals, open-toed, daisies decorating the straps.

'Matt hasn't been happy since I started managing the hotel.'

'Why didn't you say something?' Her mother reached out and touched her hand.

'I thought he'd come round in time, but if anything he's hardened his attitude.'

'Has he said why?'

Louise studied her mother's fingers: neat nails, careful half moons, bulging knuckles, the simple gold band. 'That's the trouble, Mum. We don't talk. Oh, we talk about everyday things, but the real nitty-gritty... I don't know ... it was all so painful when I came back from London.'

'I should have realised. You seemed to put it all behind you.'

'I wanted the hotel. You know how much I've always loved it. It means –' Louise's mobile bleeped. She pulled her hand free. 'I'd better get this. Maeve probably.' Her eyes fixed on the text. 'Oh God.'

'What is it? What's happened?'

'It's Matt. He's at home.'

Matt was out in the yard when she reached the house. She hesitated at the kitchen window, staring at his back. He was wearing the same clothes as the previous Sunday, his shirt half tucked in his trousers, half hanging loose. His hair stood up in tufts, and his hands were shoved in his pockets. There was a brick wall in front of him, wheelie bins lined up against it. The first summer after they were married, she'd attempted to grow climbing roses up the wall to hide the bleakness. She'd had Matt take out a row of slabs, and she added compost to the sand underneath before she planted them. The roses had tried in a half-hearted sort of way. They sent out thick green shoots with thorns that pricked her hands and arms, but the promised blooms failed to materialise, apart from occasional ones which soon shrivelled and died. It wasn't their fault – that side of the yard was in shade most of the day, and now only straggly branches clung to the wall.

Louise opened the back door. It had developed a squeak during a wet spell last spring. Most of the time she hardly noticed it, but today it shrieked across the yard. She froze, but Matt didn't move. He was eerily still, like one of those living statues that used to stand on the corner near the arts centre in London.

She took a couple of steps towards him. Closer, she could see his shirt was crumpled and his trousers had mud on them. He was barefoot.

'Matt.'

He was usually meticulous about showering, but today a sour, unwashed smell came from him. She put her hand on his arm. 'Shall we go inside?'

He turned his head. His eyes were bloodshot; a bruise bloomed yellow and blue on his cheek. She raised her fingers to it. 'What happened? Did you fall over?' He gazed at her, mute. 'You haven't been in a fight, have you?' There was no sign he'd heard her. She took his arm. 'Let's go inside. I'll make some tea.' He let her lead him across the yard and into the kitchen. She eased him into a chair and crossed to the sink to fill the kettle.

'I don't want tea.'

The kettle slipped from her fingers. Her arm hung mid-air, arrested by the sound of his voice, sudden, rough.

'Sit down.'

She turned round. His eyes were glazed as if he was looking through her.

'I said *sit down.*'

She pulled a chair from under the table. 'Talk to me, Matt. We can work this out.'

'Talk to you?'

'Yes. We don't talk to each other enough.'

He banged his clenched fists on the table. A long cut ran down the back of one of his hands, dried blood around it.

'Your poor hand.' She half rose. 'I'll get some warm water. Bathe it for you.'

'Sit down, for Christ's sake.'

She sank back onto the chair. Her eyes flitted round the room, trying to gauge how easily she could get to the door. It was impossible. 'Matt. The hotel –'

'The hotel! The fucking hotel! Jesus, that fucking hotel!' He stood up, his chair crashing backwards against the cupboard. He leaned towards her, his hands flat on the table. 'Do you know what I've been doing for the last forty-eight hours?'

'Tell me.' She kept her voice low. 'What have you been doing?'

He straightened up and a shadow passed over his face. 'You really want to know?'

She shifted sideways, trying to stand up without him noticing. That was better. She felt more confident on her feet. 'Of course I do.' She calculated the distance between them. If she could reach him before he realised. Put her arms round him. Stroke his back in that way he liked. Whisper to him.

'I've been walking round, Louise. All day. All night.

Walking the streets. Along the beach. Do you know how tempting it is to walk into the sea and keep walking until the current takes you?'

'Don't say that.'

'And all the time one question banged in my head.'

'What was it? What question, Matt?'

'If you had to choose ...' His eyes fixed on her face for what seemed like minutes, and then he glanced down and pulled something from his pocket. He smoothed it out and held it up to her.

'Remember this?' he said.

'Of course I do. It was a beautiful day.'

He was holding the wedding photo from his bedside table, the one she'd gazed at hours earlier. He moved closer and shook it in her face. 'You wanted me then. When I was useful to you.'

She tried not to turn her head away at the smell coming from him. 'Matt, I love you. Just because I'm working at the hotel doesn't mean we can't be happy together.' She clutched at the front of his shirt. 'Give me a while to find my feet, and then we'll go away for a holiday. I'll get a manager in. We can go wherever you like. Try for the baby you want.'

'The baby *I* want.' His fist came up underneath her arm and he punched it away. Her elbow exploded with pain. She bit down hard on her lip.

He flung the photo from him and dragged her towards him. 'You still haven't answered my question.'

His breath was foul in her face. 'You haven't told me what it is.'

He pulled her closer, lifting her from her feet, his fingers pinching the skin under her arms. 'If you had to choose ...' He shook her hard. '... between the hotel and me ...' Again the shaking. Her skull was going to burst ... 'which would it be?'

She couldn't speak. What could she say? *You. The hotel.* She was going to be sick.

'Answer me!'

'I can't choose, Matt. Don't make me.'

His grip tightened. He was going to punch her. She raised her hands and pushed against his chest. He didn't falter. He was so strong.

'Please put me down. You're scaring me.'

He lifted her higher. 'Choose.'

'Hotel. I choose the hotel.'

And then he dropped her. Her legs buckled. She slithered to the floor, her head hitting the side of the table as she fell.

She lay there, her cheek pressed against the cold tiles. She cradled her head in her hands. The front door slammed.

Twenty-three

'It's me ... it must be ... there's something about me ... something I do ... I don't know ... I can't believe it's happened again ... people think ... men think –'

'Louise, Louise. Stop. Here, dry your eyes.' Freda held out a handful of tissues. 'Do you want to go and wash your face?'

Louise rubbed a tissue over her eyes and nose, conscious suddenly of the stream of tears. 'I mean he picked me up and dropped me as if I was a bit of rubbish.' She pulled at the tissue until it was in shreds in her fingers. 'I can't believe it ... it's like Eugene all over again. It's me, Freda, isn't it?'

'Louise, stop it. No more talking. Let's do some breathing.' Freda put her notebook on the coffee table. 'Take a deep breath, feel it stretching your ribcage. Put your hands there. That's it, hold the breath, and breathe out. Drop your shoulders. Let your arms dangle. Now, again, a deep breath ...'

The sound of the familiar words, the repetition of the word *breath*, its soft hypnotic sound stilled the maelstrom inside her. *Breath, breath, breath.* She muttered the word, feeling the flutter of air pass over her lips.

'That's better. You seem calmer already.'

Louise kept her eyes on Freda. She looked reassuringly

the same: frizzy hair, floral skirt, only the baggy jumper replaced by a baggy T-shirt. 'I'm sorry. I didn't know where else to go. I rushed out of the house –'

'I'm glad I had the cancellation and I could see you straight away.'

'I didn't mean to barge in.'

'Stop apologising. I want to know what's happened.' Freda picked up her notepad again and balanced it on her knee. 'Last time I saw you, your parents had asked you to run the hotel and Matt wasn't happy.'

Louise related the events of the last couple of months: Matt's increasing agitation at the time she spent at the hotel, the six-month bargain she'd struck with him, the knowledge she'd created a ticking bomb. When she reached his storming out of her parents' apartment, she started to cry again. 'It's my fault. I should have been honest. You said I should talk to him, but I couldn't. I can't talk about anything. Ever since ... it's as if there's a boulder in my heart and when I try to talk about my feelings, it crushes them.'

Freda looked up from her notebook, her pen poised on the page. It was the first time she'd written in it during a session, and Louise wondered what she was writing: *This woman is crazy. Get her out of here.*

'We'll come back to Matt, Louise, but we seem to have come to the crux of things. In all our previous discussions, you never felt able to tell me exactly what happened with Eugene.' Freda tapped her pen on the page. 'But earlier on you said "It's like Eugene all over again". What did you mean?'

Behind Louise, raindrops pattered on the window pane. In the silence of the room, they grew louder, more intense, banging against the glass: a summer storm. The humidity had been building all morning and now the downpour had arrived. As the rain flung itself at her back, her eyes darted round the room. The collection of vases Freda used to have on the top shelf of the bookcase had gone. One of the vases had been green and chunky. The one in the middle was tall and thin, and she'd always wanted to cup her hands round the third one, a domed base with a lip curving outwards at the top. But now the shelf was empty. The bare wood bereft.

'Eugene was the most wonderful person I'd ever met. He was never still. Jumping from one idea to the next. As soon as he came into the room, you felt the charge of energy. A surge of particles, atoms – whatever it is that makes stuff happen, it gathered round Eugene.

'I couldn't believe it when he chose me, the one he wanted to spend time with, the one he kissed, and then the one he made love to. I'd never been all that popular with boys. But now it didn't matter. There was Eugene, and he wanted me. When he asked me to move in with him, I was so happy. He was renting a little house round the corner from the arts centre. It wasn't anything special, but I tried to make it homely. I used to buy fresh flowers every week, and I bought new cushions to put on the sofa.'

'And?' Freda asked.

'I found out I was pregnant.'

The rain had stopped, but the air in the small room didn't feel any fresher.

'You discovered you were pregnant,' Freda prompted. 'How did you feel about that?'

'I was thrilled. I mean ... it wasn't planned ... but, yes, I wanted the baby.'

'And Eugene? Was he pleased?'

'I don't know.'

'You didn't talk about it?'

'No.'

'Didn't you think that was strange?'

'Not really. We were always so busy at the centre, and there were usually other people around. We used to go out with my brother and his wife sometimes. Our house wasn't far from their flat. Eugene had let Oliver hang his paintings in the arts centre, and they got on well together. Eugene liked Jess too. In fact, I was always a bit jealous of her. He was charming to everyone, but I could tell ... well ... Jess was special for him.' The evenings the four of them had spent in the pub, or Luigi's, the Italian restaurant next door to the arts centre, flashed through Louise's head. Somehow Eugene had always ended up sitting next to Jess. 'Perhaps I imagined it. But after I told him I was pregnant, he seemed to gravitate towards her even more.'

'But you didn't know how he felt?'

'He said his mum would be thrilled to have a grandchild. We were going to Ireland after ... afterwards.'

Freda leaned forward and reached for the jug of water on the table. She poured them each a glass. Louise swallowed hers in one go. She put the glass down and felt Freda's eyes on her.

'You told me once before that you were eight months' pregnant. Were you still working?'

Louise nodded. 'I got very tired – I wasn't sleeping well – but I didn't want to be left in the house on my own, while Eugene was at the centre. When we put on evening events, I had to go home. It was often the early hours by the time he got back. There was always a reason – there'd been a party after an exhibition; he'd taken a couple of visiting writers out for a meal and one drink had led to another. And I wanted to believe him. What choice did I have?'

'But things came to a head?' Freda's voice was barely a murmur. 'In our previous discussions, you've never been able to get beyond this.'

Louise blew the damp strands of hair from her forehead. This was it: the night she'd blocked out. The night that resurfaced in her dreams. The night that woke her at ten to four.

'Louise?'

*

'I can't sleep. The baby's in an awkward position, and I've got terrible backache. I sit up waiting for Eugene. It gets to two, three o'clock, but he's still not home. I phone his mobile, and it goes straight to voicemail. I leave messages but he doesn't ring back.

'Then about half past three, I hear his key in the lock. I go out onto the landing and can see straight away something's wrong. The front door is still open. His shirt is ripped, and he's leaning over the hallstand, his head in his hands.

'"Eugene, what's happened?" I call out. I start down the stairs, but a pain grips my belly. I clutch the banister. The spasm passes and I look down again. He's staring up at me. "Why are you so late?" I ask.

'"Fuck off!" he shouts. "I'm sick of your fucking questions. Where am I going? What time will I be home? Who did I see? What? Where? Why?"

'"Don't talk to me like that." I clasp my hands under my belly. Its weight drags me down. "I'm having your baby."

'The words make him go mad. He takes the stairs two at a time. He's next to me. He stinks of alcohol and cigarettes. He gets hold of my shoulders and shakes me. His eyes are wild, crazy looking.

'"Stop it." I'm whimpering. "Stop it." Next thing there's a noise down in the hall. It's Oliver, my brother, pushing open the front door. His hair is loose, all over the place.

'"You bastard!" he screams. "You fucking bastard!"

'"What's happened? Oliver, what's happened?" I can hardly breathe. Eugene's holding my arm. He's hurting me. I try to pull away, but he grips it tighter. He's pinching the skin.

'Oliver's at the bottom of the stairs. His shirt is open at the front. The buttons are gone. He starts screaming again. "Ask that fucking bastard. Ask him what's happened."

'I turn to Eugene. He's staring at me. He hates me. I can see he does. "What's he talking about?" I say. "What have you done?"

"'Mind your own business!" He shouts the words in my face. Spit sprays my skin.

"'I'll tell you what he's done." Oliver kicks the front door shut. He's crying. My brother is crying. "My Jess," he sobs. "My beautiful Jess."

'I look at Eugene. "You and Jess?"

"'That's right. Me and Jess. I slept with her. And bloody fantastic it was as well." He twists my arm behind my back. I scream. The pain is bad. And then he shoves me. I grab at the stair rail, trying to save myself. But I can't. I'm falling. I land at the bottom. And I know straight away. My baby's gone.'

The storm had left behind a canopy of clouds, puffy as pillows. Colour had leached from the sea, and waves rippled across its surface, scuffed up by the cool breeze. White foam, like soap suds, flared out from behind the ferry as it crossed the bay. Louise sat at the open-air café on the promenade and sipped her coffee. Her eyes reached for the Breakwater. This view was in her soul: her comfort, her security, her future.

She pulled her cardigan over her shoulders, as the tension in her limbs eased. Her pulse was steady under her fingers. There was no sign of the headache that had plagued her in recent weeks. Tranquillity settled on her, like a butterfly on a leaf.

'At least the rain has cleared the air,' a woman at the next table said.

Louise smiled. 'It's a relief, isn't it?'

Twenty-four

Ollie was outside Flo's school long before she was due to come out. A class appeared while he was sitting on a nearby bench and played a game of rounders in the playground. He'd been good at games. Perhaps he could have been a cricketer. The years cascaded though his mind, spitting out alternative lives, spraying a fine mist of a nine-to-five job, the tennis court, a golfing green.

Flo had refused to see him since the visit to Plymouth, and he was desperate. He'd texted Jess's father, who usually picked Flo up, to say he'd arranged with Jess that he would meet her today. By the time he queried it, it would be too late.

Several classes were now lined up in the playground. He spotted Flo straight away and waved. She saw him – even from a distance he felt her momentary stillness as she registered his presence – but she didn't acknowledge him. He let his hand fall to his side. She was surprised; that was all. She'd been expecting Grandad.

The group Flo was with emerged through the gate, jostling each other so as not to be last. They looked back at the girl who trailed behind the rest. 'Sissy!' one of the boys shouted. 'Poo face!' another voice shrieked. The girl looked down at the ground, dragging her PE bag along behind her.

The rest of the group jeered and whooped, and Ollie saw Flo laughing.

He moved nearer. 'Hi, Flo. Over here.' She stopped and met his eyes with a cold stare. 'It's me, Flo. Grandad couldn't make it.' He waited for her face to break into a smile, for her to charge at him the way she usually did, but the stare continued. Those beautiful green eyes, so like Jess's, swept over his face, assessing, analysing, considering. One of the other girls called her, and she turned away.

He ran after her. 'Flo, wait! Where are you going?'

She didn't look round. He caught her arm. 'Don't ignore me. What's wrong?'

'Leave me alone.' She flung the words over her shoulder and kept walking, her rucksack bouncing on her back. It was green: what about the pink one they'd bought together?

'But where are you going? You can't go off on your own.'

She stopped so abruptly that he almost crashed into her. 'I don't know why you're following me, but please go away.' The words were grown up, but her voice came out in a childish squeak. Her cheeks were flushed and she looked close to tears.

'Flo, what's wrong? Come home and we can talk about it, whatever it is.'

'You don't know where my home is.'

'Of course I do. You'll always have a home with me, whatever happens.'

'I don't want a home with you. I hate you.'

'Flo, come on, we're going.' The other girls in the group were looking back. A black 4 x 4 pulled up next to them and Belinda, Jess's friend, clambered out. 'Sorry I'm late, girls. In you get.' She glanced towards Ollie and Flo. 'Come on, darling, we've got a date at the park.' She beckoned to Flo.

Ollie strode towards her, his senses rearing up at the smell of perfume wafting round her. 'I'm sorry, Belinda, but Flo can't come to the park today.'

'Oh, really?'

'No, she's coming home with me, and I've got something already arranged.'

'Sorry, sunshine, but that's not what Jess said. Yes, that's it, Flo. You get in the back with the others.'

Flo had been hovering behind him, and Belinda took her hand to help her into the vehicle.

'I won't let you take her,' Ollie insisted.

She reached into her bag with her free hand and waved her mobile in front of him. 'Her mother thinks otherwise.'

His eyes skimmed over the text: *Sorry for short notice. Please pick up Flo from school. NB – don't let Ollie take her. J*

They were standing under a tree, and the urge to smash Belinda's face into its trunk surged in his head. He'd like to see what pattern the bark made on her smug features. 'She's coming home with me.'

Flo hesitated, one foot on the step of the car, the other tethered to the ground. He saw Belinda's hand tighten on her wrist. 'Up you go, Flo,' she instructed. 'There's a good girl.'

He grasped Belinda's arm, yanked it away. 'Get your fucking paw off my daughter!'

Her lips compressed into a thin line, and her eyes grew dark. 'Oo er. Now we see your true colours. No wonder Jess is scared of you.'

'You moron!' he shouted. 'Jess scared of me? You don't know what that motherfucker she's with now is capable of!'

Belinda glanced at the girls cowering in the back of the vehicle. He felt the tremors shaking Flo's body as if he was holding her tight against him. Had he really uttered that obscenity in front of her? His baby, the little girl whose hand had clutched his as they skipped to the park, the child he'd taught to draw cats, the daughter he'd vowed to cherish and protect from any harm.

Belinda bundled Flo into the car and climbed into the

driver's seat. She leaned out, her arm resting on the open window. 'You really are a jerk, sunshine.' She pushed the car into gear, and it roared off down the street, Flo's white face pressed against the rear windscreen.

It was almost dark when Ollie rounded the corner into his road. Two pints had blunted his agitation sufficiently for him to face the flat. He fumbled in his trouser pocket for the key. He was trying to fit it into the lock when his name was called. A man in a dark suit climbed from a car on the other side of the road. 'Mr Anderson?'

The man approached. 'Are you Mr Anderson? Mr Oliver Anderson?'

'Why? Who are you?'

'I'm from the solicitors, James and Hardy, and I'm here to serve you with a petition for divorce.' The man held out a buff envelope, and scarcely realising what he was doing, Ollie took it from him.

'I take your acceptance of the petition as confirmation that you are Mr Oliver Anderson.' The man gave a little bow and turned back to his car. He climbed into the driver's seat and revved the engine a couple of times before accelerating away from the kerb.

Ollie stared after him, the envelope scrunched up in his hand.

Something slammed into the back of Ollie's knees, and he kicked his foot hard behind him.

'Oy, mate, watch what you're doing!' A man yanked Ollie's arm and twisted him round.

Ollie clenched his fists, but it was half-hearted – he was in no fit state to fight anyone. A terrier yapped and bit at his ankles. It must have jumped up and caught him in the back of the legs. He raised his hands. 'Your dog gave me a surprise.'

The man grabbed the terrier's collar and yanked him away. 'Pansy!' he hissed over his shoulder.

Ollie opened the front door and climbed the stairs to the flat, his legs complaining at every step. In the kitchen he filled a glass with water and sat at the table in the living room. He pulled sheets of paper from the brown envelope.

His eyes skimmed over the details of their marriage, the where and the when, not even a year after they'd met. It was just the two of them and they'd asked a couple on the street outside the registry office to be their witnesses. They drank flat champagne in Hyde Park afterwards and danced in the fountains under Nelson's good eye. They stayed up all night and watched the sunrise the next morning. They couldn't stop kissing.

His eyes moved further down the page: Unreasonable behaviour. The words stark and frozen.

- Lack of emotional support,

- Lack of interest in Jess's career,

- Lack of support in maintaining a household,

- Lack of financial support ...

Lack. Lack. Lack. So many lacks. But he only had two. Jess and Flo. Perhaps he could send his own petition back. Unreasonable behaviour.

- Lack of Jess

- Lack of Flo.

He turned to the second page: The Petitioner therefore prays:

1) That the said marriage be dissolved

2) That the respondent may be ordered to pay the costs of this suit

3) That the petitioner may be granted the following ancillary relief:

    (i) An order for maintenance pending suit

    (ii) A periodical payments order

    (iii) A secured provision –

Ollie covered his face with his hands, his cheekbones pressed against his palms. Perhaps he could die in this blackness. Shrivel until only his heart remained. But not a pink, healthy heart. A grey one like dirty washing up water.

He was asleep at the table when his mobile woke him. It was nearly midnight.

'Angel, hi.' His mouth was dry and his left hand numb with pins and needles.

'Sorry to ring so late: I've just got back from my mum's.'

'That's okay. Is something wrong?' He'd called in sick for the last few days, and guilt loomed over him at her voice.

'Are you coming in tomorrow?' she asked.

'I don't know. Jess has served me –'

'I think you should.'

'Why?'

'Things are happening. I think you need to be there, Ollie.'

The door of The Serendip was locked, and a sign *Closed for Refurbishment* hung in front of some sort of screen. He rapped on the door, but no one answered his knock. He took out his mobile and rang Angel. 'I'm here. What's going on?'

Her face appeared round the corner of the screen. She

pulled it to one side and opened the door a crack.

'Let me in.' Ollie had his foot on the step. 'You said to come.'

The door opened enough for him to squeeze through. Angel ran her fingers across her neck in a slicing movement. 'He's here.' She cocked her thumb towards the back of the gallery.

The place was transformed. The walls had been stripped of paintings. Instead of their rich burgundy colour, they were a stark white. A harsh strip light blazed overhead. The brown leather sofa had gone, and in its place was a life-size model of a soldier with a machine gun. It looked as if it was made from nails, screws, pieces of wire, twisted and vicious looking.

'What the hell's going on?' Ollie whispered.

Angel's eyes glistened, and her shrug was helpless.

Guy Norton emerged from the stock room. Yellow braces had taken the place of the red ones.

'You've decided to return.' The drawl was as sarcastic as ever.

'I've had some issues to sort out,' Ollie said.

'I see. Clearly your personal life takes precedence over your job. Angel and I have worked tirelessly in your absence.'

Ollie's gaze swept over the gallery. 'Why have you done this? The Serendip was great as it was.'

Guy Norton straightened his bow tie, a blue one this time. 'Simone was out of touch, hanging such bourgeois efforts. Installation art is where it's at.'

A nerve twitched in Ollie's brow.

'It's just that watercolours aren't Guy's thing.' Angel plucked at the buttons of the enormous shirt she was wearing over her clothes.

Guy put a thumb and middle finger to either side of his temples. He closed his eyes as if he was experiencing great pain. 'Angel, my dear, I thought we understood each other.

It seems I was mistaken.' He opened his eyes and fixed them on Angel. 'Not only are they not my thing, as you choose to describe them, they are hide-bound and middle-class!'

'Where are my paintings?' Ollie demanded. When the four landscapes sold, Simone had let him hang some more.

'Probably stacked in the store cupboard.'

'Perhaps you'd get them for me.'

Guy Norton shrilled a laugh. 'I don't have time.'

'They're my property. I want them back.'

'Oh, dear boy, no need to take that tone. I didn't say you couldn't have them. Merely that I wasn't prepared to get them for you.'

Ollie visualised the model of the soldier springing to life, his machine gun held steady, Guy Norton splintering into fragments.

'I'm handing in my notice,' he said. 'I presume you don't want me to work it, so I'd be grateful if you'd give me the wages you owe me.'

Guy Norton's eyebrows arched like twin arrows. 'I owe you nothing.'

'I worked a month in hand, so you owe me for that.'

'I'm not responsible for your squalid little arrangements with Simone. You'll have to take it up with her.'

Angel was tugging at his sleeve. 'Leave it, Ollie. It's not worth it.'

'She's right. There's nothing for you here.' Guy Norton stalked off across the gallery.

Ollie flung open the door. It smashed back against a table. The sound of glass tinkling followed him into the street.

Twenty-five

The morning after the showdown with Matt, Louise phoned her mother.

She answered on the first ring: 'I've been so worried. What happened?'

Louise re-lived her blouse clutched in Matt's fists, his furious eyes, her head banging as he shook her. Her ankle throbbed where he'd slammed her into the floor. 'Mum, it's fine. I'm fine.'

'Has he come round? I hope you made him see sense.'

'We had a good talk, and Matt's happy for me to take on the hotel.'

'I wasn't expecting that. He did seem very angry the other night.'

'But it's okay, now, Mum.'

'Are you sure? I mean I was never certain Matt was right for you, but –'

'I'm sure.' Louise flicked through the comments book she'd brought upstairs to read last night: *Fabulous hotel – we'll be back ... Magnificent location ... This hotel gets better and better.* She couldn't wait until she was the one responsible for such praise. 'If Dad can get the solicitor to come, I'm ready to sign the papers any time you say.'

'Isn't it a bit soon? You need to be rock solid on this.

... Hang on, Tom, I'll be there in a minute ... ' Her mother sounded breathless. 'We can delay the signing for a few weeks.'

'There's no need, Mum. I've decided.'

'So, you're sure you and Matt are happy for it to go ahead.'

'Yes, of course.' She waited, but her mother didn't say anything. 'Why wouldn't we be?'

'It seems your father and I are not the only ones who haven't been telling the whole truth.'

Louise felt colour creep across her cheeks. 'What do you mean?'

'Matt's been into the hotel. He told Maeve you've split up.'

'What? How dare he? And as for Maeve, I bet she lapped that up.'

'Well, have you?'

'What?'

'Split up? That sounds very different from Matt being happy to go ahead.'

Louise rubbed at a mark on the table, a small dark stain marring the highly-polished surface. 'He asked me to choose – him or the hotel. I chose the hotel, and he left.'

'Oh, Louise, I wish you'd trusted us more.'

'I was afraid you'd think I couldn't cope without his support.'

'You've shown how capable you are. Your father thinks the hotel couldn't be in better hands.'

Louise wanted to give her mother a hug. 'You don't know what that means to me.'

'The hotel is yours, Louise, but if you and Matt are definitely finished, there might be a delay. Your father will want things to be rock-solid legally.'

Louise took out the mirror from the drawer of her desk. The foundation had helped, but the smudge on her cheekbone from the bruise was spreading. She fingered strands of hair into place to conceal the cut on her forehead from where she'd hit the table. No one must know. No one.

She flung the mirror back in the drawer, and her hand brushed the card that had come with the flowers: *perhaps we could go for a drink.* A mobile number was written across the bottom. She tapped the digits into her phone and listened to its ringing. *Hi, this is Seb Flanders. I'm working at the moment, but leave your number and a message and I'll get back to you as soon as.*

Her mouth went dry and she ended the call. His voice brought him into the room as if he was standing next to her. She remembered the deep blue of his eyes. Clicking on messaging, she tapped in his number again: *The flowers are beautiful – thank you. Do get in touch when you're next in Plymouth. Louise.*

She parked the car round the corner and walked to the house. It was in darkness. Dusk was settling in the narrow street. A figure loomed up in front of her. She jumped. The figure crossed the road. Harmless. The next door neighbour's front door opened, and the man with the tattoos and piercings emerged, his dog straining at the lead. Her eyes followed them to the end of the road. This was stupid. She had to go in.

In the bedroom, she pulled the curtains and switched on the light. Placing the small suitcase on the bed, she flicked open the catches. She grabbed skirts and trousers from the wardrobe and flung them into the case. Returning to the wardrobe for more, her fingers got caught up in the arm of one of Matt's shirts. She held the soft cotton against her cheek. It was one of his favourites, a pale grey that he often used to change into when he came home from work. His happy shirt, he called it.

She kicked something on the floor: the frame from the

wedding photo that had been on Matt's side of the bed. No time to think about that now. She opened the chest of drawers and pulled out underwear, T-shirts, jumpers. In the bottom of the drawers were the lavender bags her mother had made. She'd smelt the sweet, piney scent every morning of her marriage. She slammed the drawer shut. Just toiletries from the bathroom now.

Downstairs, she hesitated outside the lounge. She had her hand on the front door when she remembered. She dropped the case and raced back upstairs. Oliver's painting. She unhooked it and carried it downstairs. Her life here was over.

When Seb phoned a few days after she sent her text, she agreed to meet him for a drink. He'd been working for a finance company in the City, he told her as that drink stretched to two and then three, but hated the corporate world, the business suits, the wheeler-dealing. Two years ago, after his marriage broke down, he'd plucked up courage to throw in the towel and move to the West Country to try his hand at interior design. 'The hotel would be my biggest project to date,' he told her, 'but I'd love to take it on.'

Louise wanted to say yes, to see the light dance in those amazing eyes, but it would be madness. The hotel wasn't properly hers yet, and the installation of the computer system was already a step further than she should go.

'Oh, and I should have said,' Seb added, 'the magazine Beautiful Hotels has agreed to do a four-page spread on the work. There'll be before and after photos, stories about the hotel, its history: lots of free publicity.'

Louise drained her glass of wine. Publicity. A way to announce the new ownership: father to daughter. And a chance to put her stamp on the hotel.

'Let's do it!' she said. 'But only the foyer for now.'

Seb wasn't one to waste time. He propped the mood board against the wall in Louise's office. 'The before photos are in the bag; we'll soon have finished the preparation, so I need to confirm colours with you.' He ran his hands through his hair, a habit Louise had realised in the last week that contributed to its unruliness.

'What?' he said. 'What are you smiling at?' Two little frown lines appeared between his eyebrows, giving him that puzzled look that made her think of a child struggling with times tables.

'Sorry.' She pointed to the window. 'It's the antics of that sea gull.'

'Louise, I need your okay on these colours before we can start.'

'I'm listening,' she said.

'The hotel is a fantastic Georgian building, and I want to reflect that.' He gestured towards the board covered in slicks of paint, swatches of material, pictures of furniture. 'I'm thinking pea-green for the walls, this wonderful silk paper for that central panel behind the desk, and I want plenty of gold.'

'Gold?'

'Doesn't have to be expensive gilting. You can get gold metallic paint quite cheaply.'

'But it's going to make the foyer dark. Dad always chose magnolia to keep the space light and airy.'

'No disrespect to your father, but magnolia is the most anodyne colour, bland and boring.'

'I've always thought the foyer looked good.'

Seb paced up and down the floor, his hair resembling sheaves of corn more by the second. He stopped beside her and crouched down. 'I've fallen in love with this place, Louise. Please let me try.' His blue eyes held hers.

'Sorry I didn't realise you had a visitor.' The door had opened without Louise realising: it was Maeve. 'I wanted to discuss next week's rotas, but I can see you're ... busy.'

Louise pictured the scene from Maeve's viewpoint: Seb,

kneeling at her feet, hair tousled, the words *I've fallen in love* ...

She jumped up. 'Seb and I have been discussing colours for the foyer, Maeve.' She pointed to the mood board. 'He's chosen this pea-green as the main wall colour. Inspired choice, don't you think?'

Louise arranged to meet Phyllis at a café down by the Barbican. It was nearly four weeks since she'd gone on 'leave', and the meeting couldn't be put off any longer. Louise had interviewed all the cleaning staff, and each one had protested their innocence. Two of them claimed they'd actually seen Phyllis taking money. 'Everybody knows as it's her,' one said. 'But why?' Louise asked. 'She's worked here for as long as I can remember and has always been reliable.' The woman had looked uncomfortable. 'I don't like to tell tales, but her sister died a few months back, and since then she hasn't been herself. And we're fed up with the cloud of suspicion hanging over all of us.'

Louise found a table close to the door of the café. She ordered a pot of tea and jotted down a few notes. Voices sounded above her: 'That's her. Miss Louise.'

She jumped up. 'Phyllis, thanks for coming.' She glanced at the woman hovering at Phyllis's shoulder, tall and well-built with ash-blonde hair reaching to her waist. 'I'm Louise Bradbury. And you are?'

'This is our Jodie, Miss Louise,' Phyllis said. 'My sister's girl.'

'Yes, I'm Jodie Tinder.' The woman's voice was loud and rough. 'I'm here to make sure you do the right thing by my auntie.'

It was going to be like that, was it? 'I've no intention of doing otherwise, Jodie.' Louise indicated the chairs round the table. 'Shall we sit down? Would you like tea?' She raised her hand to call the waitress over.

'No thanks.' Jodie helped Phyllis into a chair. 'We've only come to hear what you've got to say, isn't that right, Auntie?'

Phyllis nodded, and strands of hair escaped from the wispy bun. She seemed to have shrunk in the weeks since Louise had seen her, and her hands fluttered continually round her face.

'How are you, Phyllis?' Louise asked.

'How the feck do you think she is?' Jodie's voice echoed round the small café. 'Accused of theft after her long years of service.'

'I appreciate you want to support your aunt, Jodie, but I'd be grateful if you'd let her speak for herself.'

'You can see what she's like.' Jodie put an arm round Phyllis's shoulder. 'And you did this to her. She doesn't stop crying.'

'I'm sorry to hear you haven't been well.' Louise focused on Phyllis, her shoulder turned against Jodie. 'I've been looking at your records and I see you'll be seventy next birthday. We've got plans to expand the hotel over the next couple of years, and I think the housekeeper's job will become too much for you.'

Phyllis smiled. 'I'm a housekeeper.'

Louise took hold of her hands. The skin was thin and dry, bulbous blue veins criss-crossing the backs. 'So, what I'd like to suggest ...' This would be easier without Jodie breathing down her neck. '... is that you retire on the grounds of ill health. The hotel will pay you three months' wages in recognition of your long service.'

Phyllis's eyes were red and watery. 'I'm not ill.'

'You'll have to do better than that.' Jodie pulled Phyllis's hands free of Louise's grasp. 'She could take you to court for defamation of character. Stealing, my foot. You've got no proof.'

And when it came to it, she was right: there was no hard proof. 'I consulted my solicitor, and he says it's a generous offer for someone of your aunt's age.' Louise crossed her fingers under the table.

'Six months,' Jodie said.

'Pardon?'

'Bobby said we was to hold out for six months' pay.'

'Who's Bobby?'

'My other half, and let me tell you he's got a right temper on him.'

Louise juggled figures in her head. Perhaps it would be worth it to be free of this. Conversation had stopped at the tables nearby, and she sensed people were agog to see how it would end. 'I'm sorry,' she said. 'That's not possible.'

'Anything's possible.' Jodie leaned forward, and her bosom, two white mounds, nudged Louise's elbow

'Unfortunately, that's not the case. All expenditure has to be accounted for and justified, and this anomaly would be questioned immediately.'

'Whatever anomaly is when it's at home. You can't bully me with your long words.' Jodie pinched her lips together.

Phyllis began to cry. Louise watched the tears sliding down her wrinkled cheeks, and all she could think of was the housekeeper's voice: *Don't you be creasing those sheets.* She clasped her hands in her lap, the fingers interweaving, the thumbs crossed in a deep V. 'In view of your long, loyal years at the hotel, Phyllis, I am willing to offer you an additional month's pay, making a total of four months. And I'm afraid that's absolutely the final offer.'

'We'll take it.' Jodie already had Phyllis by the arm and was helping her to her feet. 'But don't think you've heard the last of this.'

The hotel foyer was a jumble of ladders, men in overalls, sheets of polythene covering the marble tiles. Dust particles hung in the air. There was no sign of Seb.

A large group, surrounded by baggage, was at reception. They'd only checked in yesterday and were supposed to be staying for several nights.

Louise crossed to the desk. 'Everything all right, Katie?'

Before she could answer, one of the group stepped forward. She was a large woman, in an anorak, despite the heat, with a pair of binoculars hanging from her neck. 'It most certainly isn't,' she said. 'How can you call yourself a luxury establishment with this ruckus going on?' She swung her arm out, indicating the whole area.

'I do apologise for the disruption.' Louise kept her voice as steady. 'I'm afraid it's unavoidable during redecoration, but it will be over soon.'

'Not soon enough for us,' a man joined in. 'We're out of here to find somewhere more ...' He smirked at Louise. '... peaceful.'

'That's a shame,' Louise said. 'Obviously you must do what's best for you, but I hope you'll consider visiting us again in the future.'

The man laughed. 'Highly unlikely.'

Katie was gesturing at her from behind the desk. 'What shall I do about what's owing?'

'Exactly. That's what we want to know.' The woman with the binoculars folded her arms.

Louise glanced down the invoice Katie held out. 'The hotel will cover the cost of your bar bill –'

'And dinner?' the man said.

She calculated. There were six of them, and they'd enjoyed a four-course meal, champagne, wine. It would be madness, but they were bound to post negative reviews online otherwise. She heard herself saying 'I think we can do that for you. Katie, perhaps you'd make up a new bill.'

Katie looked surprised, but she smiled sweetly. 'Of course.'

'Oh, and one more thing, Katie. As soon as you see Seb Flanders, can you tell him I need to see him urgently? I'll be upstairs.'

Louise paced the floor in the lounge of the flat. She'd propped Oliver's painting of The Hoe against one wall, but that emphasised the room's emptiness.

She jumped when the knock on the door came.

'Hi, Louise. I gathered you wanted to see me. Katie told me where to find you.' Seb leant against the door jamb, a wide smile dimpling his cheeks. Green paint streaked his hair, and white dust had gathered on his forehead. 'What's up?'

She clutched the edge of the door. 'Everything's up.'

'Perhaps I could come in, and you can tell me.'

In the lounge, Louise sat on the edge of the sofa, with Seb at right angles on an armchair.

'You look upset,' he said. 'Has something happened?'

'The redecoration has happened!'

'Whoa, where did that come from? I thought you were happy for me to do the work.'

'I should never have let you persuade me.' She couldn't bring herself to look at him. 'It's costing thousands of pounds; the hotel has lost several guests because of the chaos, and that colour you've put on the walls looks like ... it looks like ... vomit!'

Seb moved from the chair to sit beside her on the sofa. 'Okay, I know the foyer is a mess at the moment.' His arm was almost touching hers. 'I'm sorry you lost the guests, but it won't be for long, I promise. And don't worry about the colour – that's the undercoat.'

'But the money. My father always kept a fund for emergencies and I'm eating into it.'

'Louise, please listen to me.'

'I jumped into this. Yes, you showed me your past work, but how do I know I can trust you? You could be anyone.'

'I might have persuaded you to take on the project – I accept that – but it's not going to cost you thousands.' He pulled at a loose thread on his jeans. 'We agreed the hotel will pay for materials. Even with those fabulous curtains, it won't be thousands. I'm funding the rest myself because I'm sure the publicity generated by the magazine will get my name known. It's a gamble, but I'm trusting new commissions will follow.'

'*Gamble ... trusting ... you're sure.* It's all hot air.'

'I give you my word that it will work out.'

She looked down at the floor. She could hear him breathing. 'I think it's better if you go now.'

Twenty-six

Ollie drained his second glass of lager. He felt for the pouch in his pocket, fingering the strands of tobacco. Flo hated him smoking, and he was trying to stop, but he'd hardly slept for the last two nights, and the headaches were getting worse.

It was three pm, a dead hour in the pub. He flicked through the pages of his sketch pad. A day's drawing at Waterlow Park, and nothing worthwhile to show for it. He'd forced himself out today, but looking through this lot, what was the point?

He ordered another lager.

'On your own tonight?' The barmaid took his money and slammed the till shut. 'Usually meet your friend, don't you?'

'Dan? Yeah, I haven't seen him for a while. He's busy with his band.'

'Oh right. Are you a musician too?'

'No, I paint.'

'Cool.' She turned away to another customer.

He knocked back most of the lager in one go, blunting thoughts of the empty flat. He'd always loved their little home, but now he loathed every corner. The walls seemed to be moving, closing in on him. He kept the curtains pulled.

It was an effort even to get out of bed. He couldn't stay there much longer. More often than not, he woke in the early hours, the realisation of Flo's absence pressing on his chest. The nights when he did sleep were almost worse. Violent, terrifying dreams. Flo in danger. Being hurt. Screeching wheels crushing her. Her fingertips gripping the edge of a cliff. Sliding. Falling. And him unable to move, his feet clamped to the ground.

The old woman who lived downstairs had stopped him the other morning in the hallway: 'Are you all right?'

'I'm fine. Why?'

She frowned. 'I keep hearing weird noises. Sounded like someone screaming last night.'

He turned away. 'Must be cats,' he said.

Something had woken him. He'd come back from the pub, taken several painkillers and fallen into bed. A noise – there it was again. Piercing. Ringing. Ringing – of course. It was so long since anyone had called he'd forgotten what the doorbell sounded like. He leapt out of bed and ran to the intercom.

'Flo? Is that you?'

'Oliver, it's Mum.'

'Who?' His brain was sticky as candy floss.

'It's your mother. Are you going to let me in?'

He clicked the door release. 'It's open. Third floor.' He ran into the bedroom and pulled on his jeans and T-shirt. He was tying his hair back when there was a tap at the door of the flat.

'Mum! This is a surprise. Why didn't you let me know? The place is a mess.'

She pulled him close and hugged him as if she'd never let him go. 'It's so good to see you, Oliver.'

He laughed, afraid she'd notice his tears otherwise.

'You're suffocating me. I'll put the kettle on. Tea, coffee – oh, not sure there's any milk ... might have some wine.' He pictured the kitchen: dirty plates and mugs in the sink, his painting stuff strewn across the worktop, the overflowing bin. He pushed open the living room door. 'Let's go in here.' He yanked up the blind: dust motes swarmed in the afternoon sunlight. The hole in the carpet had grown bigger, the frayed edges unravelling as he looked at them. 'I'm sorry.'

She cleared a space on the sofa and sat down. 'I can't stay long. I've got to get back tonight. Your dad's on his own.'

'I got a shock when I saw him.'

'He's been very poorly, Oliver.' She gave him that look, the one where he hated himself and couldn't believe he was such a prick. 'I didn't realise, Mum ... stupid I know.' He ran his hands over his face.

'Okay, we were hurt ... no, your father was devastated when you didn't come ... but it's done now. Let's leave the recriminations.'

'I was too caught up with what was going on here.'

Her gaze swept over the room. 'What is going on? Looks like a herd of elephants has been through.'

He noticed the letter from the solicitor, screwed up in a ball by her foot. Snatching it up, he flung himself into the armchair and shoved it down the side. 'Does Dad know you're here?'

'He knows I've come up to London. I didn't go into detail.'

Ollie leant forward and rested his arms on his knees. He looked across at his mother. Dark rings shadowed her eyes.

'I'm sorry I didn't see you when you came to Plymouth,' she said. 'I couldn't believe I missed little Flo.'

'I'd planned to stay, but then Dad told me Louise has got the hotel, and I sort of flipped.'

'But you never wanted it, did you?' She plumped up the cushion next to her and propped it against the back of the sofa.

Christ, the number of times he'd seen that fussy little movement. If only life was as simple as a plumped cushion.

She picked up the other cushion and held it to her chest. 'What time do Jess and Flo get home?'

'Mum ... Mum ...'

'I'm not stupid. I can see you're not right.' She gestured round the room. '*This* isn't right. What's happening?'

'It's fucked, Mum. Totally fucked.' He levered himself up from the chair and went over to the window. An old man was pushing a wheelbarrow along the street. Ollie made out an overcoat, newspapers, cans of beer bundled into the wheelbarrow. A mangy looking mongrel trotted at the man's heel. How long before that was him?

'Come and sit down, Oliver.'

His mother's voice was hardly a murmur. If she was nice to him, he was lost. He needed her to shout, to rage.

'I suspected things weren't right. That's why I'm here.'

Ollie stared out of the window. The old man had reached the end of the road, and he turned the corner.

'Has Jess left you?'

He turned round. 'What makes you say that?'

His mother spread her hands wide. 'It doesn't take a genius to know that something's up.'

He sat down on the floor, clasping his arms round his knees. He wanted to crawl back into bed and curl into a ball. He didn't want this conversation.

'Tell me, Oliver. It can't make you feel any worse.'

He raised his head and fixed his eyes on the wall light. 'Jess left a couple of months ago, and she took Flo.' If he recited the facts, he might get through this. 'We'd been arguing a lot about money. She was fed up with her job, my painting, everything really. After she left, I found out she was seeing someone else. Now, Flo's gone funny.'

'What sort of funny?'

'She won't see me. Won't even speak to me on the phone.'

'Is that since you came down to Plymouth?'

'Yeah, she was angry with me for not staying.'

'Poor little Flo. She probably doesn't know whether she's coming or going.'

Ollie couldn't bring himself to look at his mother. Family, loyalty, children meant everything to her.

'I'm amazed,' she said at last. 'I always thought Jess was a lovely girl.'

'Don't, Mum.'

'I can't believe she's met someone new so soon.'

'It's not someone new.' There seemed no point keeping it a secret any longer.

He heard her intake of breath from across the room. 'Who?'

'What does it matter? She's gone.'

'It's not Eugene, is it?'

He stared at her. 'Louise always said she wouldn't –'

'Louise didn't tell me anything.'

'Then how do you know?'

She clutched the cushion tighter. 'Mother's intuition. Am I right? Is it Eugene?

'Bull's-eye. That wanker.'

'Oh my God, I don't believe this. When Louise lost the baby, she told me Eugene had been having an affair, but I never dreamt then it was with Jess. It's only recently I've pieced together all the little clues.'

'Good, isn't it?'

'This will destroy Louise.'

'Fuck that, Mum. It's not a shedload of joy for me.'

She stood up and came closer, squatting down beside him. She ran her hand over his head. 'What are you going to do?'

'I'm going away.'

'No.'

'I can't stay.'

She stood up and wrapped her arms round herself. 'You've got to fight for Flo. She needs you. That man is poison.'

'Mum, shut up. You're not telling me anything I haven't been over in my mind a million times already.'

'Would Jess let her come to Plymouth? Just for a holiday. I'd love to have her.'

'I doubt it. She's turned Flo against me. She won't want her to see you and Dad.'

Ollie scrambled to his feet and put his arms round his mother's shoulders.

'I'm sorry, Mum. I have to get away for a while. It hurts too much to stay here.' His mother felt tiny in his arms. 'But I'll write to Flo, and I'm not giving up.'

'Where will you go?'

'Somewhere. Anywhere away from here.'

Her eyes searched his face. 'Let me guess. Not Venice, by any chance?'

'You know me too well.'

'I know you've always wanted to go. But wherever, your dad and I want you to have some of your inheritance now. It should help.'

'No, Mum. I've got to prove I can make something of my life on my own.'

'We've talked about it, and it's what we want.'

'But you've just given the hotel to Louise and bought the apartment. You can't afford it.'

'Listen to me. Your grandfather was an extremely wealthy man, and as well as the hotel in Plymouth, he owned one in London.'

'What? Where? How come we never knew?'

'Your father always employed managers. The income helped subsidise Plymouth, your dad's first love. But several months ago, he put the London hotel on the market – I think he suspected he wasn't well – and the money it went for is staggering.'

'I wonder what his father would say about him selling it. You know – *duty, responsibility.*'

'Never mind that. The important thing is it's allowing us to help you and Louise now when you need it.'

'I appreciate the thought, Mum, but I can't take your money.'

'I'm not arguing, Oliver. When we die, the proceeds of the apartment will come to you. In the meantime, we're putting £300, 000 in your account. Use it wisely.'

Twenty-seven

Louise was transfixed. Instead of the chaos of the last few days, huge floor to ceiling screens had been erected in the foyer, each painted with a different Plymouth scene. Guests thronged the area exclaiming over the pictures. She peered round a screen showing the statue of Sir Francis Drake: behind it, a long ladder was propped against the wall reaching up to the cornice. A pot of paint stood at the foot of the ladder. She moved on to the next screen, this one portraying Smeaton's Tower on The Hoe. Seb was there applying masking tape to some wood panelling.

'Hello,' she said.

He looked round when he heard her voice. 'Hi.'

'Can I talk to you?'

He turned back to the panelling. 'Not the best moment.'

The ripping sound of the masking tape set her teeth on edge. 'If you could spare five minutes.' She studied his bent back, his shoulder blades spearing his T-shirt. 'I can see you're busy.'

'I'll be about an hour.'

In her office, Louise was typing up her list for the day: (5) Meeting with couple about pre-wedding dinner (6)

Interviews for new housekeeper.

She starred the first item on the list: a computerised management system. Maeve was on holiday, so Katie would have a few days to research the different systems available.

'Sorry to disturb you.'

Louise whirled round. A face was peering through a crack in the door. 'Emily, how lovely to see you.' Guilt made her hug more extravagant than she'd intended. She hadn't seen her friend for months, not since the day of her father's heart attack. 'Oh Emily, the baby.' As Emily came fully into the office, Louise took in the cream shawl, the black curls peeking over the top. 'You've had the baby.' Stupid thing to say. She remembered now: she'd had a card weeks ago announcing the arrival of Sophie Louise. She'd been meaning to send flowers, a present.

'I wasn't sure what to do. I popped a note through the letterbox at your house, but ...' Emily held the baby in one arm while manoeuvring a push chair into the office. 'I couldn't wait any longer to show her off. Hope you don't mind.'

'Of course not. I'm sorry not to have been in touch.' Louise pushed the table to one side to make more room. 'Here, have a seat. I'll order coffee.' She squeezed past the pushchair to the door and waved to Katie at the desk. The foyer was less busy, but a number of people were still studying the screens. How on earth had Seb got those painted and erected so quickly?

She turned back to the office. Emily had removed the baby's shawl. The little dark head was snuggled against her cheek and plump legs dangled from a white dress splodged with pink flowers.

Louise sat down at the desk. 'She's beautiful, Emily.' She swallowed the lump in her throat. 'Can I hold her?'

'Of course.'

Louise cradled the baby in her arms. 'Hello, Sophie.' She

held out her forefinger and a tiny hand closed round it. Her dimpled fingers were warm against Louise's cool skin. She smiled across at Emily. 'Are you getting much sleep? It must be hard work.'

'It's worth it. I love her so much.' Emily laughed. 'And you should see David with her. He's a complete softie.'

Louise stroked the delicate skin on Sophie's cheek. She bent her head and smelt the honeyed scent: milk, baby shampoo, newness. She stared at the pulse on top of Sophie's head, counting its steady beats.

'Thanks for bringing her to see me. Little Sophie Louise.'

'I didn't know whether to ... what with ... what happened to you ...'

'Don't worry. That's all over, Emily.'

The baby burped and some sick came up.

'Sophie, fancy doing that in front of Auntie Louise.' Emily held out her arms. 'Shall I take her?'

'It's fine.' Louise reached for a tissue on her desk and dabbed at Sophie's dress. 'There! That's better, isn't it, gorgeous girl?' Sophie's eyes were fixed on Louise's face. 'You're lovely, aren't you? You really are a beautiful baby.'

Sophie's mouth spread wide and her blue eyes came alive. 'Oh, look!' Louise said. 'She's smiling. She's smiling at me.'

'She likes you,' Emily said. 'You like Auntie Louise, don't you, my precious?'

The door opened, and expecting Katie with the coffee, Louise said 'Could you put the tray on the table, please?'

'Erm, I haven't got a tray.' The voice was deep, and certainly not Katie's.

Louise looked up: Seb was staring down at her. 'I see you're busy at the moment.'

She was conscious of her flushed cheeks, the baby's fingers curled round hers, the crumpled tissue smelling of sick. 'Emily's an old friend. She's come to –'

Seb laughed. 'I'll call by later. I've got plenty to get on with.' He shut the door.

'Wow, Louise! He's fit,' Emily said. 'Where did you find him?'

'Seb? He's doing some decorating for me.'

'It's a good job my David's a jealous man, or I might be tempted.' Emily giggled. 'Has Matt seen who you've got working here?'

'No, no, he hasn't.' Louise held the baby out to Emily. 'If you can take her, I'll find out what's happened to the coffee.' As she stood up, Katie appeared at the door carrying a tray. 'Oh, at last.'

Emily settled the baby in the pushchair and took a cup from Louise. 'This feels so civilised.' She dunked a biscuit in her coffee. 'I mean I'm besotted with Sophie, but it's lonely sometimes. Just an endless round of nappies and feeds at the moment.'

'I feel bad about not being in touch. It's all been frantic.'

'Are you helping out here now? I suppose your dad needs to take things easily for a while.' Emily fished a dummy from her bag and put it in Sophie's mouth. 'I should have asked before – how is he? It was such a shock when I heard. I hope you got my card.'

Louise tried to remember. So much had happened that she had no idea whether she'd had a card or not. 'Yes, it was beautiful, thank you.'

'Are you still working at the solicitors?'

'No, I've given it up. Dad isn't up to running this place any more, so I've had to take over.'

Emily paused with a biscuit half way between the cup and her mouth. 'That's a surprise. What does your Matt think?'

'He's not completely happy.'

The dummy dropped from Sophie's mouth and she started to cry, a bleak sound that cut through Louise.

'Hey ho, another feed due.' Emily pulled herself to her feet. 'I haven't got rid of the baby weight.'

'Thank you for bringing Sophie in. You must be so proud.'

Emily reached over and hugged Louise. 'It's the best feeling in the world. I recommend it.'

Louise bent over the pushchair, pulling the shawl up over Sophie's legs. 'I'll bear that in mind.'

Katie called Louise over to the desk as she passed through reception. 'I've looked at some of the computer systems on offer, and I've got a good idea which ones would work for us.'

'You're ahead of me.'

'I've been frustrated with our antiquated booking system since I started working here. It's madness nowadays not to use the Internet.'

'As you know Maeve isn't keen.'

Katie screwed up her face. 'Hope this doesn't sound rude, but Maeve will have to lump it.'

Her enthusiasm was a relief after Maeve's negative attitude. 'How about you draw up a list of the pros and cons of your top three, and we'll go through it together,' Louise said.

'Sounds great.'

'Good, oh, and Katie ...' She ran her finger round a knot of wood on the desk, '... this is just between you and me in the meantime.' She looked up in time to catch Katie's grin. 'I'd like to present it as a fait accompli to the rest of the reception staff.'

'My lips are sealed.'

The sky was a brilliant blue, but a cool breeze tugged at Louise as she stepped out of the main doors onto The Hoe. She pulled her jacket closer. September was usually a good month for the hotel and this year's late summer sunshine should have meant bumper bookings. But so far, they were at eighty per cent of last year's. It must be her fault. She wasn't a natural like her father. Then again he'd been trained from the beginning to take on the hotel. It would take years to gain the sort of experience and authority her father had.

She sat down on a bench, her eyes scanning the bay.

'Katie said I'd find you here.'

She jumped at the voice. Seb slid along the bench and sat next to her.

'I needed some fresh air,' she said.

'You like this place, don't you?' His voice was soft.

She watched the ferry, ploughing its way between the Barbican and Royal William Dockyard. She imagined herself on it, the wind ruffling her hair. She'd look over to the land, and the hotel would be only a speck in the distance, the bench where a couple were sitting talking, invisible to the naked eye.

'I love it,' she said. 'I never get tired of staring towards the Breakwater.'

'Why?'

'It's always the same, but then again, it's always different.'

'Like life, I guess.' He folded his arms and stretched out his legs. He was wearing the brown brogues, and green paint was smeared across the toe of one of them.

'How did you get those screens together so quickly?'

'A friend of mine owed me a favour. We stayed up all night doing them.'

Noticing the bags under his eyes, she felt guilty. 'I'm sorry for the way I behaved the other night. That's what I wanted to tell you this morning.'

'You were upset,' he said. 'It's always hard for people to see past the messy middle stage.'

'I know, but I agreed you should start the work.' She turned back to the sea. The ferry had disappeared, but a shaft of afternoon sunlight had set fire to the waves. 'And then I panicked when I saw the colour.'

'Well, you'll never have to see that particular shade again.'

'How much longer until you unveil it?'

'I'm hoping another couple of days.'

Louise picked the skin at the base of her thumb and watched blood ooze from it. She was longing for, but dreading, the moment she'd see it finished. If she hated it, or worse if her father hated it ...

'Louise, I wanted to ask you.' Seb clasped his hands between his knees. The veins stood out on his forearms, jagged lines of blue.

'What? Ask what?' She quelled the urge to trace her finger along one of the veins.

'I'd like to take you out somewhere when it's almost done, while the guys put the finishing touches to it.'

'But I need to be there. To supervise.'

'No.' He took one of her hands in his. 'That's the point. I want you to see the finished thing, not the messy bits while we achieve it.'

'I can't leave the hotel.'

'It will only be for an afternoon, I promise.' He let go of her hand. She'd liked the feel of it clasped round hers.

'Surely, you'll have to be there?'

'Phil, my main guy, knows exactly what to do.' His eyes met hers. 'Will you come? The day after tomorrow. Leave about midday?'

Louise's heart seemed to speed up, as if she'd just run the length of The Hoe. 'Okay, the day after tomorrow. But where?'

'It's a surprise.'

Twenty-eight

Boxes surrounded Ollie. He was trying to be organised: black marker pen in hand, labelling things: things Jess might want, things Dan's mum had agreed to store, things he was going to send down to Plymouth. His painting of the hotel that he'd done specially for his father was already packaged up and ready to go.

The biggest problem was disentangling his stuff from Jess's. The big cupboard in their bedroom was a nightmare. At the back, he'd discovered a sketch he'd done of her. Its frame long gone, the paper was dog-eared and torn in the left hand corner. He'd given her the portrait on their one-month anniversary, and memories of that night of celebration washed over him with the force of a spring tide. Cheap wine, beans on toast, the electric heater on high for once, the Norah Jones CD Jess had given to him playing *Come Away with Me*. How could she have chopped up their world like kindling wood?

He'd just decided to keep the rings he'd bought for Jess, as Flo might like them when she was older, when his mobile rang.

'Hi, Ollie.'

'Angel, I was going to ring you.' He felt bad about her. Sometimes when he woke in the night, he imagined her lips on his, her mouth warm and yielding. He wanted to kiss her again, tell her what an amazing friend she'd been. Always ready to listen to him. And she was lovely, not beautiful like Jess, but lit from within somehow.

'Ollie?'

'Sorry, I got sidetracked.'

'Are you okay? I thought you might get in touch ... you know ... after the gallery and everything.'

After the gallery. Did she mean the kiss or him handing his notice in? 'Hang on a sec.' Ollie went through to the living room, the phone clamped to his ear. He kicked a box to one side and slumped on the sofa. 'Sorry about running out on you that day. I did want to ring you, but it's been hectic.'

'Has Jess come back?'

'No, nothing like that. How's everything going? Is that bastard treating you okay?'

'It's unbelievably horrible.'

Ollie heard the crack in Angel's voice: was she going to cry?

'I can't stay long – he'll be back soon. He's a vile man. He hates everyone and everything.'

So it wasn't tears he could hear, but anger. 'What's he doing with all the paintings Simone had hung?' he asked.

'Returning them to the artists. I've brought yours home. He's got slide shows and videos on every wall now.'

Ollie had forgotten about the paintings he'd left at The Serendip. Where the hell was he going to store those?

'He says I'm a dinosaur when I complain, but I didn't spend three years studying the history of art –'

'Hey, Angel, would you be able to do me a huge favour?'

'I'll try.'

'Any chance you could look after those paintings for me?'

'Of course, but I was wondering if we could meet for a drink. I can bring the smaller ones with me then.'

'Yes to the drink, great, but ... I meant could you keep them for the next few months?'

'Don't you want to try to sell them?'

Ollie felt the groan stifled in his windpipe. He'd have to come clean. 'I'm going away. I'm trying to find places to store my stuff.'

There was a clatter at the other end. 'Are you okay, Angel? What's happened?'

'What do you mean you're going away? For a holiday?'

He pulled at a button on his shirt sleeve, unravelling the thread until the button broke free. 'I'm going to Venice.'

'Venice? How long for?'

'Not sure. Three months ... six.'

'I don't understand. I thought you were skint.'

'I was, but –'

'I thought you were worried about Flo.'

'I am.'

'I thought we were ... friends.'

'We are.' He fiddled with his cuff, flapping loose without its restraining button.

'When are you going?'

'I've booked an apartment from the beginning of October.'

'So soon. And you'll be away for Christmas.'

'Maybe.'

'What about Flo?'

'I can always come back if she'll see me.'

He waited for her answer, but on the other end of the phone, she seemed to have run out of steam.

'Angel? Are you there?'

'I don't know what to say. I'll miss you, that's all.'

'You could always visit.' He heard the words slipping easily from his mouth and then cursed. He'd promised himself six months of hard graft. Six months devoted to painting. 'But you've got your mother to look after, haven't you?'

'Look, when can we meet?'

Ollie visualised the hours ahead. More packing, and then Jess was coming to collect her stuff. He'd need a drink after that. 'What about tonight?' he said. 'I won't be free till about nine, if that's not too late.'

'Nine tonight. Where?' Angel sounded business-like, the sort of tone she used for customers.

'What about The George?' It wasn't too far for either of them, and they'd met there before.

'See you later.' And Angel was gone.

In the end, Ollie got the things Jess was likely to want down to two boxes. He was worn out from all the decision-making, the memories that every item seemed to throw up. He kept Flo's bedroom door firmly shut. She'd left a lot of things behind, and he'd consoled himself they meant she'd come back one day. He didn't think she'd leave her books, nor the little desk they bought for her fifth birthday. She used to sit there for hours pretending to be a shopkeeper, or a receptionist, or making up stories,. He remembered how he'd told her off when she'd gouged out her name with a pair of scissors, but now he couldn't resist cramming himself onto the tiny chair and tracing the letters of her name with his fingers. The bumpy surface of the wood mirrored the bumps in his heart. He stacked Jess's boxes by the front door and went to have a shower and wash his hair.

Ollie picked up the intercom. 'It's open,' he muttered. He hadn't seen Jess for ages, and apart from a few terse phone calls had had no contact for weeks. When he'd phoned to say he was giving up the flat and could she collect anything she wanted, she hadn't even asked why. He imagined her climbing the stairs to the flat: she was wearing jeans ... no, she'd probably come straight from school, so she'd have work clothes on ... her hair was loose ... no, bound to be up. She'd reached the second floor. There were ten stairs up to the third floor. Any minute now ...

The rap on the door was firm – two short taps, followed by a longer, louder one. The knock they'd always used when one of them had forgotten their key. She remembered their sign.

He opened the door. 'Hi.'

'Hi.' She didn't move, didn't make any attempt to come into the flat.

It was crazy. A decade of love and laughter shared, and now all they could say was 'hi.' He took in her face. She'd lost weight, and her features seemed more pronounced.

He opened the door wider. She took a step forward, and then he saw. Behind her was Flo.

'Are you going to ask us in, or are we going to stand here all evening?' Jess's voice grated on him. He didn't remember it being so harsh.

'Of course not, come in.' He caught her perfume as she passed, the unfamiliar lemony scent she'd been wearing that day in the coffee shop. Flo hesitated in the doorway, and he put his arm round her shoulder. 'Hello, sweetheart.' God, what should he say next? 'It's great to see you again, Flo. How's things?'

She looked at him from the corner of her eye, the long lashes shadowing her cheek, but she didn't answer. Her hands were stuffed in the pockets of her jeans. He let his hand drop from her shoulder, and closed the door.

Jess was standing in the middle of the room. 'It looks different with everything gone.'

He stared at her. She sounded so lost, so plaintive. How did she think it was for him with her and Flo gone?

'I've put the things you might want in those boxes by the door,' he said.

'Right. Thanks.'

'I don't know what to do about Flo's stuff. I haven't really touched her room.'

'Can you go and see, darling, if there's anything you want to take?' Jess said.

Flo rubbed the toe of her trainer backwards and forwards on the floor.

'You have a look, and if there's anything, I'll help you pack it up,' Jess smiled across at Flo. 'Go on. I need to have a word with Daddy.'

Flo looked up at him. 'Why are you leaving here?'

It was such a relief to hear her speak, and he tried to ignore the aggressive note in her voice.

'I'm going away for a while,' he said. 'But I'll email and text you.'

'So, I won't have a bedroom here any more?'

Jess knelt down beside Flo and put her arms round her. 'No, I explained that to you, didn't I? But you'll soon have a big, new bedroom. We can redecorate it, and you can have all your things just as you want them.'

'But what about Panda? This is where he lives.'

'Panda can come and live with us now. Go on, and I'll come to help in a minute.'

Flo crossed to her bedroom, her feet dragging on the floor. She went inside and slammed the door.

Ollie sank down on a chair, his head in his hands. 'What a mess. What a bloody, fucking mess.'

'She'll be all right,' Jess said. 'It's coming back and seeing everything.'

'Does everything include me?'

'You messed things up, Ollie. Haring off to Plymouth and then dragging her back again.'

Ollie's head reared up. 'It wasn't my fault. It was impossible to stay there.'

'And you think the answer is to run out on her?'

He clenched his fists in his lap. 'I'm not running out. I'm

going away for a while. You've obviously got no idea what it's like trying to live here on my own.'

'That's it, same old Ollie. It's all about you, isn't it?'

'Well, I didn't cause any of this.'

Jess sat down on the sofa. She pushed her hair back from her face. 'I didn't come to fight. All I want to do is collect our things, and I'd like you to sign those papers.'

Ollie had screwed up the divorce papers and stuffed them in a drawer in the kitchen.

'Ollie. Can we get on? I can't stay long.'

'Lover boy waiting for you, is he?'

'Shut up! You're such a child.'

He didn't answer.

'You always do this.' Jess pulled at her bottom lip. 'Any critical moment and you go off into one of your reveries.'

'Reverie?' He thumped the arm of the chair. 'If you think the black hole inside my head is a reverie, then you're more stupid than I ever thought.'

Jess stood up. 'I'm not interested in the boxes you've packed, although thanks for doing it. That's not why I've come.'

What would happen if he got up and put his arms round her? Held her, stroked her hair, kissed her?

'I'd like you to sign the papers, Ollie, but the divorce will go ahead whether you do or not.'

'How can it?'

She sighed. 'I'm not going into all the legal stuff, but I can get a divorce with or without your consent.'

'I don't consent.'

'That means the court will make all the decisions, including maintenance payments.'

He laughed. 'You're saying after all this that you expect me to maintain you?'

She shook her head, and he could have sworn she almost stamped her foot. 'Child maintenance. Surely, you want to contribute to your daughter's upbringing?'

'Good one, Jess!' He clapped his hands. 'I want to contribute to Flo's upbringing, more than anything, but not just financially. I want to talk to her, laugh with her, dance and skip, read, take her to the park, to art galleries, teach her to draw.'

Jess was staring at him, as if she might have realised, for the first time, what she'd done. ''I'm pregnant, Ollie.'

It was raining when Ollie left home, but he decided to walk the three miles to the pub. He raised the hood of his anorak, but the wet soaked into his jeans, and damp spread across his shoulders. A bus passed, spraying him with water. The stop wasn't far away, and he debated making a run for it. He checked the distance, blinking away the raindrops on his eyelashes. No, keep walking. One foot in front of the other. The only way. Don't question. Don't think. Don't remember.

Jess hadn't taken the boxes by the door in the end. And he hadn't signed the papers. She'd asked him for his address, but he said he didn't know. She called to Flo that it was time to leave, and she'd emerged from her bedroom, clutching Panda in front of her face. Ollie knelt down and wrapped his arms round her. He felt the tremble in her thin body. 'Goodbye, sweetheart. I love you,' he whispered in her ear. 'I'll see you soon. And I'll keep all your things safe for you.'

Angel was already at the pub when he arrived. She'd found a table and was drinking a glass of white wine. 'Ollie, you're soaked.'

He took off his anorak and hung it on the back of a chair. He eased his hair free from his collar. 'Probably wasn't the best idea to walk!'

'Can I get you a drink?'

'Lager would be great, thanks.'

While Angel was at the bar, he dried his face on his

hankie and pulled off his wet jumper. The shirt underneath seemed dry, but a puddle of water had formed around his chair. He forced his face into a smile as Angel returned from the bar with his drink.

'Thanks.' He raised his glass to her. 'You're a star.'

She sat down and sipped her wine. Her eyes regarded him steadily. 'You going away is a shock. When did you decide?'

'I'm getting more and more depressed in that flat on my own. I can't bear being there.'

'But Venice? It's so far away.'

'Not really. And I've wanted to go for years, but obviously with Jess and Flo, it wasn't possible.'

'How can you afford it?'

'I'd managed to scrape together enough money to go for a month, but my dad has given me an early instalment on my inheritance, so I can stay longer.'

'Do Jess and Flo know you're going?'

He knocked back some lager. 'Yep.'

'And?'

He shrugged. 'I imagine Jess is glad to see the back of me.'

'But what about Flo? I thought you were going to fight for custody.'

Ollie planted his elbows on the table. The legs must have been uneven and it wobbled, splashing drops of lager onto the wooden surface. He covered them with a beer mat. 'Considering she's barely speaking to me, I wouldn't stand a chance.'

'But if you don't fight for her, she might think you don't want her.'

'Are you going to lecture me? Because if so –'

'Don't be so touchy. I know how much she means to you.'

'I can't stay here and not see her. It's eating away at me.' He picked at the rough edge of the beer mat.

He looked up. Angel was fiddling with her rings. She'd told him the history of them all once: the signet ring her parents had given her for her twenty-first birthday, the one in the shape of a sea-horse she'd bought in Portugal, the amethyst – it struck him how much he was going to miss her.

'Angel, I'm sorry to abandon you to the mercies of Guy up-himself Norton.'

She raised her eyes to his. The impact of her gaze always surprised him, with its glint suggesting firelight and sweet conversation. But it was more the quality of her attention. Encompassing, enclosing, involving. When she looked at him, he knew he was her sole focus.

'I don't think I can stay there without you.' Her voice was scarcely a murmur, and he leant forward to catch the words.

'What do you mean? What are you saying?'

'Can I come with you? To Venice, I mean. I've never been and I'd love –'

'Steady on, Angel, where did that come from?'

'I haven't been able to settle since our phone call. Please think about it. I won't get in the way or disturb your painting, I promise.' She squeezed her eyes shut, and her mouth lifted in a grin. 'The thought of seeing where Veronese lived and worked ...' She opened her eyes, but there was a faraway look in them. 'He renamed one of his works to escape the disapproval of the Inquisition. He must have loved getting the better of them.'

The girl from behind the bar came to light the candle on their table. It was in a brown earthenware bowl, surrounded by pink plastic flowers.

'What do you think?' Angel said when the girl had gone. The glow from the candle lit up the lower half of her face. Her mouth was tight. He didn't want to hurt her, but none of his Venice dreams involved someone else. This was something he needed to do for himself, and he didn't want to share it.

'What about your mum?' he asked. 'How would she manage without you?'

'She's gone to live with my brother. They're buying a place with a granny flat.'

'But you'd need money.'

'I can rent out the house. My dad left it to me when he died, so I haven't got a mortgage. I'd shop at the fish market and the vegetable stalls – we'd be able to eat cheaply.'

'Angel ...' Ollie caught hold of her hands. Her skin felt warm, and he realised he was shivering. 'You know how much I like you, but –'

'Don't say *but*.'

'I have to. I'm not Guy Norton's calibre of shit, but I am one all the same. I don't know why, but I end up hurting people.' He squeezed her hands. 'You're a lovely person, and I don't want to be the one to mess you up.'

She pulled away. 'You don't know me very well.'

'Don't I? We've worked together for the last eighteen months.'

'But that doesn't mean you know much about my life. Perhaps you don't have the monopoly on messing people up.'

Ollie twisted his glass round and round. The reflection from the candle danced as he spun it. He wasn't sure what she was telling him and couldn't think what to say. There was a shout of laughter from the group at the next table, and he glanced over. A pang sliced through him when he saw the two couples. That had been his life once. Could he have it again? He'd lost Jess, but that didn't mean he had to be lonely forever. But that was for the future. Venice was his, and his alone.

'Ollie, please say yes. Or at least think about it.' Angel's hands were clasped in front of her, palms touching. 'You won't regret it.'

Twenty-nine

The boat nudged its way alongside the quay, and they stood to one side as the passengers coming over from Cremyll disembarked.

Seb caught hold of her arm when it was their turn to climb on board. She liked the feeling and smiled at him. 'This was a good idea,' she said as they settled onto the wooden seats. After a few days of rain and a cold wind, the sun was shining, and more and more people crowded on. A large woman with a dog and several parcels sat down on the other side of Seb, and he shifted along the seat towards Louise. His thigh was warm against hers, the brown corduroy of his trousers next to her black jeans. As the boat turned towards the river, the chug of the engine resonated through Louise's body. The sun was warm on her head, and her eyes grew heavy.

The woman next to Seb was talking to him, and he stroked her Labrador, ruffling the fur on its silky ears. 'You've got the touch,' the woman declared. 'She likes that.'

Out in the middle of the Tamar, the wind whipped through Louise's hair. She was wearing it loose and strands blew across her face, sticking to her lip gel. She reached up to free it and her fingers touched Seb's. He laughed. 'Great minds. Thanks for saying you'd come today.'

She hesitated. 'I don't want to get my hopes up, but will the foyer be finished when we get back?'

'Phil's promised an unveiling at five-thirty.' He took her hand and tucked it in the crook of his elbow. 'Hey look!' He pointed back towards Plymouth. 'That's Royal William Yard, isn't it? I had a great meal there last night.'

Louise didn't turn to look at the massive silhouette of the old victualling yard, now converted to apartments, restaurants, shops. It was only two minutes' walk from their house in Cremyll Street, and she and Matt often used to go there. The ferry bumped into position next to the jetty. Seb scrambled ashore and helped Louise clamber out.

She patted the *Welcome to Cornwall* sign. 'I love this moment of stepping off the boat. It's a different atmosphere over here somehow.'

'Gives you a shiver, doesn't it,' Seb said, 'when you imagine centuries of people crossing between Devon and Cornwall at this very spot.'

'And they used to row over. My grandad said it was a treacherous crossing in the old days.'

'Your grandparents used to live over here?'

'They both worked up at the house after the war. It was bombed and almost destroyed by fire. Kenelm Edgcumbe and his wife, Lilian, rebuilt it.'

'This is like coming home for you,' Seb said.

'Sort of. Mum was born at Cawsand about three miles away.' Louise passed through the gate and away from the jetty. 'But there's something I want to show you up here.' She paused in front of the clock which hung on a small stone building. When they were first going out together, she'd shown it to Matt: 'Amazing, isn't it?' She remembered her excitement. 'It was made in the late 1800s, probably not long after the hotel was built.'

'It's only some old clock,' he'd said.

Seb joined her. 'Look at this quote in the frame: *Does thou love life; then do not squander time.*' He grabbed her hand. 'Come on. Let's not squander a second of this precious afternoon. You might not talk to me any more once you've seen the new foyer.'

'Now you've got me worried.'

'I'm teasing you – you'll love it.' He darted away from her. 'Last one to the top buys the ice creams.'

Louise followed him up the grassy hill towards the house, but he was as fast as the deer you sometimes glimpsed in the parkland. She stopped half way up, a stitch biting into her side. Eventually she reached the top of the steep slope and climbed the steps. Seb was sitting on a bench waiting for her.

She was conscious that her hair was all over the place, her cheeks flushed with effort. 'I need to get back to my morning runs.' She flopped down next to him. 'I haven't had time since I've taken over the hotel.'

'Worth the climb though,' Seb said. 'What a view!'

Louise gazed at the expanse of green, the trees on each side narrowing the vista to the glittering sea beyond. Her eyes shifted to the right. If she concentrated, she imagined she could make out the hotel.

Seb jumped up. 'Shall we go inside? I'm looking forward to this.'

In the hall with its marble floor and sweeping staircase, Louise read snippets from the guide book: *The main hall was altered in a classical style by 1749 ... Between 1841 and 1844, the architect George Wightwick was engaged to enlarge the west wing gallery and add a stair turret to the east front of the house.*'

Seb leant backwards, to study the chandelier sparkling in the middle of the ceiling. 'This place is superb. What a work of love to rebuild it after the fire.'

'And it wasn't only the house they lost. Kenelm and Lilian's only son was killed in the war. There's a chapel upstairs in his memory.'

Seb stood, his head to one side, examining the objects in each room. Watching him, Louise realised how much of a butterfly she'd become. Her mind was always a frenzy of lists: the next task, the next person to see. Somewhere along the way, she'd lost the ability to concentrate on now.

It was mid-afternoon by the time they left the house. 'I'm starving,' Seb said.

'There's a café in the Orangery.'

'Lead on.'

They sat outside in the shelter of the building. Seb ate fat sandwiches filled with bacon, lettuce and tomato. Louise's scone was tame in contrast. She flicked her hand at a wasp buzzing close to her ear. A group of young girls were taking photos of themselves in front of the fountain. Their shrieks bounced around the garden.

Louise glanced over: one of the girls was doing a handstand, her long legs sticking out from her shorts, while the others clapped and counted how long she could stay up. The distraction stopped Louise focusing on Seb's fingers curved round the chunk of bread, mayonnaise oozing between the slices.

'You're so passionate about design,' she said, 'you must have a wonderful home yourself.'

'My place in Bristol is just somewhere to crash.' He wiped his mouth with a napkin. 'I'm like the cobbler with the broken shoes.'

'How would you have it, if you had time, I mean?'

'Minimalist, I guess. Leather sofas, polished floorboards, blinds at the windows, one well-chosen sculpture ... I don't like clutter.' He rested his arms on the table. 'I don't like my mind to be cluttered either. And at the moment ...' His fingers were interlocked, his forefingers in a steeple against his mouth. '... it's definitely cluttered.'

The wasp landed on the remains of Louise's jam, and she pushed the plate to the other side of the table. 'What do you mean?'

'Okay, here goes – I like you, Louise. I have from that first meeting when you sent me packing.' He ran his hands through his hair, and then as if he suddenly made up his mind, he reached over and rested his lips on hers. 'And I've wanted to do that all afternoon.'

Louise felt their softness, the warmth that lingered after they were gone. Butterflies tickled her insides. It was happening. That feeling she hadn't known since Eugene. The feeling she thought she'd never have again.

'Have I annoyed you?' Seb's voice filtered into her thoughts

The wasp, drunk on strawberry jam, dragged itself across the table.

'No, no.' She followed its inching progress. 'No.'

'No?'

'I'm not annoyed.'

'Does that mean I could ask you out to dinner one evening?'

She fixed her gaze on Seb's hair, the curls at the back of his neck, the unruliness on top. Her fingers itched to touch it. 'That would be lovely,' she said. Matt's face loomed up in front of her. 'But the thing is –'

He held up his hand: 'It's all right. I know.'

'You do?' So someone had told him about Matt. No prizes for guessing who.

'You obviously won't want to have dinner with me if you hate the foyer.' He glanced at his watch. 'Should be done by the time we're back. Let's get going.'

*

Louise hesitated as they drew near to the hotel.

Seb put his arm through hers. 'Close your eyes.'

'Don't be silly.'

'Close your eyes and I'll tell you when you can open them.'

She let him lead her through the doors.

'Okay.' Seb's voice resounded in her ear. 'You can look now.'

Louise opened her eyes. The foyer was like a film set. The walls were a rich, vibrant green that made the space seem vast. A glass chandelier hung from the high ceiling, sending beams of light spinning in every direction. Huge mirrors framed with gold hung on three of the walls, bouncing never-ending images back and forth between them. Silk paper with dark green and pearl stripes lined the fourth wall, the one behind the reception desk, while heavy yellow drapes held back with golden hooks set off the window opposite the staircase.

'It's amazing.' Her throat was tight. 'So stylish and elegant.' She glimpsed some of the staff crowded in the doorways and beckoned. 'Come and look. What do you think?'

The applause was soft at first, a rippling sound, gradually swelling. Even Chef had come into the foyer, and he gave Louise the thumbs-up sign. 'Brilliant,' he mouthed. She turned to Seb. 'It's wonderful. Thank you so much.'

He put his hands on her shoulders and spun her round. 'Better than magnolia?'

She laughed, dizzy from spinning, from the whirling kaleidoscope of greens and golds. 'Much better.' She kissed his cheek. 'I'm sorry I doubted you.' She crossed to the reception desk, now clad in warm mahogany wood. 'What do you think, Katie? Isn't it wonderful?'

'It's a triumph. And you wouldn't believe how hard they've worked.'

'Where are your guys?' Louise asked. 'I want to thank them.'

'I sent them off to the pub,' Seb said. 'And I'm ready to join them and celebrate.'

'Oh.' She hadn't expected him to disappear so quickly. 'Come to the office. I want to give you some money. Drinks on the hotel this evening.'

She turned away, but Katie stopped her. 'Louise, you had a visitor this afternoon.'

'Did I? Who?'

'He said his name was Matt.'

Thirty

Ollie stowed their luggage on the *vaporetto* at Piazzale Roma. 'San Marco! San Marco!' the *marinaio* shouted the boat's destination as some last minute tourists ran to catch it. He untied the ropes, and the *vaporetto* reversed out to the head of the Grand Canal. Angel turned to Ollie, her eyes shining. 'Here we go!'

The pilot swung the boat round and it passed under the first bridge. A water-taxi raced by, a gondola, its hull black and glossy, bucking in the churned-up wake.

The boat docked at its first stop, banging and thudding against the landing stage.

'Ferrovia! Ferrovia!' the *marinaio* called.

'It's the station,' Angel said. 'It would be romantic to arrive by train.'

Ollie frowned. 'Romantic?'

'Okay, spoil sport.' She punched his arm. 'But we are in a city made for lovers after all.'

A few people got off, but even more crowded on. The night in the pub, before Ollie had agreed to Angel coming with him, they'd had a difficult conversation.

'It would be as friends,' he'd said.

She nodded. 'Friends. I'll sleep on the sofa.'

His doubts had persisted. 'I'm going to Venice to paint. I need to prove myself.'

'I know how important this is to you, Ollie.' She'd looked upset. 'I told you – I won't get in the way.'

Ollie spread his feet wide trying to balance as the *vaporetto* ploughed through the water. Boats rocked at their mooring posts. The tide was low and fronds of seaweed clung to the steps of one of the palaces lining the canal. Sunlight glanced off the walls of the *palazzo* on his right, sliding down into the water. The light was what he'd come for, but suppose he couldn't do it justice?

'All these palaces,' Angel said. 'Such a sense of history gliding along beside us.'

His breathing steadied as he gazed at the faded grandeur of the buildings opening on to the Grand Canal.

'They're like dolls' houses,' she said. 'You can imagine their facades opening and inside will be beautiful women in wonderful gowns, and men with wigs, dancing to Vivaldi or Albinoni.'

Ollie glanced back at the rows of palaces. If he narrowed his eyes, he could almost see what she described.

'Which stop is ours?' she asked.

'San Tomá. Not far now.'

A boy of about ten or eleven approached them as they got off the *vaporetto*. '*Ciao*. Signor Oliver?'

Ollie put down his bags and stretched out his hand. 'That's me.'

The boy turned away, ignoring the hand. '*Mi segua*,' he called over his shoulder.

'What's he saying?' Angel asked.

Ollie shrugged his rucksack onto his shoulder and picked up his case. '*Follow me*, I think.' He caught sight of the boy disappearing round the corner at the end of the alleyway and set off in pursuit.

'Wait. I can't keep up.'

He hesitated, torn between Angel's plaintive voice behind him and distant glimpses of the boy. 'Can't be far now,' he called. Then ahead of him, he saw the boy had stopped. As Ollie drew level, the boy cocked his thumb at the building beside them. '*Questo é l'appartamento*,' he said and raced off.

Angel trundled her case to a halt. 'What do we do now?'

'I think this is it.' Ollie looked at the studded, oak door, at the brass name plate on the wall beside it, none of the spaces with names he recognised. He stepped backwards, straight into the path of people coming off the nearby bridge. He felt something soft under his heel and turned to find an old lady bent over, her face screwed up in pain. He put his hand on her back. 'I'm sorry. Are you hurt?' She didn't answer. '*Scusi. Scusi,*' he said. Throngs of people pushed past, jostling against them. The woman raised her stick, and Ollie braced himself for a swipe across his back, but instead, she turned and stomped off along the narrow *calle*.

'Phew! That was a close one.'

The front door of the house opened, and a man with a shock of black hair and dark glasses stood there. 'Ah, you found it.' He spoke clear, if heavily accented, English.

'The boy brought us,' Ollie said. 'I'm Oliver Anderson.'

The man clicked his heels and gave a little bow. 'Fabbio Maroni. I use the bottom flat as a workroom. I'm a carpenter.' He opened the door wider. 'I apologise,' he said. 'I was at a critical moment – the wood you understand – and I sent my nephew to meet you.'

'Do you own the apartment we're renting?' Angel seemed to have found her voice.

'No, the owner, he pay me.' Fabbio shrugged. 'To meet the guests. Come in. Let me show you.' He picked up Angel's suitcase and made for the stairs. On the top floor, he fitted a key into the lock. 'Your apartment. You will get fit climbing the stairs, no?'

He swung the door open. The combined living room and kitchen glowed with light from windows all down the long wall and across the narrow one.

'It's beautiful,' Angel said. 'What do you think, Ollie?'

He dumped his case and rucksack on the floor and took in the two sofas, covered in yellow throws, a coffee table between them. A dining table and chairs stood at the far end of the room, late afternoon sunshine pooling in the centre of the table. 'I love it.'

'Through here is one bedroom.' Fabbio led the way, lifting Angel's case onto the bed. With shutters at each of the long windows, the room was cool and shadowy. 'And here is the bathroom.' He waved at the room next door. 'This is the smaller bedroom.'

'Oh, I understood there was only one.' Ollie glanced round at the sofa, the small chest of drawers and the armchair. The room had windows on two sides.

'The sofa, it pulls down,' Fabbio said. 'Makes bed.'

'This room is lovely,' Angel said. 'It would be fabulous for painting.'

Fabbio turned to her. '*Un milione di scuse, signora.* I didn't get your name.'

'I'm Angel Beaumont.' She held out her hand, and Fabbio took it in both of his and kissed it. '*Il piacere è tutto mio,*' he murmured. Angel's cheeks reddened in a way Ollie hadn't seen before.

'Oh, I forget!' Fabbio removed his dark glasses and banged the heel of his hand against his forehead. 'I have something to help you.' He rummaged in one of the kitchen drawers and spread a map out on the table. He took a pen from his shirt pocket and drew a cross on the map. 'We are here.'

Ollie pored over the map. It was criss-crossed with *calli*

so tiny, there wasn't even space to write their names. 'What about the supermarket?'

'Is here.' Fabbio jabbed his finger at the map, but as soon as he removed it, the spot disappeared into a morass of lines. 'Now let me show you the fridge.' He opened it with a flourish and pulled a bottle from the shelf. 'Prosecco for you! And some cheese and bread in the cupboard.'

'That's wonderful, Fabbio. Thank you.'

Fabbio bowed and backed away towards the door.

Ollie flopped down onto the sofa. 'Thank God he's gone! What a creep.'

'I thought he was sweet.'

'So I noticed.'

Angel poked her tongue out. 'Don't be horrible.' She crossed to the window by the sink and pulled back the lacy curtain. 'Hey, we've got our very own canal and bridge outside the window.'

Ollie went to stand beside her. The bridge over the narrow canal was wooden, a delicate arched structure. Reflections of the tall houses on the opposite bank shimmered in the water. A gondola was moored below them, golden cushions strewn inside. The steps leading down to it were thick with moss.

'I don't even need to go out,' Ollie said. 'I've got my first paintings right here.'

Angel had her nose pressed against the window. 'I can't wait to explore.' She caught up the bottle of prosecco. 'Let's have something to eat, unpack, and then go for a wander round.'

He found glasses in the cupboard and eased the cork from the bottle. The liquid bubbled in each of the glasses.

Angel set the bread and cheese on the table. She picked up a glass and held it to Ollie's. 'To our stay in Venice.'

Anxiety flicked round him when he thought of painting. That fear of the white page that had always plagued him. 'Let's hope it's fruitful.'

Angel gulped back some prosecco. 'It will be.'

Her top lip was wet, and he stared at it. She must have become conscious of his gaze. 'What's wrong? Have I grown two heads or something?' Her eyes crinkled at the corners. 'At least I've still got all my hair.'

Ollie ran his hand over his head. The day before, passing a hairdresser, he called in on a whim and had it shorn. 'I still get a surprise when I catch sight of myself,' he said.

'I like it,' Angel said. 'And it makes you look younger.'

'Is that good or bad?'

'Good, I guess.'

It was early evening when they set out. There was no sign of Fabbio Maroni, although the door into one of the rooms on the ground floor was ajar. Whorls of wood shavings covered the floor, and the scent of cherries, mixed with an acrid smell hung in the hallway.

Ollie drew back the heavy door, and they stepped out. The hubbub of voices in the *calle*, funnelled by the walls on either side, was a shock after the quiet of the apartment. He pulled the door closed behind them.

They dawdled behind a woman with two children. The boy was bouncing a ball, but the little girl was crying, dragging on her mother's hand. The woman shouted over her shoulder at the child, a volley of explosive Italian that smacked Ollie in the chest. The child's sobbing grew louder. An image of Flo's face, plaits framing her cheeks, slid into his mind. All the times he'd told her off, the times he'd ignored her tears, the times he'd brushed aside her feelings were suddenly here in this little girl's sobbing.

They crossed over a bridge and into a *campo*. A clump

of trees stood together in the middle of the square, benches underneath them. The perimeter was lined with shops and bars and restaurants, several storeys of apartments above them. The tables outside the bars were filled with groups of people. As they passed one, a shout of laughter bounced through the air, catching Ollie in its draught. He remembered that feeling: the gusting in the chest, the lungs filling, bubbles of sound bursting from the lips – some subconscious imprint from happier times – but when had he last laughed like that?

They settled in a bar at the far end of the *campo* and found a table under the striped blue and white awning.

Ollie studied the menu. 'What would you like?'

All around them, people were drinking a sparkling orange liquid in tall glasses.

'I'll have some of that,' she said. 'Aperol spritz.'

'Okay, same for me.'

Three glasses later, Ollie felt warm and relaxed. The crowds sauntering by, the smell of pizza and panini from the tables around him, the buzz of chatter smoothed the edges of the Flo-shaped space in his head.

Thirty-one

Maeve refused to take part in the training for the new computer system. 'We'll need someone at the desk.' She examined a broken nail. 'We can't all go off on jollies at the same time.'

'It's hardly a jolly,' Louise said. 'We've got two days of intensive training on site, but you'll have to do it entirely from the video if you don't attend the sessions. Katie and the others are in the meeting room now. I'll cover reception until lunch, so that you can join them.'

'I couldn't look your father in the eye if I took part.' Maeve swept an emery board backwards and forwards over her nail. 'You know how he feels about guests being met with a bank of computers.'

'It won't be like that. We'll give our guests not only a much better front-of-house experience, but smoother reservations and billing.'

'Sounds like you've swallowed their marketing manual.'

'It's not marketing – the benefits are real. Our customer service will be quicker and more efficient.'

'Your father won't like it,' Maeve insisted.

'Maybe not, but I'm responsible for the hotel now.'

'Yes, you've told me several times already.'

Louise clutched her folder against her chest. Anger

scorched her insides. 'Maeve, I know how much my father valued you as an employee, but I won't have my authority questioned.'

'Ooh, *my authority questioned.*' Maeve pouted. 'No wonder you couldn't hang on to your men if you took that tone with them.'

Louise felt her neck and cheeks flood with colour. 'How dare you speak to me like that?'

Maeve shrugged. 'Only saying what everyone else thinks.'

'Please leave the desk immediately and don't return to the hotel until tomorrow.' Louise's voice trembled. 'You will take this as a day's holiday.'

Maeve came out from behind reception. She leaned her elbow on the desk and cupped her chin in her hand. Her face was only inches away from Louise. 'I'm going to have tea with your dad this afternoon, and we'll see what he has to say about this.'

'This has nothing to do with my father. If you come back tomorrow prepared to do as I ask, then we'll say no more about it.' She turned away and the hand gripping her shoulder made her jump.

'This might not end up how you think it will.' Maeve spun round on her heel and made for the door but stopped half way across the foyer. 'Fancy-boy Flanders is not who you think he is either.'

Louise phoned Katie in the meeting room. 'Can you come to the office, and send one of the others down to the desk?'

'What about the trainer?'

'Joe? Tell him we've got a crisis. You'll be back with him this afternoon.'

'Have we?'

'What?'

'Got a crisis?'

'Can you come now, Katie?' Louise gripped the desk, trying to stop her hands shaking.

The door to the office swung open.

'Katie, thank goodness. Who's at the desk?'

'It's okay. Sally is covering it.' Katie shut the door and sat down opposite Louise. 'But I thought Maeve was on duty. What's happened? It's not your father is it?'

Louise sipped some water. She managed to miss her mouth and liquid trickled down her chin. She fumbled with a tissue, conscious of Katie's eyes on her. Suppose she confided in Katie, only to have her side with Maeve? Her parents had had each other. From her bedroom, late at night, she often used to hear their voices, her mother's tinkling above his deep undertow. But she was on her own.

'Louise? What's happened?'

The concern in Katie voice made her decide. 'It's Maeve. We've had a terrible row.'

Katie pressed her mobile to mute and laid it on the coffee table. 'I can't say I'm surprised.'

'Why?'

'I've got to know Maeve quite well since I've been working here, but tell me what happened.'

Louise hesitated. *I've got to know Maeve quite well* – what did that mean? Buddies? Drinks together after work?

'Where's Maeve now?' Katie asked. 'She didn't abandon the desk, did she?'

'I told her to leave. And not to come back until tomorrow.'

'It must have been bad.'

'She doesn't agree with the computer system.'

'I know. She's banged on to me often enough about your father hating computers.'

'She also made some extremely personal comments.'

Katie nodded. 'She's jealous.'

'Of what?'

255

'Anyone can see Seb likes you, and as far as she's concerned male attention should be focused on her.'

'That's ridiculous.'

'She also can't bear that you've taken over from your father. From what I gather, he left a lot of the decision-making to her.'

Louise knew her father had relied on Maeve, but Katie seemed to be saying he'd let her run the show. She checked her list for the day. 'Perhaps Sally can stay on reception for a couple of hours, if you want to get back to the training. How's it going?'

'It's so easy to use,' Katie said. 'And laterooms and booking.com link directly into the central database.'

'It's a relief something's working.'

Katie stood up and straightened her top. 'You're doing a fantastic job, Louise. You should hear all the compliments we've had about the foyer.'

'People like it?'

'They love it. There's a couple who've stayed several times before, and they haven't stopped raving about it.'

'We need a proper celebration,' Louise said. 'Perhaps we can tie it in with the photo shoot.' She scribbled a note on her pad. 'I'll finalise a date with the magazine, and get Mum and Dad here for the photos.'

'You mean like an official handover?'

'Not too much emphasis on the fact that Dad's not working now, more saluting the continuation of the Anderson line.'

Katie paused with her hand on the doorknob. 'Sounds great. I could stay for a while this evening. Talk through a few ideas, if you like.'

Louise was due to have dinner with Seb. The foyer had passed its test with flying colours, and there was nothing stopping them now, he'd said. She'd bought a new dress and it was hanging on the wardrobe door up in the flat. Last night before she went to bed, she'd tried it on, strutting up and down in front of the mirror: *And here we have Louise wearing a gorgeous silk of shimmering purple.* She imagined Seb in the front row of the audience, dressed up in a dinner jacket which made him impossibly glamorous. He clapped and cheered, as she sashayed past him.

'Louise, shall we have a chat tonight?' Katie's voice dragged her back to the present.

'Let's make it tomorrow.'

Katie opened the door. 'Okay. I'll tell Joe we'll do another hour before lunch.'

'One thing before you go ...' Louise had been summoning up the courage to ask this question. 'You said someone called Matt came in asking for me.'

Katie pushed the door shut with her heel. 'Last week, you mean?'

'Yes. Did he say anything else?'

'No, just asked if you were here.'

'How did he seem?' Louise foraged around for suitable words. 'I mean – did he look unkempt? Or out of control at all?'

Katie shook her head. 'He was fine. Mind you, I didn't get the chance to say much to him because Maeve arrived and cornered him.'

'What do you mean *cornered him*?'

'She greeted him like a long lost friend and they went off together.'

'Out of the hotel?'

'Yes, I heard her asking him if he wanted a coffee. Why? Is there a problem?'

Louise shuffled papers on the desk. 'No, not at all. Matt's my ... well, I haven't heard from him for ages. I'm surprised Maeve didn't say anything about seeing him, that's all.'

*

Louise grabbed a moment to phone her mother. She didn't want to risk being overheard at the hotel, so she walked to the other end of The Hoe, her back for once turned to the sea. 'Mum, hi, can you talk?'

'Your father's having a lie down if that's what you mean.'

'So, he can't hear you?'

'He's snoring, so I doubt it. What's this about? Is it Matt?'

'No, I haven't heard from him.'

'What are you going to do? Any plans for a divorce?'

'Mum, this is not about Matt.' Louise heard the sharp note in her voice. 'Sorry, but I haven't got long and there's something I need to ask you. Has Maeve been round?'

'No, why?'

'You definitely haven't seen her today?'

'No. Is that what you wanted to ask me?'

Louise clamped the phone against her ear. 'No, but I had to make sure she wasn't there first.'

'I'm all ears; fire away.'

Louise pictured her mother in her chair near the window. If she stepped out onto the balcony, Louise would be able to wave at her. The distance between them was only the length of The Hoe, but a longing for her mother punched her in the chest. They'd spent a lot of time together when she first came back from London. She wouldn't have managed without her support.

'Go on then – what did you want to say?'

'I wanted to ask you about Maeve.'

'Why?'

'Did you or Dad ever have any issues with her? Did you find her difficult to work with?'

Her mother didn't answer. Louise waited, but the silence stretched her nerves. 'Mum? Did you hear?'

'Of course I heard. I was trying to decide how to respond.'

'You mean you did have some issues?'

'I didn't say that.'

Okay, so her mother was being cagey. What was she hiding? 'Let's just say I'm having a few problems with her. And I wondered if there was ever anything when you and Dad were at the hotel.'

'A word of warning, Louise.'

Louise held her breath. There was something. 'I know Dad thinks she's the bees' knees, but –'

'Drop it. Whatever it is you and Maeve have disagreed about, either forget it or compromise.'

'What are you saying, Mum? That I let her run rings round me?'

'Trust me on this one, Louise. Tread carefully, and don't antagonise Maeve.'

'What? You can't say something like that, and –'

'Sorry, darling, Tom's calling. I'll have to go.'

In the shower, water streamed down Louise's face and onto her shoulders. She watched the rivulets cascade over her breasts and dew-drops shine on her stomach. Her fingers traced the silver lines of stretch marks. She was glad she had them, these medals of pregnancy. They forged a permanent link between her and little Matilda, who'd lived for only half an hour. She lathered shampoo into her hair and massaged her scalp, her fingers pressing hard against her head. The shampoo stung her eyes.

She was wrapped in a towel and rubbing moisturiser into her legs when there was a knock at the door.

'Louise, are you there?'

Oh God, it was Seb. He wasn't due for ages yet. 'Hang on! Be with you in a minute.' She grabbed her robe from the back of her bedroom door, shaking her hair free of the towel and combing her fingers through it. She glanced in the mirror – her face looked scrubbed apart from a streak of black mascara across one cheek. She rubbed at it with her fist.

'Louise, it's me, Seb.'

She pulled open the door. 'I must have got the time wrong,' she said. 'I'm not ready.' Then she noticed he was wearing paint-stained jeans. The purple dress hanging on the wardrobe door reared up in her mind. She'd misjudged the whole evening. Going for dinner to Seb must mean grabbing a lasagne in the pub round the corner.

'Can I come in? I need to talk to you.' He didn't smile.

She opened the door wider, and he stepped inside.

'Would you like a drink?' she asked. 'Coffee, or I've got some lager in the fridge.'

'Nothing, thank you.'

'Is something wrong?' She took in the stubble on his chin, his eyes ringed with shadows. 'Have you had bad news? If it's the photo shoot, it doesn't matter. We can –'

'I need to tell you something.'

Louise's heart raced, each beat thudding harder than the one before. 'Go on.'

He ran his hands through his hair. 'Do you remember I told you I gave up my job in London and decided to try my hand at interior design when my marriage broke down?'

She nodded. 'You said it was something you'd always wanted to do.'

'Yes, and I don't regret the design part for one minute. Besides I wouldn't have met you otherwise.'

'What are you saying?'

He sat down, his hands clasped, his head bent. 'I'm still married. I go back to London most weekends. See my wife and children.'

'Children?' she whispered.

'Two boys. I've tried for their sake, but the marriage is over. My feelings for you have confirmed it.' He looked up. 'You must hate me for not telling you from the beginning, but I didn't know I would end up falling in love with you.'

His gaze pierced her, and she looked away, her eyes on

the floor. The cream rug was stained where she'd spilt a cup of coffee the other night. She'd scrubbed at it for ages, but the brown flecks remained.

'Talk to me, Louise. Tell me what you're thinking.'

Her head was a jumble. A wife and two children. A whole life she'd known nothing about. Did he make love to his wife when he went home?

Seb took one of Louise's hands. His skin was cold. 'I'm going back this weekend to tell her it's over. I don't want to start our relationship on a lie. It's too important for that.'

Her mouth was dry, her tongue sticking to the roof of her mouth. She swallowed, trying to find saliva.

'Do you hate me?'

She shook her head. How could she hate him with her own secret throbbing inside her?

Thirty-two

Ollie set up his stool tucked away in a corner of Campiello Barbaro. It was one thing to paint scenes from the apartment windows, but another to be exposed, in this city made for art and artists.

He took his palette and brushes from his rucksack, and set his bottles of water on the ground at his feet. His gaze ranged over the *campo*: the tree in the foreground, surrounded by a circle of grass, the moss-covered cast iron fountain, the back of a *palazzo* with its ornate windows. Where should his focus be? He glanced to the left, to the stippled canal. Of course, the scene had to be about the bridge.

He balanced the watercolour block on his knees. The rough paper would work best, its textured surface capturing the pigment. He mixed the colours he'd need for the sky and the water: cobalt blue, and then a touch of burnt sienna added for the part of the canal furthest away, and ultramarine for the foreground water. He pencilled in an outline of the bridge to fix the proportions in his mind, and then soaked his brush and covered the top part of the paper with a wet wash. While the wash dried, he did some rough drawings of the bridge in his sketch book.

'Hey, that's good!'

Ollie was pleased with the way the steps down from

the bridge had gone. He'd added a strong wash of French ultramarine and teased it around with a damp brush to add depth at the base. He was creating ripples in the water of the canal when the man's voice boomed over his left shoulder.

'Come and look at this, darl.'

A pair of red trainers with yellow laces approached. They stopped next to the black boots already at his side.

'I love it!' The female voice had a strong Australian accent. 'It's our bridge, Jason, isn't it?'

'It sure is.' The man crouched down, so that his eyes were level with Ollie's. 'Do you know, my wife and I came here on our honeymoon because of that darned bridge.'

'Did you?'

'Hey, darl, our artist is a Brit.'

The man's face was so close, Ollie could see the thread veins reddening his nose, and smell the spicy scent of his aftershave.

'Yes, this little lady fell in love with it in the film *Summertime*, and insisted we came here. Did you ever see that film?'

'No, I haven't.' Ollie wanted to add flecks of pink to the water to reflect the house above it, but needed to rinse his brush.

'Oh, you should.' The woman's piercing eyes and blonde hair falling round her shoulders reminded him of Jess. 'It's the most romantic film ever. Katharine Hepburn –'

'I don't see many films,' Ollie said.

The man put his arm round the woman's shoulder and pulled her close. 'How about I buy this painting as an anniversary present?'

'Oh, it's not for sale.' Ollie spread his hands over the painting.

The woman looked on the verge of tears. 'But it's wonderful. You've captured the bridge perfectly.' She turned to her husband. 'Can't you persuade him to sell it?'

Ollie stood up, knocking his stool over. It crashed onto the jar, sending it flying, and paint water splashed over the woman's trainers.

'I'm sorry.' He grabbed a cloth and dabbed at the dirty stains.

She touched him on the shoulder. 'No worries. They're an old pair of sneakers.'

He straightened up. 'That was really clumsy of me.'

She was grinning, a toothpaste-advert sort of grin. 'But there is one way you can redeem yourself.'

'Hey, darl, you're one clever girl.' The man kissed his wife on each cheek and turned back to Ollie. 'You can make it up to us by selling us the painting.'

They were persistent – Ollie had to give them that. 'Okay, it's yours. But I don't want any money.'

'Are you crazy?' The man pulled a brown leather wallet from his shirt pocket. He thumbed through the notes. 'How about this?' He handed Ollie a fifty-euro note.

'It's too much. I can't take it.'

The man brushed Ollie's protests aside. 'Do you have something we can put it in to protect it?'

'Jason, the shop gave us this for the calendar.' The woman took out a manila envelope with a stiff backing from her shoulder bag. 'It's perfect.'

Ollie stared after the couple as they crossed the *campo* and climbed the bridge, arms entwined. Pausing on the top, they waved. Maybe they would put the painting on their wall when they got home to Australia, above the shelf decorated with Murano glass animals. 'Honey, do you remember the artist who didn't want to part with his painting?' the woman would say when their anniversary came round. And he'd laugh, a loud ready sound. 'Strange guy,' he'd say. 'Fancy not wanting to sell your work.'

Ollie was packing up his stuff when a man stopped next to him. '*Buon giorno,*' he said. He was wearing the gondolier's striped shirt and black trousers and a straw hat with a red ribbon hung from his hand. He gestured towards the palette and the sketchbook. '*Sei un artista*?'

'*Si. Acquerelli*. Watercolours. Do you paint?'

The man replied in a stream of rapid Italian. His tone was aggressive.

Ollie didn't understand a word. '*Inglese*,' he said. 'Do you speak English?'

The man pointed again at Ollie's painting equipment. 'You have licence?'

Ollie frowned. 'What licence?'

'To occupy public space.'

'You mean I can't just sit and paint?'

'Need licence to sell.'

'*Grazie*.' Ollie turned away. He piled his paints and palette into his rucksack, conscious of the man's eyes watching every move.

On the way back to the apartment, Ollie stopped off at the newspaper stand next to Accademia Bridge. He selected a postcard: gondolas tied to their mooring posts at Piazza San Marco. He'd sent Flo several already, but she hadn't replied. Resting on his rucksack, he wrote: *The gondolas glide up and down the Grand Canal. Perhaps one day soon, you'll be here to see them, sweetheart. I miss you, Daddy x*. He called in at a *tabacchi* and bought stamps for *Inghilterra*. He dropped the card into a post box. It landed with a soft plop.

The front door slammed shut behind Ollie, and Fabbio's head appeared from the downstairs apartment. Wood shavings clung to his T-shirt and tight black jeans.

'Ah, Signor Oliver!' He flicked back his mane of black hair. 'You have good day?'

Ollie thought of the fifty euros in his back pocket. 'Yes, very good.'

Fabbio turned away. 'Come with me.'

Ollie put down his rucksack and stool. When he reached the doorway of the apartment, he stopped. A line was strung across the room with washing hanging from it. He stared at the bra, a pair of panties, a petticoat. Items of clothing hung from hooks around the walls: a raincoat, jeans, a shirt: they were all made from wood.

'Is good, yes?' Fabbio's mouth spread wide in a grin.

The folds in the raincoat, the cuffs on the shirt, the straps of the bra were chiselled meticulously. 'They're amazing,' he said. 'What wood do you use?'

'Crimolo, an old Italian pine from the Dolomites.'

Ollie ducked under the washing line and reached out to the coat. The wood was smooth and soft to the touch.

Fabbio was nodding and smiling. 'The signora, she loved them.'

'Angel? She's seen them?'

'*Si*. She come in this morning. I give her cappuccino *e cioccolato* éclair.' He put his fingers to his lips and kissed them. 'Tonoli's at the end of the *calle* – the best *pasticceria* in all Venice.'

Ollie backed away towards the door. 'Thank you for showing me your work.'

'È un *piacere*. Any time.'

The apartment was empty when Ollie reached it. He put his painting things away in the studio and flicked the switch on the kettle. Angel had been as good as her word: after the first few days when they'd explored the city together, she'd left him alone to paint. She'd return in the afternoons full of the places she'd been to, the sights she'd seen. Her descriptions were so vivid, he felt as if he'd crossed to the Lido on the *vaporetto*, haggled at the Rialto fish market, cried as the thought of the Jews herded into the Ghetto.

Angel had taught him the meaning of the different street names: *ria terra*, a filled in canal; *fondamenta*, a pavement running beside a canal; *calle*, a street running between buildings. 'If you understand the names, you understand some of the history,' she said. 'Like our street, Calle dei Preti o del Pistor.'

'That's a right mouthful,' Ollie said. 'What does it mean?'

'The priests and the baker.'

He'd laughed. 'Religion and bread. What more do you need?'

But that afternoon, without Angel there, he felt jumpy, oppressed somehow by the quiet. He didn't fancy coffee after all and went to the fridge. There was half a bottle of white wine from the previous evening and he poured a glass. He stood looking out of the kitchen window at the people crossing the bridge. A woman was bumping a pushchair up the steps. Every time they reached another step, the child clapped. He let the lace curtain fall and turned away.

Angel had left her laptop open on the table. He could check if information on the artist's licence was available. He gulped back some wine and sat down. Clicking on the mouse, he waited for the screen to come to life, but instead of the browser, a document headed *Venice Reflections* appeared. He started to read.

Ghosts

Afterwards, crossing the water
to return from cemetery to city,
the *vaporetto*'s feathered wake.

Dead children tug at my wrists;
I drag the weight of their unknown lives
with me through the twists of narrow *calli*.

Ollie looked up from the laptop. So this was what Angel had been writing. He didn't go to the cemetery on the island of San Michele with her, but he recalled how upset she'd been afterwards. He turned back to the screen.

My eyes stare back from shop windows,
fainter than the dazzling masks
patterned with a theatre of bright colours.

Behind the curves and cut-outs…
air in place of faces. Next door, handless
gloves in pairs of flattened leather.

Stitched with buttons and bows,
man-sized and child fingers;
their softness distanced by glass.

No more warmth within them
than the rows of *bambini* graves
with their photos and dates: *nata*

and *morta* engraved almost hand
in hand. Even the tourists shushed
by the cypresses' sad whispers.

The full moon now a night mask,
the porcelain face of a not-quite baby doll,
while the gloves beside my window self

are the pinned ghosts of shadow lives.
I imagine squeezing my hand
to fit these neat stitched seams,
then clapping life into cold fingers.

The cypresses' sad whispers. The full moon now a night mask.
The words were haunting. He repeated the lines 'Nata.

Morta. Nata. Morta. Born. Died. Born. Died.' His night-mares drummed in his brain, Flo's fingers slipping from his grasp, the drop to death below.

Feet sounded on the stairs and he snapped shut the laptop. Angel hadn't mentioned she was writing poetry, and he didn't want to be caught snooping. The door crashed against the wall and she staggered into the room.

Ollie jumped up. 'Are you okay?'

She carried shopping bags in each hand and was breathing heavily. 'Good job we're not far from the supermarket.'

'I'd have come with you if I'd known.' He took the bags from her.

'I wasn't sure what time you'd be back. Your first day out painting.' She crossed to the kitchen area and started unpacking the shopping. 'How did it go?'

'I've got some news.' Ollie poured her a glass of wine.

'Okay, that's the perishable stuff put away.' She settled down on the sofa and pulled the beret from her head. 'Sounds exciting.'

Her brown curls twisted in corkscrews, and Ollie had to resist the urge to reach out and smooth them. 'Here's your wine,' he said. 'You won't believe what's happened.'

'Try me.'

'I sold my painting.'

She laughed. 'Ollie, that's wonderful. What was it?'

'Ponte San Christoforo.'

'My favourite bridge.'

He raised his glass. 'It's thanks to you I went there.' He leant forward to kiss her cheek. She turned at that moment and their mouths collided. Her lips tasted of wine.

She pulled away. 'I'm pleased for you, Ollie.'

Over supper of grilled mackerel and roasted vegetables, Angel told him about her day. 'I got off the *vaporetto* at

Giardini and walked to Sant' Elena. It's completely different down there, very quiet and green. And I saw this amazing sculpture.'

'Oh?'

'It's half hidden in the water, and I almost missed it.' She put down her knife and fork. 'It's a woman lying on her side. She looks as if the tide has washed her up, but she can't reach the land. There's seaweed wrapped round her limbs, and they're massive. Her bare feet are huge.' Angel picked up her fork again and speared a piece of red pepper. 'This is going to sound totally stupid, but I wanted to lie down next to the woman. The sea would have been freezing, but in some mad way I imagined my warmth seeping into her.' She met Ollie's eyes. 'Crazy, aren't I?'

At the beginning of November, the weather turned cold. It seemed as if the knife-like wind would never stop blowing. Sometimes Ollie could hardly hold the paint brush, his fingers were so stiff. Angel came home from the market and said it was called the Bora, which occurred when cold air crossed the mountains and descended to the coast. 'Fuck the Bora! Fuck the Bora!' Ollie stamped his feet and blew on his hands to get the circulation moving.

One day he set up his easel in Piscina San Samuele. The triangular-shaped building there fascinated him. He'd been back several times to study the effects of light striking the walls at different times of day. On that particular morning, another artist was working at the other end of the square, and Ollie nodded to him as he sorted out his paints and palette.

It had been drizzling earlier, and the smoky quality the rain lent to the light was fabulous. While he painted, sounds of a piano drifted from one of the apartments above him. A light, tinkling that ricocheted off the wall opposite, swelling its volume. Then a man's voice shouted, a door slammed, and the music stopped.

He was about to pack up because his feet were numb when an American stopped to admire his work. The man said he'd like to buy the painting and asked if Ollie had others he could see. Ollie showed him one of Ponte dei Pugni, and another of the view from Guidecca across to St Mark's: the man said he'd take all three. 'I'm always on the lookout for good watercolours,' he said, 'and these are spectacular. Can you give me your email?' Ollie couldn't believe it. He rolled up the paintings, and tucked the notes the man gave him into his wallet.

As his buyer walked away, Ollie heard a noise behind him. He turned round and saw two men in the uniform of the *carabinieri* standing with the other artist. They were gesticulating at him, their hands on the guns at their waist. His heart pounded. He'd applied for a licence, but the amount of red tape was a minefield. He bundled his paints and palette into his rucksack and strode off, not daring to look back.

For the next few days he painted in the apartment, but eventually, lured by watery and diffuse winter sunlight, he risked going out again. He got up early and caught the *vaporetto* to San Zaccharia. Tourists usually swarmed around there, but it was eerily empty at that hour of the morning. He set up his painting things near the water, close to where the gondoliers moored their boats for the night. He wanted to catch the dawn striking the church of San Giorgio Maggiore across the wide basin of the lagoon. The tide was high and little waves slopped over the edge, almost reaching his boots. He soaked his brush with water and added raw sienna. He applied the wash to the paper, adding ultramarine blue into the wet paint and graduating it down.

Where the light glimmered to the left of the church, he painted yellow ochre to warm the sky. Around him, the city came to life: pigeons roosting in the eaves of St Mark's Basilica swooped down to peck at the ground; yawning tourists appeared from their hotels; a boat from Hotel Cipriani over on Guidecca bobbed across the waves. Ollie drew in the outline of the church. He'd have to wait until the wash was completely dry before he could paint it.

By about ten o'clock, he'd done as much as he could and he headed back to the apartment. He stopped at Tonoli's on the corner and bought cakes. As he climbed the stairs, he heard a male voice. He raced up to the top floor and pushed open the door.

Angel was lying on the sofa, a rug covering her. Fabbio knelt beside her, clasping her hand in his. They both looked up, surprise in their eyes, and Fabbio leapt to his feet.

'What's happened?' Ollie asked. He dropped his rucksack on the floor. 'Are you all right?' He perched at the end of the sofa near Angel's feet.

'Ow!' Her shout reverberated in his ears.

Fabbio patted her shoulder.

'What's going on?' Ollie stared at Fabbio's hand on Angel's pink jumper. Black hairs covered his fingers, and sprouted down the side of his hands and up to his wrists.

'I've hurt my ankle,' Angel said. 'I was coming back from the vegetable boat and I tripped on the bridge. The steps were slippery in the rain.'

'You poor thing. It's not broken, is it?' Ollie lifted the rug. Her ankle was swollen and a bruise was spreading over the entire foot.

'I don't think so, but it really hurt when I tried to put any weight on it.' Angel touched Fabbio's hand. 'Luckily Fabbio came along, and he half carried me back to the apartment.'

'I bet he did.'

'What?'

'It doesn't matter.' Ollie knelt down beside the sofa. 'Have you taken any painkillers?'

'We haven't long been back.'

'You need an ice pack on that ankle, and it should be elevated.' Ollie looked up at Fabbio. 'Can you go to a chemist for us?'

Fabbio spread his hands wide. 'Chemist?'

'Pharmacy?'

'Ah, *farmacia*.'

'Yes, *farmacia*. Do you understand – an ice pack? Cold. *Freddo*.'

'*Si, si*, I go.'

Ollie breathed out as the door slammed behind Fabbio. Angel's eyes were closed, deep grooves between her brows and round her mouth where her lips were drawn tight.

'I'll get the painkillers,' he said. 'If it's not better tomorrow, we'll have to go to a doctor.'

Angel didn't answer. Her eyelids flickered as if she was drifting off to sleep. He leaned forward and stroked her hair.

Thirty-three

Ollie woke with a start. The shutters were closed and darkness engulfed him. There was a noise. A weird, dragging sort of sound. He sat up. There it was again. His scalp prickled. It was here inside the apartment. A dragging, and a soft moan.

He leapt from the bed. Two paces and he was at the door, flicking the light switch. Angel was clinging to the door frame of the bathroom, pain etched across her face. She blinked in the sudden glare.

'Why didn't you call me?' He took her in his arms. Her nightdress, damp with sweat, clung to her, and he was aware of her soft breasts against his chest.

'Sorry,' she whimpered. 'I need the loo, but my ankle ...'

'It's okay. I'll help you.' He put his arm round her waist and half carried her into the bathroom. 'I'll wait outside. Call me when you're ready.' He closed the door and slid down the wall to the floor. He was only wearing boxer shorts and he shivered as the cold air settled on his skin.

The loo flushed, and he heard the sound of running water.

'Ollie.' Her voice was different, not at all her usual rich, deep tone.

'I'm here.'

The door opened, and she stood there balancing on one leg. The other was bent, her swollen ankle dangling in mid-air. He put one arm round her back and hooked the other behind her knees. 'Ready?' She circled her hands behind his head. Her palms felt sweaty as if she had a temperature. He swung her up and edged sideways out of the bathroom and into her bedroom. Her hair tickled his cheek. It smelt of sunshine and oranges. He lowered her onto the bed, and she sank back, breathing heavily. The bedside lamp cast soft shadows on her face, highlighting her cheekbones. He remembered their kiss and the sweetness of her mouth.

'Can you get me a clean nightie from the middle drawer, please?' she said.

He turned away as she pulled the flimsy material over her head and flung the old one on the floor.

'Anything else?' he asked. 'More painkillers?'

She opened her eyes. 'I took some while I was in the bathroom.'

He resettled the pillow under her foot. 'Try to keep it raised. I'll leave my door open. Call if you need me.'

'Don't go.'

'But ...'

'I don't want to be on my own. Stay and talk to me.' She patted the bed. 'Come in or you'll get cold.'

'Are you sure?'

'Yes.'

'Okay. I'll be back in a minute.'

He switched off the light in his room and went into the kitchen. He turned the tap on and poured a glass of water. A lamp on the building opposite cast an orange glow on the inky water of the canal. Was he doing the right thing? 'It would be as friends,' he'd said to Angel. What else could he offer her when his whole life was messed up? And yet, now they were here, he wanted more. He'd been ready to punch Fabbio when he got home and found him bending over Angel. He drained the glass and the cold water burned his gullet.

'Ollie.'

'Be there in a second.' He rinsed the glass and stood it on the draining board. His fingers lingered on it. When he took his hand away, he would have decided, and he didn't want to get this wrong.

He slid into bed next to Angel and pulled up the cover.

She shuffled closer until her head was resting on his shoulder. 'Ollie, can I ask you something?'

He leaned back and squinted down at her. 'Why does that question make me nervous?'

'Are you happy?'

It was the sort of question he would have run away from before. Would have prevaricated and quibbled: *What's happiness? Happiness is transitory. How can you know if you're happy?* He remembered the song he used to sing with Flo when she was little: *If you're happy and you know it, clap your hands. If you're happy and you know it, stamp your feet.* That was where happiness belonged – in a child's world of hand clapping and foot stamping. But that was then. Now, happiness seemed a reality. It was Angel. She had this gift of spreading tranquillity like a crisp white sheet freshly laundered.

'You make me happy,' he said.

She kissed his shoulder. 'What a lovely thing to say.'

'The only thing that stops me feeling happy is Flo. I miss her so much.'

'Is it really bad?'

'I have horrible dreams. The same ones over and over again.'

'Do you want to tell me.'

He hesitated. Talking about them might only make them worse.

'Come on. It's not good to bottle things up.'

'There's one where we're out for a walk, and she slips over the edge of a cliff. It's a drop of several hundred feet, and I'm hanging onto her hand, but her fingers keep sliding away. I'm trying to shout for help, but ...'

Angel stroked her hand across his chest. 'Cry if you need to. I know how hard it is.'

'You don't! You don't!' He pushed her hand away. 'How can you?'

'Let me explain.'

'What?'

'I know I haven't got a child, but I do understand loss. How it peels away layers of skin, eats into you.'

Ollie heard the break in her voice. 'Go on.' He lay very still.

She turned off the bedside light. 'I can only talk about this in the dark. It happened ten years ago, but even now I can't expose it to the light.'

'I'm listening.'

'When I was doing my degree, I fell in love with Justin, another student. He was studying medicine. He was four years older than me, and as soon as I finished university, we got married. He was a junior doctor in A and E, and one morning, he texted me and said he was leaving the hospital shortly. I got up, had a shower, and started cooking bacon and egg. He was always starving after a long shift. There was a knock at the door. I thought it was him, forgotten his key. It was the police. He'd fallen asleep at the wheel and been in a head-on smash.'

'Oh, my God.' Ollie cradled Angel in his arms. 'I'm so sorry.'

'We'd only been married for two months.'

He kissed her mouth, her cheeks, her eyelids. Her tears tasted salty. He placed his lips in the hollow of her throat. Her pulse throbbed against his mouth.

'I want to look after you,' he whispered. 'I won't let anything bad happen to you again.'

'What about something good?'

He hardly dared breathe. 'What did you have in mind?'

'Make love to me.'

It was several days before Angel was able to hobble round the apartment. Ollie shopped and cooked, and after he'd helped her to shower and dress, he carried her to the sofa. Her convalescence coincided with days of heavy rain, and they spent the time talking.

'I'm scared I'll lose Flo forever,' he said, following yet another phone call where he'd met a brick wall. Flo was always out, busy or didn't want to talk to him. Just once she'd come to the phone.

'How are you?' he asked.

'Good.' She sounded distant, not his little girl.

'How's school?'

'Good.'

'Are you having much homework?'

'No.'

There was something he had to know. He shouldn't ask, but he couldn't stop himself. 'Are you still living with Nana and Grandad?' He couldn't stand it if she was in the same house as that prick.

'I've got to go now.'

He'd thrown his mobile across the room and flung himself onto the bed. Angel lay down next to him and stroked his back.

He turned to face her. 'It's my fault, isn't it?'

'Why do you say that?'

'I shouldn't have run away. I should have stayed and fought for her.'

'You tried.'

He sat up. 'Not hard enough. I couldn't stand it when she stopped talking to me.' He remembered that awful day when she went off with Belinda rather than him.

'Do you want to go back?'

He thought about it: no work, knocking on gallery doors again. Eugene was rich; he could give Jess and Flo whatever they wanted. 'I don't know.'

'There's your painting. You're just starting to get sales.'

'Suppose I give it another couple of months?' he said. 'If I can sell more paintings, get a few contacts, I'll have something to offer Flo.'

'Sounds a good idea.'

'Would you come with me?'

'Of course.' She wrapped her arms round him. 'I love you. I always have.'

Another day, he told her about the rows with his father. 'I don't want to run a hotel, but I hate myself for disappointing him.'

'And what if you'd taken on the hotel and given up painting?' Angel was sitting at the table, slicing mushrooms.

'I'd have hated him instead.'

'It's hard for me to understand – my parents didn't mind what I did as long as I was happy.'

Ollie stopped stirring the Bolognese sauce he was making. 'I suppose it's different when there's a family business to consider, but my father took it too far. He put the hotel before everything, even my mum.'

'Still, wouldn't you feel better if you made it up with him?'

The sauce had thickened and smelt good. 'I guess I would. And do you know what I've just realised?'

'What?'

'I've done the same thing – put painting first.' He laughed.

'Don't tell me I'm like the old man after all!'

It seemed no matter how many hours passed, their conversation never ran dry. While Angel read or wrote in her notebook, he painted in his studio, but after an hour or so he missed her. Her wild curly hair. Her freckles. Her wonky little finger. The air of stillness that surrounded her. Why on earth hadn't he seen it before? Even Fabbio, who called in every day to see how Angel was, didn't irritate him now he realised he'd been jealous.

At the beginning of December, the weather was foggy and damp. Mist veiled *calli*, trailed across *campos*, hung over the canals. The days passed in permanent twilight. Although it was not the intense cold of the Bora, the damp chilled Ollie to the core. The mist added another dimension to the interplay of light and water, so he forced himself out each day, but managed only a couple of hours before retreating to the warmth of the apartment. Angel had made friends with a couple of Australian girls who were working as interns at the Peggy Guggenheim museum, and sometimes she met up with them for coffee or lunch.

One day when she was out, he opened up the laptop and clicked on the *Venice Reflections* folder. He scrolled past *Ghosts,* to the next poem, *Ponte San Christoforo.* That was the bridge he'd painted, the one Angel had discovered and taken him to. He scanned the words.

> Almost a wedding picture. The waterfall
> of steps fans downwards to the *campiello*
> like the ivoried flounces of a bride's train.
>
> Brick buildings bless cream stone with hints
> of cherry: the pink of rosé wine.
> Or soft lips. The curves of arches, trees

and window boxes filled with the petals
of a live confetti fixed in wide-angled stillness.
Sunlight glosses my perfect photo.

The bridge? Not a frown, but a mouth
opened in rippling smile with the water.
The lapping sound of their gentle kiss.

Gondola couples glide through and past;
their eyes entwined, oblivious to footsteps
crossing over. I watch the day deepen

until the last splash of rosé tilts
the skyline towards sleep. All bridges
now the mouths of half-sighs;

the water a tongue curved
towards the city's heart.

He read the poem a second time. The description of the
bridge – *The waterfall of steps* – was exactly what he'd tried
to paint. The words evoked the scene as vividly as his picture. He moved on to another poem.

La Resistenza

the sculpture for Venezia alla partigiana

No mermaid; her legs locked heavy
and useless behind her, cast
to lie alone by the Giardini.

That was the sculpture Angel had raved about. He still
hadn't seen it – he'd gone to look one day, but it had been
high tide and scarcely visible.

Muscles bound in bronze, dressed
in seaweed rags. The bare soles of broad feet
made for standing steady.

Tides shiver across her green skin,
wash away the sunlight
before her flesh has time to warm.

Yet, strength shines from her lone stance,
the sculpted poise and grace
with which she holds her weight

against incessant water and skies.
There is song still in her lungs
for those with the will to hear it.

Ollie repeated the words aloud: *Tides shiver across her green skin, wash away the sunlight before her flesh has time to warm.* That was what Angel had said – she'd wanted to warm the woman. He read the poem again. It might have been about the sculpture, but it could just as easily be a description of Angel: *the sculpted poise and grace with which she holds her weight ...There is song still in her lungs for those with the will to hear it.*

He checked the time. Two-thirty – she'd be back soon. One more, he'd read one more.

'What are you doing?'

He looked round at the voice. It was Angel, her arms full of shopping, her hair glassy with raindrops.

She kicked the door shut behind her. 'I said what are you doing?'

Thirty-four

'You must be thrilled to have inherited this wonderful, historic hotel, Louise.' Jasmine from *Beautiful Hotels* was recording the interview on her smart phone. 'How did you feel when you found out your father was giving it to you?'

They were sitting in the lounge. Flames leapt from the logs burning in the huge fireplace. Louise glanced up at the portrait of Jasper Anderson, the first owner of the hotel. Blood on his hands through slavery, her mother had told her once. 'But don't mention it to your father. He won't hear of anything that taints the Anderson line.' Old Jasper's eyes were narrowed, his mouth set. *You'd better do us proud, girl,* his expression warned.

'I had mixed feelings,' she said.

Jasmine raised her eyebrows. 'Oh, why was that?'

'On the one hand, I was delighted because I've always loved the hotel. But my dad was handing it over as a result of illness, which obviously I wasn't happy about.'

'And what have been your biggest challenges so far?' Jasmine crossed and uncrossed her legs. She was wearing pink tights and purple ankle boots. 'It can't have been easy.'

'The challenges?' Louise repeated. God, where should she start?

'I know our readers would love to hear what goes on behind the scenes.'

'It's certainly been an interesting few months.'

'Yes?'

'Running a big hotel is ...' *Choose your words carefully,* Jasper Anderson boomed. '... not easy.'

'I'm sure it's not.' Jasmine tapped her pen against her teeth. 'Perhaps if you could outline one or two challenges for our readers. You know – difficult guests, unpaid bills, managing staff – chefs for example. They're temperamental, aren't they?'

'Oh no. Chef is a dream, a total professional. He's organised a lovely buffet for this afternoon.'

'And the other staff?'

Louise met Jasmine's gaze. Why was she going on about staff? Perhaps she'd heard something. Had Maeve been complaining about her? Since their row, Maeve had watched one of the training videos, although she'd made no attempt to use the computers. She spent the day drifting round the hotel, chatting and smiling at everyone. Something was brewing.

'The Plymouth has a number of long-serving staff,' Louise began. 'They were used to my father and his way of doing things. I wouldn't have been surprised if they'd found it difficult to adjust to a new person.' She hesitated, savouring the expectant look on Jasmine's face. 'But without exception, they've proved loyal and supportive. In fact, I couldn't have managed without them.'

'What are you most proud of so far?' Jasmine asked.

Louise's eyes moved to Jasper Anderson again. *See, I'm doing okay. We Andersons are made of stern stuff.* 'Our bookings have largely held steady.' Not strictly true, but Jasmine didn't need to know that. 'In fact, we're noticing an upturn since the introduction of our computerised system.' The upturn hadn't come yet, but it would – Louise was sure of it.

'The new foyer has been much admired, and we're hoping to move on to the rest of the hotel as soon as possible.'

'And Seb Flanders ...' Jasmine paused. 'Will you work with him again?'

'Seb has a great feel for the period of the hotel, and I'd love to see what ideas he has.'

'Louise.' Katie poked her head round the door. 'Your parents are here.'

Louise jumped up. 'Thanks. I'll be right out.'

'I'll come with you.' Jasmine turned off her recorder.

'I'd rather have a couple of moments on our own. It's the first time they've seen the new foyer.'

'Fab! I can get their immediate impressions.'

Louise thrust her hands behind her back. 'Please wait until I call you, Jasmine. It's likely to be emotional for them.'

Jasmine's otherwise smooth brow puckered. 'As you like.'

Louise hesitated in the doorway. Her mother and father were standing just inside the hotel entrance. They were holding hands, and looked small and lost in the big space.

'Mum, Dad, great to see you.' She crossed the foyer and hugged each of them. 'Thanks for coming. The *Beautiful Hotels* people are here. They want to get some photos, and perhaps ask you one or two questions.'

Her father had put his dark suit on, the one he wore for special occasions, and it hung loosely on him. His gaze ranged over the foyer, checking every inch of it.

'It's lovely, isn't it, Tom?' Louise's mother had a fixed smile on her face, and she nudged his arm.

'Your mother said it was green.'

'It's called pea green, Dad. Apparently, it was a popular colour in the Georgian period.'

'Same as all this gold stuff, I suppose. It looks dramatic, I'll give it that.' He waved his hand in the direction of the walls. 'I don't know what was wrong with magnolia.'

Louise took them over to the desk to introduce them to Katie.

'I love the paper on this wall,' her mother said. 'Very sumptuous, isn't it, Tom?'

Her father nodded, but Louise saw his attention was focused on the two computers. She crossed her fingers.

He straightened his jacket and cleared his throat.

Was this it? What was coming?

'It's not as bad as I expected, Louise.' He smiled. 'Well done.'

She hugged him. 'Thanks, Dad.' The smell of his after-shave sent her careering back to the days when he was fit and strong. Her dad who could conquer the world.

'Just one thing,' he said.

'Yes?' Her heart thudded.

'Where's the grandfather clock?'

She knew she should have insisted on a place for it in the foyer. 'It's in store at the moment, but –'

'It will be in here though?' Her father twisted round. 'What about there? If you squash up the sofa, you should be able to fit it in.'

'Yes, Dad. I'll get it sorted.'

There was a noise over by the door. Seb had arrived with the photographer, and Maeve was with them. 'Oh, here's Seb Flanders, the designer.' She felt her cheeks flushing as she said his name. 'You must meet him.'

Maeve hovered round them while Louise completed the introductions.

'You've done a wonderful job, Mr Flanders,' her mother said.

'Please call me Seb.' He glanced at Louise. 'Everybody does.'

'It must take tremendous vision. I can't visualise what a room will look like from a minute paint sample and a scrap of material.'

'I know what you mean,' Seb said.

Louise kept her shoulder turned, but somehow Maeve contrived to be in her eye line. 'Maeve, perhaps you'd ask Jasmine to come through. She can organise the photographer now Mum and Dad are here.'

The photographer was called Elaine; she was very tall and very thin, emphasised by skin-tight white jeans. Bracelets clattered up and down her arm as she wielded her camera. She took photos of Louise and her father, Louise and both her parents, Louise on her own.

'Look up.'... 'Look at each other.' ...'Come on, give me a bit more.' ...'Let's have a smile: it will soon be Christmas.' The bracelets jangled. 'Wonderful.' ... 'Pretty.' ... 'Super. Now, shall we have one of you, Seb, with Louise?'

'Yeah, sure.' The corners of Seb's mouth lifted in a half smile, and he gave a little shrug. His blue eyes slid past hers.

'That's wonderful!' Elaine clicked her camera repeatedly. 'Just one more. I'd like you both to turn inward and look towards the mirror.'

Louise and Seb moved closer together. His arm touched hers: he must be able to feel her trembling. Seb's face was inches away. She'd had a wedding photo in this pose. Seb wasn't smiling. Still couldn't meet her eyes. She knew it: he was going to stay with his wife.

'Fantastic. I've got everything I need.' Elaine was studying her camera. 'All yours now, Jasmine.'

As Louise turned away, she caught a whisper, not much more than a sigh of air: *Louise*. It was Seb. 'Can we talk later?'

'Where?'

'The bar on the front. Where we met before.'

'Seven?'

He nodded. 'Seven.' And moved away.

She called to Katie at the desk. 'Can you have the buffet brought into the lounge, please?'

Louise waved good bye to Jasmine and Elaine. 'It's been great. Thank you.'

Jasmine had gone out of her way to put her parents at ease. She'd listened patiently while Louise's father related details of every single Anderson who had owned the hotel, leading up to himself: 'And now Louise.' He beamed.

'So, this is an historic occasion,' Jasmine said. 'The first time the inheritance has passed from father to daughter.'

'That's right,' her mother had said quickly.

Louise remained waving until the taxi turned right at the bottom of Elliot Street. Thank God: it had been a success.

Louise crossed the foyer to the lounge, expecting her parents to be waiting for her.

But only her mother was there, on the sofa chatting to Seb.

'This young man's been telling me all about his work.' She touched Seb on the arm. 'I think he's so talented.'

'Where's Dad?'

'He said he wanted a wander round. He's chuffed to bits to be back in the place.'

'I'll see if I can find him. We can wander round together.' Louise shut the door.

She glanced in the dining room, and the smaller sitting room they called the snug. She checked the kitchen but the staff said he hadn't been in there. She raced up to the flat, but that was empty.

Downstairs, she stopped at the desk. 'Have you seen my father anywhere?'

Katie pointed. 'He's in your office, I think.'

Louise made out the silhouette of someone sitting at the

desk. She patted her pocket: the key was there. Her father had handed over all his keys when they signed the papers. Perhaps he'd kept the office one for old times' sake. She raked her mind for what she'd left on the desk: the invoice for the new computer system. The notes she'd made in preparation for another meeting with Maeve. It had been such a rush this morning.

She pushed open the office door. Her father was slumped over the desk, his forehead almost touching the keyboard.

'Dad!' She darted forward. 'Are you okay?'

He raised his head and turned his face towards her. She was expecting pallor, sweaty skin. Instead, tears streamed down his cheeks.

'Dad, whatever's wrong?' She grabbed some tissues and held them out. He made no attempt to take them.

She dropped to her knees, wiping a tissue over his cheeks. 'What is it? What's happened?'

He shook his head, his hands gripping her arms. She took one of them and rubbed it. It felt icy cold.

'Tell me,' she said. 'Has someone upset you, or do you hate the foyer?'

'I miss it,' he muttered. 'I miss it every second of every day.'

'Oh, Dad.' She wrapped her arms round his waist. His head rested on her shoulder, and wet from his tears seeped through her top. 'It must be tough for you.'

He sat up abruptly and dragged the tissue across his face. 'I'm a stupid old man. Don't take any notice.'

'Of course you're not. You put everything into this place.' She straightened his tie as she'd seen her mother do countless times. 'I'm sure I'd feel the same.'

'You're doing a great job.' He ran the back of his hand over her cheek. 'Can't say I'd have chosen pea-green myself, but it looks good, I'll give you that.'

'You don't know how relieved I am to hear you say that.'

Louise stood up. 'But it's hard for you being right next door. Why don't you take Mum away for a few days or even longer? Have some fun and forget about the hotel.'

'Your mum keeps on at me about that, but this place is in my soul. And there's your brother as well. I can hardly think about him without my stupid eyes watering.'

The door of the office swung open. Louise turned, expecting to see her mother, but it was Maeve.

'Here you are, Tommy,' she said. 'I've been searching for you.'

Louise looked from her father to Maeve and back again. *Tommy*?

'You've not been crying, have you?' Maeve said.

He shoved the tissue in his pocket. 'Course I haven't.'

'Come on, you silly fool.' Maeve pulled him to his feet. 'Let's get out of here.'

'Wait,' Louise said. 'I'll get Mum.'

Maeve manoeuvred Louise's father through the door. 'No need to worry her. I'll take him back to the apartment. Now, no more crying, Tommy, do you hear me?'

Louise ran to the lounge. Her mother and Seb were looking at something together, their heads close.

'Mum, you need to come.'

Her mother twisted round. 'What is it? It's not Tom?'

'He's upset, and Maeve insisted on taking him back. I think you ought to be there.'

'Oh. She'll take care of him.' There was something in her voice. An edge, Louise had never heard before. She moved round the sofa and sat down next to her mother. 'What is it, Mum?'

Her mother was staring down at a photo album on her lap: some of Seb's work Louise surmised. She looked across and caught his eye.

He nodded. 'I've got things to do. I'll leave you to it,' he said. 'It's been lovely to meet you, Lindy.' He stood up. 'See you again soon, I hope.' His eyes jumped to Louise, and her heart did a little dance. 'Keep the album for now. I'd love to know what you think.'

Louise's mother seemed to come out of a trance. 'Yes, yes. You must come over.' She patted Louise on the hand. 'Make sure you bring Seb to see us.'

Louise took the album and laid it on the coffee table. Her mother continued to stare at her lap as if it was still there.

'Mum, something's wrong, isn't it?'

'I don't know what you mean.' Her mother twisted her hands round and round. The knuckles bulged, and her wedding ring was cutting into her flesh.

'It's Maeve,' Louise said. 'There's too much stuff stacking up against her.'

'Maeve's worked at the hotel for a long time.'

'But she called Dad *Tommy*.' The logs in the grate shifted, sending a shower of sparks up the chimney. 'He's never been known as Tommy, has he? Stupid baby name.'

'There are things you're better not knowing.'

A knot tightened in Louise's stomach. *Don't antagonise Maeve*, her mother had said.

'A secret, you mean.'

Her mother flapped her hands around her head, as if her hair had been invaded by a swarm of insects. She'd always hated secrets. 'It will come out in the end', she used to say.

'I have to work with Maeve.' Louise said. 'Her attitude is not good for the hotel. She does what she wants, when she wants. I can't have someone like that in the place.'

Her mother's mouth was pinched, and her skin looked bleached, as if the blood had leaked away. 'Okay, I'll tell you, but when I do, you'll wish I hadn't.'

'I'm listening.'

'Your father had an affair with Maeve –'

'What! That's crazy.'

'Louise, I would never have told you this, but I can see the situation is impossible.'

Her mother was wearing a dress which Louise didn't recognise: blue silk with white spots. Her hair had been newly blow-dried, and her eyes looked pretty with grey shadow and a soft line of mascara. She'd dressed up for today. She hadn't been anywhere she needed to dress up for ages. She must have been so looking forward to it.

'I say he had an affair with Maeve, but it was more a case of she had an affair with him. She flirted with him, and he fell for it.'

'I can't believe what you're telling me. How could Dad have been so stupid? With her of all people.'

'He's not the first, and he won't be the last to make a fool of himself.'

'When was this?'

'Fifteen years ago.'

Blood oozed from Louise's thumb where she'd picked at the skin around the nail. 'Why on earth did you keep her on at the hotel? How could you bear to see her every day? Always in the office with Dad.'

Her mother shrugged. 'I had no choice. The affair lasted two months – that was when Tom told me about it.'

'Couldn't you have found a way to get rid of her?'

'By then she was pregnant.'

Louise gasped. 'Pregnant.'

'Apparently a baby was the last thing on Maeve's agenda. Your father gave her money for an abortion and two months' holiday pay.' Her mother's voice was a monotone. 'We thought that would be the end of it, and we'd never have to see her again. But she came back when the two months was up.'

'Couldn't Dad have made her redundant?'

'She demanded money.'

'You mean blackmail?'

'He was to pay her so much per month, and she had to keep her job, or she'd tell everyone he'd raped her and bullied her into having an abortion.'

'My God.' Louise couldn't believe she'd had no inkling. 'Does Oliver know?'

'No one knows. Just Tom, me, and her.' Her mother rubbed at the fabric of her dress.

'Weren't you tempted to call her bluff? Even if she had told people, it was only her word against his.'

'I said that, but Tom wouldn't take the risk.'

'And you've had to live with it all these years.'

'I wouldn't be surprised if the stress contributed to his heart attack.'

Louise banged her fists down on her knees. 'She's not getting away with it any longer.'

'There's nothing you can do, Louise. The shame would kill your father.'

Thirty-five

'I wish you'd asked me first.' Angel stabbed her croissant with a knife.

'I stumbled on them, and once I started I wanted to read more.'

'If I hadn't come in when I did, would you have told me you'd found them?'

'Probably ... I don't know ...' Ollie admitted. 'I did feel guilty.'

They were sitting outside their favourite café bar, *Ai Artisti* having cappuccini and croissants. The morning air was cool, but for the first time in ages the sky was an unbroken blue, and the sun a brilliant yellow circle, straight from a child's painting. 'You looked as if I'd caught you out in some horrible secret.'

'I'm really sorry. Will you forgive me?'

She gave a half laugh. 'It's not exactly a major crime, is it? You probably think I'm making a fuss about nothing.'

'Not at all. I'd hate people to look at my work before I was ready to show it.'

She shrugged. 'Well, now you've read them, what do you think?'

'I don't know much about poetry, but I really like them, especially the one about the sculpture.'

'Are you just being kind?'

'Of course not! Your poems touched something.' He thumped his chest. 'Here in my heart.'

'I'm so glad you like them.' She was wearing a red beret set at an angle on her hair. The words *a riot of curls* slipped into his mind. The cliché was made for her.

She pushed the last of her croissant into her mouth. Crumbs stuck to her cheek, and he brushed them away. She smiled and little wrinkles creased the skin around her eyes. He never got tired of gazing into them, that rich, milky-brown colour, containing depths he'd never fathom. All the time working together in London and he hadn't seen how beautiful she was. How could he call himself an artist when he'd been so blinkered?

'So, am I forgiven?'

'Forgiven. But don't do it again!'

He turned at a noise: 'What the ... !' A sparrow was pecking at the crumbs on his plate. 'Shove off, you cheeky bugger!'

His phone buzzed and he fished it out of his pocket. An email: *Hi Ollie, Just checking in. Want you to know your work's going down a storm here.*

Was this real? 'Christ, that's amazing!'

'What?' Angel was staring at him.

He beckoned to the waiter. 'Aperol spritz. *Due, per favore.*'

'Ollie, you said you were working when we got back.'

'Fantastic news.'

'Are you going to share it, or sit there grinning like the cat that got the cream?'

He read the email again to convince himself it was true. 'You remember the paintings I sold to an American guy a while back?'

'The ones where you were lucky not to be arrested?'

'Don't remind me. I'm sure that prick of an artist only called the police because the American didn't buy his work.'

He made his words sound bullish, but he recalled how scared he'd been.

'Suppose the police had arrived while you were in the middle of the sale.'

'Yeah, they didn't though, did they?'

The waiter arrived with the drinks and a bowl of crisps. Bells began to chime, the sound echoing around the walls of the *campo*.

'Do you want to hear my good news or not?' Ollie heard the belligerence in his voice, and instantly wished he could retrieve the words.

'Of course, I do.' Her hand rested on his neck. 'I didn't mean to spoil the moment.'

'I know.' He touched his lips to hers. 'And you're right about the risks. I'll try again for the licence.'

'And the good news?'

'That was an email from the American guy. He'll buy as many paintings as I can do. Turns out his business is buying and selling Venetian art, and people in the States are raving about mine.'

Her fingers tightened on his shoulder. 'That's wonderful. I'm so pleased for you.'

'When I think I couldn't get anyone interested back home. And now, I can paint and sell, and paint and sell.'

They strolled back to the apartment, pausing, as always on Ponte dei Pugni to match their feet to the marble footsteps cut into the bridge in memory of the fist fights between rivals in earlier times.

'Don't you wish time travel was possible,' Angel said. 'I'd love to be whisked back to another era.'

'It would be smelly and dangerous, I should think. Nothing like Venice is today.'

'But it would be authentic. Real people's lives.' Angel

leaned over the bridge, staring down into the canal. 'Venice is more like an historic theme park.'

'I thought you loved it here.'

'I do, but I wish I could get more a sense of what it was like in ... say ... Veronese's day.' She turned and spread her arms wide along the parapet of the bridge. 'Or imagine living here when Byron stayed. I might have watched him swim from the Lido up the Grand Canal.

'But you're viewing the past through modern eyes. To them, it wouldn't have been dramatic but where they lived.'

Angel reached up and circled his throat with her hands. 'If I want to imagine myself as a courtesan in Casanova's time, I will.'

'Then I'll have to come back and rescue you from his wicked clutches.' He took her hand. 'I never thought I'd end up being jealous of someone who died centuries ago!'

Angel's ankle was aching so they stopped at a bench in Campo Santa Margherita. The men at the fish stalls were packing up, and seagulls wheeled round them, their shrill cries filling the *campo*. Some children were playing hopscotch nearby, their mothers engaged in intense conversation.

'I love sitting here, people watching,' Angel said. 'Wondering what their lives are like. I mean take that old woman.'

The woman was muffled up in a black astrakhan coat with a trilby pulled low over her eyes; a little dog peered out from her wicker shopping basket.

'I can see her in an apartment at the top of some decrepit *palazzo*. The rooms are overstuffed with antique furniture, fussy knick-knacks, Murano glass. Her husband died last year, and she pours all her love into that dog.'

Ollie stared after the woman. Now that Angel had described it, he could picture the apartment, and the woman did look lonely.

*

They stopped off to buy a pizza for lunch. 'And shall we get a bottle of prosecco?' Ollie asked.

'I thought you were painting this afternoon.'

He caught hold of Angel's waist and twirled her round. 'That was before my good news. Now, I intend to devote the afternoon to gluttony and lust.' He kissed her mouth. 'But not necessarily in that order.'

Angel stood on tiptoe and nuzzled her cold cheek against his. 'I'm all for a bit of lust.'

Ollie had a shower when they got back to the apartment. The water streamed down his face and onto his shoulders. He rubbed shower gel over his chest and soaped his belly. Soon he'd be inside Angel, in her soft, wet darkness. She'd wind her legs round him, ankles clasped. Her breasts would push against his chest, and he'd reach down to take a nipple in his mouth. He'd push deeper and deeper, and she'd give that little cry.

He stepped out of the shower and hitched the towel round his middle. He peered at his reflection in the mirror. The gaunt, sunken cheeks had disappeared; the hunted look that used to stare back at him was gone. He'd put on some weight since they'd been in Venice, and his skin looked smooth; his eyes clear and bright.

Angel was playing music in the living room, and strains drifted through the door. He recognised the song and hummed along. *Bless the Broken Road* was one of her favourites. 'It's our story,' she told him. 'We had to go along a broken road to find each other.'

He hung the towel on the rail and pulled on a pair of jeans. Angel was at the table in the living room, her notebook in front of her.

She looked up. 'I had an idea about that woman with the dog; I want to get it down before I forget.'

Ollie kissed the top of her head. He loved the feel of her hair, springy and untameable. 'And there was me thinking you'd be lying in bed panting with anticipation.'

'Panting is on hold.'

'Now who's the spoilsport?!'

'Give me ten minutes.' Angel waved her hand toward his jacket hanging from the back of the chair. 'Oh, and your phone's gone several times while you've been in the shower.'

'I'll have a look later. I don't feel like talking to anyone at the moment.' He trailed his fingers across her breasts. 'Except you.'

'But it might be the American with an even bigger order. Or perhaps it's Flo.'

'I wish.'

'Check it and see.'

Ollie yanked the phone from his pocket. He tapped the button and the screen swirled into life. 'What the ... ? Five text messages from Jess.'

Angel got up and stood next to him. 'What do they say?'

He clicked on the first one. 'It says *ring me.*'

He clicked on the next. *It's urgent.* 'Christ, what can it be?'

He stabbed at the messages:

Ollie, where are you?

Ollie, has Flo phoned you?

He scrolled down to the last one:

Flo's gone missing.

'Phone Jess,' Angel said. 'See what's happened. Flo's probably round at one of her friends.

Ollie couldn't move.

She took the phone from him and his eyes followed her finger as she clicked on contacts. She pressed Jess's name and held the phone to his ear. 'It's ringing.'

'Where the hell have you been?' Jess's voice screamed out of the phone.

'What's happened? Where's Flo?'

'She's run away.'

'What? When? How long's she been gone?'

'Has she phoned you?'

'Of course she hasn't.' His knuckles were white round the phone. 'How long?'

Jess was weeping. Her tears saturated his ear. 'She wasn't in her room this morning. We don't know when she went.'

'Have you phoned the police?'

'They're searching for her now.'

'And she's definitely run away? She's not with one of her friends?'

'No, we phoned everyone. And she's taken her rucksack and all the money from her piggy bank. She'd saved up about thirty pounds.'

'Which rucksack?'

'What does it matter?'

'Which one?'

'The pink one.'

'Oh, Christ.'

'Ollie.' Jess's voice was tiny. 'Suppose –'

'Listen, I'm coming back, as soon as I can get a flight.'

'I'm scared.'

'Hang in there, Jess. It will be all right.'

He dropped the phone on the table. 'Fuck. Fuck. Fuck.'

Angel wrapped her arms round his waist.

'She's run away.'

'I know. I heard.'

'Anything could have happened.'

'Look at me.' Angel gripped his face between her hands. 'You go and put some stuff in a bag. I'll check the flights.'

He ran into the studio and grabbed the painting things from his rucksack. He flung them away from him. Tubes of paint rolled across the tiled floor; his palette struck the chest of drawers. In the bedroom, he dragged clothes from the wardrobe, stuffing them into his rucksack. It was the 14th December. He was thirty-nine. If anything had happened to Flo, there was nothing to live for.

Angel called from the other room. 'I've got some flights.'

He stood in the doorway. His guts hurt as if someone had kicked him. He couldn't focus. Angel was at the laptop, but her face was blurred.

'Sit beside me, Ollie.'

He pulled out a chair and sat down next to her. What was that smell? She always smelt so lovely, fresh, like spring. But there was a stink in his nose, like rotting flesh.

'There's one direct flight per day at this time of year, and you're too late for that.'

The screen was bright; his eyes hurt.

'You can catch that flight tomorrow, as long as there are seats.'

'No, I'm going today.'

'There's an *Alitalia* flight this afternoon. You might just make it if you get a water taxi to the airport.' Angel put her hand on his knee. 'But it stops over in Rome. You won't get to Heathrow until nearly midnight.'

He stood up. 'Can you get me a ticket?' The fog in his mind cleared. He saw Flo, her blonde hair in plaits, her green eyes wide and scared, the pink rucksack bumping on her back. 'I've got to find her.'

Thirty-six

The pub was empty when she arrived apart from a noisy group at the bar. Seb was sitting at a table tucked away in the corner. A bottle of Sauvignon Blanc and two glasses were on the table. He stood up as she approached.

'Thanks for coming.' He pulled out a chair and she sat down. 'Is this okay? I wasn't sure whether to get the wine or not.' He lifted up the bottle and held it over the glass. 'Yes?'

'Thank you. I'd love some.'

He poured out two glasses of wine. 'Today went really well. You must be pleased.'

'Relieved. Mum and Dad seemed to like the foyer.'

'Yeah, and what a lovely lady your mum is.'

Louise thought of her mother in her blue dress with white spots, leaning towards the mirror brushing the grey shadow onto her eyes. How had she coped all these years? Kind and generous to a fault, and all the time covering up the biggest lie.

'You look very pale, Louise.' Seb's fingers brushed the back of her hand. 'Are you all right?'

'I'm tired. I was more anxious about today than I realised.'

'Are you sure it's that? It's not because of me, is it?'

He had that ability to focus on you as if you were the only person in the world who mattered. As if he could see inside your head, assess the complex system of lobes and nerves and cells, understand your thoughts and emotions. Know the truth. She studied the painting above his head, daubs and splashes, dots and streaks of black and grey that looked as if they might have been thrown on the canvas. Perhaps that's what Seb could see inside her head. A turmoil of black and grey.

'Louise, talk to me. Are you upset because of me?'

She lowered her gaze to his. His eyebrows speared downwards into a frown. Stubble pricked his chin and a nasty-looking scratch marked his cheekbone.

'Let's just say you haven't helped.' The words shocked her. Her real thoughts were usually tucked away in her heart, where they burrowed and buried their sting. 'You ignored me when you came into the hotel yesterday. What was I supposed to think?' He'd been in reception discussing the photo shoot with Katie, but he hadn't come near the office.

Seb put down his glass. Expressions rippled across his face, as if he was trying out which story to tell her. 'You're right,' he said. 'I should have explained. I thought it would be better to put it off until after today.'

'Put it off. That sounds ominous.' She gulped back some wine.

'I've made such a mess of this.' The signet ring he normally wore on the fourth finger of his left hand was missing. The skin was paler there, with a slight depression below the knuckle. 'I've managed to upset my wife, my kids – and now you.'

'What's happened? You said you were going back to talk to your wife.'

'And I did. I told her I'd been unhappy for a long time. That I liked the new life I'd made, and that I'd met someone else.' He flicked a beer mat across the table, and it slid off the other side and dropped onto the floor. 'She threatened all sorts of things. Told the kids what a bastard I was. They begged me not to go, and ... well, I chickened out.'

'So, this is goodbye?' She should have known it was too good to be true. The likes of her didn't find lovely men.

'I thought it was going to be. I agreed I'd stay, and I told myself I'd keep away from you. I knew you deserved an explanation, but I couldn't do it. I thought if I could get through today, I'd be able to go away and forget you.' He took hold of her hands. 'But I was kidding myself. I can't go back to that life.' His eyes met hers, and their blueness overwhelmed her all over again. 'But leaving my boys is so hard.'

Sky blue, sea blue, Seb blue. 'I'm sorry,' she whispered.

'I consoled myself with the thought of you. Us. What I hoped would be a new life together.'

'But?'

'When I was talking to your mother this afternoon, she told me about ... your husband.'

Oh, shit. Why did she have to go and do that?

'I should have come clean before,' Louise said. 'But I push things away I don't want to deal with.'

'So, what's the situation? Your mother said she didn't know if you and your husband have finished for good or not.'

'We're finished.' She made her voice as firm as she could. 'But we haven't done anything formally yet.'

'And your husband's okay with it? I like you, Louise. I like you a lot, but I don't want to get in the way of your marriage, if it's still got a chance.'

'It hasn't.' An image of Matt's face, contorted with anger, skimmed across her mind. 'I'm going to ask him for a divorce as soon as possible.'

Louise climbed the steps up to The Hoe. She'd been on the go for more than twelve hours, and her muscles ached each time she lifted her leg. She glanced up at her parents' apartment as she crossed towards the hotel. How had they lived with that hurt between them?

After all the activity of the afternoon, it was peaceful in the foyer. Mike was behind the desk, and he looked up smiling when Louise went over.

'I know what you're going to say: what am I doing here so early.'

'I thought Donna was covering this evening.'

'Her daughter is sick. She phoned me and asked if I'd do a couple of hours' overtime.'

Another problem to deal with. She'd have to insist all changes to staffing went through her or Katie. 'I'll be in the office, Mike.'

'Before you go ...' Mike nodded towards one of the armchairs. 'Someone's waiting to see you.'

She glanced over at a man reading the newspaper. The paper obscured his face, but she noticed his muddy trousers and scuffed shoes. She looked back at Mike. 'This is a funny time to come calling. Who is it?'

'You'd best check him out,' Mike said. 'I'm here if you need help.'

A few feet away from him, Louise hesitated. It was Matt, but how different. His hair was long, and an unkempt beard covered most of his face. But he was wearing a suit and what looked to be a new white shirt with a dark blue tie.

'Hello, Matt. This is a surprise.'

He stood up: the sleeves of the jacket finished way above his wrists and the trousers flapped around his ankles.

'It's good to see you, Louise.' His voice sounded more ragged, throatier somehow, as if he'd been chain-smoking.

'Why didn't you let me know you were coming?'

'How?'

'Phone me.'

'I haven't got a phone.' His arms hung limply by his sides. His head was bowed, his eyes wary. Like a dog who's been kicked too many times.

'Would you like a drink?' she asked. 'Coffee? Tea?'

He shook his head. 'I want to talk.'

'What about?'

'Us.'

Louise sat on her computer chair and indicated the sofa to Matt. She felt even more uneasy now they were in the enclosed space of the office.

'How have you been, Louise?' His gaze was fixed to the floor.

'I'm okay. It's busy ... the hotel, you know ... it's full on.' She stopped. That was the wrong thing to say. 'What about you?'

'Me?' He looked up and met her eyes for the first time. 'Not okay. Not busy. Not full on.'

'Oh.'

'I'm a mess, if you want the truth.'

If that was the truth, then, she didn't want it. She needed him to say he was getting on all right, it was a good thing they'd separated, and they should talk about divorce.

'Are you living at the house?'

'No, I need to be at the hotel,' she said. 'I thought you'd be there.'

'I haven't been back since that day.'

'Why not? You loved that little house.'

'I loved it when it was our home. Our little world, where we would bring up children.'

'The house is miniscule, Matt. There was barely room for the two us, never mind ...' The words died in her mouth as she saw his face twist. 'If you're not living there, where have you been staying?'

'Dossing down on mates' floors. Up country a bit. Somerset, Gloucestershire.'

'What about work?'

'I got sacked.'

'Right.' Louise cast a surreptitious glance through the window to the reception desk. Mike was talking to one of the guests. He was pointing to something in a book. They were nodding, smiling. She wanted to be out there. Away from this atmosphere that made her scalp crawl. 'Why have you come, Matt?'

He stood up and moved towards her. She pushed back hard against the chair, her hands gripping the edges. He dropped to his knees, taking one of her hands in both of his. 'Louise, I want you to listen. I've got something important to say.'

She stared at the flecks of grey in his beard.

'I've been to hell and back since you left me.'

She shrank away from the pinpricks of his gaze.

'Let's try again. We can make it work.'

'You picked me up and dropped me, Matt. I was scared.'

'I'm sorry. I didn't know what I was doing.' His grip tightened. 'If you'll give me another chance.'

'I can't. We want different things.'

'You loved me once.'

Did she? Those first days when she came back from London, she'd been beside herself with pain. Losing Matilda was more than she could bear. She wanted to die. Matt had been there. She'd gone out with him for a while before she went to London, and she remembered he was kind. When they met again by chance after she came back, he started calling at the hotel. Asked her out for a drink. 'You should go,' her mother had said. 'You can't stay cooped up in here all the time.'

'I'll get another job,' he said. 'You can go back to the solicitors. We'll find a bigger house if that's what you want.'

He was pinching her fingers, he was holding them so tightly. She tried to pull her hand free, but he gripped it more.

'It wouldn't work, Matt. The hotel is my job now, and you know how you feel about it.'

'But you don't have to be here. Your dad can come back.'

'He's a sick man.'

'Someone else then.' He jerked his head towards reception. 'Him at the desk – he can do it.'

'Mike's the night porter. You don't know what you're talking about.' Her eyes searched the room, anything so as not to look at him kneeling in front of her. Propped up on the filing cabinet was the mood board Seb had produced for the foyer. She made out the swatch of material, the richly-coloured brocade he'd chosen for the windows, the silk wallpaper that now hung behind the desk. She was going to ask Matt for a divorce as soon as possible she'd told Seb. Why wasn't she doing it?

Tearing her hand free, she moved behind the chair and planted her palms on the back. 'The hotel is mine now. You asked me to choose, remember? And I chose the hotel.'

'You don't mean that, Loulou.'

'Don't call me that!'

'But that's my name for you.'

'It's not. My brother's the only one who calls me that.'

He sank back on his heels and leaned forward until his forehead rested against the floor.

'Matt, please get up.'

He struggled up, so that he was on all fours. 'I need you to see how much you mean to me.'

'We finished forever that day in the kitchen.' The leather of the chair was sticky with sweat from her palms.

'I don't understand.'

'It's over.'

'But you and me –'

'There is no you and me. Please get up and go.' She turned away and straightened the brochures piled on the window sill, tears blurring her eyes. She heard a sound behind her. It took every ounce of strength not to turn round. Suppose he was coming closer? She waited, spine coiled. And then the office door slammed. He'd gone.

Thirty-seven

Ollie turned his phone on when the plane's wheels hit the ground at Rome airport. The woman next to him tutted and sighed. 'Fuck off,' he muttered under his breath. She'd been reading some Italian gossip magazine ever since they left Venice, giggling with her friend across the aisle.

He leapt up the minute the seat-belt sign was switched off, and squeezed past the woman. She complained loudly in excitable Italian. He yanked his rucksack from the overhead locker and pushed into the queue waiting to disembark. Shifting from foot to foot, he forced down the panic rising in his chest. No messages or calls from Jess. No news. Just one text from Angel: *My heart is with you, my darling.*

No news. No news. No news. What the fuck were the police doing? She couldn't have gone far. Why hadn't they found her? He should let his mother know. But she'd be devastated. He wouldn't tell her yet.

As soon as he got inside the terminal building, he pressed on Jess's number. The ringing pierced his ear. Why didn't she answer? People swirled round him, pushing, chatting, gesticulating. No one was crying. No one was yelling at people. No one was screaming inside.

'Hello.' Peter, Jess's father, answered. 'Where are you, Ollie?'

'Rome airport, waiting for my connection. What's happened?'

'Nothing new. There's been no sign of Flo, no sightings apart from a possible CCTV image.'

'Was she on her own?'

'Apparently.'

'Where? Where did they see her?'

'They can't be sure it's her, but near Holloway Road tube station last night about ten pm.'

Holloway Road. Was she trying to get to the flat? But she knew he wasn't there. She wasn't stupid.

'The police have put out a national Child Rescue Alert, and they're doing house to house ... the Missing Persons Bureau....' Peter's voice cracked.

Ollie had always got on well with him, with both Jess's parents. They must be going through hell as well.

'We've got a support officer here all the time, and she's wonderful.' He sounded stronger; he must have gathered himself. 'Everyone's doing what they can. Eugene's set up campaigns on Facebook and Twitter.'

'I don't want that bastard involved. This wouldn't have happened if he hadn't arrived on the scene.'

'It would have helped if you hadn't disappeared.'

'You've got a nerve, Peter.' He turned his back on the crowd round the departure board. People were staring at him. He breathed in and let the air escape until his lungs felt empty. It was no good alienating the man. 'Is Jess there? Can I speak to her?'

'She's asleep. The doctor's given her a sedative. I'll have to go – the police are here.'

'It's not ... ?'

Peter hesitated, and Ollie heard a male voice in the background.

311

'No, there's no news.'

'Ring me the minute you hear anything.'

'Of course.'

The time inched by. Seconds and minutes took on a life of their own, seeming to run backwards instead of forwards. Ollie lost count of the number of times he checked the departure board. The flight for Heathrow was up there, but the boarding gate remained blank.

He circled the departure lounge over and over again. His eyes flitted over couples, asleep, heads resting on each other's shoulders; squalling babies in pushchairs, their teddy bears thrown to the floor; parents trying to calm fractious children. He was searching for a sign. He didn't know what, but some talisman that would keep Flo safe. That would mean she'd be there when he arrived.

He slumped down onto a seat and took his mobile from his pocket. He clicked on Angel's number.

'Ollie, any news?'

'Nothing.'

'Have you spoken to Jess?'

'She was asleep. I spoke to her dad. The police are pulling out all the stops apparently, but so far, nothing.' A man sat down beside him and started eating a huge beef burger. Ollie gagged at the smell. He got up and moved away. 'There is one thing – they think they've got a CCTV image of her from last night.'

'Last night?'

'Yes, which means ...' Ollie bit down hard on his lip. 'She was out all night. Anything could have happened to her by now.'

'I know it's easy for me to say, but try not to imagine bad things.'

'I can't help it. My mind's in overdrive.'

'Do you want me to come? I can get a flight lunchtime tomorrow.'

The need to see Angel, feel her arms round him, to bury his face in her hair made him cry out. A group standing nearby turned round.

'Ollie, are you okay? Look, I'll pack some stuff now.'

'No, no. You stay there. The thought of you in our apartment is my only bit of security. Let's wait and see what happens.'

'Take care, my darling.' Angel's soft breathing came down the line. 'I love you.'

'I love you too.'

It was nearly two am when the taxi dropped Ollie outside Jess's parents' house. The lights were blazing in both the downstairs rooms and the hall. What did that mean? She'd been found. The lights were a celebration. His legs sagged under him as he walked up the path to the front door. He hardly had the strength to lift his hand to the knocker.

The door opened and a policewoman stood there. 'You must be Ollie. Come in.'

'Anything?' he said, his voice hoarse.

She shook her head. 'I'm afraid not.' She held out her hand. 'I'm Detective Constable Phillips, but please call me Judy. And I'm so sorry about Flo. We're doing everything we can to find her.'

He climbed the remaining couple of steps and hesitated inside the front door. 'Where are they?'

'Jess and her dad are in the kitchen. Her mother's lying down.'

'Ollie, thank God you're here.' Jess appeared in the doorway. But it wasn't the Jess he remembered. Her beautiful blonde hair was greasy and lank. Her eyes were slits surrounded by red, puffy circles. Her belly pushed against the black jumper she was wearing. Somehow he'd forgotten she was pregnant.

He dropped his rucksack, and they moved towards each other at the same moment. Then she was in his arms, and she was weeping, the worst sound he'd ever heard. A kind of shrieking, like a fox in the night.

It felt strange holding her, stroking her hair, whispering 'Ssh, ssh.' She was the Jess he'd loved for all those years. The woman he'd thought the most beautiful in the world. The woman he'd be with forever. The woman who'd given him Flo. But she wasn't his Jess any more. The arc of her belly pressing against him confirmed that.

Peter came out of the kitchen. 'Come and sit down. You're both exhausted. I'll make tea, and Judy and I will go in the other room, while you two talk.'

Ollie wrapped his arm round Jess, and she leaned against him, as they moved down the hallway in a weird procession, Peter at the front, the policewoman behind them. He helped Jess into a chair at the kitchen table and sat down next to her.

'I need to make some phone calls,' Judy said. 'I'll be in the sitting room, Peter.'

'Do you want tea, Ollie, or would you prefer a beer?'

A beer. The normality of an evening in the pub. Watching the head foaming on top of the beer. Flicking off the cap on the bottle of lager. No, alcohol would muddle his head. Clear wits, that's what he needed. 'Tea is fine, thanks.'

Peter put the two mugs on the table. 'Shout if you need me, Jess.'

She nodded, and reached for the box of tissues on the table. She wiped her face and blew her nose. 'I didn't think I had so many tears in me.'

Ollie sipped the tea. 'Talk me through what happened.'

'Flo went to bed as usual about eight-thirty.'

'Where? Here?'

'No, we're living with Eugene in Highgate now.' She clutched his hand. 'I'm sorry, Ollie. But with the baby and everything, it seemed ...'

'It's okay. But she might turn up there.'

'That's why Eugene's staying in the house. In case.'

'So, she went to bed ...'

'Yes, we'd been reading a book together. You know like we used to – she reads one page and I read one page. A new one we got from the library on Saturday. *Bella Donna*. It's the first in a series, and I said to Flo –'

'Jess, what happened then?'

'I ran a bath and I could hear her singing and chatting to herself. I went in to say good night about nine, and everything seemed to be okay. She snuggled down, and she said "I love you, Mummy," and I turned the light out.' Jess's body shook with a fresh storm of crying. 'I went to wake her up this morning ... oh God, yesterday morning ... and she wasn't there. Ollie, suppose something terrible's happened ... suppose someone's got her.'

He heard Angel's voice in his head. 'Try not to imagine bad things.'

'She wouldn't have gone if it wasn't for me,' Jess said.

'What do you mean? I don't understand.'

'She was unhappy because I left you and took her with me.'

'But she refused to see me or talk to me.'

'She was protecting herself. I used to hear her crying in her room after she'd seen you.'

Oh, fuck, he should have pushed harder. He should have been there every day, demanding to see Flo.

'She doesn't like Eugene. She doesn't like it because I'm pregnant. She said to me "You can't have a baby with him. What about Daddy?"'

He put his arms round her, resting his cheek against her hair. He could feel the contours of her head – she was too thin. 'It will be all right. It will be all right,' he said. And he missed Angel. He wanted Angel.

Thirty-eight

Louise splashed cold water on her face and cleaned her teeth, but the fug of the night remained. It was eight-twenty and she was always up before seven. Must have slept right through the alarm. Pulling on her dressing gown, she rang down to reception.

'Katie, I'm glad it's you.'

'Hi, Louise. Everything all right?'

'I've got a migraine. Can you hold the fort, and I'll be down later?'

'Of course, but I'll have to go – some guests are waiting.'

'Is Maeve there?'

'She's around somewhere, but I'm not sure where.'

Typical. She was probably off talking to the kitchen staff, or filling the new housekeeper's ears with her poison. 'Can you tell her I'd like to see her in my office at midday, please?'

'She'll want to know what it's about.'

'Just ask her to be there.'

'Will do.'

Louise switched her laptop on. She typed disciplinary procedures into the search box. She had two hours to work on her strategy.

She'd chosen a black knee-length dress, black tights and her grey shoes, the ones with the heels. Her hair was piled high in a loose bun, and she'd spent more time than usual on her make-up, especially her eyes, concealing the circles and puffiness of the sleepless night. The paperwork was on her desk, and she read and reread her notes.

By twelve-fifteen Maeve still hadn't arrived. Louise paced up and down the office. She checked her phone for messages and emails. Nothing. Maeve was doing this on purpose. Showing who had the power. Well, she was making a mistake this time.

Louise sat down. She leant back in the chair and swiv-elled from side to side. She muttered her speech: *I've asked you ... Difficult issues ... No choice ... Disciplinary –*

The phone rang and she snatched it up.

'It's Katie. I've had a message from Maeve.'

'It had better be good.'

'She's been delayed.'

'What does she mean *delayed*?' Louise clamped her fist round the paperweight on her desk. She squeezed the cold glass until her hand hurt. 'She's supposed to be here working today.'

'She said she had an important meeting, and she'd get there as soon as she could.'

'This is beyond a joke. *I'm* her important meeting.'

'I hope you don't mind me saying so, Louise ...' Katie sounded breathless, as if she'd been running. '... I think she's playing with you.'

'I don't think: I know. But her time is running out.'

Louise waited at the window, her arms folded. Her hands circled her upper arms, her fingers pinching the soft flesh. Outside it was grey and drizzly. A mist hung over the sea, blocking out any view of the distant headlands or the Breakwater. Drake's Island was just visible. She'd learnt its history at school, and this little mound of land out in the Sound had always fascinated her. Not much more than six acres, it had witnessed Francis Drake setting off to sail round the world, the imprisonment of Roundheads after the Civil War, barracks for soldiers waiting to fight off the French and Spanish.

So, Maeve was a bitch of the first order; Matt was probably lying drunk somewhere; Seb hadn't texted her. Did any of it matter? Would it be recorded anywhere in hundreds of years' time? Her seagull landed on the window sill, its beak bright yellow and vicious-looking. Its beady eyes glared at her. Eyes that could spot prey: catch insects on the wing, plunge-dive to snatch up a fish. *Pull yourself together, Louise,* its eyes seemed to say. It matters – all of it.

She turned as the door opened and Maeve rushed in.

'Sorry I'm late. The traffic's terrible.'

'Where have you been?' Louise remained standing by the window. She felt the gull at her back, heard its squall through the glass. 'You were down to be on duty this morning.'

Maeve plonked herself on the sofa, and her skirt rode up to her thighs. She pulled at it and smiled up at Louise, as if the problem of tight skirts was a shared preoccupation. 'Well, I popped over to see your father – he was exhausted, poor love, after yesterday's excitement – and then I went into town because I'd seen some pictures that would be perfect against Seb's green wall.'

Louise sat down at the desk. 'You're not employed to do either of those things, Maeve. Your job is to run reception.' She hesitated: how much to say in one go? Maeve would have a ready answer for everything thrown at her. 'The fact that you're not doing it properly is why I've called you in today.'

Maeve widened her eyes. 'I don't know what you mean. I've worked here for more than twenty years. I know this hotel inside out, and I run the reception desk with as much precision as a commander runs his ship.'

'But that's the point – you don't.' Louise's eyes strayed to the document on her desk: *Notice of Disciplinary Meeting*. She mustn't let herself get swamped with Maeve's protests. 'We now have a computer system in place, which you refuse to use.'

Maeve shook her shoulders, bristling like a hen. 'I'm protecting your father. If he thought I'd collaborated in something he expressly said –'

'Maeve, I'm going to stop you there.' Louise picked up the document. 'I haven't asked you to this meeting so that we can engage in claim and counter-claim. I would like you to read this, and tell me you understand what it says.' She handed over the sheet of A4.

She watched Maeve's eyes skim the first couple of lines. How long before she started protesting? One ... two ... three ...

'But this is ridiculous!' Maeve slapped the paper with the back of her hand. She held it between her thumb and forefinger. 'Disciplinary meeting!' She grabbed her glasses from the top of her head. 'Disciplinary action against you will be considered with regard ... failure to implement company policy ... what a load of bullshit.' Her eyes blazed. 'Failure to fulfil job specification ... bullying of other members of staff.' She flung the paper away from her. 'I've never heard anything so pathetic.' She stood up. 'I've got better things to do than stay here to be insulted.'

'Maeve, this is serious. I handed you the notice of the meeting rather than send it to your home, as I thought we might air some issues informally first.' Louise forced herself to meet Maeve's eyes. 'Clearly I made a mistake.'

Maeve bent down and picked the sheet of paper up from the floor. 'And that's not the only mistake you've made.' She tore the paper in two, and then ripped the pieces across again. 'We'll see what your father has to say about this.'

Louise stood on the slipway at Admiral's Hard and gazed out across the Hamoaze to Cornwall. The wind bit into her and she pulled her anorak tighter, stuffing her hands into her pockets. A small group of people huddled together waiting for the ferry. The tide was in and boats at anchor rocked and bobbed. The cold struck her cheeks, and she lifted her face to the wind.

'Where's Maeve?' she'd asked Katie after the meeting.

Katie had shrugged. 'She came out of your office like a demon, snatched her bag from the drawer and disappeared out of the door.'

Louise's teeth ached where she'd ground them together. 'I need to get out, Katie. Can you cope for an hour or two?'

'Of course. I'm guessing the meeting didn't go well.'

'You could say that.'

The ferry eased in beside the slipway, and the waiting passengers climbed aboard. 'You coming, love?' the sailor called. 'We're leaving now.'

Louise shook her head. 'Not today.'

He untied the ropes from the bollards and waved to the pilot. The little boat reversed and ploughed out into the river, cutting across the choppy waves. Her dad used to wait here for her mother when they were courting. A photo of them on their wedding day stood amongst the family pictures on the grand piano in the smaller sitting room. They'd got married in the tiny church in Cawsand and then sailed over to Plymouth, her mother still in her wedding dress, for a reception at the hotel. She thought of her father having sex with Maeve. Where had they done it? In one of the hotel bedrooms? She hated him for it.

Hands gripped her waist and twisted her round. 'Hello, you playing hooky?'

'Seb!' She jumped backwards and almost missed her

footing on the slope of the slipway. 'You gave me a fright. What are you doing here?'

'Saving you from an icy plunge.' He smoothed her hair back from her face, and brushed her mouth with his. His touch was so gentle, it was as if she'd dreamt it.

'How did you know I'd be here?'

'Just a hunch. Katie said you'd gone out for some fresh air. I searched along the front, and when I couldn't find you there ...' He laughed. 'Seems I know you better than you think I do.' He walked to the end of the slipway and stared down into the water. 'There's hundreds of fish here.'

She studied his back, the grey jerkin with the collar turned up. A watery sun had emerged from behind the clouds and its light rested on his shoulders. Her insides flipped at the thought that he'd come searching for her.

'So, it's true,' she said.

He glanced over his shoulder. 'What?'

'There are plenty more fish in the sea.'

'Hey, you!' He ran back up the slipway and pulled her close to him. 'Don't you consider any other fish. Not when you've got this one completely hooked.' He put his hand under her chin and tilted her head backwards. 'I've been thinking. We've had a couple of false starts, but I'm certain now of what I want.' He bent down and kissed her. 'You.'

Heat spread across Louise's chest and inched up her neck. 'I saw Matt last night after we met. He turned up at the hotel.'

'I knew it: he wants to give it another go, doesn't he?'

She put her fingers to his lips. 'Maybe he does, but I don't. And I've told him that.'

'You mean ...'

'Yes, we can be together at last.'

Seb covered his face.

Louise clutched the handrail. The cold metal stung her skin. 'I thought it was what you wanted.'

'It is.' He looked up, a grin spreading across his face. 'I was ... overcome for the moment.'

'Shall we go back to the hotel?' she said.

'There is just one thing.'

What now? What other hurdles did they have to leap?

'We haven't been honest with each other, Louise. We've both kept secrets.'

'I know.'

He stared into her eyes, forcing her to meet his gaze. 'If we're going to have a relationship, we have to talk. Say how we're feeling.'

'I don't find that easy,' she said.

'Then we'd better go back and start practising. I want to know everything about you.'

'That makes two of us.'

'Don't worry. I intend to bore you silly.'

'I could ask Chef to send up dinner to the flat,' she said, 'and I think I've got a bottle of champagne in the fridge.'

'And then?'

She smiled. '*And then* sounds wonderful.'

Louise opened her eyes. The darkness was thick in the bedroom. She made out a glint on the opposite wall where the mirror hung, and next to it the outline of the wardrobe, her white bath robe hanging from the door. She moved her head so that she could see the clock: two am. Hours before they needed to get up. She slipped her hand between her thighs. It felt hot and moist. 'Beautifully wet,' Seb had murmured, spreading her legs wide. Her belly stirred at the memory.

He was lying on his side away from her, and she wrapped herself round him, fitting her body to the long curve of his back, his bottom cupped in her lap. She put her arm round him and ran her fingers over the smooth skin on his chest.

His light breathing stirred the silence. The scent of his after-shave, familiar, yet teasingly strange on the pillow, brought back his kisses, her mouth still full and plump from them. She closed her eyes.

She sat up. What had woken her? It was three-fifty, that hour again. But her teeth weren't clenched; there were no tears of distress; no hangover of lurid dreams. Still, something wasn't right. She reached out and touched Seb's warm shoulder. He was there. He wasn't a figment of her imagination. He hadn't had sex and disappeared. They were going to be together. She'd be happy again.

She heard something. Voices. Shouting. She slid out of bed and padded to the door. She peered out. Definitely shouting. But more. A high-pitched, shrilling noise. An alarm.

'Seb! Seb!' She turned on the light and ran to the chest of drawers, dragging out some old jeans and a thick top. 'Seb! Wake up!' She pulled on socks and shoved her feet into her trainers.

'What? What's happened?'

'It's the fire alarm.'

Her mobile rang. 'Louise, it's Mike.'

'Is it real? Is it a fire?'

'Afraid so.'

'Oh, God.'

'I'm checking the rooms on the first floor.'

'I'll do the second. The fire brigade?'

'On their way.'

She clicked the phone off.

Seb was standing at the door, dressed. 'What shall I do?'

'The third floor. Check every room is empty.'

'Okay.' He reached for her hand. 'It will be all right. We can do it.'

'Get out as soon as you can. One of the fire escapes at the side of the building. Not the stairs.'

'Right.'

She raced down to the second floor. The smell of smoke was strong, an acrid, jagged stink in her nose. Mist encircled her: wisps of white. The smell grew stronger. Noxious fumes trickling up the stairs. She pulled open the fire door, and it closed behind her. The mist cleared, and she ran along the corridor, knocking on doors, flinging them open. 'Anyone here?' She pushed at one door, and it opened a crack, but wouldn't budge any further. 'Hello? Is someone in there?'

'Hello.' The croaky voice of an elderly man.

'You need to get out. There's a fire.'

'My wife ...'

She remembered now. The old couple, Mr and Mrs Hyde. They'd checked in the day before yesterday. Insisted on room twenty-one on the second floor. Four-poster, sea view. They'd spent their honeymoon there and were celebrating their diamond anniversary. Their family were arriving this afternoon for a party.

'I can't open the door, Mr Hyde.'

'My wife has collapsed.' He sounded close to tears.

'Where is she?'

'Behind the door.'

The screech of the alarm pierced her head. Sliced it in two. They wouldn't get out. They'd all die at this rate. 'Can you move her a bit, Mr Hyde? So that I can squeeze through?' She raced to the end of the corridor – the other rooms were empty – and chased back. The door was ajar. The woman lay crumpled on the floor, her legs bent at an awkward angle. He was cradling her in his arms, stroking her face. 'Muriel, wake up. Come on, my darling.'

Louise hooked her hands under Mrs Hyde's arms. 'We have to get out now.'

'I'm not leaving her.'

'You won't have to.' She managed to get the woman up onto her knees. Her body flopped to one side. She let out a low moan. How long had gone by? Was the hotel empty? 'Mr Hyde, get on that side of her. I'll go this side, and we'll pull her onto her feet.'

Mrs Hyde was overweight and heavy, but between them, they hauled her up.

'Jimmy,' she muttered. 'Where's my Jimmy?'

'I'm here, my love. We've got to go. Try and walk.'

'Hold her a second.' Louise grabbed a dressing gown from the bed and wrapped it round Mrs Hyde's shoulders. 'Put that on her. I'll be back in a second.' In the bathroom, she soaked small towels in cold water.

Her mobile rang. It was Seb. 'Louise, where the hell are you?'

Sirens wailed in the background. Voices. Screaming.

'Just coming. Been struggling with an old couple. Can you meet us on the fire escape?'

'Right, but get out now.'

She handed Mr Hyde a cloth. 'Keep that over your nose and mouth. I'll do Mrs Hyde's.' She put her arm round the woman's waist and held the cloth to her face. Half-lifting Mrs Hyde off her feet, she pulled her along. She got cramp in her arm. Pain streaked along it. She had to hold on. She couldn't let the woman go now. 'Nearly there. Nearly there.' Mr Hyde had dropped behind them. 'Are you okay, Jimmy?' she shouted. He didn't answer. He'd better be all right.

They reached the fire escape. She pressed her elbow down on the handle and stumbled out. She gasped. The smell of smoke bombarded her nostrils. Choked her. She held a cloth to her face. Below her, three fire engines were lined up on The Hoe and more in Elliot Street.

Seb leapt up the final steps two at a time as she manoeuvred Mrs Hyde through the door.

'Thank God, you're out. I was scared shitless.'

'Can you take her?' Louise's chest hurt when she breathed. 'I'll help her husband. He's a bit more with it.' She staggered when Seb lifted the weight from her, banging her head against the wall. Seb had Mrs Hyde in his arms. She turned back. 'Come on, Jimmy. Hold the rail. It might be slippery on the stairs.'

He gripped her hand, and they set off. Down one step. Pause. Down another. It was never-ending. 'It's my knees,' he said. 'I'm sorry.'

'Don't apologise. Let's just get down.'

'Where's Muriel? Is she all right?'

'She'll be fine, Mr Hyde. Careful, round the corner here. We're going down the next flight now.'

They reached the ground at last. A paramedic appeared and led Mr Hyde away to an ambulance.

Louise bent over, her head hanging forward. She felt sick. She gasped for air, each breath tight and raw. Dragging herself upright, she limped round to the front of the hotel.

She heard the crackle of fire; a loud bang, something exploding or falling. Firemen swarmed around in front of the building, shouting to each other, pulling hoses. A huddle of people had gathered at the far end of The Hoe. Please God, all the guests were out.

'Get back, Miss,' a fireman said. He pulled his helmet down and waved his arm towards a fire engine. 'We've got a water cannon coming through here.'

'I'm Louise Bradbury, the owner. Is everyone out?'

'As far as we can tell.'

'How did it start?'

'We don't know yet. Perhaps an electrical fault. A spark from a fire.'

One of the other men called to him. 'We're ready now, Charlie.'

'Righto. On my way.' He glanced back at Louise. 'We'll save the building if we can.'

Louise stared up at the hotel. She'd lit the fire in the main lounge yesterday after her meeting with Maeve. Holding a match to the kindling, watching the flame take hold was always something she enjoyed. Usually she went round the hotel before she finished for the night, checking everything. Making sure the guard was in front of the dying embers. Last night, she'd been up in the flat with Seb. She hadn't thought about anything else.

Her eyes scanned the building constantly. What was going on? What was happening in there? Oh, God! A glow in the window over on the far left-hand side. That was the store room in front of the kitchens. A flame appeared. Another. Flickering, glittering light. The sound of glass cracking. An explosion.

'Louise.' Her mother's voice next to her, her eyes wide.

'Mum.'

'Where's your father?'

'What do you mean? I haven't seen him.'

'He's not in the apartment. I woke up. I heard the noise, but he's not there.'

Louise forced her eyes back to the hotel. 'You don't think –'

'He wouldn't be so stupid, would he?'

'Where is he then?'

Her mother started to cry.

'It's okay, Mum. I'm going to check.' She ran to the main entrance. Through the glass, she saw the foyer was filled with smoke. She pulled open the door. The stench was thick and putrid. Her eyes stung. She couldn't see a thing.

'No, Louise, you can't.' Her mother's faint voice reached her ears. 'Louise. Come back.' The sound, thin as a reed, echoed in the air.

Thirty-nine

Jess let her father take her up to bed as a sliver of pale light emerged in the sky.

'You grab some sleep as well, Ollie,' he said. 'We don't know what today's going to bring. The police might want you and Jess to do an appeal on TV.'

Another liaison officer, Viv, arrived to relieve Judy. She made coffee. The noise of the kettle and the clattering of cups jarred Ollie's nerves. She sat down opposite him at the kitchen table. 'Do you want to talk?' She spoke out of the corner of her mouth, as if she'd watched too many gangster movies.

'I feel so useless. There must be something I can do.'

'Best leave it to the police. They know what they're doing.'

'But what made her go? If we knew that.'

'Your wife said Flo was unhappy because of the marriage break up.' Viv had short mousey-grey hair and narrow eyes. They made him feel like a criminal. 'She might have gone looking for you.'

'But she knew where I was. I sent her loads of postcards.' A picture of him leaning on the wall next to Rio de Toletta, the postcard of the gondolas in his hand, his words on the card: *Perhaps one day you'll come here and see them* swerved

329

into his mind. Surely she wasn't trying to get to Venice? No, but Grandpa – 'I'll come with you,' she'd said. 'I'd visit you if you were ill.' And there was her stricken expression, her angry cry when he threw the exercise book into the sea at the Mayflower Steps: 'What did you do that for?'

'Plymouth!' he shouted. 'Get them to check the hotel.'

Viv went into the hall, and he heard her talking on the phone. She came back and sat down at the table. 'They've made a note.' She pushed the cup of coffee towards him. 'Your drink's going cold.'

A wave of longing for Angel struck him in the gut. He needed to hear her voice: her strength sharpened his. Venice was an hour ahead. A bit longer and he'd ring.

'This appeal,' he said, 'what would it involve?'

'You and Jess would speak to the media. Describe what happened.' Viv had a soft west-country burr, belying her sharp features. 'How would you feel if Jess's partner joined you for the appeal?'

'Jess's partner?'

'I meant Eugene McBride. Perhaps you don't know –'

He shoved the cup away from him. 'Oh, I know Eugene all right.'

'As Flo's step-father, Eugene –'

'Step-father? He's got no relationship to my daughter.'

'I understand how hard this is for you, Ollie.' Viv took out her pad and started writing. 'But we have to take him into account. Flo was living in his house.'

'What are you saying? He might have something to do with it?'

'In the case of missing children, we always look at the family, the people who are closest to them.' She kept her gaze on her notebook. 'Stranger abduction is very rare.'

A cry burst from Ollie's mouth.

'I'm here to support you and Jess. Let's pray we get some news today.' Viv smiled her thin-lipped smile at him.

'Pray?' Ollie snapped. 'Do you think some old bearded man in the sky can help us?'

She spread her hands wide. 'I don't know. If it were me, I'd try anything and everything.'

He kicked the leg of the chair. 'That's the thing though, isn't it? It's not you.'

Ollie dozed off, his head resting on the kitchen table. Viv was knitting, and the gentle clacking of the needles was the last sound he heard as he allowed his eyes to close.

When he came to, he had pins and needles in his hands, and his head hurt. His fingers found the deep ridge in his forehead where the table had dug into him. He rolled his shoulders, trying to ease the pain. Viv wasn't there. Her knitting was on the table, but there was no sign of her. He screwed up his eyes to make out the time on the cooker: eight-forty five. He'd slept for two hours. The kitchen was filled with wintry sunshine streaming through the glass of the back door. The cat appeared at the window, its mouth open in a wide miaow. He got up to let her in. She stepped over the sill onto the work top, nuzzling her head against the back of his hand. 'Hello, old girl,' he said. Jess's parents had got her as a kitten when Flo was a baby. They'd grown up together.

There was a knocking at the front door. A commotion in the hall. Someone screamed. He closed his eyes.

'Ollie! Ollie!'

Fists hammered against his chest. He opened his eyes.

'They've found her! They've got her, Ollie.' Jess flung her arms round his neck. She was kissing him.

'Found her? Is she –?'

'She's alive. She's okay.'

The room was full of people: Jess's parents, Viv, another police woman, a man who introduced himself as Detective

Inspector Jones. 'She's at the station, Mr Anderson. We found her an hour ago.'

'Where? Where was she?' Ollie couldn't take it in. His head was going to burst.

'In a café at Paddington station. She'd told the staff she was waiting for her dad to pick her up.'

'Isn't it wonderful?' Jess was holding onto his arm. 'I can't wait to see her.'

'Paddington?'

'Yes, as you suggested she had a train ticket for Plymouth.'

'Oh, Christ.'

'We understand you have family there, Mr Anderson?' the detective said.

He covered his face with his hands. His heart was racing. He breathed in ... Flo was alive ... out ... she was safe ... in ... He opened the kitchen door and stumbled into the garden. The patio was hard and cold under his bare feet. He pulled his phone from his pocket and clicked on Angel's name.

'Ollie?'

'They've got her. She's safe.'

'Oh.' Angel sounded as if she'd been holding that breath in since they'd got the news 'Have you seen her?'

'No, they've taken her to a police station. I should think we'll go there now.'

'Thank God. Are you all right, darling?'

'I'm shell-shocked.' The cat must have followed him, and she wound herself in and out of his legs. He looked down. She was licking his toes. 'I need to see her and hold her.'

'I'm coming over, Ollie. I've booked my flight.'

'When?'

'Tomorrow. I hope that's all right.'

'It's wonderful.'

Flo was sitting at a table, doing some colouring with a woman police officer when they arrived. She looked up and met his eyes as he pushed open the door. In that split second, he saw the depth of her fear and pain.

And then she smiled. 'Daddy.' She jumped up, the chair crashing into the wall behind her, and flung herself into his arms. She wrapped her legs round his waist, and clung to his head, her face pressed against his.

'It's okay. It's okay,' he whispered. 'You're safe now.' His cheek was wet with her tears.

'I'm sorry, Daddy.'

'Sweetheart, it's all right.' He stroked her hair; her beautiful hair that she brushed every morning until it shone, was dull and knotted. 'You gave me and Mummy a scare, but all that matters is you're safe.' He turned and put his arm round Jess. 'And here's Mummy. Shall we all have a hug?'

Flo reached out to Jess. 'I'm sorry, Mum.'

'It's my fault.' Jess couldn't stop kissing Flo. 'I let you down.'

Ollie pulled them both close. 'Let's make a promise,' he said. 'We've all let each other down, and we won't do it again.'

Flo nodded, and held out her clenched fist. He scrunched his fingers into his palm and fitted his knuckles into the hollows of hers. 'Agreed?'

Flo tapped the back of his fist three times with hers. 'Agreed.'

He glanced at Jess. 'What do you say?'

She looked from him to Flo: this was their secret sign and she'd never been part of it. But she scrunched her fingers up and held out her fist. She tapped the back of Flo's three times and then his. 'Agreed,' she said.

When they got back to the house, Peter pulled open the front door before they were even out of the car. After all the emotion at the police station, Flo was subdued. She said hello to her grandad, but turned away from his kiss. She clung to Ollie's hand as if she'd never let it go again. Ollie saw the shadow flit across Peter's face. 'Give her time,' he said. 'I expect she needs a good sleep.' He went to carry on up the path towards the house, but Peter caught his arm.

'I need a word.'

'What now?'

'Yes.'

'You go in with Mummy, Flo. I'll be there in a second.'

'But I want you, Daddy.' She stuck her thumb in her mouth.

'Come on, Flo, baby,' Jess said. 'Grandad wants to talk to Daddy.'

Ollie watched them close the front door behind them. 'What the hell is it, Peter? Can't it wait?'

'No.' Peter looked down at the ground, as if now he'd got Ollie's attention, he didn't know what to say.

'Hurry up. I need to be with Flo.'

'You left your mobile here when you went to the station.'

'I didn't even think of it,' Ollie said.

'It kept ringing, and I didn't know what to do.' Peter kicked away a stone that was on the path. 'I answered it in the end.'

'And?'

'It was your mother. There's been a fire at the hotel, and your father and sister are in hospital.'

'Jesus Christ! Are they going to be okay?'

'I don't know. She wants you to go as soon as you can.'

Forty

The drill bored into Louise's head. She twisted from side to side. Pain. She had to escape. *Take it away. Please take it away.*

'What did you say?'

There was a voice. A trickle of sound. She couldn't see. Her eyes hurt.

'Louise, are you awake?'

Oh, God ... nausea ... she was going to be sick ... There was something in the way ... something on her face. She lifted her hand. Heavy. Too heavy. She tried again ...

'What is it? What do you need?'

... it wouldn't wait. She managed to drag the thing from her face. Sick. Retching. Throat raw. She fell backwards, the taste of vomit in her mouth.

'Louise, darling.'

The voice was clearer.

'Here, let me wipe your face.'

Coolness over her skin. Gentle hands. Moisture on her lips.

'Louise, I'm putting your oxygen mask back on.'

A different voice. Lighter. A woman. 'Talk to her, Seb. Tell her you're here.'

Seb. She knew that name. Someone was stroking her arm. Fingers. Soft. Butterfly kisses.

'Louise, darling, it's me, Seb. Can you hear me?'

Yes, she knew that name. Seb. Wasn't he –?

'Tell her to squeeze your hand if she can hear you.'

'Squeeze my hand, Louise.'

She tightened her fingers.

'Oh, thank God. She can hear me. Darling ... I love you.'

'Let's get her more upright.' The other voice.

Hands under her arms. 'If you could lift those pillows.'

Pillows. She was in bed.

'That's better. She should be more comfortable now.' The female voice. 'I'll be back in a few minutes. Moisten her lips again.'

She forced open her eyes. It was bright in the room, although a blind was drawn at the window. The thing was over her face again. She lifted her hand to it. It was plastic. Pinpricks jabbed her eyes. Grit. They were full of grit. And they were so dry. She blinked. Tears, she needed tears to wash them out. Tears meant sadness. She'd had a baby once. Matilda. She died.

Louise woke up. Her throat felt tight and each breath tore at her chest. Seb was sitting next to the bed. His head had fallen forward and his eyes were closed. He must have been there for hours. It was his voice she'd heard. She remembered now. His hair was standing up in peaks. She wished she could smooth it down. She loved the feel of it under her fingers. The oxygen mask was still on her face, its edges biting into her cheeks and chin. When would they take it off?

Seb came to with a start. He sat back in the chair. His eyes ranged round the room, as if he was seeing it for the first time. His face was pale and drawn.

'Seb?' It was the first time she'd spoken out loud, and the word sounded harsh and scratchy.

'You're awake.' He pushed himself up from the chair and came over to the bed. He put his arms round her and rested his head against hers. 'Thank God, you're safe. I thought I'd lost you.'

She pulled off the mask. 'I went back in.' Memories were emerging. 'There was so much smoke. I couldn't see or breathe ...'

'I know. Don't try and talk yet.'

'Dad ... I thought Dad was in there, but I couldn't see –' A fist squeezed her heart. 'Dad! Was he in there? Did they ...?'

Seb drew her head towards his chest. 'They got him out. But he's in intensive care.'

Forty-one

Ollie leant his forehead against the cool glass of the train window. He stared at the scenery racing past, a kaleidoscope of fields, rivers, roads, houses, blurring into one. He usually enjoyed train journeys, but today, his mind was cut in two. Flo, arms limpet-like round his waist, 'Don't go, Daddy. Don't go.' The hotel, a burnt shell, his father and Loulou in hospital. What would he find when he arrived?

After Peter had given him the phone message, he'd tried to ring his mother, and then his sister, but couldn't get answers on anyone's phone. He had a quick shower, pulled on a clean shirt and underwear and repacked his rucksack. Peter would take him to the station.

Flo sat on his lap in the kitchen. Jess was on the opposite side of the table, drinking a cup of tea. Her face looked grey.

'I have to go, sweetheart,' he said. 'Granny and Grandpa need me.'

'I need you, Daddy. You've only just come back.' Her eyes bored into him.

He stroked her hair away from her face. 'I don't want to go, but I have to see what's happening at the hotel. I need to make sure everyone's all right.'

She was sucking a strand of hair, which she pulled from

her mouth abruptly. 'I can come with you. Help you.'

He wanted to agree, couldn't bear the light of hope in her eyes, know he would have to dash it. 'I've no idea what I'm going to face when I get there.' He gripped her hands. 'You've been through a big ordeal. You have to recover.'

'But I'm fine.'

'You can't go with Daddy today, Flo. The police want to talk to you again, and you need a bath and a good long sleep. Nana's made your bed up for you.' Jess's words were slow and slurred. She looked as if she desperately needed a rest herself.

'But it's not fair.' Tears squeezed out from between Flo's lids.

Ollie felt Jess's eyes on him, the desperation in them: *Do something. Sort this out. Please.*

'I tell you what ...' he said. 'Let me go to Plymouth without any more fuss, and I'll come back to get you in a couple of days. I'll have sorted things out by then.'

'I'll take you, Flo, if that's what you want,' Jess said. 'You can spend some time with Daddy in Plymouth.'

Ollie smiled across the table at Jess. 'Thanks. See, sweetheart, you'll soon be there.'

Flo got off his lap and moved round the table. She curled her arms round Jess's neck. 'Do you promise?'

'I promise.'

The train pulled into Totnes station. Ollie blinked at the lights. Twilight had settled outside in the last hour, grey shadows lurking in fields deepening to mauve, and then to black, as the train sped through the countryside. Half an hour to Plymouth. He took out his phone and sent a text to his mother: *Be with you in an hour Oliver x* and another to Angel: *On my way to Plymouth. There's been a fire. When you land, can you get train to Paddington, and come down tonight. I'll meet you at station. I can't wait to see you. O xxx*

Forty-two

Seb wasn't there. The nurse, one Louise hadn't seen before, was twiddling knobs on the machine next to the bed.

'How's my dad?' she asked.

The nurse turned. 'I'm not sure. I'm Sally, by the way, but I'll find out for you.' She placed her hand on the cream bed cover. 'I understand he was exposed to smoke for substantially longer than you. His carboxyhaemoglobin levels are high, and there is the complication of heart disease.'

Louise stared at the nurse's hand, reddened and dry-looking. 'When can I see him?'

'We want to do a chest x-ray on you and a bronchoscopy.'

'A bronchoscopy? I don't like the sound of that.'

'I'm afraid it's not very pleasant. You have a tube passed down your throat into the windpipe and then into the bronchi.' Sally moved to the end of the bed, and jotted something down on Louise's notes. 'If it troubles you, you can have a sedative beforehand.'

'I feel better. Is it necessary?'

'The damage from inhaling smoke can take time to materialise. You might seem okay, and then suddenly deteriorate.'

'But I need to be with my mum. She's coping with this all on her own.'

'I think your partner – Seb, is it? – has gone to see her in ICU. He said he wouldn't be long.'

Louise lay back on the pillows. She'd just had a coughing spasm. Perhaps it was a good thing they were doing this broncho thing. Her chest still felt tight and she wheezed when she breathed. If only she'd checked the hotel last night, she might have noticed something amiss. Why hadn't Mike realised sooner? He was usually so conscientious. When she'd opened the door of the flat, the stench of smoke was already strong. But the alarm in the flat and on the landing hadn't gone off. They'd been inspected the previous month. Her father had been scrupulous about that and drummed into her how essential it was. She pictured the foyer. The photos for the magazine were stunning. But it was all ruined now.

She turned her head towards the door. Where was Seb? He'd been gone for ages. Maybe he'd come with the news her father had regained consciousness. Oliver was on his way, her mother had said, when she looked in earlier. It would be lovely if her father was awake when he got here.

The door opened, and Sally came in, looking over her shoulder. 'If you'd wait here a minute.' She moved to Louise's bed.

'There's a policeman to see you. Are you happy for him to come in?'

'What does he want?'

'To update you on the fire, I think. Would you rather wait until you have someone with you?'

'No, send him in.'

'I'll stay in the room.' Sally turned back to the door.

The policeman wore plain clothes. He was tall and burly,

with a red face. 'I'm Detective Sergeant Mills,' he said. 'Thank you for seeing me. The nurse has told me I can only stay a few minutes.'

Cold air emanated from his coat, sending shivers along Louise's arms. She pulled the covers up to her chin. 'I gather you've got some news for me.'

He pulled up a chair. 'I'll sit, if that's okay. Seems less formal.'

'Not long, Sergeant,' Sally warned.

'No, I understand. May I call you Louise?'

She nodded.

'We're liaising with the fire service on the causes of the fire at your hotel.' He took a notebook from his coat pocket. 'There will have to be a thorough investigation, of course – fire personnel are working in the building now – but initial findings suggest arson.'

Louise's stomach flipped. 'Arson? You mean started deliberately?'

'Looks like it. It seems there's evidence of some fire alarms being tampered with, and possible signs of petrol at the back of the building, near to where the fire is thought to have started.' His pen was poised over the notebook. 'I don't want to distress you further, but do you know of anyone, anyone at all who might have a grudge, and could possibly have done this?'

She shook her head. 'No one I can think of.'

Sally moved forward. 'I think that's enough, Sergeant. Louise is still very fragile.'

Forty-three

Ollie took a deep breath and pushed open the door. Louise was sitting up in bed, her face red and blotchy. His mother stood next to her, holding her hand. A man he didn't recognise, a small guy with blond hair, was on the other side of the bed.

He let the door swing shut behind him. It closed with a soft whoosh. His mother looked over. 'Oliver, you're here.' She sank onto a chair, her head in her hands. The sound of her sobbing filled the small room.

'What's happened?' he said. 'Are you all right, Loulou?' He moved closer to the bed, and put his hand on his mother's shoulder. He could feel her bones through her jumper.

'I'm okay,' Louise said. 'But ...'

Ollie looked from one to the other. The blond guy had his head bent. Louise was crying. Ollie knelt down next to his mother. 'What's happened? Is Dad worse? Which ward is he in?'

His mother turned towards him. 'Tom's gone, Oliver. He never regained consciousness. He died an hour ago.'

'Ollie, talk to me.'

Angel's breath was warm on his shoulder. They were in

bed at his parents' apartment. He pulled her closer, running his hand along the hollow in her back, over the mound of her buttocks. Her breasts pushed against his chest. He lowered his head and took one of the nipples between his lips. He sucked and felt it grow hard in his mouth.

He pulled away and flung himself back on the pillow.

Angel leant up on one elbow and gazed down at him. The light on the bedside table created a halo effect behind her head. He reached up and ran his fingers over her eyebrows, across her cheekbones. 'I'm sorry.'

She kissed him. 'Don't be silly.'

'I want to make love to you, but ... it doesn't seem right the day the old man dies.' He pinched his nose between his thumb and forefinger to stop the tears. 'I can't believe I won't see him again.'

'I know. Cry if you need to.'

'What's the point? I walked out on him when I couldn't get my own way over the hotel.' The memory of the shrunken man he'd left the day he came with Flo, slammed its fist into his chest. 'What sort of son am I?'

Angel lay down and wrapped her arm round him. 'We know people are going to die one day, but somehow, it's always a shock.'

From the living room came the soft undertow of the television. Seb had said he'd watch for a while before going to bed. He seemed nice. Louise deserved someone good, after Eugene, and it turned out Matt was no better. He hoped his mother was asleep. She must have been exhausted after all that crying. They'd been a real love match, her and Dad.

Ollie was up first the next morning. He stood at the window, gazing at The Hoe and into the greyness of the bay beyond. He was suddenly aware of his mother beside him, and put his arm round her shoulder.

'Your father loved this view,' she murmured.

'It's beautiful.'

'He said he wanted to die sitting in his chair looking out towards the Breakwater.' She clutched a tissue against her mouth. 'Instead, he suffocated in that rotten, poky office.'

'The hotel meant the world to him.'

'I hate it.'

The venom in his mother's voice took him aback. 'I didn't know that.'

'Oh, at first, I loved the space and grandeur.' She shivered: she was only wearing a thin dressing gown. 'But it ate up every bit of your father's strength and commitment. There was no room for us, his family.'

'You never said.'

'How could I? I loved him, and it was his life.'

'Don't you want it rebuilt?'

'I'd be happy to see it knocked down, but it's up to Louise. And she's as mad about it as your father was.'

'I'll help her, if it's what she wants. I feel I owe it to Dad as well.'

'What about Venice, your painting?'

'I can always go back for short stays. I've got a great contact in the States who'll buy whatever I can paint.'

'That's good. And Angel? She might not want to stay here, and I can see how good she is for you.'

'I'm glad you think so, Mum.'

'I want you to be happy, Oliver. You and Louise.' His mother sighed. 'I'm glad she's met Seb. Someone who'll cherish her at last.

'Seb's a designer, isn't he?'

'He's brilliant. You should have seen what he did with the foyer.'

'Perhaps he'd help if we decide to rebuild the hotel.'

'He'll do it if Louise wants it.'

'Mum.' The sky was lightening, red streaking across the white clouds.

'What is it?'

'I can't see the painting I did for Dad anywhere. Didn't he like it?'

A red glow appeared over the headland, the hills iridescent as the light built.

'He loved it, but he was waiting for you to tell him the best position to hang it.'

Ollie took Angel for a walk. Seb had gone to the hospital to see Louise, and his mother wanted some time on her own. Ollie could barely look at the hotel: the charred remains of one side of the building, the pall of smoke still hanging over it, the scaffolding. A fence had been erected all round, and groups of onlookers huddled beside it.

Angel stopped. 'You've been holding out on me, Ollie Anderson.'

'How?'

'You didn't tell me the hotel was so big. It must have been beautiful.'

'I suppose.' His nostrils stung from the stench of smoke. 'Let's go down to the front.'

They leaned over the rail and gazed down at the waves.

'When I was at school I used to spend as much time as I could mucking about in the sea or swimming in the pool. And over there ...' He pointed across the water to a slice of land sticking out into the sea. 'That's Mount Batten, where I did all my painting.'

'I'd love to have seen you when you were a little boy.'

They walked on towards the Barbican. When they reached the Mayflower Steps, Ollie stared down at the spot where he'd thrown the exercise book. The water was choppy, the wind whipping up little waves that splashed against the wall. A seagull bobbed up and down. Physically the book was long gone, but the words it contained: *my grandad gave it to my dad and my dad will give it to me* scarred his thoughts.

Angel pulled up the collar of her coat. 'Can we go in somewhere for a hot drink?'

They wandered back towards the Tinside Lido and climbed down some steps into a café. 'It's not exactly inside,' Ollie said, 'but we're out of the wind here. What would you like? Cappuccino and a croissant? Remind you of Venice.'

'Sounds good.'

He waited until the coffee and pastries arrived. 'Can I say something?'

She stopped buttering her croissant and looked up. 'Go on.'

'You know how much we both love Venice.'

'Yes.'

'I've been happier there with you than ... but ... Flo ...'

She covered his hand with hers. 'I know what you're going to say.'

'I can't bear to leave her again.'

'I know.'

'And Louise and Seb –'

'Ollie you don't have to explain.' She drew patterns on the check tablecloth, her finger circling round and round. 'I love Venice, and our life there, but you're needed here at the moment.'

'But you're not going to want to come back. Look at the fantastic poetry you've written there.'

'I'll go back to pack up our apartment, but there's no point being there without you.'

He sipped his cappuccino, and the milky froth warmed his throat. He didn't have any right to ask her. But he couldn't risk losing her. 'Would you consider ...?' His tongue felt too big for his mouth. 'How would you feel –?'

Her lips brushed his. 'I'll live here with you – if you'll have me.'

'You will?'

The woman at the next table was nodding and smiling. Ollie caught her eye, and she gave the thumbs-up sign.

'We're back, Mum,' Ollie called as he opened the door of the apartment. They hung their coats in the cupboard and went into the living room. His mother was sitting at the table, her head in her hands, and Seb's arm was round her shoulders.

'What's happened?' Ollie looked from to the other. 'It's not Louise, is it?'

'No, she's okay,' Seb said. 'Bit upset after the bronchoscopy, but okay.'

'What then?'

'We've had a visit from the police.' His mother's voice was frail, suddenly an old lady's.

'The arson – they know who did it?' Ollie planted his hands on the table, leaning over her. 'Was it Matt? The bastard.'

Angel pulled him back. 'Ollie, wait. Give your mum and Seb a chance.'

'Matt's dead.' Seb turned away as if he was trying to control his emotions. 'A walker found his body in undergrowth up on Dartmoor. An empty bottle of whisky and several packets of tablets were nearby. The tablets were nearly all gone.'

Forty-four

Louise sat in the chair, watching Seb bundle her few belongings into a bag. It would be strange to see the outside world again, a world irretrievably changed. She was wearing the old jeans and baggy sweater she'd pulled on the night of the fire. Although they'd been washed, the fibres had soaked up the stink of smoke, and she couldn't wait to get out of them. All her clothes had been in the hotel. And not just her clothes, everything she owned.

Seb zipped up the bag. 'That's it, for what it's worth. I'll buy you new stuff as soon as you're settled at your mum's.'

'I can't wait to get out of here,' Louise said, 'but I'm scared.'

He crouched down by the chair. 'Of what?'

'It's all going to be real then.'

'It won't be easy seeing the hotel.'

'And Dad,' she said. 'There'll be no Dad.'

His blue eyes were fixed on her face. 'Louise, I've got something to tell you.'

Her legs started trembling. 'Not more bad news?'

'I'm afraid so.' He fiddled with the zip of the bag. 'Matt's dead.'

She gasped. Razor blades seemed to slice the soft flesh of her throat.

'I know it's a shock, but I had to tell you.'

'How? When?'

'It looks as if he killed himself.'

She couldn't speak. Her windpipe was clogged with words.

'Louise?'

She stared at her hands, the criss-cross of creases on her palms. There was a lifeline, wasn't there? Was Matt's short? She'd never checked.

'Louise, say something.'

'He drowned, didn't he?'

'No.'

'He talked about walking into the sea until the current took him.'

Seb shook his head. 'He was found in undergrowth. Seems to have been a mixture of alcohol and drugs.'

'It's my fault.'

'Of course it isn't. You mustn't think like that.'

A bout of coughing shook Louise. She struggled to catch her breath.

Seb held out a glass. 'Here, take some sips from this.'

The water was cold. She wiped her mouth on a tissue. 'He begged me to try again, but I told him to go away.'

'You couldn't have known he would do this.'

'Did he start the fire?'

'I can't see how. Apparently he'd been dead for several days when he was found.'

Tears tingled at the back of her nose. 'Poor Matt. What have I done?'

'You mustn't blame yourself.'

'All he wanted was a home and family.'

Forty-five

The train from Paddington was late. Ollie jogged on the spot, trying to keep his impatience at bay. At last, it slid in beside the platform, and there was a great clanging of doors. Jess and Flo climbed down from a compartment near the front. Flo had her pink rucksack on her back and was trundling a case behind her. He caught both of them up in a hug.

Jess kissed his cheek. 'I'm so sorry about your dad,' she whispered.

'Thanks. I'm finding it tough.'

She indicated Flo with her eyes. 'I've told her, but she hasn't said much.'

'How are things after ... you know.'

'We've had a long talk, and she's beside herself with excitement. But it all depends on you.'

'Mysterious.'

Flo put her hand in his. 'Daddy, I've got a surprise for you.'

'That sounds lovely. Have you done me a drawing?'

'It's a bigger surprise than that.'

'Can you show me when we get back? Granny can't wait to see you.' He set off for the exit, Flo hanging on his hand and chattering about the journey. He realised Jess was way behind.

'Hey, let's wait for Mummy to catch up.'

She drew level with them. 'Actually, Ollie, I need to talk to you on our own.'

He hesitated. 'But –'

She glanced over her shoulder. 'Dad's here.'

Ollie followed her gaze. Her father was standing some distance away. He came forward and shook Ollie's hand. 'Sorry to hear your bad news.'

'Thank you. But I don't understand. I thought –'

Jess's stare silenced him. She nodded towards Flo. 'You're going to go for a walk with Grandad, aren't you?'

Flo's eyes filled with tears. 'But I want to stay with Daddy.'

'You know what we agreed on the train, Flo.' Jess's voice was stern. 'I need to discuss things with him.'

Peter held out his hand. 'Come on, little one. Let's find something we can do.'

'What's the big mystery then?' Ollie said when Peter and Flo had left. He'd ordered a coffee, and Jess had a glass of water.

She took tablets from her bag and swallowed a couple. 'Heartburn,' she said.

He nodded. 'I wasn't expecting to see your dad.'

'He wouldn't hear of us coming on our own.'

'Is he planning to stay?'

'No, we're going back to London. There's a train in a couple of hours.'

'But I thought –'

'I doubt either Louise or your mum would welcome me.' She pointed to her stomach. 'Not with this on show.'

Ollie wrinkled his nose. His mother had said he'd have to book Jess into a B & B. She couldn't have Louise upset.

'It's okay.' Jess touched his hand. 'I'd hate me if I was Louise.'

He drained his coffee cup. 'I'll have to get back. Mum's expecting us. What's all this about?'

Jess twirled her empty glass round and round. 'Flo wants to live with you.'

He breathed out. 'You mean permanently?'

'If she settles down, maybe, yes.' She kept her eyes on the glass. 'I presume you'll be staying in Plymouth now. I mean with your mum, and Louise and everything.'

'Of course I'd love to have her.' Oh God, this was a dream come true. 'But what about you? You'll miss her so much.'

'I'll hate it, but I can't risk her running away again.'

'Has something happened?' Ollie clenched his fist. 'If that prick has touched her –'

Jess caught hold of his hand. 'No, no, it's nothing like that.'

'What then?'

'She says she won't live with Eugene. She can't stand him.'

'That's my girl. Knows a rotten apple when she sees one.'

'Ollie, we need to get this sorted.' She kept her hand on his.

'But before you were fighting to keep her to yourself.'

'I was so wrong. This has been a wake-up call.'

He stared at her hand. A few months ago, he would have given the world to feel her touch, but now all he could think was how different it felt to Angel's. Four fingers, a thumb, a palm – a hand was a hand wasn't it?

'So, can she stay?'

'Of course she can.'

'You'll need to sort out a school for after Christmas.'

'I'll be living with Mum in the meantime, until we can find somewhere of our own.'

'We?'

'Yes, I've met someone.'

'I thought so.'

'Why?'

'You're so different from how you used to be. I guessed there was no chance for us.'

A jolt ran through his body. 'You mean you want to?'

'I don't know what I want any more, Ollie.'

He clasped both her hands in his. What was she saying? That she didn't want to be with Eugene? Before he went to Venice, he used to lie awake at night and wonder what he'd do if she asked him to take her back. He'd have jumped at the chance. One hundred per cent. And bollocks to Eugene. But being in Venice with Angel, it was as if he'd finally ripped the plaster off the wound of their break-up and barely a scab remained.

'I've messed up big time,' she said. 'I know that, but I've got to live with it. I can't separate another child from its father.'

'You don't have to stay with that psychopath if you're not happy.'

'He's not that bad, Ollie. He's got a temper, but he does love me.'

'If he's ever violent towards you ...'

She pulled her hands free and rested them on her belly. 'He wants this baby. I know what he, what *we*, did to Louise was unforgivable, but he won't mess up this time.'

Ollie walked along the platform behind Jess and Flo. They had their arms round each other, their heads bent as they talked. He was conscious of Peter's silence beside him. Were they doing the right thing? Suppose Flo couldn't cope when it was time to say good bye. They stopped at the open door of one of the carriages. Peter helped Jess up the step. He hugged Flo, and when he turned away, Ollie saw his eyes were filled with tears. He climbed onto the train without looking back.

Jess leaned out of the carriage window. 'I'll see you very soon, my darling.'

Flo clutched Ollie's hand. 'See you soon, Mummy.'

'I'll miss you, baby.'

'I'll miss you. I'll ring you every day. My new phone is so cool – thank you.'

Another train drew into the station, the noise drowning out their conversation. People got off. Others got on. The guard walked alongside the train slamming doors shut.

'We'll be up to see you before you know it, Jess. I'll bring Flo when the baby's born.' Ollie said. 'And I'll look after her.'

The guard raised the green flag and blew his whistle.

'I know you will,' Jess said. 'I'll go to my seat now.'

The train began to move. It picked up speed.

Flo waved until it was a blur in the distance. She turned to Ollie, her eyes glistening in the lights above them. 'I wish Mummy could have stayed here with us.'

He squeezed her hand. 'I know. What about we make her a card when we get back? I think she'd like that.'

'Can we make a big one?'

'Whatever you want,' Ollie said. 'But we'd better go: Granny wants you to help her with Christmas decorations.'

They walked along the platform and made their way towards the exit. Outside a thin drizzle was falling. 'Look at the rain in the lights, Daddy,' Flo said. 'It's all sparkly.'

Forty-six

The apartment was quiet at last. It had taken ages to get everyone sorted, but finally they'd gone. Louise was lying on the sofa, and Ollie tucked the blanket round her.

'I'm not a complete invalid,' she snapped.

'Seb left me strict instructions to take care of you.'

'He'd wrap me up in cotton wool, if he could.'

'It's going to take a while.'

She didn't answer.

He pulled open the door and stepped onto the balcony. He'd promised Flo he'd wave to her when she got out on The Hoe. They were standing in a group waiting for him. His mum was hand in hand with Flo: they were going in search of a Christmas tree. Angel was setting off to buy presents, and Seb was armed with a list of things to get for Louise.

Flo's arrival had made Ollie's mother smile again. 'You're so beautiful, my precious,' she said. 'Your grandpa loved you.'

Ollie had explained to Flo that Angel was his girlfriend. She didn't say anything, just looked at him with that intense gaze of hers, and he was afraid he'd blown it. But later on when Angel suggested reading a book she'd bought as an early present, Flo agreed. He studied their two heads close together, one dark, one fair. Perhaps, together, they could make this work.

As he stepped back into the apartment and closed the door, Louise's mobile rang.

'Can you get that?' she said.

He clicked accept. 'Louise Bradbury's phone.'

'This is Detective Sergeant Mills. Is Louise available?'

He held the phone out to her. 'It's the police.'

She shook her head.

He lifted the mobile to his mouth again. 'I'm Oliver Anderson, Louise's brother. She's resting. Can I help?'

'We've got news for her. Perhaps you could let her know we've charged Robert Tinder with arson.'

'Robert Tinder?'

'He's more commonly known as Bobby, and has served a prison sentence for GBH. We understand his wife's aunt was housekeeper at the hotel until recently.' The policeman paused. 'Apparently she left in difficult circumstances. It's looking like a revenge attack.'

Ollie glanced at Louise. Her eyes were wide with questions.

'Do you think he acted alone?' he asked.

'We're almost certain he had inside help. He wouldn't have been able to disconnect those alarms otherwise. We've questioned all the staff, and there's a warrant out for the arrest of Maeve Crawley.'

'What are you waiting for?'

'She's done a runner, I'm afraid. But we'll find her; she won't get away with it.' He cleared his throat. 'I'll call round tomorrow to see Louise.'

Ollie put the phone on the low table where Louise could reach it. 'Did you hear that?'

'They've charged someone?'

'Yeah.'

'It's Maeve, isn't it?'

'No, a man called Bobby Tinder. Mean anything to you?'

Louise's already pale face turned ashy-white. 'Oh my God, Jodie Tinder, Phyllis's niece.' She picked at the bloodied skin on her thumb. 'I was sure Maeve had done it.'

'The policeman said Tinder had inside help, and Maeve's disappeared.'

'I knew it,' Louise said. 'But I thought it was her and Matt.'

'Who is this Bobby Tinder? I don't understand.'

'It's a long story.'

'I won't be going anywhere.' He perched on the arm of the sofa. 'I'm ready to help get the hotel up and running again, if that's what you want.'

Louise's fingers plucked at the blanket. 'It's not.'

'I'm meeting the insurance assessors tomorrow, and we'll get the hotel back as good as – no, better – than it was before.'

'You can. I don't want anything to do with it.'

He squatted beside her. 'I don't understand.'

'I gave it everything I had, and look what happened.' She tried to stand, but sank back on the sofa as a coughing fit overtook her. 'Seb and I are going away, as soon as I'm well enough. You can do what you like with the hotel.' She pushed herself to her feet. 'I'm going upstairs to lie down.'

'What is it, Loulou? Why are you so angry with me?'

'You really don't get it, do you?'

'I know I didn't support you when Eugene –'

'No, you didn't support me. You blamed me because my boyfriend slept with your wife.' Her voice was hoarse. 'But I've got over that.'

'What is it then? Tell me.'

'I loved the hotel. It was in my blood, but Dad didn't think I was good enough. He wanted you.' She flung the blanket away. 'And he was right, wasn't he? The hotel was destroyed on my watch.'

She made for the stairs and he ran after her. 'Loulou, the fire wasn't your fault. You have to believe that. And I know you'd have been brilliant at running it.' He took her hands. 'I should have realised what the hotel meant to you. I was too caught up in my own troubles, and I couldn't see beyond my fights with Dad.'

'If only he'd believed in me.'

'I don't think he believed in either of us when it came to it.'

'What do you mean?'

'He wanted us to live up to some vision he had – me in charge and you as the dutiful helper, like Mum has been all her life.'

She sat down on the stairs. He squeezed in beside her and put his arm round her shoulder. 'But I'd have made a complete mess of it. The hotel would have been bankrupt in time. You're the one with the skills to run the place. Same as you ran the arts centre while Eugene did nothing but lord it over everyone.'

'Do you think so?' She smiled, and for a second he glimpsed the old Loulou.

'Let me help you restore the hotel. I know you and Seb will make a great team.'

'I'll have to talk to him,' she said. 'But I would love to see it come back.'

'Then let's do it, but you'll be in charge. Don't forget – *I'm an artist!*'

Ollie stared out of the window at the bay. The sky was heavy and grey, the sea leaden. Heavy drops of rain started to fall, splashing noisily on the tiles of the balcony. There was a noise behind him, and he spun round. Angel was standing in the doorway.

He crossed the room. 'That was quick. Did you forget something?'

She shook her head, and he saw the shine of tears in her eyes. He caught hold of her shoulders. 'What's happened? Have you hurt yourself?'

'No. It's nothing like that.' Her voice trembled.

'Angel, my darling, come and sit down.' He led her over to the sofa. 'Tell me what's wrong.'

'I've just had a phone call from my mum.' She was clutching her mobile.

'I expect she's missing you because it's Christmas.'

'It's not that.'

'What then?'

'You know she went to live with my brother and sister-in-law after she broke her hip.'

'Yeah, that's how you were able to come to Venice.'

'Well, they've had a huge bust up. Turns out the atmosphere's been toxic for weeks.' Angel twisted her bracelet round and round on her wrist. 'My sister-in-law told my mother to get out. She had to stay in a hotel last night.' She pulled a tissue from her pocket and scrubbed at the tears on her cheeks. 'Ollie, she's in a terrible state.'

'What did your brother say?'

'He's a coward. He does as he's told.'

Ollie put his arm round her and pulled her closer. 'What are you going to do?'

'I'll have to go back to London this afternoon. I can't abandon her on her own in a hotel over Christmas.'

'Could you bring her to Plymouth?'

She gave a half laugh. 'Don't you think there's enough going on here as it is?'

'You're probably right.' He rested his head against hers. Her curls tickled his cheek. 'And after Christmas? What then?'

'I might have to move back into the house with her.'

He felt sick at the thought of her going. 'I'd come with you, but I can't leave Flo and Mum.'

Her eyes met his. 'I know.'

'Where does this leave us?'

'I suppose we'll have to see. If we want to be together enough, perhaps there's a way.'

He leant forward and kissed her. Her lips were soft and warm. 'We'll find a way,' he whispered. 'This is just another bump in the road.'

'*The Broken Road*.' She stroked his cheek. 'You remembered.'

'Of course. But we can make it smooth again.'

'Daddy, we're back!' The front door crashed open, and Ollie jumped up. Flo stood there beaming. 'We've got an enormous tree. Grandma's waiting in the hall – she needs you to help her bring it up.'

Ollie blinked back tears and smiled at her. She ran to him and he wrapped his arms round her. He could do this. He could be a lark if he tried hard enough. He owed it to everyone. He took Flo's hand. 'Come on then. Let's go and get this tree.'

Acknowledgements

My thanks to:

Lorna Fergusson of Fiction Fire, whose mentoring and support gave me the motivation to kick-start my 'stuck' novel. To Emma Darwin, whose invaluable editorial feedback helped to make the book much stronger. To Sue Jenkinson of the Evesham Hotel, who provided insight into running a family hotel. To friends who read early drafts and offered invaluable insights, Helen Shaw, Joan Corrigall, Elisabeth Drake, Wendy Logan, and especially Mairé Davies and Joanne Phillips. To my writing group who read even earlier drafts and offered detailed feedback. To my writing students who kept me exploring the craft of writing. To Jane Dixon-Smith of JD Smith Design who made the outside of the book as polished as I hope the inside is. And to Trevor and my family for their love and support.

Reading Group Guide

A free guide to *The Broken Road* is available for reading groups. The guide contains discussion topics and background to the book.

To receive a copy of the guide, please go to:
www.lindsaystanberryflynn.co.uk/contact